FORGOTTEN PROMISE

TRINITY MASTERS: CROSSROADS CONTEMPT

BOOK ONE

MARI CARR

LILA DUBOIS

CROSSROADS
CONTEMPT

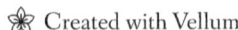

TRIGGER WARNINGS

The Trinity Masters series is a romantic suspense and all books contain explicit sex and depictions of violence (action scenes).

FORGOTTEN PROMISE

She holds the key to their survival.
Kailani's family have kept a secret for generations. She never thought it would put her in jeopardy until the night her phone rings and a stranger says, "Our society is under attack."

With danger all around her, Kailani is forced into a deadly race across the country to find the others who share her secret. But she's not going alone. Because before that call, she had an entirely different crisis on her hands–her arranged marriage to two men, including the man who broke her heart, Benjamin.

A centuries old secret becomes a race against time and the survival of the Trinity Masters hangs in the balance. Kailani, John, and Benjamin may not survive the mission. But even if they succeed, the fate of their trinity is at stake due to past mistakes and present tensions. And in the end, Kailani may seize the power to dissolve their marriage.

WELCOME TO TRINITY MASTERS

Before the birth of a young nation, a society was formed. Like-minded men and women, who knew the great experiment of their country wouldn't survive without support, came together and—in secret—formed the Trinity Masters.

If you know the way in, you'll find their headquarters deep under the Boston Public Library. If you saw the list of members, you'd know their names, recognize great scholars, artists, politicians, and soldiers.

The founding members were individuals of vision, power, and creativity. They knew that without deep bonds to both strengthen and protect, their country would fail. The rules of the society were set: the best among them would be invited to join and reap the benefits of membership. But there's a price each member must pay—they agree to an arranged marriage. The marriages create those much-needed bonds. However, a stool with two legs will fall but with three legs...

The arranged marriage is between not just two but three people.

They meet at a binding ceremony, after which the newly

formed trinity is given a month to get to know one another. Sometimes, they are given a task by the leader of the society—the Grand Master. Once formed, trinities are final, with no appeal and no second chances for those who disobey.

The punishment for disobedience is both creative and brutal.

But the Trinity Masters isn't the only society based on the arranged menage marriage concept. Time and treachery allowed the Americans to forget about their European counterpart...the Masters Admiralty.

Formed during the Black Plague, the Masters Admiralty is ruled by the Fleet Admiral, but their membership is larger, their society more complex, than that of the Trinity Masters. Divided into nine territories, their borders drawn long before the modern borders of European nations were decided, the Masters Admiralty has nine territory admirals, and not all of the territories get along.

Recently, the two societies met again, the distance between them the result of betrayal and greed. The Grand Master of the Trinity Masters and the Fleet Admiral of the Masters Admiralty have a tentative alliance, though relations are strained.

Both societies have faced treachery from within, as well as attacks from those who hate what they are. It's up to the members, to the trinities, to protect and defend not only their spouses but the societies themselves...

INTRODUCTION

If you're new to the world, here's a refresher on what's been happening for the Trinity Masters and Masters Admiralty...

The current Grand Master of the Trinity Masters is Juliette Adams, descendent of founding father John Adams. She inherited the position when her brother, Harrison (Forbidden Legacy), fell in love with a nonmember and was forced to step down.

Juliette never expected to inherit the title, and when she did, her first action was to dissolve her own trinity (Hidden Devotion). Essentially betrothed since she was a child to two other legacy members, she grew up loving Devon Asher, until the day he broke her heart. Juliette had no idea that dissolving her trinity would reveal a conspiracy within the society because their third, Rose Hancock, was poised to betray them all...

Now married to Franco Santiago, a man who should have been a legacy member, but whose name was purposefully erased from their history, and Devon, Juliette is struggling to manage and lead the society while also unraveling a host of mysteries and dangerous secrets. Rose (Beloved Sacrifice) is now one of Juliette's counselors, and was pivotal in repairing the relationship between the Trinity Masters and Masters' Admiralty, as well as tearing down the conspiracy she was forced to serve.

Meanwhile, in Europe, Fleet Admiral Eric Ericsson is dealing with an ongoing threat from an old enemy while also struggling with some very personal grief. Colum O'Connor is the Archivist of the Masters' Admiralty, holder of all records and information. The archive is kept in Dublin, the only place in Europe that doesn't belong to one of the Masters' Admiralty's nine territories. Colum and Eric are grieving for the same woman (Bravery's Sin), and Eric pushes Colum to befriend Franco in the hopes that it will give Colum something to focus on besides the loss he suffered.

Colum travels to Boston to meet with Franco, but Franco doesn't show. Colum is getting ready to leave when Franco, bloody and disoriented, stumbles down the steps of the Boston Public Library and tells Colum that Juliette and Devon have just been kidnapped.

CHAPTER ONE

B oston
One hour and forty-five minutes since the Grand Master was kidnapped

WALKING into a dangerous crisis felt like coming home. She trusted pain and catastrophe more than joy and contentment, and in many ways, this was normal to her. More normal than the peaceful existence she'd been enjoying this past year as a happily married woman with two wonderful husbands.

Rose sized up the situation and then turned to her small clutch, which she'd dropped onto a chair when she entered the suite. Ten minutes ago, she'd made a dramatic entrance into the hotel—running through the lobby in a ball gown with two tuxedo-clad men at her heels. Ideally, she wouldn't have drawn attention to herself, but that was the sort of dramatic moment that people noticed.

Luckily, the front desk clerk who'd watched her didn't know she was the one responsible for setting the hotel on fire several years ago. She'd been in a dark place for, well, most of her life, only now beginning to experience a calm, peaceful happiness.

She glanced behind her at the man who, like her, had found his own happy ending, except now...now that was falling apart.

Rose finished digging the small pill case out of her clutch and raced over to Franco Santiago. He was covered in blood, but when she first approached him, he'd assured her that none of it was his. She didn't fully believe him, but there didn't seem to be any fresh blood, which meant he wasn't actively bleeding. Now if she could just get him to stop panicking long enough to provide coherent information, they could begin crisis management.

"Open," she said to Franco.

The Irishman seated beside Franco eyed her warily. Rose didn't know who he was, and as far as she was concerned, he was their primary suspect. A suspicious nature was one of Rose's best qualities. But questioning the Irishman had to wait. Because until Franco could give them the whole story, all they had were the frantic calls that had brought her, Sebastian, and Lachlan to the hotel.

Franco looked at her, opened his mouth to say something, and she popped a pill in.

"Swallow."

He grimaced, but she saw his throat work.

"What was that tablet?" the Irishman asked suspiciously.

"Who are you again?" Rose countered.

"The Archivist. Colum O'Connor."

"He's Masters' Admiralty." Lachlan Howard tapped his wrist piece to end the call he'd been on.

Rose glanced around the room again, assessing who was here. Besides her, there was Sebastian, who held the same position within the society she did, and Lachlan, a Warrior Scholar

—one of a group of on-call security professionals. Each Warrior Scholar was former military, with refined and dangerous skill sets. But by day, they were graduate students, most in fields entirely unrelated to their previous occupations. Rose had heavily encouraged Juliette to create the Warrior Scholar corp.

Juliette...

Rose looked at Franco.

Juliette was Franco's wife, and she, along with Franco's other spouse, Devon, had just been kidnapped.

It was terrifying and horrible...except it was even worse than that.

Because Juliette Adams wasn't just a humanitarian activist and Boston socialite. Juliette was the Grand Master of the Trinity Masters. Leader of America's oldest and most powerful secret society. The identity of the Grand Master was a closely guarded secret; in fact, Rose wasn't even sure if Lachlan had known exactly who the Grand Master was before tonight.

Juliette and Devon's kidnapping wasn't just an attack on Franco's spouses; it was probably an attack on the Trinity Masters itself.

"Right, so..." the Archivist said, pulling her attention back to the one person in the room whose presence Rose didn't understand.

"Why are you here?" she asked.

"Wait, Price is in the elevator," Sebastian cut in.

Rose didn't see why they had to wait. Price Bennett was, like Sebastian and Rose, one of the Grand Master's counselors. They served as advisers most of the time, fixers when needed, and their identities within the Trinity Masters were also secret. Price was the one counselor Juliette had retained from her brother Harrison's tenure as Grand Master, but Price had taken a passive role within the council, acting more as a form of institutional memory.

"Are we safe?" the Archivist asked.

"The hotel is secure," Lachlan said. "I have two men in the lobby, one on the roof, and the others are checking on the library."

"You don't answer to him," Rose told Lachlan while eyeing the Irishman.

"The library is compromised," Sebastian said. "We shouldn't bring attention to it."

Lachlan raised his brows. "They won't." His tone made it clear he was insulted by Sebastian's comment.

There was a knock on the door, and Price walked into the room. "What happened?"

"Are we waiting for anyone else?" Lachlan asked, looking at Franco.

Rose stepped in front of Franco, answering for him. "No. We need to act."

"We need to find them," Franco snarled.

It was shocking to hear the normally clever, sweet man sound so feral.

"We will." Lachlan walked over and crouched by Franco. "I will. We're already on it. But it would help if I had more information."

That seemed to calm Franco. Or maybe the anxiety medication she'd given him was taking effect.

"Can you tell us what happened?" Lachlan asked.

"They took them. Juliette and Devon. They're gone."

The heartbreak in Franco's words made Rose's own heart ache, and she checked the urge to grab her phone to text Marek and Wes, just to make sure they were okay. She'd been at the symphony with her husbands when her phone buzzed in her clutch. Given that she'd put it on "emergency mode"—a custom setting that looked like the phone was off but would vibrate if calls from certain numbers came in—she hadn't hesitated to leap from her seat when she felt it go off.

Despite it being incredibly rude, she had raced out of Symphony Hall and answered, only to hear Franco's frantic voice saying almost exactly the same words he'd just said to Lachlan. It was the Irishman who'd gotten on the line, provided the name of the hotel, then ended the call.

Wes and Marek had followed her out, her husbands knowing she wouldn't have gotten up without a good reason. Sometimes it still shocked her, the closeness she felt, the bond between the three of them. All she'd had to do was look at them, and Marek had said, "Where?"

Together, the three of them had run down Huntington Avenue toward Copley Square, not bothering to get a taxi since they'd be faster on foot.

Sebastian had beat her to Franco's room by a few minutes. It was Sebastian who had stopped Wes and Marek at the suite door. Rose's husbands had turned around and gone to check them into a room in the hotel, promising to stay close if she needed anything.

She'd assumed Sebastian had barred the way because they weren't members of the council, and therefore didn't have clearance to be in this room right now. Rose glanced at "the Archivist," and wondered if Wes and Marek being stopped at the door actually had more to do with the fact that Marek was former Masters' Admiralty, and Wes had spent years living in England.

Rose's journey to happiness had involved a decades-old mystery and spanned continents, bringing her into contact with the Trinity Masters' European counterpart, the Masters' Admiralty. The European secret society was far older than the Trinity Masters, and the two organizations had fallen out of contact, thanks to treachery and lies. Now a tentative relationship was being forged, but that didn't mean Rose liked the Archivist's presence here tonight. It was suspicious.

"Yes, they're gone," Lachlan agreed, focused on Franco. "Where were you when this happened?"

"Just have him start at the beginning." Sebastian looked like he was ready to shake the information out of Franco.

Lachlan cast Sebastian a cold look. "Mr. Stewart, please don't interfere."

Franco took a deep breath, then shook his head as if clearing it. "The library. They were taken from the library."

"Where in the library?"

"The back, the Boylston Building."

The Boston Public Library was old, at least in the context of the United States, and was actually two buildings joined together. When people mentioned the Boston Public Library, they were usually referring to the Central Library. A stately Renaissance-style building with grand reading rooms, it was both a tourist destination and a favorite of students from one of Boston's many universities. The entrance was on Dartmouth, looking out on Copley Square and facing Trinity Church.

This whole section of the city was built on what had once been water. When they filled in the back bay, one of the original architects had an underground building constructed in secret. That underground structure, directly below the library, was the Trinity Masters' headquarters, accessed via a hidden elevator. The fact that they were taken from the library implied that whoever had taken Juliette and Devon knew where headquarters was. Hence, the location might be compromised.

While the Central Library was the famous tourist destination and aesthetic study location, there was actually a second building, linked to the first, referred to as the Boylston Street Building, which was a more modern library. Carpets instead of marble floors, computer stations, dedicated spaces for children and teens, it was the library used by Bostonians for day-to-day needs.

"Not in the rare books room?" Lachlan clarified. The rare books room was where the secret elevator was hidden.

"No. I mean we were near the rare books room. They were planning to go down to headquarters, but I was staying up top because I was meeting with Colum."

At that, everyone looked at the Irishman, whose eyes widened slightly. He leaned back, as if putting space between him and Lachlan would lessen the danger he only now realized he was in.

"We were in a little side room on the second floor, near the connecting hall. You know, the connecting hall where the travel books are?"

Rose nodded, though she did not, in fact, know what Franco was talking about.

"They have a good travel section. The library, I mean. I don't know why they put it in the hall. They should have it somewhere more central. Travel books are both inspirational and aspirational."

Lachlan nodded at Franco and without looking away, said, "What did you give him?"

Rose knew Lachlan was speaking to her. "Anxiety medication."

"Okay." Lachlan cleared his throat. "Franco. I want you to tell me what happened when they took Juliette and Devon."

Franco's face started to crumple.

"Tell it like a story," Colum said, in his lilting Irish accent. "Not that it happened to you. Only but it's a story you're telling."

Franco nodded. "Right. I can do that. I'm on drugs after all. Good drugs. Thanks, Rose."

Rose could feel Sebastian staring at her, but she ignored him.

Franco took a breath. "Some people came down the hall, I think they were in the Washington Room, or maybe just came from that direction. They wore masks, medical masks, not bank robber masks."

The tension was thick in the room, Franco's measured words an improvement over the frantic repetition of "they're gone," but still frustratingly slow.

"We weren't talking about trinity stuff, so we didn't have to stop talking. Devon was discussing something with the remodeling—we're not done with the house yet. I was looking at the travel books because, well...books."

Colum shrugged. "What else would ye be doing?"

"Right?" Franco turned to him. "They had a few books from this new—"

Lachlan cleared his throat and Rose took a steadying breath, the tight bodice of her formal gown digging into her ribs. Franco's attention shifted back to Lachlan, and he nodded slowly, almost bobbing his head.

"What did the men do?" Lachlan asked.

"They walked right up to Devon and...and they shot him."

The silence that followed that statement was broken only by the heavy sound of Franco's breathing.

"I heard the pop. It was loud. Juliette screamed, and they grabbed her. One pressed a gun to her head. She looked at me, and I thought I was about to see someone blow my wife's brains out."

Rose's heart broke for him. Franco's unnatural calm, thanks to the anxiety medication, somehow made the words worse than if he'd been sobbing or raging as he said them.

"But they didn't. One of them put a needle in her neck, and then a bag over her head. It was so fast. I ran toward them, but someone hit me. I tried to fight." Franco stopped, shook his head. "No. I fought. I did. I fought." His expression didn't change, but a tear slid down his face. "It wasn't enough. I tried to get to Devon. They had him on the ground, and I think they were...helping him? I grabbed him, tried to drag him away, but they stopped me. I think they hit me again. I was on the floor watching as they put them, both of them, into carts. Big laundry carts."

There was silence when he finished.

"Check his head," Lachlan said to no one in particular.

Rose leaned forward, but it was Colum who got up on one knee on the couch and started gently ruffling through Franco's hair.

"He's got a fecking big knot on the back of his head."

"If he has a concussion, the drugs probably weren't a good idea," Sebastian said.

"How about you get him some ice?" Rose countered.

"Okay, Franco. We're going to go over it again," Lachlan said.

Rose sat as Lachlan methodically walked Franco through the attack again and again. Each time, he asked slightly different questions, refining what they knew.

It was bad.

At least five men had attacked. Two men had taken down Devon, one shooting him in the chest, the other putting pressure on the wound once he was down. Another two had taken Juliette, one grabbing her, the other wielding the syringe. There must have been a fifth person, probably a lookout, who hit Franco. The man who'd had the syringe carried a duffel bag, and possibly had some medical training, because from what Franco remembered, it seemed like they'd done some initial triage on Devon before loading him up and taking him away.

Lachlan finally rose, and Price stepped in, holding out a bag of ice to Franco.

Franco stared at it. "What's this for?"

Colum took it and held it to Franco's head.

"Ow."

Lachlan tipped his head to the far corner of the suite's living room. Rose joined him at the window, Sebastian and Price only a step behind her.

"It wasn't an assassination," Lachlan said. "They would have left the bodies."

"If Devon was shot in the chest..." Price shook his head. "Immediate field triage increases his chances dramatically."

Rose had to turn away and look out the window.

The cornerstone of the society was arranged marriages, and occasionally, there were childhood betrothals. That's what had happened with Rose, Devon, and Juliette. She'd grown up knowing that they would one day be her spouses.

That had unraveled when Juliette unexpectedly became the Grand Master and broke the betrothal. If things had gone the way Rose's parents had wanted, Rose would currently be married to Devon and Juliette. She'd be their third, not Franco.

Rose's family had been a collection of bigoted assholes who referred to themselves as purists, and because of them, she'd never let herself get too close to Devon or Juliette, even back when they were betrothed. Still, she'd cared for both of them, as much as she'd allowed herself to. The idea of them dead...

"Ransom?" Sebastian asked. "Should we be expecting a call?"

"Unclear," Lachlan said, "but we'll take measures. We have some good K&R people amongst the Warrior Scholars. However, I think we should assume this is an attack on the society itself."

Sebastian and Price both looked at her.

Rose raised a brow. "It's not me."

Yes, in the past she might have tried to burn down and blow up the society, but nowadays, she was married and boring and in therapy.

"If you've been hiding information and protecting more purists—" Sebastian started.

Rose bared her teeth in a maybe-smile. "I haven't. I'm loyal and Juliette trusts me."

"Last time we were attacked it was you," Sebastian doggedly went on.

"And if your brother hadn't—"

"No." Lachlan sank a command into that one word. He didn't say "stop" or "shut up." Just "no," but it cut Rose off mid-sentence. He was right, fighting amongst themselves didn't help, and bringing up the past only served to distract them from what they should be doing right now. Which was finding and rescuing Devon and Juliette.

"We assume this is an attack on the society. Headquarters should be considered compromised, meaning no one goes down there. Like I said, I have people checking the library now, but if possible, we should close the entire building, just to be safe."

Price nodded. "I'll call Lee Hager. He's the Director of Operations and a longtime member."

"If this is an attack on the society, did they take Juliette to weaken the Trinity Masters or to get information?" Rose asked.

"The faster we find them, the less time they have to torture information out of them," Lachlan said too loudly.

"Fuck," Franco breathed, his eyes glossy, though he was unnaturally calm.

"Price, can you get security footage for the area around the library?" Lachlan continued.

Price owned Bennett Security, a massive private security firm that had access to things it definitely shouldn't.

Lachlan started laying out what he needed, and Price tapped his phone as Lachlan spoke.

Rose touched Sebastian's arm, tilting her head to indicate she wanted to talk in private. They walked over to the corner where no one would overhear. She glanced at Colum and Franco, sitting silently on the couch. Colum held the bag of ice to Franco's head. Franco's eyes were half closed. Rose knew that reality would hit him like a ton of bricks when the drugs wore off, but at least he'd have a little time.

"What happens if we can't rescue them?"

Sebastian's jaw muscle flexed, his face stamped with anger. "Ready to declare them dead?"

"No, you emotionally immature asshole, I'm saying the Grand Master is gone. My whole life has been a series of worst-case scenarios becoming reality, so I like to be prepared."

"We'll find them."

"Unless we find them in the next few hours, we need to have a plan. What about when Izabel Serra, Rowan Greene, and Brennon Reyes come back for their marriage ceremony?"

"Is that why you're in Boston?" Sebastian eyed her.

"No, I'm in Boston to kidnap my former fiancés. Yes, dumbass. Izabel is a friend, and they had a little reception after their binding ceremony last night, and tonight we were at the symphony together." Rose gestured to her dress. "We're supposed to be flying back to the West Coast tomorrow."

"If Izabel, Rowan, and Brennon just had their binding ceremony, they aren't due back for a formal marriage ceremony for a month."

Rose had forgotten that there was a month between the binding and marriage ceremonies.

"We'll have Juliette and Devon back by then," Sebastian insisted. "Until they're back... We'll just put everything on hold. No major decisions or ceremonies."

"The Trinity Masters is full of dangerous, powerful people," Rose countered. "Even if we keep this a secret, not having a leader is a bad idea."

"Fair. If the Grand Master is incapacitated..." Sebastian's expression went blank. "I...I don't know what, or who, takes over. Maybe we do? As counselors?"

"What about the keyholders?"

The question came from the couch. Colum was looking at them and had apparently been listening in.

Price and Lachlan stopped talking and turned to look at the Irishman.

"If the Grand Master is killed or compromised, doesn't one of the keyholders become your acting Grand Master?" Colum asked.

Rose looked at Sebastian, who met her gaze and then spun to Colum. "Who the hell are the keyholders?"

CHAPTER TWO

B oston
   One month before the kidnapping

KAILANI IONA WALKED out of the dressing room. The room beyond felt like a cave, and not just because it was underground. Dark, save for the lights that illuminated a giant triquetra medallion embedded in the stone floor, the altar room was something she'd heard about from her parents when they told stories about their own marriage.

She'd been excited on her way here, nerves only settling in as she accessed the secret elevator at the back of a closet in the rare books room of the Boston Public Library. The weight of the library rested on the roof of the Trinity Masters' underground headquarters.

Now her stomach was in knots, and Kailani's knees shook as she followed a path of lighter stone in the floor to a chair on the edge of the medallion. When she was close enough, she could see the looming form of two other chairs. Two other robed figures were following their own paths, and as one, they stepped around to the front of their chairs and sat. There was a moment of quiet before the Grand Master appeared from the darkness.

A black robe with a deep hood hid the Grand Master's face.

A legacy of the Trinity Masters, Kailani had looked forward to the day when she would be called to this altar and introduced to her future spouses.

The day Kailani had received her invitation to join had been one of the happiest days of her life because being a legacy —the child of Trinity Masters members—didn't guarantee her own inclusion. She was essentially fast-tracked thanks to her name, moving to the top of the list, but she had to earn her place, prove herself worthy.

Unlike her own plain robe, the Grand Master's had a chain of gold disks across the chest, draped from shoulder to shoulder.

The Grand Master was the reason she was here today. The leader of the society arranged each of the trinity marriages, selecting trios and binding them together with a purpose. Sometimes it was to protect one of the members or to ensure a brilliant scholar or artist was supported. Sometimes it was in an effort to spur scientific advancement. Other times it was to solidify alliances that were necessary to maintain the strength of the union.

"When you joined the Trinity Masters, you made a vow. You pledged your lives to our cause and our way. The time has come for you to meet your partners, your lovers, your spouses. When I call your name, stand and lower your hood," the Grand Master said.

The voice was feminine. Several years ago, the position of Grand Master had changed hands, and though no one knew the identity of the society's leader, the shift from a man to a woman, as evidenced by the voice, had been a topic of much gossip and speculation.

Kailani's *tutu* had said "about damn time" when she'd heard it was a woman.

"John Wilson."

Kailani gripped the arms of her chair, leaning forward slightly as one of the robed figures stood. Members had choices when it came to the ceremony—they arrived robed and were meant to reveal themselves when their name was called. Some people just took down the hood, some stripped the robe off, revealing underwear or lingerie, while others stripped off the robe and were naked underneath, showing that they came to the marriage open and vulnerable.

John Wilson shrugged off the robe, and Kailani got her first good look at her future husband.

He was white, with brown hair and a close-cropped beard. He was taller than her, which wasn't saying much, and he wasn't completely naked. He wore a pair of solid black boxer briefs that hugged his muscled thighs. He glanced at her, and though she knew he couldn't see her face, thanks to the lights and the hood, she smiled.

He looked slightly uncomfortable—he tried to put his hands in his pockets, but there weren't any, so dropped them to his sides—but his gaze was sharp, assessing.

John Wilson. Good name. Good-looking man.

Some of Kailani's nerves settled.

The Grand Master shifted, the movement barely visible since they stood on the edge of the cone of light. Still, it was enough to attract her attention, and when Kailani looked over, the Grand Master's hood was turned toward her. Kailani froze, waiting for her name to be called, but it wasn't her name the Grand Master said.

"Benjamin Dara."

The Grand Master was looking right at her as she said the name. That look was a warning...a threat.

Because the Grand Master had to know that the last person on earth Kailani would ever marry was Benjamin Dara.

Benjamin—always "Benjamin," never "Ben," or God forbid "Benny"—stood and shrugged off his robe.

Tall with lean muscles, Benjamin was black, with close-cut hair and a goatee. He was also a grade-A asshole.

Kailani stared at the Grand Master, wishing she could see into the darkness of the hood. Why would the Grand Master do this to her? She had to know about her and Benjamin's history...

"Kailani Iona."

Kailani sprang to her feet. She'd bought beautiful lingerie specifically for this, but there was no way she was taking off her robe now. She shoved back her hood and met Benjamin's gaze. The shock she felt was reflected in his expression.

Kailani turned to the Grand Master. "Grand Master, with all due respect, we can't be married because—"

"You can."

Those two words fell like a hammer. Kailani rocked back on her heels.

The rest of the ceremony passed in a blur. Kailani went through with it because there was nothing else she *could* do. When she'd joined, she'd pledged to obey the Grand Master. She knew the penalties for betraying the society.

Finally, the Grand Master said, "A trinity marriage isn't easy, but if you love and trust one another, you will never be alone."

When it was over, Kailani raced back to her dressing room.

She had her clothes on and was out in the corridor in under ten minutes. Her plan was to get out before she had to see

Benjamin. She needed time to regroup and think, and she certainly wasn't going to go to the hotel with her fiancés. Ordinarily, newly bound trinities stayed in a special suite at the Park Plaza for a few days, as the first part of their month-long get-to-know-you period. They also started making decisions about merging their lives together.

Oh my God. In thirty days, she would have to come back here and get married to Benjamin Dara.

Unfortunately, Benjamin and John seemed to have the same "rush out" plan she did because as she stepped into the corridor, they walked out of their own dressing rooms.

Kailani froze, then stormed past Benjamin.

He reached out, caught her arm. "Kailani."

She yanked her arm away. "Don't touch me."

John rushed over to them, his gaze assessing. "You two... know each other."

"You could say that." Benjamin was looking at her in a way that made Kailani's blood heat. No, it made her blood boil because she hated him.

"Ah." John looked between them. "I'm guessing you don't get along?"

"The Daras are amoral assholes," Kailani said.

Benjamin scoffed. "Don't be naive. Your family's money isn't exactly lily-white."

"Wait, your families? This has to do with family history?" John asked.

"Yes," Benjamin said.

"No," Kailani countered. "Benjamin is an ass all on his own without taking into account his family's willingness to destroy things to ensure fourth-quarter profit."

"Who are your families?" John asked slowly.

"The Daras own Ironclad Airlines, Endaragon Energy, and

a couple of weapons manufacturers that make them part of the military industrial complex," Kailani explained.

"And the Iona family is in politics and hotels. They own large chunks of Hawaii and want to maintain the status quo there to ensure they don't have too much competition," Benjamin interjected.

"That's bullshit," Kailani snarled.

"It's true, and your tree-hugging is laughable, given that you need tourists for your business to survive."

"Your families own airlines and hotels. Right." John blinked.

Kailani turned to him. "John, I'm so sorry. I'm making a terrible first impression." She slid her arm through his. "Maybe we can go to dinner to get to know one another. I promise I'm a very reasonable individual, normally."

"We'll all go," Benjamin said.

"Absolutely not," she shot back.

"Why? Are you still mad about that time we hooked up?"

The way he said it, almost with pity, made Kailani feel small and stupid all over again.

"Wait, you dated?" John asked.

"Of course not," Benjamin said. "We're legacies—our parents are members of the Trinity Masters. We grew up knowing we'd have arranged marriages, so we didn't date. What would be the point? But we were friends when we were younger, and once the hormones kicked in, there was a lot of hooking up."

Kailani felt sick because Benjamin was right. It wasn't his fault that she'd fallen in love with him when she was nineteen. She'd been naive, painfully so, but thought she was worldly. She'd seen herself and Benjamin as "Romeo and Juliet"—their families' businesses and interests were at war, but she and Benjamin would fall in love, and that would fix everything.

She'd imagined that their love would be so pure and powerful that the Grand Master would see that and place them in a trinity together to codify the relationship.

Actually, at nineteen, wildly in love with a boy who'd swept her off her feet, she'd taken the fantasy a step further, dreaming that she and Benjamin had the only duo marriage in the society. At the time, she couldn't imagine sharing him with anyone, even a third in their marriage.

She'd apparently forgotten how "Romeo and Juliet" ended because she'd been shocked when everything had fallen apart.

They'd spent a magical summer traveling and having sex and doing every romantic thing two young people with money and time could think to do. And in the fall, when they were both due back at college, Benjamin had casually kissed her, said "that was fun," and a week later, she saw a picture of him with another girl.

Maybe she could have recovered from that, but two months later, a bill her senator uncle was sponsoring had the legs cut out from under it. Lobbyists known to work with the Dara family solidified opposition to the legislation before it was even fully written.

Kailani had tearfully confessed to her uncle and grandparents that she'd mentioned the bill to Benjamin when they were together. Benjamin had given that information to his family, who in turn had used it against her own family.

Kailani's uncle and grandparents hadn't been mad, just disappointed.

And Kailani had spent the next few years wondering if Benjamin had started that summer fling with her specifically to get information from her. Time and distance told her that wasn't the case, that the Daras were too powerful and well connected for that legislation to have been more than a nuisance. Instead, his betrayal had been a casual crime of opportunity that had fractured not only her trust but her relationship with her beloved grandparents and uncle.

Maybe if she'd been able to avoid him in the years since, Kailani could have made this work. But their jobs for their respective families had brought them into opposition again and again. And every time they clashed, he made her feel like that naive young woman who'd fallen in love one summer.

"I'll call for dinner reservations once we're upstairs," Benjamin said, glancing at his phone.

"I'm not going to dinner with you," Kailani repeated.

"Kailani, don't be dramatic."

Goddammit. He always made her feel so stupid. Rage made her throat tight, her hand clenching around John's arm.

"They can force me to marry you, but they can't force me to like you. They can't force me to go to dinner with you or live with you." Kailani felt bitter satisfaction when Benjamin's eyes narrowed. "I'll marry you. I'll walk back in here a month from now and say the vows, but I'll never be your wife. Plenty of trinities live separately."

"That's not fair," Benjamin ground out.

"Fair?" Kailani smiled, and she knew it was bitter. "Don't be naive, Benjamin. Life isn't fair."

"This seems like a fairly major issue," John said quietly.

"I won't be held hostage in my own marriage." Benjamin took a step toward her, looming over her.

"You don't like that idea? Guess what, I don't care."

"You're going to be my wife."

"In name only. As far as I'm concerned, after the ceremony, I don't ever want to see you again."

John cleared his throat, but before he could say anything, the sound of footsteps interrupted.

Devon Asher turned the corner into the corridor. A robe

hung open from his shoulders, showing off a casually expensive dress shirt and pants.

"The Grand Master sent me to find out why you're still here and not on your way to the hotel."

Kailani swallowed hard. Devon was another legacy, and if he was here, it probably meant he was on the Grand Master's council. The council members' identities were meant to be a secret, so the fact that the Grand Master had sent him, essentially revealing the fact that he was a counselor, didn't bode well.

"We have a problem," Benjamin said.

"No, we don't," Kailani countered.

"Uh, yeah, we do," John said with an apologetic look her way.

"You have time to work through whatever problems...whatever history...you have," Devon said.

"Time won't help. Kailani is refusing to be in the trinity," Benjamin said.

"Asshole," Kailani breathed, but Devon was looking at her with a merciless gaze that reminded her that, according to gossip, Devon worked for the CIA. She wondered if he was the one the Grand Master tasked with "disappearing" problem Trinity Masters members.

"I am not refusing anything," she said. "I know my duty. I'll be back here in a month to get married."

"You're refusing to go to dinner with me. You're refusing to live with me, to really be my wife," Benjamin countered, and there was emotion in his voice she couldn't name.

"Kailani?" Devon asked.

"Do the rules of the society say I have to live with my trinity?"

Devon didn't say anything.

"Do the rules force me to have sex with him?" She raised a brow.

"No," Devon said softly.

"Then there's no problem." Kailani turned to John. "Would you like to get some dinner?"

"I think we should stay here and talk it out."

It was killing her that John probably thought she was a bitch. Kailani's throat was tight, and she was on the verge of angry tears. She had no intention of crying in front of any of these men.

"Gentlemen, if you'll excuse me?"

Kailani turned and walked away, Benjamin's words seeming to follow her.

"Devon, I need to lodge a formal request for the Grand Master to dissolve this trinity."

CHAPTER THREE

Oahu
One month later, and two hours after the Grand Master was kidnapped

KAILANI MADE her sixth trip across the living room, aware that if she kept this up, she was going to wear a path in the carpet, which would piss her off...because it was fluffy and new and clean. The Hale'ekolu hotel was one of Honolulu's oldest and most exclusive properties, known for restrained elegance and the ever-important spirit of aloha. Owned by her family for generations, the Hale'ekolu had been undergoing major renovations the past few months, this bank of suites the first to be completed.

She sighed as she glanced out the window of the hotel room, staring at the grounds below. She couldn't wait until the construction was finished, the view of the beautiful gardens currently marred by scaffolding, small excavators, and building materials. It was the off-season, though in Hawaii, that wasn't saying much since the hotel was full ninety percent of the time. Still, they'd discounted room rates and were paying extra to have the work completed before summer.

Kailani pressed her forehead against the glass and closed her eyes, warding off the coming headache. She hadn't had a peaceful night's sleep since that damn binding ceremony, too many bad feelings she thought she'd managed to overcome crashing down on her again.

Shortly after the binding ceremony, Kailani had caught a flight to L.A. for one night, wanting to apologize to John for her behavior after the binding ceremony. The poor man had been collateral damage, caught in the middle of her battle with Benjamin.

The LAPD detective had been understanding once she'd explained—more calmly—her reasons for not wanting to marry Benjamin. She'd focused primarily on the contentiousness between their families, barely mentioning the summer romance she and Benjamin had shared because she was too afraid of revealing how much their break-up had hurt her at the time.

John had confided that after she'd left headquarters, Benjamin asked Devon about dissolving the trinity. Kailani had heard that much, but John filled her in on the parts she'd missed.

According to Devon, there was no appeal process, no way to dissolve a trinity, but he'd promised to talk to the Grand Master. Of course, Devon had also stressed that if they didn't hear from the Grand Master before the month was up, the three of them would be expected to return to Boston and get married.

Kailani had been shocked to discover there was even the tiniest bit of hope, and unfortunately, she'd clung too tightly to it, jumping every time the phone rang, praying it was their reprieve.

During her visit to California, she'd gotten the sense John was hoping for the same outcome she and Benjamin were. And she couldn't blame him. There would be no happily ever after for the three of them if the Grand Master refused to dissolve the trinity.

Since then, she and John had spoken a couple of times on FaceTime. After each conversation, she found herself more and more disappointed the two of them hadn't been paired up with a different third, anyone besides Benjamin, because she didn't question for a second that John was someone she could come to care for, even love.

If only the phone would ring.

If only the Grand Master would grant their request.

If only it hadn't been Benjamin beneath that hood.

If only...

Ugh.

She could hear her grandmother's powerful, raspy voice, chastising her for working herself into a state over something she had no control of. Tutu, a no-nonsense woman, would simply look at her and say, "*Ku'uipo*, you're alive and breathing, so behave like it."

Kailani had no idea why those words had always worked, but dammit if they didn't sink in and soothe the rough edges.

Today...they weren't having the desired effect, as she forced herself back to the couch and made herself sit down.

No more pacing.

No more freaking out.

She could do this.

She'd known this day was coming ever since returning from her trip to Boston four weeks earlier, and while she'd tried to distract herself with work, the overwhelming feeling of dread had never fully lifted.

She jumped, startled, when there was a knock at the door.

Even though she'd been expecting it.

Time's up.

She took a deep, steadying breath, then rose and crossed the room.

Kailani opened the door, and her smile came easily when she saw John.

"Aloha, John," she said. "It's so nice to see you again."

"It's good to see you too, Kailani." John stepped into the room. His smile was warm and friendly, and her heart panged a little as, once again, she wished things were different.

Kailani hadn't recognized his name or handsome face at the binding ceremony, which made sense as she'd since learned that—unlike her and Benjamin—he wasn't a legacy. His name had been put forth for membership by the mayor of L.A.

A detective in the major crimes division, John had the best homicide closure rate in the country, cracking over two hundred cases, most with confessions, and he was still young, only thirty-five.

John held his duffel bag, and her stomach sank at the sight of it, even though her own suitcase was packed and ready at her apartment should things not go the way she hoped today.

"Go ahead and put your bag down here. This suite will be yours. I thought we could chat, in private, before heading down to lunch."

Her smile faded when she heard another voice at the door.

"Hello, Kailani."

She scowled, her voice cold when she said, "Benjamin."

Turning away from Benjamin, she offered him no other greeting or even an invitation to come in. Instead, she walked over to the couch and sat back down heavily.

"Good to see you too," Benjamin said, sarcastically dragging his ridiculously oversized suitcase into the suite.

What the hell did he have in there?

Kailani pointedly ignored him.

They were all here together at John's request. He had contacted both of them via email a few days earlier, asking if the three of them could meet in Boston a day or two prior to the wedding ceremony.

It was Benjamin who'd suggested meeting at Hale'ekolu, as he was in Japan for business, and his flight was stopping in Hawaii on the way back to the states anyway. John was going the wrong way by flying west to Hawaii first, but she was grateful they were here because in truth, the timing of the binding ceremony couldn't have been worse. She was knee-deep in the renovation project and her absence meant more work for her family if she left the hotel.

"How have you been?" she asked John, who claimed the spot next to her on the couch.

"Busy. While L.A. is sometimes short on water, the same can't be said for criminals. I've just closed a case. Double homicide."

"You cracked it?" Benjamin asked as he sank down in an overstuffed chair across from them.

Kailani was curious about Benjamin's question, as well as his familiarity with John.

John nodded. "I did. Finally. The media surrounding the case hindered us for a while, as we were forced to work our way through hundreds of calls from people who thought they saw or heard or knew something. In the end, it was one of those calls that panned out and pointed us in the right direction."

John must have read the confusion on Kailani's face. "Benjamin had a layover in L.A. last week prior to his business in Japan. We met for lunch."

Kailani nodded, grateful for his explanation, even though she felt guilty for thrusting John into the middle of their drama.

"So...no word from the Grand Master?" John asked, addressing the elephant in the room.

Benjamin shook his head. "Not yet. If we don't hear from her soon..."

He didn't bother to finish. They knew time was running out. If they didn't hear from the Grand Master within the next twenty-four hours, the three of them would be hopping on a plane bound for Boston tomorrow...to their wedding ceremony.

John's expression was pensive, even troubled. Their two FaceTime calls had been surface-y. She'd apologized each time, and after that, the two of them had limited their discussions to work and personal interests such as favorite movies, reading preferences, and why Hawaiian poke was the greatest food on the planet. John, foolish man, insisted tacos were the best. They hadn't broached the subject of the disastrous binding ceremony since Kailani's in-person visit.

"What do we think the likelihood is that we'll hear from them?" John asked.

Kailani shrugged helplessly because she had no idea.

"My working knowledge of how the Trinity Masters is run is limited. My actual experience begins and ends with the invitation, initiation, and basic orientation," John confessed. "Because of my job, I haven't had the opportunity to travel to Boston for the quarterly meetings, and I haven't attended any of the gala events. There's always been a case to work."

Kailani reached out and grasped his hand. "I'm sorry this was your introduction to the trinity marriage."

Benjamin made a sound between a scoff and a snort, but she refused to acknowledge it—or him—in any way.

John squeezed her hand. "I appreciate the apology, but it doesn't solve the problem of what we're going to do if the Grand Master says no to dissolving this trinity."

"Devon said—" Benjamin started.

"Devon said he would talk to the Grand Master," John interjected, "but—if you'll forgive my paraphrasing—he also said the three of us need to figure our shit out. Which we've yet to do."

"John," she said, but he interrupted her, just as he had Benjamin.

"You're both legacies," he said, and while it wasn't a question, Kailani nodded anyway. "What are your parents' relationships like?" he asked.

Kailani smiled. "I have a dad and two moms, and the three of them have a very close, loving relationship."

John rubbed his jaw. "All three of them?"

"Yes. They all share a bed." She paused. "My moms have a romantic relationship with each other as well as with my father, if that's what you're asking. I have an older brother, and the two of us were raised as siblings, despite the fact we have different biological mothers."

"That sounds nice," John said, turning his attention to Benjamin. "Your parents the same?"

Benjamin shook his head. "No. I have two fathers and a mother, but all three of them have their own bedrooms. My fathers are best friends, as close as brothers, both in love with my mother."

"I see." John was taking in all that they were telling him, and Kailani realized just how wrong they were not to have had at least some of these discussions prior to now.

She shouldn't have walked away after the binding ceremony, but the moment Benjamin took off that robe, a lifetime of pain and anger came bubbling to the surface. She'd needed distance to sort through all the emotions, but they wouldn't give it to her.

So, instead, she'd run fast and far, licking her wounds and leaving far too much unsaid.

"My parents have a loving relationship," Benjamin hastened to add. "But...well, my dads are straight, so I suppose their relationship is a bit different from the one the Iona family shares."

"Different," John mused, and Kailani got a sense he was trying to figure out what to say next. "Were you hoping for a relationship like your parents?" John asked Kailani.

She nodded. "I was. I dreamed of the day I would meet and fall in love with my partners, building a life, a family together. To be perfectly honest, I wouldn't have been upset if the Grand Master had given me a wife and a husband. I've always been jealous of the closeness between my two moms."

"And, Benjamin, did you want the same relationship your parents have?"

Benjamin didn't respond immediately, then he admitted, "Not exactly like theirs. I always imagined I'd share a bedroom with my trinity."

"Even if your trinity included another man?" John asked.

"I grew up in this society, John," Benjamin said. "As legacies, we knew there would always be a chance that one of our partners would be the same sex, and especially in modern times, most legacy members make sure they're prepared for whatever form the trinity takes."

"Is that your way of telling me you're bi?" A slight grin crossed John's face.

"Most of my past lovers have been female, but I have...on occasion..." Benjamin playfully wiggled his eyebrows the same way he used to when they were younger and he teased Kailani. The look was achingly familiar, reminding her of that brief moment in time when she'd been madly in love with him. It took her breath away and her heart panged. She hated that he could still provoke such strong emotions in her.

Love, hate, heartbreak, joy, anger, fun. She'd experienced it all with Benjamin.

"What about you?" Benjamin countered. "Have you ever been with a man?"

John leaned back, resting his arms along the cushions of the couch, his hand resting just an inch or two from Kailani's shoulder. She was tempted to scoot closer, overwhelmed by the desire to touch him, and to have him touch her. She'd felt an instant attraction to him at the binding ceremony, and it had grown as she got to know him better.

But she kept her distance, aware that she had no right to muddy those waters, especially not until they picked their way across this minefield.

"I grew up in foster care," John announced.

Kailani's eyes widened. Family was one of the subjects neither of them had broached before today. Now she wondered if that was because John had been hesitant to talk about it.

"I didn't realize," she said softly.

John sighed. "These are the things we should have been saying to each other over the past month. Now...we've left it all too late."

His tone was gentle, but she felt chastised by the words just the same.

She leaned toward him, brushing his hand with her shoulder, closing the distance between them despite knowing she shouldn't. While Benjamin provoked too many emotions inside her at once, all she felt right now as she looked at John was guilt. "I know. I'm sorry."

John brushed her hair away from her face, tucking it behind her ear in a way that was equal parts sweet and sexy. He gave her shoulder a gentle squeeze, then turned his attention back to Benjamin.

Kailani glanced over, saw the dark expression on Benjamin's face.

"I spent some time in a group home, an orphanage," John continued. "Hit puberty there. So did the guy I was sharing a room with. We did some exploring. Mainly just touching, hand jobs, blowjobs."

"That's it?" Benjamin asked.

John nodded. "That's it."

Benjamin considered that, rubbing his jaw. "Even though you're not a legacy, you must have given some thought since joining about what your trinity would look like."

"I have," John confessed. "I've thought about it a lot. My desires are very similar to yours and Kailani's. I want a relationship—physical and emotional—with my spouses. That matters more than what's in someone's pants."

He looked at Kailani, his voice soft. "Kailani, if the Grand Master doesn't call, if we do get married, are you still refusing to be a part of it, still unwilling to live with Benjamin?"

John had clearly come to Hawaii with an agenda. Given the way she and Benjamin had done all the talking after the binding ceremony, then cut off all meaningful conversation since then, the least she could do was offer him honesty.

She stiffened, aware how cold this would sound, but she had a right to protect herself. And protecting herself meant keeping Benjamin out of her life. "Being in a trinity doesn't mean I'm obligated to live with, or sleep with—"

"Dammit, Kailani! I'm not going to sit here and listen to this anymore." Benjamin slapped his palm on the arm of the chair before standing. She stiffened, ready to pick up the fight where they left it a month earlier. "Stop being so obstinate. It's beneath you." He stared at her for a moment, expression unreadable. "You can't still be pissed off about the airport."

Kailani rose, rage at his dismissal of all the pain he'd caused, making her lean toward him angrily. "You want to talk about the airport? Fine. You wanted to expand Honolulu airport so your family's airline could have more gates, but it would have increased emissions by thirty percent, and done even more damage to the air quality on that part of the island."

"We were going to put seventy million dollars' worth of solar panels on the airport building as part of the improvements!"

Kailani resisted the urge to roll her eyes, keeping her tone cool and irritated. "The fact that you think that's some magnanimous gift is—"

John raised his hand and his voice. "Enough! Sit down. Both of you."

Kailani fell silent in an instant, stunned by the vehemence of his tone. She'd formed an opinion of John during their too-brief acquaintance, assuming his success as a detective stemmed from his mild mannerisms and his peaceful way of relating to others. In her mind, she'd placed him in the role of "good cop," drawing out all those confessions because he was relatable and an easygoing guy.

But now, with his face flushed, his shoulders stiff, his voice deep and loud, she was rethinking that, as she was introduced to the "bad cop" for the first time.

She and Benjamin exchanged a quick glance, and she could see he was as shocked as she was by John's aggression because both of them resumed their seats immediately.

"I've spent the last month listening to what the two of you aren't going to do. So now it's my turn, because I think you need to know what I'm not going to do. I am *not* going to be the 'child'," he finger quoted, "stuck in the middle of your contentious divorce. I am *not* going to shuffle from one home to the other, always playing the mediator in your arguments. I am *not* going to split my time between the two of you because you can't let go of the past and move on. I joined the Trinity Masters because I wanted the stability I never had as a kid. So I'm telling you right now...if the two of you don't knock this shit off, I'm going to—"

Kailani's phone chirped loudly, cutting John off mid-threat. She wasn't sure if she was glad of that or regretful because the masochist in her wanted to know what he was going to do.

Her heart started to race as she pulled the phone from her pocket.

The display said only "333."

"It's the Grand Master." She snuck a quick glance at Benjamin, then focused on John.

"Why are they calling you?" Benjamin frowned and pulled out his phone, checking the display to see if he'd missed a call.

"I guess we're about to have our answer." Kailani put her phone on the table and answered on speaker. John and Benjamin both leaned in, their expressions different but equally hard to read.

"This is Kailani," she said in greeting. She didn't expect this to be a conversation. Either their request was granted, or this call was to tell them what, if any, punishment there was for even asking.

"Keyholder."

Kailani froze, time seeming to stop for a moment.

"Our society is under attack."

Holy shit. Was this really happening? Was she getting *the call*?

"Please gather the others and open the door. The top lock position is now the acting Grand Master."

John was frowning, looking between her and Benjamin. Benjamin looked confused, and he shook his head at John. Both men looked at her. Kailani recovered enough to grab the phone, stabbing the screen as she tried to take it off speakerphone.

"Be careful," the voice on the other end of the line said. "Our secrets may be compromised."

Just as she managed to turn off the speakerphone, the call ended.

Kailani stared at her phone. That was a call she'd never expected to get. After all, her mother, grandmother, and great-grandmother had never received the call when they were the keyholders.

She looked at John and Benjamin. The issue of their marriage, which had consumed her thoughts and kept her from sleeping this past month, was no longer the biggest crisis in her life.

"We're not...I can't go to Boston. I don't think you have to either." She rose. "I'm sorry, I have to go."

"What was that?" Benjamin demanded. "That wasn't about our marriage."

"No, it wasn't," she agreed as she headed for the door. "It wasn't an answer to our request, but right now I have another... duty...that's more important."

John somehow beat her to the door, holding it open for her. "I'm coming with you."

"*We're* coming with you," Benjamin countered. "He said be careful. There's danger." Benjamin's face was stark as he followed her down the hall.

She was practically running, but Benjamin's long legs meant he could keep up with her at a walking pace.

"You're in danger?" Benjamin looked at her for confirmation.

Kailani didn't answer as she raced down the stairs, John and Benjamin beside her.

Again, John beat her to the exit, but this time he blocked it, his gaze bouncing from her to Benjamin and back. "Who, or what, is a keyholder?"

CHAPTER FOUR

I f Kailani thought he was going to walk away when she was in danger, she'd lost her damn mind.

Then again, apparently she thought he'd meekly accept getting shut out of his own marriage, so maybe she *had* lost her mind.

Benjamin trailed behind Kailani and John as she speed-walked through the hotel. Hale'ekolu was a beautiful property —Waikiki oceanfront, but at the northern end of the beach. The bulk of the grounds were elevated by a natural stone rise in the shoreline, making it truly oceanfront rather than beach-front. The elevation and the curve of the shore meant Hale'ekolu offered some of the most iconic views of Diamond Head.

They exited the large L-shaped building that was the modern part of the hotel. Kailani's shoes made a tapping sound on the stone floor of the open-air hallways. The modern multi-story hotel bracketed a cluster of older buildings. The property had started as a small residential hotel back before Waikiki was one of the most famous beaches in the world.

The fact that Hale'ekolu could afford to keep the spacious grounds—including a large grassy lawn, winding garden paths, and historic trees—undeveloped was a sign of how well the hotel was doing. Most other oceanfront properties had torn down older, shorter buildings, parking high-rises on the beach in order to maximize the number of ocean-view rooms.

In a place where every square inch of real estate was nearly priceless, the presence of the two-story original hotel, the style uniquely and classically Hawaiian with a Dickey roofline, deep porch, and dozens of second-floor balconies—one for each set of folding wood-framed glass doors—was a testament to the influence the Iona family wielded.

Thinking about her family had Benjamin looking around warily as he followed Kailani. He'd only met her grandmother once, but it had been enough.

Kailani nodded and murmured greetings to the construction crew as they passed by a doorway covered in plastic sheeting. The signs of improvements were everywhere, scaffolding and plastic, the occasional cart of tools. One of the casual dining restaurants and the wine bar were closed due to the construction, but the two fine dining restaurants, located in the original hotel, were still open. He'd checked before the plane landed, hoping that they could sit down and have a meal together. He also had the names of half a dozen other restaurants in a note on his phone, and reservations at each of them. Ideally, if they were going to dinner, they would do so on neutral ground, meaning not at the Hale'ekolu, but Kailani wasn't one to give up a home-court advantage.

"Where are we going?" John asked as they followed a garden path away from the towering new section of the hotel, headed for the original hotel building.

"You two are going nowhere." Kailani looked back over her shoulder, her gaze meeting his for a moment.

Benjamin's heart lurched, and he hated himself for the reaction.

Kailani's gaze shifted to the building in front of them. "Actually, you can go sit in the restaurant."

"Hibiscus or Makai?" Benjamin asked as they walked between two giant elephant ear plants, emerging onto the wide covered porch of the historic building.

Kailani shot him a suspicious look.

"Yes, Kailani. I know the names of your hotel's restaurants. It's not nefarious, you have one of the only Michelin-star and Forbes five-star restaurants."

"Forbes rates restaurants?" John asked.

"Not exactly as well-known as Michelin stars," Benjamin said.

Kailani shook her head. "I can't...I need to go. Here." She turned and hurried toward the ocean-facing end of the building. A hostess stand was positioned on an adjacent open set of double doors, a plaque on the front of the podium bearing a stylized flower and the word "Hibiscus." Behind the hostess, white-draped tables waited for diners, most of the tables outside on the porch, which he thought might have been called a lanai in Hawaii. The space had an indoor-outdoor feel, thanks to the series of tall double doors, all of which had been opened, allowing a seamless flow between the interior and exterior. A single hibiscus bloom in a bud vase waited on each table.

"Hi, Sue, can you get these gentlemen a table and a bottle for me?" Kailani smiled at the hostess, who'd been checking something on a tablet. "I know the staff is still prepping, so don't worry about that."

"Actually, Sue, we don't need a table, but thank you." Benjamin smiled at the elegant young woman with a flower behind her right ear, who was too professional to react to his countermanding her boss.

Benjamin put his hand on Kailani's back and steered her through the double doors, into an interior hallway. A grand staircase near the center led up to Makai, the fancier restaurant that sat atop Hibiscus. A few stanchions on the far side of the stairs roped off yet another construction zone.

He'd counted on Kailani's professionalism to not make a scene. He'd been right. She let him guide her into the hall, but she didn't stop there, instead turning to take them down a small side hall. They passed the bathrooms, stopping before a narrow door with a "staff" plaque.

"Kailani." Benjamin reached for her, but stopped himself, dropping his hand when he realized that he'd been planning to grab her shoulder to hold her still, to force her to stop running and actually talk to him. Instead, he cleared his throat. "What's going on?"

"I can't tell you."

"That call came from the Trinity Masters," he countered. "We're all members." Benjamin gestured from himself to John. "You need to tell us what that was about."

"Do you really think that you know every secret the society has?" Kailani's smile was surface-pretty, but cutting. "Don't be *naive*." The emphasis she put on the last word wasn't lost on him.

Benjamin felt his back teeth creak as he clenched his jaw, but he didn't say anything. The same way he hadn't said anything all those years ago.

"Okay, you're saying that call was from the Trinity Masters, but it doesn't have anything to do with the three of us and Benjamin's request." John had one shoulder leaning up against the wall, his pose casual, relaxed, which seemed odd.

"Yes." Kailani glanced at the staff door. "I'm sorry, but I need to—"

"That's a pretty big coincidence." John shook his head

slowly. "Can you explain it to me again because I'm not getting it?"

Benjamin frowned at John. Was he serious? In their admittedly brief interactions, John always seemed intelligent. Also, there was something vaguely familiar about the way he was talking.

"The Trinity Masters has secrets, layers of secrets," Kailani said. "I'm not saying I know all of them because I'm sure I don't, but there is one...thing...my family was trusted with. That call was related to my family's..." She paused, clearly choosing her words carefully. "Inherited duty."

John nodded slowly. "And you think you can't tell us about it."

"I can't."

"If you don't tell me what's going on, I can't help you." John pushed away from the wall. "If I don't know the full story, I can't help, and I want to help."

Benjamin blinked as he realized what John was doing. Why his words felt vaguely familiar.

John was questioning Kailani like she was a suspect. Benjamin had heard detectives saying nearly exactly the same things in the true-crime documentaries that were his guilty pleasure.

Kailani let out a frustrated breath, her words rushed. "Thank you for wanting to help, but this is something I have to do alone. I know this probably seems crazy, but it's a coincidence. The fact that the call started with 'keyholder' is proof that this has nothing to do with us. That was them asking me to initiate emergency procedures."

"Emergency procedures?" John asked. "That plus them telling you the society is under attack makes me think this is something you shouldn't be handling by yourself."

Benjamin wanted to jump in and demand answers, but he

bit back the urge. John's questioning method was clearly more effective.

"I won't be alone. That's actually part of it."

"There are other keyholders," John said.

Kailani jerked in clear surprise. "I...yes." John's faux confusion was gone, his eyes sharp with intelligence. "And one of the keyholders is going to be the acting Grand Master because our current leader has been attacked and is incapacitated in some way."

Kailani only stared, eyes wide.

"You're the Grand Master's...designated survivor," John concluded.

It was Benjamin's turn to be shocked as he looked between John and Kailani. All the pieces were there, between what they'd heard on the phone call and what Kailani had revealed under questioning.

The Grand Master was dead, and now Kailani was the Grand Master?

Benjamin realized in that instant that there was a new absolute worst-case scenario for his life, and he was living it. Fuck.

Kailani opened her mouth, then closed it. "Damn it," she breathed. "I shouldn't have let you hear that call. It's not... exactly like that."

"It's not?" John asked. "Because it sounds like the Trinity Masters have procedures in place to maintain leadership in case of assassination or attack. And it sounds like maybe they chose a designated survivor from a legacy family, who lives as far away from Boston as they can, while still being inside U.S. borders."

Benjamin looked at John. He felt oddly proud of how intelligent he was. This was a man he'd be honored to marry.

Except he wouldn't be truly married to John because Benjamin would accept nothing less than a real trinity marriage. Even if their marriage wasn't dissolved, it would be in name only as Kailani had made it clear she was unwilling to be a part of it.

"I can't stand here and argue with you two. I don't have time." Kailani sounded almost panicked as she turned and opened the staff door.

Her anxiety was triggering Benjamin's own. He forced it down and looked at John. "That was cool, man. How you questioned her."

He'd kept his voice low, he thought. Too low for Kailani to hear.

As with everything related to her, it didn't go as planned. She must have excellent hearing because she whirled on them. "Questioning?" Her expression went slack, then morphed into a cool, professional mask that hid everything she might be feeling. "You questioned me like I'm a suspect."

John shot Benjamin an irritated look, then faced Kailani. "No, I asked you questions in a way designed to get information from people in crisis."

Kailani's expression didn't change as she marched into the office on the other side of the staff door.

The room was small and cluttered, but in a tidy way, with a tiny desk, file cabinet, and a large wire shelving unit with assorted dishes and a few shelf-stable grocery items. The most interesting part of the room was a large wall safe half hidden by the racks. That must be what she'd come for.

Benjamin started to follow her, but Kailani swung the door shut in his face.

KAILANI LOCKED the door from the inside. She'd worry later about the fact that John had managed to get her to say more than she should have, and between her words and what he'd heard on the call, all but pieced together the secret of the keyholders.

Kailani crouched and released the brakes on the wheels for the ceiling-height rack that half-hid the safe. The dining manager and executive chef who used this office thought they kept spare cash and physical copies of hotel records in the safe. She carefully maneuvered the heavily laden rack away from the wall enough that she could slip behind it.

The safe had a simple, if large, combination dial, and it took her only seconds to spin the numbers and pull on the handle. As she swung the safe door open, she heard one of the men rattle the handle of the office door as they tried to open it, but she'd thrown the dead-bolt lock, which had been installed specifically for this situation.

A memory of the voice on the phone made her gut churn with anxiety, and she yanked open the wall safe.

Kailani had seen, and used, plenty of safes in her life. She knew what she should see when she opened that door—shelves and boxes, some probably lined in felt or acetate, depending on what was being stored. Instead of the interior of a secure box, she was looking at the bottom of a spiral staircase.

This wasn't the door to a safe, it was the doorway to the *waihona*.

Translated to "depository," the *waihona* was part of what she and her family maintained and protected as keyholders. Hidden deep within the original hotel, the *waihona* was a vault, the contents of which even she, as a keyholder, was ignorant of. She was fairly certain her grandmother knew, had placed things into the *waihona*, but *Tutu* never talked about it.

Kailani stepped over the lip of the opening, ducking to fit through. When she entered the stairwell, battery-operated lights clicked on, illuminating narrow spiral metal stairs.

Normally she left the door open when she came here, but

there was the possibility that Benjamin—wait, Benjamin and John; she needed to mentally categorize John as dangerous too —would come through the office door, so she reached back and pulled the safe door closed, locking herself inside. She touched the matching handle and combination dial on the inside of the safe door, reassuring herself that she'd be able to get out, even as no one else could get in.

The rectangular shaft of the stairwell always made her claustrophobic, and the air was warm and stale. The walls were dark wood, the stairs black. The widely spaced emergency lighting had an odd green tint.

She started up, her shoes ringing against the metal. At the top, there was a tiny landing and another door. Kailani reached under her shirt and pulled out a thin gold chain. An ornate key dangled from it. She'd worn it every day since she became the keyholder. On the occasions when she couldn't hide it under her clothes, she wore it on a waist chain.

She undid the clasp and fitted the key into the center of an old-fashioned lock. It had been a year since she'd opened this door, but she oiled the complex hidden lock mechanism every few months.

The lock creaked, metal scraping, and then there was the heavy sound of tumblers dropping. The sound kept going, click after click, thunk after thunk. Turning her single key had caused a chain reaction, unlocking the massive mechanical system hidden inside the hollow door.

Finally, she swung it open, revealing a small room. Like the stairwell, it was made of dark wood, and the air here was even more stale. These rooms weren't airtight, but they also weren't hooked up to the modern HVAC system. The entire *waihona* was hidden within the center of the original hotel, the two restaurants, small reception rooms, and wine bar that took up most of this building acting as camouflage to protect this secret.

Literal gold bars were stacked along the side walls, the only visible things in the room.

Kailani glanced at the door directly opposite the one she'd entered. That door was wider, nearly the entire wall. That door, and whatever it contained, was the heart of the *waihona*.

Instead of a single keyhole, there were three, set in a triangle in the center of the door.

She didn't know which of the three locks her family's key fit because she'd never been in the interior room. The contents were supposedly enough to ensure the survival of the Trinity Masters.

What she needed now was the names of the other two keyholders. Once she had their names and locations, she'd go get them, bring them back to Oahu, and then, together, they'd insert their keys into the inner door. While each of the three keys could open the outer door, the inner door's locks were all slightly different.

And whoever's key fit in the top lock became the acting Grand Master.

Which also meant that, until she did her duty, the secret society was leaderless.

Kailani turned and pressed on the wall beside the door. A hidden compartment popped open. Inside was a sealed letter. The position of keyholder, and the physical keys, were passed down through families. Each time the keyholder changed, the retiring keyholder notified the Grand Master. In turn, the Grand Master sent that information, via physical note, to the Hale'ekolu. The sealed envelope was then stored in the *waihona*. A year ago, the last time she'd been in here, Kailani had come to place a new letter in the compartment and remove the old one, which she'd burned without ever opening.

Carefully, Kailani opened the envelope.

Two names. One in L.A., the other in upstate New York.

She memorized the addresses, then put the letter back in the compartment and closed it. Her hands were shaking, her leg muscles trembling, and she exited, locking the door behind her before she descended the stairs and unlocked the vault door from the inside. She put the shelving rack back in place and finally opened the office door.

The first thing she heard was the muffled blare of an alarm. Benjamin was standing by the door, his face a hard mask. John came running around the corner, skidding to a stop.

He looked at her, took a quick breath, then said, "The hotel is on fire."

CHAPTER FIVE

John ran beside Kailani, who had her phone to her ear. He took a moment to look her over, checking to see what it was she'd gotten out of that wall safe. Whatever it was had to be flat enough that she'd shoved it into a pocket without creating a bulge.

They stopped near the entrance to the currently closed-due-to-construction casual dining restaurant. It was on the ground floor of the modern part of the hotel and had an adjacent open-air dining area with a small stage. He knew a fair amount about Kailani's family hotel, and Benjamin's family's various businesses, due to his background research over the past month.

The fact that the hotel had world-class musicians playing on the patio of their casual dining restaurant was a sign of just how fancy it was. Too fancy for someone like him. He'd come from humble beginnings and while he made a decent living, he was still very thrifty. John had spent too many years in bad living situations, homes where food wasn't always guaranteed.

All those years of being hungry ensured he didn't spend money on frivolous things.

Kailani halted near a wall of plastic sheeting with a zipper in the middle. Even the construction zones looked elegant.

Here, the siren was nearly deafening, and bright white lights flashed from behind the plastic. To their left, confused hotel guests were starting to fill the open-air hallways while elegantly uniformed hotel staff directed them out of the building.

Kailani shoved her phone into her pocket—she probably couldn't hear anything over the alarm—and then reached for the zippered doorway. John lunged, realizing too late that the zipper might be hot, but she yanked it open and pulled back the plastic. Beyond was a plain white utilitarian hallway, slowly filling with smoke.

"The kitchen," Kailani yelled.

Then she pointed at the small spigots in the ceiling of the hallway.

The fire suppression system. Which was not on. John checked the floor. No water, no foam. That wasn't right.

A second later, a hotel employee, the flower behind her ear somehow still in place as she ran, led a pack of firemen toward them. John backed away, nudging Benjamin with his shoulder, and pulling Kailani with them via a hand on her arm.

The Honolulu Fire Department poured through the plastic doorway.

A moment later, the fire alarm shut off, and the sudden quiet made his ears ring.

"There's another group of firemen, they came in the loading zone," the staff member—wait, no, this was the hotel manager, according to her name tag—told Kailani.

"Have you started the door-to-door?" Kailani asked.

"Yes. Starting with these floors." She pointed to the section of building above the restaurant kitchen.

"Was anyone inside?" Kailani's words were calm, but John could see the tension in her as she waited for the answer.

The manager shook her head. "The construction crew wasn't working on the kitchen this week, and most of them are gone for the day anyway."

Some of Kailani's tension dissipated. "That's right. We're waiting on parts."

John had been doing his level best to ignore what his gut was saying, but that was too much. He cleared his throat. "Kailani, can I talk to you for a second?"

She frowned at him, but something in his expression must have told her that he wouldn't interrupt unless he had something critical to say.

They stepped away, Kailani angling herself so she could still see everything.

"You don't think this is a coincidence," Benjamin said, proving once again that he was quick, though he didn't have a great filter. "You think that this is an attack."

John started to shake his head at the second part of Benjamin's statement, but Kailani's attention whipped to them. "An attack? No, the construction probably triggered a fire."

"And the fire suppression system didn't go off?" John asked gently.

"It was probably accidentally unhooked or damaged or..." Kailani looked over her shoulder, expression stark.

"The Grand Master was attacked, if you're the designated survivor—"

Kailani shook her head. "No one knows. The identity of the keyholders is a secret from everyone except the Grand Master, the council, and the keyholder families."

"Unless the society is being attacked by someone who *does* know," Benjamin countered.

"You mean a member? Regular members don't know about me, about the keyholders. You didn't."

Benjamin's jaw muscle flexed.

John cleared his throat. "Or this is a distraction."

They both looked at him.

"It feels like a distraction," he said. "If I took this case, and found out there was a fire at the same time someone accessed a safe..."

Kailani shook her head. "But that would mean they'd have to know I was going to the vau— Safe. Or about to. They'd have to know about the keyholders, and no one knows."

"Unless they were able to get the information from the Grand Master," John said softly.

Kailani looked ill. "I...I have to go. I should already be at the airport trying to catch a flight." She glanced around. "But if this was an attack, if someone knows about the keyholders and the..." She shook her head. "I can't leave the hotel defenseless."

"If you're about to get on a plane, you're going to be defenseless," Benjamin countered. "You can't fly commercial."

"Why can't you just call these other keyholders and tell them to come here?" John asked.

"It used to be that way," Kailani said. "It used to be you'd send a coded telegram, but when commercial air travel became easier the orders were changed. I have to go in person."

"Can you just change the protocol and text them?" John asked.

"I need to follow the instructions I have," Kailani insisted. "Which means getting on a plane."

"But you, personally, may be in danger," John said.

Kailani's expression was stark. "There wasn't... There's no plan for what we do if someone knows about the keyholders."

"You need security, both additional security at the hotel and for yourself," Benjamin insisted.

"I need to call my brother, Makani," Kailani said, pulling her phone from her pocket, dialing, then stepping away to speak.

Benjamin muttered something under his breath that sounded like "shit."

John gave him a curious look, and a disgruntled Benjamin admitted, "Makani isn't exactly my biggest fan."

"So what you're saying is you've pissed off the entire Iona family at some point in time?"

Benjamin lifted one shoulder in a casual shrug. "In a nutshell, yeah. At least she's not calling her *tutu*. I'm hoping to avoid running into her grandmother while I'm here."

John shook his head, torn between amusement and the same frustration he'd been feeling ever since meeting these two at the binding ceremony. Separately, they were both nice people and he'd enjoyed their conversations and getting to know them.

It was when they were together that things took a turn.

Kailani returned to them. "Makani is on his way."

The hotel manager walked over. "Ms. Iona, the police are here. They're helping with crowd control in the parking lot."

Kailani murmured, "Excuse me," to them and walked away just as the firemen emerged from behind the plastic.

A half hour passed before Kalani returned.

"Everything okay?" John asked.

"Yeah. The fire's out."

"That's good."

"It is, but..." She ran a hand through her hair, releasing a long, slow, exhausted breath. It made sense. "They're calling in the arson investigator."

None of them reacted to the news that this was probably deliberate. It was hardly a surprise.

"I'd hoped it was just an accident." Kailani smiled grimly at John. "An accident and a coincidence."

"What's next?" John asked, determined to help her.

"I..." She considered his question, then shrugged. "I have to go. I should stay because there are a lot of things happening at once. But I don't have time—" Kailani stopped talking, her attention drawn toward the walkway behind him.

John turned and saw a man, who had to be Kailani's brother, approaching them. Well, he was walking toward the kitchen. He hadn't spotted Kailani yet.

The resemblance between the two siblings was remarkable considering the fact they were actually half brother and sister. Makani had a dark tan that seemed to indicate that while his sister spent most of her time in the office, his work tasks allowed him to spend more time outside.

Either that or he spent his off-hours surfing, his twill board shorts and graphic button-down definitely giving that impression. All he needed to do was flash them the "hang loose" sign to confirm John's suspicion.

Makani shared the same shiny straight black hair as his sister, the stylish short cut brushed back away from his forehead, though his eyes were lighter than Kailani's, his a pale brown compared to her black. They both had thick lashes highlighting the delicate almond shape.

Makani was muscular, but not in a bulky way. He was medium-build and height, a few inches shorter than he and Benjamin. Of course, John suspected there weren't many people taller than Benjamin. John, accustomed to typically being one of the tallest guys in the room, wasn't used to looking up at others.

Makani wasn't alone. Two other men, who gave off law-enforcement or military vibes, walked with him, breaking off to go speak with the firefighters.

Makani frowned as he took in the chaos. Then his eyes landed on Kailani and his expression cleared.

Walking over, he reached out to tug her into his arms. "Kailani," he said, pressing his cheek against the top of his sister's head. Kailani had spoken about the closeness of her family, and it was apparent now in the way Makani held his sister. It was an affectionate, protective embrace, and John realized he didn't know which sibling was the elder. They looked to be very close in age, which was entirely possible considering they had different mothers.

Kailani was the first to break the embrace. "I'm fine, *i hawawa.*"

"It's not silly to be worried about you. We are in the middle of—" He stopped talking, his gaze traveling from John to Benjamin and back again. It appeared Kailani had filled her brother in on more than just the fire when she called him, which meant the Iona family knew at least something about Kailani's role as keyholder. John studied the man's face, wondering if he could press him for the answers Kailani refused to give.

"Makani, this is John Wilson," Kailani said, introducing him. "John, this is my brother."

"Aloha." Makani reached out to shake his hand. "My sister tells me you're a homicide detective in L.A. It's an admirable profession, but I can't imagine it's easy. Figure you've seen some shit in your time."

"I have," John replied simply. He couldn't help but wonder if Kailani had told her family the truth behind their binding ceremony, that she was rejecting the match, and that they'd lodged a request to dissolve it.

Makani turned his attention to Benjamin and scowled.

"Dara. I didn't think you were stupid enough to show up here, so I didn't put you on the 'banned from property' list. My mistake."

"Iona," Benjamin fired back, making no attempt to be friendly. "I see you're carrying on the tradition of welcoming hospitality."

Jesus. John closed his eyes briefly, praying for patience. The Trinity Masters were in danger. Now was not the time for a pissing contest.

"Who are those men you arrived with?" Kailani asked, glancing across the grounds. The two men were talking to one of the firemen.

"Private security. I placed a call right after I hung up with you," Makani explained.

"Good to see you're following my suggestion," Benjamin said smoothly.

John mentally willed Benjamin to shut up.

Makani's smile was more a baring of teeth, but he ignored Benjamin's words, continuing to talk to his sister. "I asked them to meet me here. I'm going to set them up in rooms here in the hotel, and they're going to pretend to be guests."

John frowned, concerned that the Iona siblings weren't taking this matter seriously enough. "You aren't evacuating the hotel?"

Makani shook his head. "I got a preliminary report as I came in. There's no structural damage, or smoke or fire damage to the upper floors. Even the kitchen isn't too bad. Plus...the guests provide another level of security because, at any given time, there are countless people exploring the grounds, enjoying the gardens. There is enough activity in and around the hotel that it would make foul play difficult. Too many witnesses."

"Which is cold," Benjamin interrupted.

Makani didn't acknowledge Benjamin's comment. "I believe the reason the fire was started here is because this kitchen was closed. Easy access because none of the guests would be hanging out around here."

John agreed...with both men. Using the guests as an added layer of protection was smart...and indeed cold. "Are there cameras on the grounds that we could check?"

Makani nodded. "There are. That was actually going to be my next stop after checking out the damage and making sure this one was okay." As he spoke, Makani wrapped his arm around Kailani's shoulders, ruffling her hair as she tried to swat him away.

John watched their interplay with interest, that same sense of longing he always experienced whenever he witnessed families—especially close ones—interacting together sneaking in. It wasn't a new feeling, so he'd become quite adept at handling it. After so many years, he'd learned how to acknowledge the desire without letting it bring him down.

"Will you be okay to handle everything without me?" Kailani asked, her voice lower as she turned her body toward her brother, her back to them. She lifted her hand, indicating she wanted to speak to her brother in private. The two of them took a few steps away, annoyed when they realized he and Benjamin were dogging their steps.

John chuckled at her efforts. "Kailani, I'm sure your brother is more than capable. So what's our next move?"

She shook her head. "*My* next move," she replied, stressing the pronoun.

"How can we help you if you keep pushing us away?" John asked.

Kailani narrowed her eyes at him. "Stop using that voice with me. You're not going to get me again."

Benjamin snorted, trying to cover up the sound with a cough as Makani looked confused.

"I need to fly to the mainland immediately. I hate to leave you here to deal with all of this, but..."

"Kailani," Makani said. "I understand you have a duty to perform."

Makani turned around and gestured at a third man John hadn't noticed, lingering near the gardens, leaning against a tree.

"Who is that?" Kailani asked.

"You're taking a bodyguard with you."

Kailani scoffed. "No. I'm not."

Makani crossed his arms. "There's no way I'm letting you go anywhere alone."

"She won't be alone," John interjected. "I'm going with her."

Kailani was already shaking her head.

"We're both going with you," Benjamin added.

John closed his eyes wearily, trying to figure out how he could politely tell Benjamin to shut his pie hole and let him do the talking.

As expected, Kailani stiffened, annoyance that was almost alarming rolling off her. Whatever was between her and Benjamin, it wasn't minor, wasn't easily resolved, which meant if they were still getting married...

He frowned, wondering what impact this keyholder thing, and the apparently missing Grand Master, was going to have on the three of them.

But that was a problem for a later time. Right now, if he didn't step in, Kailani and Benjamin would just argue and fight.

"Kailani, you need to get to the mainland and do your keyholder duties, right?" John asked. "But you also need some personal security. If this fire was arson, it's possible that whoever attacked the Grand Master is coming after your hotel, you, or both."

Kailani and Makani nodded.

"Benjamin, you own a whole airline, which means you can get us, all three of us, on a flight."

"I can get us on a private plane."

John turned to Kailani. "The safest, fastest way for you to travel is on Benjamin's plane."

"Saying this is killing me, but I agree," Makani said.

Benjamin shot him a grateful look, then focused on Kailani. "The pilot will need to file flight plans. Where are we going?"

Kailani looked resigned but only for a moment. Then she straightened her shoulders and said, "L.A. We're going to your hometown, John."

CHAPTER SIX

Benjamin turned from speaking with the flight attendant. Besides the attendant, there was a pilot and copilot to fly the Challenger 300 aircraft.

He'd been braced for Kailani to say something about what a waste this flight was—there were eight seats and only three passengers, plus most of the small cargo area was empty. He wasn't a complete asshole, so normally, given enough lead time, his head of travel would have arranged to lease empty space in the cargo hold to shipping companies or freight services, and the empty seats would either be sold to people who otherwise might have chartered their own jet or used for charity. He'd spent plenty of flights sitting in the back row with his head-phones on while a Make a Wish child and their family used the front set of four seats.

John was sitting in the second row, a forward-facing seat. Benjamin hadn't missed his raised brows and slightly shocked expression as they breezed through security and were driven out onto the tarmac in order to board the jet.

Kailani had taken the first-row seat, which was rear-facing and put her directly across from John, leaving Benjamin to sit alone on the other side of the narrow aisle. He chose the forward-facing seat so he could see Kailani's face.

Since walking into that hotel room, things had been moving at a sprint. Now they had five hours of enforced downtime, and he intended to use those to get some answers. Benjamin looked at John and internally acknowledged that if anyone was going to get answers out of her, it would be the detective.

They sat silent but attentive during the safety briefing. Benjamin could have given the safety demonstration he'd heard it so many times, but he politely paid attention. John was leaning forward, nodding as if he was memorizing the instructions. Given that they'd spend all but thirty minutes off this six-hour flight over open ocean, with no land in sight, the reality was if the plane went down, even if they didn't die on impact, they were dead. Benjamin chose not to say that. See, he wasn't a complete asshole, no matter what Kailani said.

Forty-five minutes later, they'd reached their cruising altitude and each had a drink in hand. The attendant retreated to the small galley space at the front, slipping on a headset once they were seated. The headset allowed the attendant to speak to the pilot and copilot and provided passengers with the kind of privacy anyone who flew in a plane like this expected.

Benjamin looked at John. Their gazes met, and Benjamin inclined his head, yielding the lead to the detective.

John undid his seat belt and sat forward, elbows on his knees. "Kailani, why don't you tell us what's happening."

Kailani seemed to wilt for a moment, and Benjamin tensed. She shouldn't, couldn't, look tired or vulnerable or soft. He could deal with assertive, pissed, even passionate but poised Kailani.

Kailani who looked like she needed help or protecting?

Benjamin swallowed hard, then took a too-big sip of the sparkling wine the attendant had served, the bubbles burning the back of his throat.

"John, don't treat me like a suspect." Again, she sounded tired instead of regally dismissive the way he was used to.

"I'm not. And I'm sorry about that."

Benjamin felt John's gaze on him and gave a small grimace of apology. He shouldn't have pointed out what the other man was doing.

"I wasn't treating you like a suspect, but I *was* questioning you. Most people, unless they're highly skilled romance authors, tell stories and give information in a fractured way that makes sense only to them. Some people start and stop, some have a circular conversational pattern. Either way, it means it can take three and four times as long to get all the relevant information, and I didn't think we had time."

"That's the thing. There shouldn't be a 'we.' No one should know about the keyholders."

"If we'd gotten married?"

"Then you'd know, yes. Because one of our children, if we decided to have them, would take over as keyholder."

Benjamin surged to his feet, pacing to the back of the plane. The movement helped burn off some of the anger and helped keep him from saying the things he wanted to say. Things like: "*You mean yours and John's child, because you made it very clear I'd never be your husband, let alone in your bed.*"

"Let me ask this, then." John sat back, turning in his seat so he could see both of them. "How often are trinities dissolved after the binding ceremony and before the wedding?"

Benjamin returned to his seat as he realized where John was going with this.

"I...I don't think that it's ever happened," Kailani said softly.

"The only reason that Devon agreed to mention this to the Grand Master is, I'm guessing, because you're legacies."

"And because he knows some of our...history," Benjamin said.

"But if the Grand Master chose to dissolve it, it would be totally out of the ordinary, correct?"

Benjamin nodded, but Kailani was looking out the window.

"Kailani, does your keyholder status give you some special pull?" John pushed.

"No." She sighed. "No, it doesn't, and if I had tried to use the fact that I'm a keyholder to get special treatment...I think that might have put my whole family in danger."

"So realistically the three of us are...were...getting married. We went through the binding ceremony."

Kailani leaned her head back against her seat, watching them through her lashes. "I see your point. As my fiancés, you have the right to know about the keyholders."

John spread his fingers, saying nothing. Benjamin stayed silent too. He'd noticed John switching between tenses when it came to their marriage. Benjamin had figured that by this point in time, he'd either be back to being single or on his way to Boston to be forced into a loveless marriage where he was always on the outside looking in.

Option three—the society under attack, Kailani responsible for the safety and continuity of society leadership—was one he'd never imagined.

"I'll tell you...what I can. There's some information I don't think I'm meant to share with anyone. I wouldn't even tell Makani."

"That's fair." John relaxed into his seat. Benjamin held still, not wanting to do anything to alter the moment or make Kailani change her mind.

"You heard and figured out some of it," she began. "But let me just start at the beginning.

"During WWI, the Grand Master at the time saw the potential to lose a whole generation of members, including the person who was meant to become the next Grand Master, most likely his son."

"The Grand Master is a hereditary position?" John asked.

"Most people think so," Benjamin answered. "My family does."

"Does anyone know who it is?"

Benjamin shrugged. "Everyone likes to guess. We used to make a drinking game of it at the legacy house. Everyone would declare that their father, brother, etc., was the Grand Master, and we'd decide if they were lying. If we believed them—meaning, if they were either a good liar, or possibly telling the truth—we drank."

"I'd forgotten about that." Kailani's expression softened into a smile and she turned to Benjamin. "Remember what's-his-name? Last name was Madison. He was good. We all drank."

"Maybe he was telling the truth about his father being the Grand Master."

"The current Grand Master is a woman," John pointed out.

"He had a sister, I think." Kailani looked into middle distance, remembering, then shook her head.

"Sorry to get us off track," John said.

"No, you're right, the story only makes sense if you know that the position of Grand Master is hereditary, though it's not like a monarchy." Kailani finished her drink, and Benjamin rose to get her another one. "I know that people can be chosen and voted in," she said.

"Yes," Benjamin agreed from the galley, where he took a fresh flute and poured. "My parents said the same. I think I have an ancestor who was on the Grand Master's council."

"The Grand Master probably knew that the U.S. would enter the war. Probably guessed what was coming after the sinking of the *Lusitania*. He saw the potential to lose an entire generation of Trinity Masters members, and he thought it was possible that Boston would be attacked."

Benjamin had recently started the phase he swore he'd never go through—reading and watching war documentaries—and he could easily imagine a Grand Master in 1915 playing out worst-case scenarios and seeing places like Boston and New York under fire from German ships.

"He created a backup plan. Both a person and a place that become the acting core of the society in times of crisis. And he chose a location as far away as possible from Boston for the vault, and a family with deep ties to that location." Kailani smiled. "What's now the Hale'ekolu was only a collection of what we'd call rental cottages, with one main house. We built the old hotel, the one that's still there, specifically to house the *waihona*."

"By vault, you mean that wall safe?" John asked.

Benjamin met Kailani's gaze, and from her perfectly blank, give-nothing-away expression, he knew there was more than just a simple wall safe.

"It's called the *waihona*. Nowadays we say that translates to depository, but I think the term vault probably fits better. And no, there's more to it than the wall safe."

"Isn't it risky to have something like that in a semi-public place?" John asked.

"No," Benjamin and Kailani said in unison.

She nodded to him, so Benjamin explained. "Like her brother said, the guests would be part of the protection. The constant presence of people does more to hide something than all the security in the world. It's the same with the headquarters under the library. If someone were to attack, they'd risk mass casualties, including the death of innocent bystanders, which in turn brings major attention from both the media and law enforcement."

John looked taken aback. "That's smart but...calculating."

"It is," Benjamin agreed.

"My great-great-grandmother was the first keyholder," Kailani said, pulling their attention back to her. "At the time, they chose a woman, since she couldn't enlist and there was no chance she'd be drafted. She was given a very specialized key, a literal key. But she wasn't the only one. The Grand Master identified two other families, making sure they weren't based either on Oahu or in Boston. They also have keys, keys that were passed down the way mine was."

"Three keyholders." Benjamin leaned on the arm of his seat to be closer to them, to his trinity. "And together you're the acting leadership? Or you decide who becomes Grand Master?"

"No. The keys decide." Kailani put her hand over her chest, an absentminded gesture. "I guess you could say the Grand Master who created the keyholders decided, over a century ago. Each of the three keys opens the first door of the *waihona*. To open the second door, you need all three keys." She held her hands up, forming a triangle with her fingers. "The keyholes are set in a triangle, and whichever key fits in and opens the top lock, that person becomes acting Grand Master."

"Shouldn't you know which key fits in that lock?" John asked. "If the same families have the same key, you'd know based on the last time this happened."

Kailani shook her head, her expression strained. "The keyholders have never been called before."

"But if this is what happens every time a Grand Master dies..."

"It's not," Benjamin said. "When the Grand Master dies or steps down, their heir takes up the position of Grand Master." Benjamin looked at Kailani. "Which means the current Grand Master either doesn't have an heir...or isn't dead."

"The person who called didn't say, but I think you're right," Kailani agreed. "If the Grand Master was permanently out of the picture, I think there are other plans, protocols to select the new Grand Master if the old one didn't have an heir."

"So the Grand Master has been incapacitated in some way," John said. "Hence a temporary transfer of leadership to one of the keyholders."

"Exactly. But we won't know who it is, which keyholder, until I get the other two keyholders and take them back to Oahu."

"Again, why can't you just call them?" John asked. "It sounds like your instructions are outdated, and if time is a factor..."

"I've been thinking about it," Kailani said. "And even if I did disobey and go rogue, I don't think the others would believe, or act on, a phone call. My family is the only one contacted by Boston when the keyholders are activated. The others, their instructions say that someone will come in person to tell them it's happening. They won't get their key and come to the Hale'ekolu unless they see a fellow keyholder show up on their doorstep, key in hand."

"That's a hell of a risk," Benjamin said. "It means potentially days without an acting leader while the keyholders travel."

"True. But I guess it was the safest thing they could come

up with at the time. Nothing about the keyholders has been updated in...I think since my *tutu's* time. Except the names of who actually has the keys and their location. That's why I went to the *waihona* earlier. The Grand Master sends a sealed letter every time there's a new keyholder. We don't open it, we just put it in the *waihona* until we need it. I just got a new letter last year, so hopefully we're going to the right place."

"Back to the fire. It's possible someone else knows," Benjamin said. "The arson at the Hale'ekolu might have been set by the same entity that attacked the Grand Master. Or it's a hell of a coincidence."

"I don't like coincidences," John said. "We need more information about what happened in Boston. Can you call Devon? I assume he's close enough to the Grand Master that he'd know what's going on."

Benjamin nodded. "He's probably on the current council."

"That wasn't his voice on the phone though," Kailani said.

"No, but Devon on the council explains why he was there during our binding ceremony. And why he said he'd talk to the Grand Master." Benjamin pulled his phone from his pocket, connecting to the satellite Wi-Fi. He sent a text, figuring he'd wait to call if Devon didn't text back.

"If they know about the Hale'ekolu, is it possible they know the names and identities of the other keyholders?" John said. "Do we need to warn them?"

"That's a good point," Benjamin said.

"I can maybe believe that someone knew about the *waihona*," Kailani said. "It hasn't changed or moved since it was created, and whoever donated or provided the contents probably had to be told where it physically was."

"So you think that only you, only the hotel, is compromised."

"As far as I know, the only person who knows the exact

names and addresses of the other keyholders is the Grand Master, and the keyholder families. It's possible someone accidentally said something about the Hale'ekolu over the years. That's more likely than some outsider having access to current keyholder information."

"It might not be an outsider," John said softly. "And there are ways of getting information from someone."

"You mean they might have tortured the information out of the Grand Master," Benjamin said.

"If you were going to torture the leader of American's most powerful secret society, is this what you'd ask about?" Kailani countered. "The Trinity Masters have plenty of other, more valuable secrets."

"True," John conceded.

They sat in silence for a few moments, each of them lost in their own thoughts.

"I should warn the other keyholders." Kailani grabbed her purse. "Maybe it's breaking protocol. Maybe it's the wrong thing, but if the fire was an attack... I might already be too late to warn them."

"You're fine," John said soothingly. "Because you're right, everything you said is right. Their identities are probably safe."

"And if they're not?"

"Then we'll deal with it."

"I should have done it already. The instant you said it." She took out her phone, staring at it for a long moment before she started typing.

"They're probably fine," John said again, shooting a helpless look at Benjamin. Benjamin wished he knew how to comfort Kailani, but experience had taught him that whatever he said would be the exact wrong thing.

It only took her a few minutes to send two messages.

"What did you say?" Benjamin asked.

"I sent them the key emoji and the little danger symbol. I don't want to risk anything more. It...it might be enough. Or they might think it's spam. Or the numbers I have were for landlines and the messages don't get there at all." Kailani leaned back, her shoulders slumped, as if the weight of her responsibilities was crushing her slender frame.

"We'll help you," Benjamin declared, hoping against hope that for once, he wouldn't fuck it up. "Tell me where we're going and I'll arrange travel. I'll hire a car service when we get to L.A."

For a moment Kailani stiffened, then their gazes met, and she visibly relaxed. "Thank you, Benjamin."

Hearing her say his name made his heart clench, even as his gut churned with regret.

The attendant got up and started to prepare food. They fell silent, keeping conversation sparse, and surface level as tables were raised between the seats, John and Kailani now looking like they were on a dinner date as the four-course meal was served.

By the time they were finished eating, Kailani seemed exhausted, and when she leaned back and closed her eyes, Benjamin turned to the window, looking out at the tops of clouds and the endless blue-gray of the ocean.

"I'm going to go get a bottle of water," John said quietly, climbing out of his seat.

Benjamin thought about telling him he could call the attendant, have one brought to him; but instead, Benjamin found himself rising and directing John to the back of the plane, where there was a self-service wet bar. He took a bottle of mineral water from the small refrigerator, then grabbed a glass for himself.

John looked from the water to Benjamin's bottle of whiskey, and set down the water.

"Good choice." Benjamin took down a second glass and poured, adding a splash of water to each glass.

John frowned at the splash of water. "Why are you watering it down?"

"Adding a splash of water helps open up the nose, the scent, and brings out some of the subtler flavors."

"Ah. I guess this is one of those things rich people know." John took a sip, his brows rising. "That's nice."

"I know plenty of rich people who'd put ice in this glass like barbarians," Benjamin assured him, leaning against the wall.

They sipped in silence for several minutes.

"It's possible that Kailani will be the acting Grand Master."

"One-in-three chance," John agreed.

"And if she is the Grand Master, there's an upside to this we haven't mentioned. She'll have the power to dissolve our trinity." Benjamin forced a smile as he said it.

John's expression didn't change. He didn't look relieved or happy about that, which was probably to be expected, since he hadn't objected to the trinity in the first place. He also didn't look surprised—he'd realized the same thing.

"Even if it's not her key, if she's not the acting Grand Master, it's very possible whoever is will dissolve it, as a favor to her," Benjamin went on.

"And if the current Grand Master comes back?" John asked. "Will they allow that?"

"I don't know." Benjamin's emotions were a mess, so he locked them up. "Maybe she'd call us to the altar again, since there's clearly a reason she wanted us in a trinity. Maybe the aftermath of whatever is going on will take all her attention, and our marriage will be the last thing she, or anyone else, cares about."

"So it's possible you and Kailani will get what you want," John said quietly.

Benjamin looked over to where Kailani was asleep in her seat, her head tipped to the side, displaying the long, slim line of her throat. She was lovely, even more lovely now as a grown woman than she'd been as a teenager.

"Yes," Benjamin said softly. "We'll get what we want."

CHAPTER SEVEN

Kailani kept her eyes closed, feigning sleep.

It had been a fucking day, between the keyholder call, the fire, and now this trip to the mainland with... God...at this point she didn't know who Benjamin and John were to her.

There was a chance that at the end of this mad dash journey, she would be the Grand Master of the Trinity Masters, and the society was under attack.

Dealing with that had to take precedence over everything else. Including the future of...her trinity. Because if she did become acting Grand Master, she would have the power to dissolve her own trinity.

That should feel like a relief, but when she considered leading the entire secret society, all she felt was panic and a fair amount of nausea.

How would it look if her first act if she became Grand Master was to serve herself and end the engagement, rather than focus on the needs and interests of the society?

Her mind was whirling over a million things, so many that

trying to hold her own against Benjamin simply wasn't possible. He kept her on her toes on good days. This was not a good day.

She needed time and space to think. To take a breath.

Since being alone wasn't an option, she'd decided to create her own space, even if all that entailed was sitting here with her eyes closed.

Her naptime act must have fooled them. Benjamin and John must have believed she was asleep because they spoke for a few minutes in hushed tones before falling silent. Sneaking a peek, she saw that each of them had slipped in earbuds and were looking at their phones.

She might have expected the quiet to soothe her rough edges, and after everything she'd been through today—not to mention a month's worth of anxiety since the binding cere-mony—she was surprised she hadn't fallen asleep for real.

Unfortunately, she couldn't.

It was this damn plane.

It was evoking too many memories, things she'd buried away for ten years, refusing to give them even a passing thought.

The last time she'd been on one of Dara's private planes, she'd been nineteen years old and head over heels in love with Benjamin.

She might have expected to feel the same anger that always struck her whenever she and Benjamin were together, but sitting here, jetting across the ocean with him, was having the opposite effect, reminding her too much of the good times—brief though they had been.

She and Benjamin had embarked on a summer romance, one that had lasted four weeks, three days, and a handful of hours. He'd been her first love, and in truth, her only love.

It wasn't that she'd been so devastated by their break-up that she refused to fall in love. She wasn't that much of a sad sack. Her lack of romances since him had more to do with the Trinity Masters, her job, and—if she was being honest—a change in her ability to trust others.

She'd licked her wounds over Benjamin for almost six months, then she'd done what any strong woman would do. She'd picked herself up, dusted herself off, and started dating again. However, with experience came wisdom, so she'd held back parts of herself from the men she went out with and slept with because they hadn't been members of the society. Falling in love would have been stupid, as her future partners weren't hers to choose. She'd made that mistake with Benjamin and she wasn't going to do it again.

When she was twenty-four, one of her mothers had a stroke. Mom had recuperated, and was fine now, but it had been a long haul. As such, Kailani had taken on more responsibility within the family businesses—a lot more. It wasn't unusual for her to work sixty-, sometimes seventy-hour weeks. Not because her family expected that but because she genuinely enjoyed what she did.

As for her ability to trust—not just men, but everyone—it had definitely been impacted by Benjamin's perfidy. He'd shaken it when he'd betrayed her by casually using information she'd given him to turn around and damage her uncle's career.

Kailani dared to sneak another peek through lowered lashes, glancing across the aisle at her ex. John and Benjamin appeared to be following her lead, both of them partially reclined, eyes closed, trying to grab some rest while they could.

Kailani took a moment and studied Benjamin in profile, her mind drifting back in time...

"Tell me where we're going," she demanded for the fiftieth time. It had been a long flight, almost all of it over water, so she assumed they were headed for Europe. The problem was that didn't narrow it down much.

Benjamin merely shook his head. "I'm not spoiling the surprise, so you can stop asking."

"How will I know if I packed the right things?" she said, trying a different tack.

"If you don't have the clothes you need, I'll buy them for you."

Kailani rolled her eyes, though she was used to Benjamin's continual attempts at spoiling her by buying her flowers, jewelry, and clothing. "Or I'll buy them for myself."

Benjamin had grown up with the proverbial silver spoon in his mouth, and apparently he'd dated too many women in the past who took advantage of that.

Kailani was not that woman.

Her family had money in their own right, but that didn't mean she intended to live her life as a trust-fund baby. She was three years away from finishing her degree in Environmental Sciences, which she planned to put to use by changing some aspects of how her family ran their hotels.

Benjamin wrapped his arm around her shoulder and placed a soft kiss on her cheek. "I'm looking forward to having you all to myself for four whole days. It's going to suck when we have to go back to school next week."

Kailani had opted to spend her summer break in Boston rather than returning home to Hawaii. Something all her East Coast friends thought was complete madness. She had tried to explain that Hawaii, during the height of the tourist season, wasn't exactly a good time for the locals, even the Nu'uanu Valley where her family lived. She much preferred the slower, quieter spring and fall seasons.

Benjamin had just one more year of college, and like her, he'd decided to steal a few months for himself, proclaiming he had the rest of his life to work, and since he was joining his family's business right after graduation, this was his last summer as a "free man."

Benjamin was looking down at his phone, checking his texts, so she took the time to study him in profile. They'd known each other since they were children, both legacies of the Trinity Masters. Despite that fact, their families seemed to work on opposing sides more often than not. She and Benjamin had met and become friends at a time when they were too young to give a shit about stuff like that.

The friendship portion of their relationship changed a few weeks earlier when they reconnected at a party at the legacy house. Seven legacy kids from some of the oldest Trinity Masters families had gotten together to purchase the property as a home base in Boston, and since then, it had been called everything from the frat house to the Fortress of Solitude. Benjamin was staying there while in Boston, and along with his summer roommates, had decided to host the party for the legacies in town that changed everything for the two of them.

She wasn't sure what had changed, but it was as if they both opened their eyes at the same time and said, "Oh. Wow. There you are," truly seeing each other for the first time. They'd spent the entire party sitting on a couch in the corner just talking for hours about anything and everything, long after everyone else had left or passed out.

And they had been talking ever since, inseparable.

Benjamin put his phone down and caught her staring at him. He gave her a charming grin, flashing his perfect, straight white teeth at her. He had an amazing smile and her heart skipped three beats.

"You are so beautiful," he murmured, cupping her face so he could steal a kiss. Kailani had been kissed by plenty of guys in her life, but she decided right then and there, none of those any longer counted as kisses. Those past weak attempts faded in the face of Benjamin's long, slow, sensuous kisses. "I can't get enough of you," he admitted, pressing his forehead to hers.

His affectionate nature was one of her favorite things about him. She'd had a handful of boyfriends, and even lovers in the past, but none of them had ever looked at her or made her feel like Benjamin. It was as if she was vital to his happiness. He was equal parts passionate and cuddly and when she talked, he listened. Really listened.

He pointed toward the window, his lips brushing her ear when he whispered, "Surprise."

Kailani gasped as the Eiffel Tower came into view as their private jet descended. "Paris!" She had admitted to Benjamin that first night at the legacy house party that she'd never been to Paris but hoped to go after graduation from college. The fact he remembered touched her.

"I can't believe this," she said, turning to hug Benjamin, the embrace ending when the flight attendant stopped by to ask them to put their seat belts on as they prepared to land.

The next few hours were an absolute whirlwind as Benjamin showed her around Paris—by limousine—pointing out some of the more famous attractions, promising they'd return to spend more time at each over the course of the next few days. He'd built an incredible itinerary.

They'd ended their first night with a private dinner cruise on the Seine, which offered an incredible view of the Eiffel Tower.

"Come on." Benjamin took her hand. Kailani hadn't been surprised to learn that the Daras owned a luxurious apartment in Champs de Mars with an amazing view of the tower. "Let me show you around."

Kailani followed him through the apartment, in awe of the intricately hand-painted ceilings, elaborate marble work,

Versailles parquet floors, crystal chandeliers, and grand staircase.

Finally, he led her into the master bedroom.

"Holy shit. That bed is huge."

Benjamin laughed. "It's an emperor king."

"Of course, it is. Because the Daras can't just be kings...they have to be emperor kings," Kailani teased, though there was no denying the truth behind her jest. The Daras seemed determined to own the world, which was the reason for so much contentiousness between their families.

Benjamin, as always, took her jest in stride. "Sounds richer, doesn't it? Besides, if I'm the emperor king that makes you the empress queen."

"Well, I do like the sound of that."

Benjamin grinned as he picked her up and carried her over to the monstrous mattress, tossing her into the middle. Sometimes she was amazed how well they fit...physically. Benjamin was a big guy, tall and broad, while the best word to describe her was petite. She wasn't ashamed to admit that his strength and muscular build were big turn-ons for her.

Kailani came up on her knees and crooked her finger at him, inviting him to join her. There had been too many kisses, glancing touching, longing looks since they'd left Boston. She'd spent close to twelve hours with her arousal set on simmer. She was ready to turn up the heat, to boil over in his arms.

Benjamin didn't accept her invitation, so she scooted to the edge of the bed, reached out, gripped his shirt, and pulled him toward her. Benjamin met her halfway, bending down and kissing her hard. She wasn't a passive lover, but she'd realized since sleeping with Benjamin, that had less to do with sexual preferences and more to do with a poor choice of partners. They'd needed guidance. A lot of guidance.

That wasn't true of Benjamin.

Benjamin broke off their kiss before she was finished, resisting her attempts to pull him back to her and onto the bed. He gently pried her hands away from his shoulders, then took a step back.

"Take your clothes off," he said, his voice gruff.

"I will if you will," she tossed back.

He narrowed his eyes briefly, but then, to her surprise and delight, he began to unbutton his shirt.

She took a moment to admire his smooth, sexy chest, his well-defined pecs and abs. Sometimes she felt the urge to pinch herself, to remind herself this was real. That he was hers.

Distracted, Kailani frowned when Benjamin obscured her view, his arms crossing.

"What did I tell you to do?"

Sometimes she liked pushing his buttons, testing him to draw out his alpha side, but not tonight.

Tonight, she just needed to fuck. Hard.

Kailani unbuttoned her blouse, slipping it off her shoulders. Benjamin's gaze missed nothing. She expected him to step closer, to take over, but instead, he held that sexy pose, arching one eyebrow impatiently. "If I have to tell you again," he started, leaving the rest of that threat unspoken.

It wasn't the first time he'd said something similar when she didn't follow his commands. So far, she'd never tested that limit, never forced him to enact...whatever came next.

One night, she was going to play that card, deny him so that she could see where it led them. She trusted him completely, so she knew he wouldn't hurt her. No, she had a good idea that the second part of that threat would most likely come with an explosive orgasm.

She gave him a saucy wink as she climbed off the bed so that she could strip off her pants, panties, and sandals.

Benjamin remained still, watching her, still wearing too

damn many clothes. Kailani had a good idea how to change that situation.

Once she was naked, she climbed back on the bed, crawling to the center slowly, ensuring that Benjamin got a good long look at her ass as she did so.

She yelped when he spanked her. Just one sharp slap, the loud sound of it shocking her as much as the sting. She had never been spanked. Not even as a kid.

Benjamin paused for a second, and she suspected he was taking stock, trying to feel her out. When she looked over her shoulder and wiggled her ass provocatively, she expected him to laugh.

Instead, his eyes grew dark with desire and he slapped her other ass cheek. It burned—actually, it hurt—but not in a way she found intolerable. When he laid down five more smacks, her body reacted before her brain could process what was happening. Her pussy clenched tightly and she was suddenly slick with arousal, something Benjamin discovered for himself when he slid two fingers inside her.

"Jesus, Kailani."

She moaned, pushing back to draw his fingers in deeper. "Please."

"Please what?"

Benjamin was a big fan of dirty talk...his and hers, and as such, he liked to make her ask for what she wanted.

Initially, she'd been somewhat shy about asking in such specific detail, but once she figured out it was a guaranteed way to get her from point A to B quicker, she forgot to blush.

"Please take off those damn pants and shove that big fat dick of yours inside me. Hard and fast. Please," she said again, just to make her point.

"Goddamn, you've got a mouth on you," he said, even as he

started stripping off the rest of his clothes. The mattress sank as he climbed on behind her. "I like it."

She giggled when he tickled her sides, trying to crawl away from him.

Benjamin held her back with one hand on her shoulder. "Where do you think you're going?"

Holding her in place, he ran his fingertips along her slit, from clit to ass, before switching directions and doing it again. And again.

Kailani trembled with need. "Benjamin."

She felt him twist away briefly, heard the nightstand drawer, then the crinkle of foil.

Finally, the head of his cock brushed her opening. "I've been wanting to do this all day," he admitted.

Apparently, she wasn't the only one impacted by what felt like one long day of foreplay.

They both groaned, then sighed as he slid inside in a long, slow thrust.

He held steady for just a moment. Perhaps he meant to give her time to adjust, but she'd waited long enough.

Kailani moved first, pulling away slightly, intent on taking control.

Benjamin growled, his fingers tightening on her hips, as he gave her exactly what she'd asked for, taking her so hard she struggled to remain upright.

When she was right there on the precipice, he reached around her waist and stroked her clit.

"Oh my God, Ben!" she gasped, unable to say his whole name as wave after wave of pleasure inundated her.

Benjamin fucked her through that climax and the next, offering her no break, no time to recover. She fell from her hands to her elbows, her strength gone, but still he fucked her like it was their last day on Earth.

Neither of them had talked about what came next week because they didn't like to think about living so far away. Kailani was determined to make it work, dedicated to a long-term relationship.

She cried out when he pulled out. "Wait, you haven't—" she started to protest.

"Roll over," he said. "I want to see your face when you come again."

Kailani shuddered, uncertain if she would survive one more. He helped her into the position he wanted, kneeling between her outstretched thighs.

She'd expected him to come back gentler, but Benjamin had taken her at her word. Guiding his cock back inside, he resumed the same powerful, overwhelming pace.

"Benjamin," she said, her voice hoarse from her cries.

"One more, Kailani. With me." He found her clit once more and then, he got exactly what he asked for.

She was a rag doll in a tornado, tossed into an abyss she didn't want to escape. He was right there with her.

He gave her three more hard thrusts and then... "Fuck. Kailani!"

Neither of them sought to separate as Benjamin held himself above her, kissing her. These weren't hungry or passionate kisses, but in her mind, they were so much better. Finally, he placed his forehead to hers, stole one last kiss, then pushed away.

Kailani lay on her back, wishing she could freeze time. Because this was the moment. The one she wanted to last forever.

Benjamin walked to the master bath, cleaned up, then returned. He crawled in next to her, then slid his arm under her pillow, inviting her to curl up against him. It had become what Kailani thought of as their "falling asleep" position.

She wrapped her arm around his waist, his chest her pillow, fighting sleep, even though she was beyond exhausted.

She just wanted...needed to stretch this perfect night out forever.

Benjamin's breathing deepened and she could tell he was close to falling asleep. She couldn't let him do that without telling him, without letting him know...

Benjamin cupped her cheek, drawing her face up to look at him. His smile was gentle, soft. "You know I think this is the first time I've really been...happy."

Kailani's heart simultaneously broke and melted. "Really?"

"Yes. You make me feel...so happy."

The look in his eyes and the tone of his voice told her to read between the lines. To hear the words he couldn't say.

That he loved her, the way she loved him.

It was too soon to say it, but when he kissed her, she felt those words like a vow. A promise that he would love her forever.

Then that sweet kiss turned very, very sexy.

It had been a beautiful moment. At nineteen, she'd thought that look was a promise. One she'd believed in with her whole heart.

Kailani slowly opened her eyes.

And it had been forgotten the very next week.

CHAPTER EIGHT

They landed in Van Nuys. John didn't really consider himself a snobby Angelino, but seriously...Van Nuys?

"Seriously...Van Nuys?" He looked at Benjamin, who was signing something for the attendant who'd greeted them in the small private terminal, which was a building only slightly larger than his house, set nearly a mile from the main airport terminal.

"It's the only place that had a runway available at the time we needed," Benjamin said apologetically.

"Wait, what's wrong with Van Nuys?" Kailani looked around.

"Nothing, it's just...not L.A."

Kailani's lips twitched.

"The San Fernando Valley is not L.A.," John declared. "Though I have some friends on the Van Nuys P.D. Their vice department is no joke."

"We might be waiting a while for a car," Benjamin said apologetically. "Given the time, most of the dispatch offices are closed." It was 3:30 in the morning, and the attendant who'd unlocked the terminal doors had looked half asleep. "Let me call some people I know, they might have their private drivers available, or the number of a driver I can call directly."

John looked at the two of them, these people who both were and weren't his. They were Schrödinger's marriage.

"This is my town," John said. "I'll get us a ride."

He might internally think that north of the 134 was too far away to deal with, but L.A. was his, and while they were here... he'd show them a little bit of his city.

John pulled out his own phone.

Ten minutes later, they waited on the curb in the dark. When a Van Nuys police cruiser pulled up, John stepped forward.

"Detective Wilson?" the officer asked through the window.

"Yes, thanks for the ride."

"Detective Espinoza says she still owes you." The officer sounded like he was reciting the message. "And that this isn't that big of a favor."

John laughed. "Okay, tell her I'll think of something." He turned to his companions and then gestured at the cruiser.

"This is our ride?" Benjamin asked stiffly.

"Yep." John opened the back door for Kailani.

Kailani stared at him, and John felt a little guilty, but she gamely slid into the backseat. Out of habit, he put his hand on the top of her head to make sure she didn't hit it.

Benjamin helped him load the bags in the trunk. John opened the driver's side back passenger door for him.

"I've never been arrested," Benjamin pointed out.

"You're not under arrest."

"Then how about I sit in front?" Benjamin eyed him.

John winced internally, realizing that despite all his wealth and power, Benjamin was a black man, and police interaction—

even if it was getting a ride in a cop car—would feel different for him.

"If you want to, you can," John said, because he wasn't an asshole. "But that would be significantly less amusing for me."

Benjamin's serious expression melted into a surprised smile. Then he shook his head and with an exaggerated sigh, slid into the backseat. John shut the door before circling around and climbing into the passenger seat.

"Buckle up, it's the law," the officer said.

Soon, they were on the 405 South, and despite it being nearly four in the morning, there was traffic. It was light compared to what they'd be up against during the day, so they were making good time. It helped that as cars spotted a cop in their rearview mirrors, they slid out of their way.

John turned in his seat. "I want the two of you to think about what you've done." He used his best scolding voice.

Kailani grinned. "This is weirdly fun. People keep looking at us."

"The windows are heavily tinted, so they can't see you, ma'am," the officer said.

"Why is it sticky?" Benjamin's pained expression made John smile, and Kailani outright laugh.

"Do you want me to answer that, sir?" the officer asked.

"I don't know...do I?"

"Probably not."

Benjamin cleared his throat. "I will be burning these clothes." He sighed. "I expected to feel scared or stressed."

It was an unexpected admission for the hyper-controlled Benjamin, and John stayed quiet, not wanting to interrupt this admission.

"Instead, I just feel...sticky."

Kailani dissolved into laughter. Benjamin looked at her, his expression soft and pleased.

In record time, they were pulling up outside John's small Craftsman in Culver City. It had been in good shape when the Trinity Masters, via some made-up grant, helped him buy it. He'd protested he didn't need it but had been told by the head of the foundation supplying the grant, aka a Trinity Masters member, that renting left him vulnerable to manipulation, and the Trinity Masters intended to protect him from that.

It was large by Culver City Craftsman standards, just under two thousand square feet. He'd bought it from the son of the original owner, so almost everything in the place was original. He didn't know shit about maintaining a home, let alone an historic one, but he was learning. When he bought it, there were spots on the outside where the paint was peeling, so the first major improvement was to repaint the whole thing.

Rather than just picking a color, he'd gone on several architectural tours, attended lectures, and even done some volunteer security work for the L.A. Conservancy in exchange for help selecting the exact right shades of green and yellow to match the historic Craftsman aesthetic.

The officer helped them unload the bags onto the sidewalk in front of his house. John watched Kailani and Benjamin as they studied his house. He felt a weird urge to apologize for his home, despite the fact that he'd never imagined he would actually own a home in L.A.

He picked up his own bag in one hand and headed up the bush-lined walkway. His porch was three steps up and deep enough that he could have put a full-sized table and chairs there. His door was dark wood with a small inset glass window and framed by wide trim painted a yellow-orange color. Calling it either yellow or orange didn't do it justice, he'd been told. The official name was Rockwood Amber.

John swallowed the urge to tell them this, to explain about the paint just to fill the silence.

He unlocked the door and stepped inside, holding it open for first Kailani, and then Benjamin.

"I want to check in with Makani," Kailani said. "I texted him, but I want to call."

"Did you hear back from the other keyholders?" Benjamin asked.

"No." Kailani looked worried.

"You can use my home office."

John pointed to a narrow interior door with a stained glass panel depicting a California Live Oak. The room on the other side was cozy, with a large picture window that faced the porch. He had a desk in there, but he always kept his papers tidy, so he wasn't worried about a mess.

Kailani slipped in, closing the door behind herself.

John looked over when Benjamin put a hand on his shoulder.

"Can I have a tour?" Benjamin asked.

"Yeah. I'm mean, sure." John cleared his throat, trying to overcome the awkwardness he felt.

He took a breath and turned to the living room. All those architectural tours he'd taken came in handy because he soon relaxed as he showed off the significant Craftsman elements of the home. He pointed out the details in the hand-glazed green tiles around the fireplace. He talked about the half wall of built-in bookshelves that separated the living room from the dining area, an open-concept style that was wildly unique when the house was originally built. He took Benjamin into the kitchen, with its original cabinets, the upper inside with imperfect hand-blown glass.

From the room that was probably meant to be a bedroom in the back of the house, he pointed out the large oak tree that dominated his backyard, that the bedroom's small fireplace was a miniature of the larger one in the living room.

It shouldn't matter if Benjamin liked his house, but for some reason, John needed him to love it as much as he did.

In the hall that connected the two bedrooms and bathroom, they met Kailani, who must have gone exploring, looking for them.

"John," Kailani said softly. "It's a lovely house, it's just..."

"Empty," Benjamin finished in his forthright way. "It *is* lovely. But it's empty. Did you just move in? Is your stuff in storage?"

John looked around. True, there wasn't much here. He shook his head.

"How long have you lived here?" Kailani asked.

"Three years."

Benjamin's eyes widened and Kailani bit her lower lip, he suspected to keep from blurting out her own surprise.

John wasn't offended. "I know the place is...sparsely decorated."

Benjamin raised his brow as he snorted. "One of my parents' houses has a minimalist aesthetic—Mom went through a phase. It was like living in a modern art museum. And even that had more furniture than this."

John let the other man's comments roll off his back. After all, he'd just put the billionaire in the back of a police cruiser.

Regardless, when Kailani and Benjamin stared at him, he realized they expected some sort of explanation, so he forced himself to come up with one. "Work keeps me busy," he lied.

"What does that mean?" Benjamin asked, calling him on it instantly. "You know you can buy furniture online and get it delivered, right?"

"I'm aware," John said sarcastically. "But the truth is I don't need much."

Kailani looked around again and frowned. "Yeah, but...you need more than this."

"You have one chair," Benjamin said, stabbing his finger toward the dining room, where a single chair sat positioned near the half wall. He didn't have a table, so if he wasn't eating on the couch, he usually used the wide top of the half wall as a table, either standing or sitting beside it.

From the first moment he met Benjamin and Kailani, he'd felt the Grand Canyon-sized divide between him and his future spouses. He'd spent more than a few restless nights wondering if the differences between them would cause problems somewhere down the line, because the hard truth was he didn't see the world the same way they did. They were used to looking at life from the windows of luxury hotels, private jets, and limousines. His view came through the dust-covered windshield of a cop car.

Kailani and Benjamin had grown up with loving parents and wealth beyond anything he could imagine, legacies to the secret society John was still trying to figure out. They'd never known a single second of hunger or homelessness, while those two states had been second nature to him growing up.

"I have a bed, a couch, a—"

Benjamin cut him off mid-list. "We're not counting those as two things. You have a futon, for God's sake. That's one piece of furniture. Plus, it looks like you've got a coffee table that's seen better days, doubling as your dining table, and—"

It was John's turn to interject. "I also eat there," he pointed to the half wall, "and at the kitchen counter sometimes."

Kailani looked like she wanted to argue that point.

Benjamin rolled his eyes. "You live like a frat boy."

"I don't like clutter," John said stubbornly.

"A couch isn't clutter," Benjamin announced. "I'm getting you a couch."

John started to argue, but Benjamin had already walked away from them, phone in hand.

Was he buying the couch right now?

Kailani reached over and placed her hand on John's forearm, and he felt the same warm buzz that always accompanied her touches.

When she'd pushed down the hood of her robe at the binding ceremony, she had taken his breath away. She was truly one of the most beautiful women he'd ever seen, with her tanned skin, dark eyes, and delicate features. Then, with her face flushed and her eyes sparking with anger as she looked at Benjamin, he'd felt drawn not only to her looks but her spirit.

"I could help you decorate if you want," she said.

He appreciated her offer, and he knew it was sincere.

The three of them had squandered their month, wasting too much time on Kailani and Benjamin's past without giving the present a second glance. He wanted to get to know them, and he wanted them to know him as well.

He didn't know what the future held, but the more time he spent with them, the more he realized he wanted them to be a part of his.

"I told you I was in foster care," he said, feeling slightly nervous. He didn't talk about his childhood because he hated pity, hated the way people suddenly started looking at him differently, like he was somehow...broken.

"You did," Kailani said softly.

"I never managed to find a permanent placement, so I was moved around a lot. Sometimes, I didn't get a lot of warning ahead of time, which meant there wasn't much time to pack up my stuff. After a while, I just made sure everything I owned would fit in a trash bag."

"A trash bag?" she asked.

He gave her a crooked, self-deprecating grin. "I didn't get my first suitcase until I was in my twenties." He pointed toward the front door where he'd dropped his duffel bag. "There it is."

He'd hoped the joke would lighten the moment, but it missed the mark.

Kailani's hand, still on his arm, squeezed gently, and he saw the sheen of tears in her eyes. "I'm so sorry."

And there it was...the sympathetic voice, the pity. Somehow, coming from Kailani, it felt much worse, so he changed course, unwilling—actually unable—to tell her more.

This was still too new—their relationship, as well as his attempts at opening up to someone. Right now, all he could handle were baby steps.

So he shrugged casually, assuming an it's-no-big-deal air. "I guess I just got used to living a minimalist lifestyle."

Kailani's hand fell away, obviously sensing his huge one-eighty.

Benjamin walked back over to them. "I've ordered you a few things."

John nodded, trying to process the fact Benjamin had bought him an actual couch. "You bought me a couch?"

"No, I bought you a Mission-style panel sofa, two Mission-style armchairs with matching side tables, and Craftsman Tiffany-style lamps." As Benjamin spoke, he walked around the living room, indicating where everything would go. "I also commissioned a size-appropriate dining table and chairs—a replica of the set in Gamble House." Benjamin glanced around, his gaze assessing. "That will do to start. The bed...we need to measure to see if an Alaskan King will fit." Benjamin put his phone in his pocket. "My people will handle delivery and installation, but they'll need someone to open the door. Do you have an assistant...I mean, a neighbor with a key?"

John blinked. Benjamin was decisive and overbearing, but based on what he'd just said, he hadn't simply ordered furniture. He'd ordered the *right* furniture.

Kailani tilted her head, then said, "That was nice of you," to Benjamin.

"It's been known to happen," Benjamin retorted, sarcastically but with humor.

Kailani reverted to form, rolling her eyes.

Before they could pick up the bickering again, Benjamin's phone rang. Glancing at the screen, he cursed softly. "This is a work thing. Give me a minute?"

John nodded as Benjamin stepped into the kitchen and answered.

Kailani drifted back down the hallway, stopping in front of his bedroom. "I really would like to help you decorate," she said, walking into the bedroom that served more as a walk-in closet, considering he still slept on the futon in the living room. He'd been meaning to order a bed. He just hadn't made the time.

"How much do you think all that furniture he just bought costs?" John asked, feeling slightly ill at the thought.

"Do you really want to know?"

He shook his head. "I need to tell him to cancel the orders. That's all...fuck," he said, running his fingers through his hair. "Too much."

"You can ask," Kailani said, smiling, "but he won't do it. Benjamin can be very generous when he wants to."

"I bet that hurt to admit."

She laughed. "You have no idea how much."

"I don't get it, Kailani. You're a kind and rational woman, but whenever Benjamin is around..."

"I'm a raving bitch."

"I wouldn't have used those words, but since you did, I'll allow them." John was overcome with the desire to reach out and...what? Hug her? Kiss her? Carry her back to his frat-boy futon and...

He shoved all those thoughts aside.

"I hate how I behave when I'm around Benjamin, but it's like I can't help myself. It's a habit I can't seem to break."

"Are you trying?" John asked.

She smirked. "Not really."

Ever since the binding ceremony, John had been curious about what was at the heart of Benjamin and Kailani's animosity, but he'd never found the right time to ask. He'd considered starting the conversation during one of their FaceTime calls or with Benjamin that day at lunch, but he hadn't known them well enough to broach the subject comfortably.

After everything they'd been through today, he decided it was time. "Can I ask what happened between the two of you?"

Kailani sighed. "That's a hard question to answer. It all started so long ago."

Before she could say more, Benjamin walked into the room, and Kailani fell silent. John's window of opportunity had closed.

"So, what's next?" Benjamin asked, just as Kailani's phone began to ring.

"Hold on, this is Makani, I wasn't able to get a hold of him earlier," Kailani answered, but rather than retreating to the office, she stayed with them.

They listened to her side of the conversation, and after only a few minutes she hung up. Tension that hadn't been there a moment ago was back in her shoulders.

"Makani used the emergency contact protocol and was able to talk to someone at headquarters. He told them about the fire, which is now confirmed as arson by the investigator. Whoever he spoke to said that there had been no further attacks on that end."

Benjamin pulled out his phone, frowning at the screen. "Devon never called or texted me back."

John really wanted to know who was answering the phone for the Trinity Masters, if Devon, who was clearly one of the inner circle, wasn't.

"Makani was also promised backup. Headquarters is sending a couple people to Hawaii. Makani has their names: Tate and Levi. They are coming with their trinities, and though the spouses aren't security experts, more people means more eyes."

"Do we think they're counselors, like Devon?" John asked.

"No...Makani said they were 'Warrior Scholars' but I'm not sure who or what that is."

Benjamin frowned. "I think it's a new thing, something this Grand Master is, was, doing."

"We should find out," John said. "We need to know all the players."

"I'll call a friend," Benjamin promised.

"Any word on whether the names of the other keyholders were compromised?" John asked.

"No. And I just checked again. Still haven't heard back from anyone," Kailani said.

"We should hire security, bodyguards," Benjamin said.

"No," Kailani said again. She checked her phone. "It's six in the morning, but where I'm going is an hour away according to Google maps. Hopefully I'll catch the keyholder at home before they leave for work..." Her voice trailed off as she looked at Benjamin, then John, and back. "You're not going to let me go on my own, are you?"

"Nope," John said. "We're going with you. I'll drive."

CHAPTER NINE

The massive house in Malibu had tall windows and walls of glass, the white of the building a backdrop for the greens and browns of palm trees and massive coastal sunflowers. Situated on a hill, no doubt with gorgeous views, the dwelling's modern architecture was both geometric with lots of straight lines and corners, and delicate. The curved uphill drive let them out onto a large level area flanked by an L-shaped garage on one side and the house on the other. A white sports car was pulled up near the steps at a casual angle.

"That gate probably meant security," John said as he climbed out of the driver's seat.

"Or it's just about privacy," Benjamin said. "Gates with call boxes can be a pain unless you have full-time staff to respond to requests to enter."

John looked over and shook his head.

Kailani had been nervous when they pulled up at the address and found a solid black-and-gray gate at the foot of the driveway, but as John pulled closer, and while they looked among the vegetation for a call box, the gate had swung open automatically.

If there'd been a call box, she wasn't sure what she would have said. Should it have been cloak-and-dagger—should she recite the Trinity Masters' Latin motto? Should she just say her name and hope that curiosity meant they let her in?

"Are you alright?" Benjamin asked quietly.

She looked up into his face, and for the first time in over a decade, her first impulse wasn't to defensively brace herself or launch her own verbal attack.

"Yes, just...thinking about what I'm going to do."

Aware that this was taking too long, that it had been over twelve hours since she'd gotten the call, Kailani squared her shoulders and walked up the handful of wide, shallow steps to the massive, smooth white front door.

She raised her hand and knocked. She'd googled the name of the person she was here to meet and found a picture, so she knew who she was looking for.

A figure moved through the house, just a shadow until they walked by the glass wall beside the door.

Kailani put her hand to her throat, fingers hooking under the chain.

The door opened.

Preston Kim stood in the doorway. He wore exercise clothes and had a towel slung around his neck. His gaze moved from her to John and Benjamin, who'd taken up positions behind her.

Kailani hooked her fingers under the chain and pulled out the key, letting it rest on her shirt.

Preston's gaze dropped to it, his eyes going wide with surprise, before he shifted his attention to her face.

Kailani met his gaze. "Can I speak with you privately?"

. . .

JOHN STOOD in the foyer next to Benjamin, feeling out of place. Put him in a back alley, questioning suspects or witnesses, surrounded by the worst humanity had to offer, and he was just fine. Throw him on a private plane or in—fuck—a Malibu Barbie mansion like this, and his confidence wavered.

The man who'd opened the door had invited them in, then excused himself and Kailani without a word of explanation.

They weren't there more than a second or two before another man and a woman appeared.

"Preston?" The woman called out to Kailani and Preston's retreating backs as she and the other man approached him and Benjamin, still hovering by the front door.

The four of them stared at one another. Then the man stuck out his hand. "Lance." That was followed by a quick round of introductions. Benjamin smiled when the woman introduced herself as Carly.

"You two care to explain that?" Lance asked with a nod to where Kailani and Preston had disappeared.

John hoped Benjamin, as the legacy, would take lead on the conversation because he wasn't exactly sure what was known, not known, and who could be read in on the situation. The fact Kailani pulled Preston out of the room told him some level of secrecy was required, but how much?

John suddenly regretted not making more effort to attend Trinity Masters meetings and galas. He had used the connections afforded him through the society, but only those close to home that would have an impact on the cases he was trying to solve.

"I'm afraid you're going to have to ask Preston," John said.

Neither Carly nor Lance seemed appeased by that response.

"You're Carly Kenan, aren't you?" Benjamin asked.

Carly nodded.

"I'm a huge fan of your games," he said to her. "Can't tell you how many all-nighters I had to spend in college, completing assignments, because I squandered the days and weeks preceding playing *End Times*. My buddies and I were addicted to it...the role-playing, the off-the-chain graphics. When I look back, I figure it was a miracle I managed to graduate on time."

John wasn't sure what exactly *End Times* was, though he'd heard of it from other officers at the precinct. Video games hadn't been a part of his childhood, and by the time he reached adulthood, he had a career and wasn't interested in playing catch-up on them, just so he could hang out online with some guys from work for gaming nights. Regardless, he appreciated Benjamin's not-quite-too-obvious attempt at distraction.

Carly grinned half-heartedly, clearly distracted as she looked over her shoulder at the closed door to the room Preston and Kailani had escaped to.

"I hear that a lot," she said, not adding more. So much for distraction.

Meanwhile, Lance remained silent, his arms crossed, glaring at them in such a way John might have felt threatened if he wasn't used to employing the same technique. Lance's entire demeanor screamed military. If John had to guess, he'd go with former Marine. There was something about the upright way Lance stood, the tight way he held himself. What's more, Lance kept placing himself just slightly in front of Carly, even though she'd already made a couple subtle steps to move back to his side.

Benjamin cast a sideways glance at John as the silence slipped well into the awkward range.

John decided it was his turn to take a stab at dispelling the tension. "Something smells wonderful," he observed, not lying. He wasn't sure what they were baking, but his mouth had been watering since they walked into the house. They'd eaten on the plane, but not since then, and his stomach was telling him it was breakfast time.

He expected Carly to comment, so he was surprised when Lance unfolded his arms, a huge grin covering his face. "Homemade cinnamon rolls. My own recipe. We were just about to have some with coffee."

Carly stepped next to her husband and slid her arm through Lance's affectionately. "Lance is the world's greatest when it comes to baking."

Lance gave her a sweet kiss on the side of her head. "I think you're biased, babe. Biased, but not wrong."

The two of them laughed easily, and just like that, the tension was broken.

"There's plenty if you want to join us." Lance gestured toward what John assumed was the kitchen, the rest of them following him toward the delicious smells emanating from there.

Benjamin walked next to him, giving him a subtle shoulder bump in silent approval for his success in breaking the tension.

Upon entering the kitchen, Carly set about pouring them all coffee, asking him and Benjamin if they preferred sugar and cream, while Lance, who'd donned an apron that said, "I bake because punching people is frowned upon," plated up the most mouthwatering cinnamon rolls John had ever seen.

Once they were all served, they sat around one end of what he supposed was the kitchen table, though it was a part of the massive, long kitchen island. Everything in the kitchen was glossy and white, but it still felt homey rather than sterile. Behind and beside them, a corner where two glass walls met offered a panoramic view of the ocean.

"So," Carly began, and John braced himself, afraid she was going to ask them why they were there. Which meant he was surprised when she asked, "Are the three of you a trinity?"

Well, hell. He didn't have an answer for that question either.

KAILANI STEPPED into the small home office with a view of the steep hills of the Malibu canyons. When she heard the door close, she turned to Preston.

"Keyholder," she said softly.

"Yes." Preston shook his head in disbelief. "It's real? And it's...happening? Wait, did you text me last night?"

Kailani nodded. "We've been activated. I opened the first door to get the names. You're my first stop."

"Why have we been activated?" Preston asked. "What happened?"

"I don't know. But something did, which means we need to get back to the *waihona* as fast as possible."

"*Waihona*," he repeated the word slowly. "Is that a Hawaiian word?"

Kailani realized he didn't know where he was supposed to go. "Yes. It's on Oahu, in the Hale'ekolu hotel."

"I've stayed there. Really nice place."

"Thank you, my family owns it."

"And the *waihona*, that's the treasury?"

"I think of it as the vault," she said, "but my family calls it the *waihona*."

"And we need to open it...because if headquarters falls, whatever's inside is meant to keep the society together." It wasn't quite a question.

"Yes," she agreed.

"And one of the three of us is acting Grand Master," Preston said grimly.

"There's something else you should know." Kailani wished she had more facts, less conjecture, but Preston deserved to have all the details. "It's possible that whoever attacked in Boston knows about us."

Preston's shoulders went stiff. "No one knows about the keyholders."

"No one *should* know," she agreed. "But it's possible they know, and that the *waihona* is the next target. Someone tried to burn down the hotel an hour after I got the call."

Preston walked over to lean against his desk. "Walk me through it, everything that's happened."

"Um. Sort of," John replied to Carly's question.

"What does that mean?" Lance asked. "Either you're a trinity or you're not."

Benjamin sighed. "Our binding ceremony was bad."

Carly burst out laughing as if he'd said something genuinely hilarious. But John noticed Lance wasn't quite as amused.

Carly leaned toward her husband, still grinning widely, and gave him a quick kiss on the cheek. "You're going to have to let it go, Lance."

Lance shook his head. "It's not funny, Carly."

She rolled her eyes but didn't respond, turning her attention back to them. "I bet your binding ceremony wasn't as bad as ours."

Benjamin and John exchanged a glance, and despite the fact basically everything in their lives was still up in the air, they turned back to Carly at the same time.

"Challenge accepted," John joked.

"Okay," Carly started. "Once all three of our names were announced and the ceremony reached the end, Preston and Lance both kissed me. But—"

Lance scowled. "You realize there's no way I'm going to come out of this story without looking like a complete ass."

"Aw, I know," she said, without the slightest amount of guilt. "That's why I'm telling it."

Lance narrowed his eyes, but there was no anger in his expression. He leaned toward his wife and gave her a quick, hard kiss, then said, "Just know there will be consequences for this later."

Carly snorted. "If that's your way of threatening to punish me, it would be just as effective to say, 'I dare you.'"

Benjamin leaned forward in his chair, looking too interested in hearing how Lance fucked up.

"When Preston turned to kiss Lance, Lance pushed him, told him to essentially fuck off."

John looked at Lance, who grimaced.

"Believe me," he said. "If I could go back and rewrite the whole beginning of our story, I would."

"It got worse than that?" John asked sympathetically.

"Hell yeah. I tried to seduce Carly without Preston there, picked a fight, stormed out, then..."

"Let's just say that by the next morning, I was on a plane back to California alone after telling Preston and Lance I wanted nothing to do with them or the trinity," Carly replied. "Can you top that?"

John waited for Benjamin to respond, curious what he'd say.

"Kailani and I dated back when we were both still in college. I didn't think it was that bad of a breakup, but when my name was called and she realized it was me—"

Lance relaxed. "Ha. You fucked up way before the binding ceremony, didn't you?"

Benjamin started to shrug, then nodded. "Yeah. Kailani stormed out and said she wouldn't marry me. She caught a flight back to Hawaii and yesterday was the first time we've seen each other since. Today was supposed to be..." Benjamin caught himself before saying the rest. If he admitted today was supposed to be their wedding day, he'd also have to explain why they were in California instead of Boston. "We asked the Grand Master's counselor if it was possible to dissolve the trinity, but we haven't heard back from her."

Carly took a sip of coffee. "I considered doing the same thing, though it didn't get quite that far. For what it's worth, I've never heard of any trinity being dissolved. Can I ask you something, Benjamin?"

He nodded.

"Are you resistant to the trinity as well?"

John was shocked when Benjamin shook his head without a moment's hesitation. "I want a trinity marriage. I want to be married to spouses who want *me*." He snuck a glance at John. "I'm not willing to accept anything less. And neither of them should have to either."

"Then can I offer you some advice?" Carly asked.

Benjamin leaned forward eagerly. "Please."

"Talk to her. I know that sounds like ridiculously vague advice, but Preston, Lance, and I could have solved so many of our problems if we would have stopped throwing up roadblocks, stopped running away, and just talked."

Lance smiled at him and Benjamin. "Once you're ready for the conversation, text me. I have a recipe for a souffle that is guaranteed to put your girl in a well-fed, mellow mood."

Carly laughed, even as she elbowed Lance playfully, then crooked her thumb at him. "This guy is the reason I have to work out an hour every day. I obviously don't know either of you well, but I genuinely hope your marriage is a happy one."

"Is someone protecting the WAIHONA?" Preston asked once she'd finished explaining the chaos of yesterday.

"Yes. My brother."

"He knows enough to protect it?"

"All of my family knows about the *waihona*—where it is, that it's our duty to protect it. The hotel was actually built around it. However, no one but the keyholder knows exactly how to access it."

"Good that your brother is there, but is that enough?"

"My brother, Makani, was able to talk to someone in Boston, I'm guessing one of the counselors, and they're sending additional guards."

"My father was a counselor," Preston said softly. "We can call him if we need more information."

"Right now, I need to make sure you get on a plane, and then I need to go get the last keyholder."

"I'll go pack for us."

"Us?"

"My trinity is coming with me," Preston said.

"But it might be dangerous there," she said.

Preston's lips twitched. "You're not married yet?"

"No."

"Okay, then let me explain something. I realize that it's dangerous, and yes, I could go on my own, but if my husband and wife found out that I went into a dangerous situation without telling them, or without taking them with me...that would definitely be *more* dangerous for me." He was smiling but sobered. "Worse, it would hurt them."

Kailani thought about how John and Benjamin had insisted

on coming with her, on staying with her, despite both knowing the danger.

"They'd understand," Kailani said stubbornly. She wasn't even sure why she was arguing this point. "You'd be following orders, doing your duty to the Trinity Masters."

"True." Preston studied her for a moment. "But my trinity comes first. Always."

Before Carly could say more, Preston and Kailani joined them in the kitchen. Preston crossed the room, pressing a kiss to the top of Carly's head before moving over to give the same to Lance.

It was hot.

He glanced over at Benjamin to try to catch his reaction to the two men. Benjamin had observed them as well, and then... turned to look at him, naked desire laid bare for John to see. Nice to know his attraction was returned.

"Impromptu vacation," Preston said to his spouses. "Pack a bag."

John thought it spoke to the level of trust between the trinity when Carly asked, "Snow or sand?"

"Sand," Preston replied.

John leaned back as a wave of...not quite jealousy...but longing passed through him. He wanted the kind of relationship Preston, Carly, and Lance had.

And he wanted it with Kailani and Benjamin.

Kailani slid into the backseat so Benjamin's long legs could take the front passenger spot.

John turned on the car. "Where to? Where's the last keyholder?"

"For this, I'll need to fly."

"I'll come with you," John said.

"We'll," Benjamin corrected. "We'll need to fly." Benjamin's jaw clenched. "Even if you want to go commercial, I'm coming with you."

"Why?" John asked. Kailani could only see part of John's face reflected in the rearview mirror, but what she could see bore an odd expression.

Benjamin turned to face him, anger and tension radiating off him. "Why am I coming? Because even if I piss her off, Kailani is one of my oldest friends and I care about her."

Kailani knew her mouth was hanging open in shock. Benjamin's words hit her in the chest, an almost physical blow.

The urge to push back, to say she'd take care of it, that she'd book them seats on a flight out of LAX, was riding her. A decade of seeing Benjamin as the enemy was a hard habit to break. Had he seen her as the enemy the way she'd always assumed, or as a friend, even after everything they'd been through?

Kailani touched Benjamin's shoulder. "Can your plane fly us to New York?"

He twisted, looking back at her, and she ignored the faint surprise in his expression.

She wasn't changing her stance on Benjamin, she assured herself. What he'd said didn't change anything. She was just being smart and using available resources to get to the third keyholder as fast as possible.

Benjamin cleared his throat. "I'd be happy to."

"Good thing we put the suitcases in the trunk," John said cheerfully as he put the car in gear and started down the drive. "It's not far from here to Van Nuys."

Benjamin pulled out his phone to make arrangements as John navigated the morning commute traffic. Kailani looked out the window, and though she knew this was the same Pacific Ocean that surrounded her island, it was a cold and cool gray-blue that made her miss the bright blue water of home.

CHAPTER TEN

B oston
  Seventeen hours since the kidnapping

HIS HEAD THROBBED, but luckily his heart had gone numb.

Franco stared at his hands as he sat on the couch in the hotel suite that was their base of operations. Not their temporary headquarters. No, that was now somewhere on Oahu. The keyholders were one of dozens of different charters, backup plans, rules, and protocols that existed within the Trinity Masters, most of which were secret even from the general membership. Maybe some were forgotten rather than secret. Since joining and taking it upon himself to catalog and uncover every scrap of information, Franco had uncovered more lost, forgotten things.

Learning those secrets, decoding the clues, had been fun and felt so important before yesterday.

Now all Franco wanted was his husband and wife back.

Out of habit, he went to run his hands through his hair. Colum grabbed his wrist before he could. The Irishman, who'd been an academic pen pal before yesterday, had seemingly appointed himself as Franco's companion and nurse. His duties included stopping Franco from touching the lump on his head.

Everyone else was dealing with something, handling something.

Franco had no background in security or investigation; he had no skills that would help find the two people he loved more than life itself.

"Follow that line of investigation," Lachlan was saying. The Warrior Scholar had taken command of the investigation, using a combination of his fellow soldiers-turned-academics, Bennett security employees, and other members who had the kind of dangerous skills they needed right now.

Sebastian looked nearly as bad as Franco felt, his face grim as he scanned security footage. They'd already had both live people and analysis software go over all the security tapes they'd gathered, trying to track where Juliette and Devon had been taken. Now Sebastian was watching to see if he recognized anyone. Lachlan had said they needed to strongly consider this was an inside job, that someone within the society had betrayed them. Since no digital membership roster existed, they couldn't just run facial recognition software to compare the faces of every member against the videos. But Sebastian had memorized the membership, had studied most of them.

Franco stood, unable to sit any longer. The doctor who'd come and put staples in his head had forbidden Rose from giving him any more tranquilizers, since it was risky with the head wound.

Right now, exhaustion was doing the work of numbing his emotions. They'd been up all night, and it was now lunchtime. Seventeen hours since Juliette and Devon had been taken.

Seventeen hours was a long time.

Franco walked over to the window, looking down on the streets of Boston. A storm had blown in about four a.m., and rain lashed the streets. The sky to the east was an angry, roiling gray. It matched his mood.

Even with the rain, there were people on the streets, huddled in raincoats since it was too windy for umbrellas. The people were going about as if the world hadn't just ended. As if it was acceptable to walk and talk and smile while somewhere out there, Franco's spouses were being hurt. Tortured. Killed.

Franco slammed the side of his fist into the glass so hard it shuddered.

Lachlan's voice stopped for a moment, but it was Colum who put a hand on Franco's shoulder, pulling him away from the window.

"Ye won't be helping anyone doing that," he said, his thick accent oddly soothing. "Sure won't you have a cup of tea?"

"No," Franco said softly.

"Just one in the hand."

Franco shook his head.

"Sure didn't the lord himself stop for a cup of tea on his way to the cross."

Franco blinked and looked up. "What?"

Colum handed him a cup of tea. "Drink."

"Did you just imply that Christ stopped for a cup of tea on the way to his crucifixion?"

When Colum grinned, Franco laughed. It was rusty, and flirted with the line of being hysterical, but it stopped him from imagining Juliette beaten and bloody, Devon dead with a bullet in his chest, or alive but with fingers missing from torture.

The tea was strong, with milk and a little sugar, and though Franco had grown up on Cuban coffee, the tea was comforting.

"Don't worry. I brought my own tea bags. We didn't have to

use that English crap." Colum pointed to the tea bags that room service had brought up with the tea and coffee service someone had been smart enough to order.

"You carry tea bags with you?" Franco asked.

"This place may claim to be as close to Ireland as you can be off the island itself, but they serve English Breakfast. Not a box of Barry's in all of Boston."

The suite door opened, the beep indicating it was someone with a key. Rose raced in, her expression pinched with worry. At some point, she'd changed out of the ball gown into jeans and a sweater. They'd tried to get him to change, to shower, but Franco didn't want to be warm and clean and comfortable while Devon and Juliette were...

A vivid memory of Juliette locked in the attacker's arms, her eyes wide over the hand that covered her mouth, slammed through Franco.

"We have another problem," Rose announced.

Lachlan ended his call, turning to her. "Go."

"Juliette and Devon aren't the only ones missing."

For the second time in as many days, they were on Benjamin's private plane. John had been a bit shell-shocked during the first flight, awestruck by the sheer luxury surrounding him. It beat the hell out of flying economy, where he had to practically shoehorn himself in, his knees pressed too tightly against the seat in front of him.

This time...his first thought was "a man could get used to this," especially when—once they were in the air—the flight attendant came around with mimosas, promising that lunch would be served at noon.

John accepted the mimosa, though he suspected one drink would put him out. He'd managed to grab an hour, maybe two, of restless sleep on the previous flight. His eyes were scratchy and dry, yet he felt oddly wired. He was no stranger to pulling long hours. There had been many times when he was in the middle of working a case where he'd remain awake for forty-eight hours, even more.

"If either of you are tired, several of these chairs fully recline," Benjamin offered when none of them had bothered to speak since boarding.

Kailani, who had been looking out the window, turned her attention to them. "I'm not sure I could fall asleep."

While he felt the same, he hated the dark circles under Kailani's eyes.

"Maybe you should try," Benjamin suggested. "Once we land in New York, we'll be on the move again."

Benjamin's words were spoken kindly, laced with concern, but John didn't miss the way her eyes narrowed slightly before she seemed to come to her senses. She was still struggling to overcome too many years of anger, and while he thought—or maybe hoped was a better word—she was coming around, they weren't out of the woods yet. Their trinity remained on shaky ground and would until one of them reached across the void.

He recalled Carly's advice, her suggestion that they talk, and it occurred to him that he was in the best position to lead the charge, lead by example.

Kailani was hesitant to reopen old wounds and John could tell Benjamin was walking on eggshells, trying not to take a bad situation and make it worse. So how could he ask them to be vulnerable if he wasn't willing to do the same?

John took a sip of the mimosa before placing it in the drink holder. The three of them had claimed the same seats they'd had on the previous flight, he and Kailani facing each other, Benjamin next to him across the aisle.

"Preston and his trinity seem very close," he remarked, a

weak opening, but when he considered all the things he wanted to say to these two people, it felt like the easiest opening.

"They do," Benjamin agreed, glancing at Kailani, before adding, "for their less-than-stellar beginning."

"What do you mean?" Kailani asked, taking the bait.

"According to Carly, their binding ceremony was as rocky as ours," John responded, aware Benjamin most likely wouldn't. "Apparently, Preston and Lance nearly came to blows at the end of it."

Kailani's gaze slipped to Benjamin's briefly, but she looked away quickly. "How did they resolve their problems?" she asked John.

"They talked to each other."

Kailani's deadpan look made it clear she was unimpressed with the answer.

"What if I start?" John suggested.

"Start?" Benjamin asked.

"Talking, telling you about me, about what led me to the Trinity Masters."

Kailani smiled softly, tiredly. "I'd like that."

Benjamin grinned and nodded. "Me too."

John took a deep breath...and opened a vein.

"Who?" Lachlan and Sebastian asked at the same time, both jumping to their feet in response to Rose's declaration.

"Izabel Serra and her new trinity."

"They were just called to the altar," Franco said.

"I know," Rose said. "Her family arranged a little post-binding ceremony reception, and last night the six of us went to the symphony together." Rose waved her hand through the air, as if waving that information away as unimportant. "I was supposed to have lunch with her today."

A grim anticipation settled over the room, everyone's attention on Rose, except Colum's. He'd picked up his phone and was staring at the screen.

"She didn't respond to any of my texts about canceling. I went by her condo—she has a place here, and they were going there rather than here, the hotel." She gestured around, indicating the suite. Normally this suite was reserved for new trinities for several nights after their binding ceremony, to give them a neutral place to get to know one another.

"Her door was unlocked. Not broken, just unlocked. But when I went in..." Rose pulled her phone from her pocket and passed it around. The probably once-elegant living room was demolished—furniture overturned and broken, paintings off the walls, and...

"Is that a tranquilizer dart sticking out of the wall?" Franco asked, handing Rose back her phone.

"Yes," Lachlan said. "They must have missed with the first shot and forgotten to retrieve the dart."

"They drugged them too." Franco had to force down the memory of that needle going into Juliette's neck.

"Who's her new trinity?" Lachlan asked.

"Brennon Reyes and Rowan Greene," Rose said.

Lachlan looked up sharply. "They took Rowan Greene?"

"We should assume so," Rose said. "Why are you making that face?"

"Rowan Greene is a Night Stalker."

Everyone looked at Lachlan, who shook his head and explained.

"He's 160th Special Operations Aviation Regiment."

"Shit," Sebastian muttered. "That's right. Fuck."

"Explain," Franco demanded, heart slamming against his ribs.

"Listen, Devon is certainly dangerous and skilled enough

that in a fair fight, I'd put money on him. Juliette is more dangerous, but not in a hand-to-hand combat way. Rowan..." Lachlan shook his head. "Rowan is the thing you should be afraid of in the dark. The Night Stalkers are who the Army sends in when they want something taken care of under the cover of darkness. They'll jump out of a helicopter, silently neutralize every target in a building, rescue or recover whatever their mission objective is, and be back in their Little Bird helicopter before anyone on the ground knows there's a problem."

Franco hadn't thought he could be any more terrified for his loves, but if the same people who'd taken Juliette and Devon had managed to kidnap Rowan...

Lachlan and Sebastian spent the next five minutes organizing an investigative team to check if the trinity stayed until the end of the symphony and then go over to examine Izabel's condo. A team had worked through the night trying to find Devon and Juliette, but nothing yet. Maybe there would be more clues at the condo, other clues. Maybe this was a good thing.

Franco winced as soon as he had the thought, guilt biting at him.

Lachlan cleared his throat. "We may need to take some decisive, risky actions. Which means I need to know what my chain of command is." Lachlan looked from Sebastian to Rose, his gaze finally settling on Franco.

Franco felt everyone looking at him, but he wasn't in charge. He couldn't be, for so many reasons.

"They keyholders are gathering in Oahu," Franco said. "And you sent people to protect them and the temporary headquarters."

"A counselor needs to go there, for continuity," Rose said. "To be with the new Grand Master."

"Not the new Grand Master," Franco snapped, though a

nasty little voice inside his head reminded him of that other rule, that last line in the charter document that created the keyholders. "The *acting* Grand Master."

"Right," Rose said softly. "That's what I meant."

"That still leaves a temporary leadership hole, and I may need someone to give the green light," Lachlan said.

"I'll do it."

The voice came from Colum's cell phone. They all turned to the Irishman. He held up the phone, turning it so they could see the screen, see that he was on a video call...

With the Fleet Admiral, Eric Ericsson.

Sebastian froze, Lachlan frowned, Rose's expression turned sharp and predatory, and Franco...Franco wanted to laugh. If Juliette and Devon had been here, he *could* have laughed, but they weren't, which meant he had to take this seriously, had to deal with the fact that the Fleet Admiral knew what was happening. Knew they were wounded and vulnerable.

"I'll make the calls," Eric said. "You can blame me if it's FUBAR."

"You are not taking over the Trinity Masters," Rose snapped.

Lachlan casually folded his arms. "I've handled coups before. If he tries—"

"This isn't a coup. I have my own pack of idiots to deal with, I don't need additional idiots." Eric smirked, then his expression sobered. "But it sounds like you're under attack. I can send the MPF. They're hunting cults and bombers, but they can be on your shores in six hours."

"Hang up the call," Rose snapped.

Colum didn't react to her order.

Rose walked over, a slight smile on her face, every step calm and measured. The hair on the back of Franco's neck stood on end. She slid up to Colum, so close to him that her body brushed his, her smiling face tipped up to his.

"May I?" Rose murmured to Colum.

"Uh..." Colum appeared to be having trouble forming a sentence with Rose in his personal space.

She slipped the phone from the Irishman's hands, taking a half step back. She was still smiling as she spoke. "Fleet Admiral."

"Tell Marek I said 'hi' and his grandmother is still the best."

"I will, but I want you to know something."

Across the room, Sebastian looked alarmed and started forward.

"While we appreciate the offer of help," Rose purred, "don't think that we're weak."

"I don't, I—"

"We will not let you take us over. The Trinity Masters will not become another territory of the Masters' Admiralty. And if you try, remember this—"

"Rose, don't!" Sebastian lunged for her, tried to grab the phone.

Rose turned, both her body so Sebastian couldn't grab her hand, and the phone screen so that it was facing Colum.

"Just remember," Rose said softly. "We have a hostage. Your Archivist."

CHAPTER ELEVEN

"I never knew my mother," John started, swallowing deeply.

"Never?" Benjamin asked, somewhat surprised.

While John had told them he'd been in foster care, he hadn't gone into any detail. No doubt they'd thought his entry to the system had come later in his life.

"My mother left me next to a dumpster in a back alley right after I was born. Umbilical cord still attached."

"Oh my God, that poor woman." Kailani's eyes widened and she covered her mouth with her hand. "Was she young? Or postpartum depression?"

The fact that Kailani's first instinct was to worry about a young woman who'd abandoned a newborn made him love her a little bit.

Benjamin's eyes were sympathetic, though his expression was somewhat aghast.

"Not too young to know better. She was a known associate of a mid-level drug dealer and probably an addict herself. Her arrests were for petty larceny, vandalism, and one solicitation charge that didn't go to trial."

"She put a newborn in a dumpster," Benjamin said, as if he was still trying to process the willingness to literally throw away another human.

John held their gaze, even when every instinct inside wanted to look away, to shut up. He forced himself to forge on. "Guess I was lucky to be born in June. The weather was mild."

"Don't," Kailani whispered. "Don't do that."

He knew what she was talking about because he'd done this to her once before. Tried to lessen the heaviness with misplaced humor, tried to make light of something that hurt like hell. His mother had tossed him out like garbage.

He gave her a slight nod, a sad smile. "I was found by a busboy at the restaurant that owned the dumpster when he was taking out the trash. He called 911. I was treated at the hospital and stayed there while the cops tracked down my mother. She was arrested for child endangerment, and DCFS found a great-aunt who was willing to take me in."

Kailani leaned forward, reaching out to take his hand in hers. He gave it a squeeze, grateful for her touch before releasing it.

"Just a great-aunt?" Benjamin frowned. "No other family?"

"Nope, that was it. There was an uncle, but he was incarcerated. My birth mother's parents were dead."

Neither Kailani nor Benjamin asked about his father, or any potential relatives on that side. They'd clearly deduced, the way he had, that there was nothing there he could have wanted.

"My great-aunt died when I was four," he continued. "So I was shuffled into the system. The first placement was the stereotypical story you always hear about couples who take kids in for the money."

"Were they abusive?" Benjamin asked, shifting in his seat so that he was more fully facing him.

"Let's just say my foster mother wielded a mean wooden spoon." He was attempting to keep this tone light, but the truth was he'd never shared this with anyone.

"Jesus," Benjamin muttered.

"I was taken out of that placement when I was eight, after my teacher saw the bruises on my arms and back. For the next ten years, I moved five more times, sometimes into people's homes, twice I stayed at a group home, until I finally aged out at eighteen."

"Were they all bad places?"

John shook his head. "No. Not all of them. I actually liked the group home, despite the fact it felt more like an institution than a home. The people who ran it were kind and there were always other kids to play with. Plus, we got three meals there and even snacks if we wanted."

"Snacks?" Benjamin repeated as if he couldn't conceive of a world where a snack felt like a big deal.

"Did that mean you weren't always fed?" Kailani asked.

"Not always. It's why I liked school. I could get breakfast and lunch there for free. It was the summers that were tough."

Kailani wiped her eyes. "John," she said brokenly.

He shook his head. "No, Kailani. That's the wrong response. I'm not telling you this story because I want sympathy. I'm telling you because I want you to know me, to understand me. My upbringing made me the man I am today. It taught me courage, strength, and perseverance."

Benjamin reached across, placing a strong hand on his shoulder. It was a friendly touch, but when John looked over, he realized it was much more than that. Because John had seen this look on Benjamin's face before, during the unguarded moments when the other man had been looking at Kailani.

There was caring and affection, but also a hunger that stirred John's.

John dropped his own shield and let Benjamin see the same desire reflected back. Benjamin's hand tightened, then slid down John's arm until it fell away.

Both men held the gaze a second longer then turned their attention to Kailani, her lids heavy with recognition...and need.

Sexual tension crackled in the air between them, and for the first time, John felt a flare of hope.

Time to finish this.

Time to make them understand.

"When I was invited to join the Trinity Masters," John continued, "there were obviously key points that were meant to be the selling factors. I was told I would be introduced to influential people who could help me advance in my career, and that has happened. They promised doors would be opened, that I'd have the power of the secret society behind me, guiding me, helping me achieve great things. They even helped me get the house. And all of it sounded good, but none of that was why I joined."

"Why did you join?" Kailani asked, her voice still thick with emotion.

"Because of the arranged menage marriage. The Trinity Masters were offering to give me a family. One that would never leave."

KAILANI HAD THOUGHT her heart couldn't ache any more for John after hearing about his childhood. But his reason for joining the Trinity Masters?

It shattered her, shook her, left her feeling like...God...the world's worst person. John had no doubt been looking forward to the day he'd be called to the altar, the day he'd meet his forever family.

And she'd...

She looked out the window, her fingers pressed tightly against her mouth as she blinked hard, trying not to cry.

John didn't want her tears, told her they weren't necessary, so she would try.

"Thank you for telling us, John," Benjamin said, and Kailani was grateful that at least one of them had managed to pull themselves together. Because she'd seen the same horror she'd felt listening to John's story, reflected on Benjamin's face.

Out of the three of them, she and Benjamin had the most in common. Living parallel lives, both from loving, wealthy parents and homes where they wanted for nothing—no, where they got everything they wanted—and legacies of the society.

Placing the two of them in a trinity together should have felt like a no-brainer because they had shared experiences and lifestyles. It was John who must have felt like the odd man out this entire time.

Here he was...a man who'd grown up essentially alone, never truly receiving unconditional love, never knowing from day to day where he'd be sleeping or if he'd have food to eat. And yet, he'd had the courage to open up his heart to them, to risk even more rejection after a lifetime of it.

Guilt suffused her.

"John," she finally whispered, facing him, hating the tear that slid down her cheek before she could swipe it away. "I'm so sorry."

"It's okay, Kailani," John asked after a moment. "I didn't tell you that story as a way of comparing pain or mitigating yours. We all feel what we feel."

"Yes, but—"

John shook his head. "No. I don't want your apology. But maybe...maybe you could help me understand you too?"

She knew what he wanted, what he needed, and there was no way she could deny him. "Ask me."

"Why do you hate Benjamin?"

She blew out a long, slow breath and gave John—and Benjamin—the truth. "I don't hate him," she admitted because it *was* the truth. She didn't hate him. He infuriated her.

"It's just sometimes..." She glanced over at Benjamin, whose expression was unreadable. When it had been John speaking and sharing, she'd been able to tell exactly how Benjamin felt because she could read it on his face.

When it came to her—to them—it was as if she suddenly went blind.

"Sometimes," Benjamin prompted, his tone neutral, even.

"Sometimes, you're an ass," she said, only half serious.

Fortunately, Benjamin heard the joke half and he smirked. "Only sometimes? Damn. I'm doing better than I thought."

John chuckled, as Kailani narrowed her eyes, his smart-ass comment tweaking her the same way it always did.

"Listen, Kailani—" Benjamin started.

John held up his hand, cutting him off. "No. It's not your turn, Benjamin. I was allowed to speak without interruptions. Kailani deserves the same."

Benjamin muttered something under his breath, probably cursing. He was a forthright, opinionated man. And because he had wealth and power, he wasn't accustomed to being told to wait his turn.

"Thank you," Kailani said to John, grateful to have the opportunity to finally let out all the resentment she'd been harboring for too many years. "You can be ruthless and amoral."

"I am not my family's businesses. I am not Ironclad Airlines or Endaragon Energy."

"Aren't you? Your fathers may still technically be in charge, but you're the driving force behind most major decisions. I know you're the one who chose to continue hub-based flights rather than point-to-point routes, which would potentially reduce emissions."

"And raise flight prices," he countered. "Making air travel unattainable for many. Point to point would also mean that our staff would spend more time away from home," he countered. "Hubs allow flight attendants to go home at the end of their shift."

"You're persisting with coal heating despite knowing it's both bad for the environment and unsustainable. Your family's lobbyists made sure the dozens of environmental protection bills my uncle sponsored or co-wrote were neutered before they ever made it to the floor."

"Do you have any idea how massive an infrastructure overhaul would be needed to change even one town to electric heating? Never mind having to remodel the home of every damn person."

"Ah, yes, and God forbid you tackle something difficult, or that the company redirect some of the record profits into that infrastructure change."

"Don't be naive."

"Don't you dare call me naive! Wanting better, expecting people to do better, isn't naive."

There were other examples, she could have kept going, but Kailani fell silent, her words drying up as a mix of anger and old hurt swirled through her.

John, too astute, leaned forward. "But that all sounds like business stuff, a smoke screen. None of that is the root of the real problem between the two of you, is it?"

Kailani sucked in an unsteady breath, trying to decide how to respond. Then she recalled everything John had shared. She shook her head. "No. It's not," she whispered. "You keep getting me to confess more than I want to, Detective."

John shrugged and said, "I'm good at my job."

"That's an understatement," Benjamin mumbled.

Kailani looked across the aisle at her first love, her first heartbreak, her nemesis, and then...she gave them the truth.

BENJAMIN SAW the moment Kailani made her decision to open up to them. In truth, he'd been waiting for her to do so since John posed the question. He knew the rift between them ran much deeper than all those excuses she'd listed.

"We were together one summer." Her words were softer than her previous list of complaints, and he could tell this part was hard for her.

He closed his eyes briefly, swallowing deeply. He'd purposely put that summer out of his mind for nearly a decade. It made life a lot easier...and less painful. However, being on this jet with her again had brought the memories back, and it had taken everything inside of him not to pull her into his arms, kiss and cuddle her as he had back when she'd been his. And he had been hers.

They'd been together one summer—just six weeks—yet even now, after all the hard feelings, the anger, the hurt, he still considered that the best time in his life.

"You said that," John replied, when Kailani fell silent.

"I was nineteen, Benjamin was twenty-one. At the time, I'd had other boyfriends, so I didn't really think of him as my first love. In hindsight..." Kailani looked at him with such sadness that it took all his strength not to go to her, to pull her onto his lap and hold her.

"You *were* my first love," she admitted. "Those other guys

before you...I thought..." She shrugged, letting him fill in the blanks.

Benjamin swallowed hard, trying to dislodge the lump in his throat. "You were my first love too, Kailani."

He saw the instant skepticism in her eyes, borne from too many years of distrust. Whether she believed it or not didn't change the truth. She was his first love, first true—not based solely on a young man's hormones and lust—love.

But he didn't try to convince her of it.

Not now.

Not yet.

He wanted to hear the rest.

"It was a whirlwind summer romance," she said, turning her attention back to John.

Benjamin got the sense it was easier for her to tell John the story, to pretend he wasn't there.

"Sounds nice," John said. "What kinds of things did you guys do? Movies? Bowling?"

She laughed, John's words reminding Benjamin once more of how different their lives were.

"More like impromptu jaunts to New York City to see Broadway shows, cruises around Boston Harbor on his boat, trips to BDSM clubs, and weekends experimenting with kinky sex, a week at the beach on Martha's Vineyard, and—"

"The trip to Paris," Benjamin interjected.

"Jesus," John said, grinning at Benjamin. "Sex clubs, huh? Looks like I need to up my dating game."

The three of them laughed, and it occurred to Benjamin it was the first time they'd shared a joke, all of them letting go for just a second to enjoy the humor of it.

This could be so perfect, he thought, even though it was too soon to hope for such. They still had miles left to cover...literally and figuratively.

"Paris," Kailani said, picking up the crumb he'd dropped. "I'd never been, my family preferred to vacation in Asia, not Europe," she confided in John, "but it was number one on my bucket list of vacations."

"My number one is Monte Carlo, followed closely by Venice and Switzerland," John said with a grin.

"Seriously? Monte Carlo?" Benjamin said. "I have to admit that wasn't what I'd have guessed. You strike me more as a backpacking-in-the-wilderness kind of guy than a craps-table one."

John laughed. "I've done some camping in my time."

"Why Monte Carlo?" Kailani asked.

"Two words. James Bond."

Kailani laughed as Benjamin rolled his eyes. "Bond fan, huh?" he asked.

"The biggest. *GoldenEye* was my favorite."

Benjamin scoffed. "Dude. That was Pierce Brosnan."

John didn't take offense. "I know, I know. I liked Roger Moore and Sean Connery too, and I think Daniel Craig is great, but there was something about Brosnan's Bond that really captured my attention when I was younger. I didn't get to go to the movies much growing up, so most of my cinema knowledge comes from what was playing on TV. Seemed like there was always a Bond movie somewhere on cable, and I loved them. The intrigue, the mystery, the suave hero chasing down larger-than-life villains."

"I think I'm starting to understand your choice to become a cop," Kailani said, smiling widely.

"Bond may have influenced my decision to go into law enforcement. That and the fact I didn't have a clue how to become an MI6 agent," he joked.

"What a shame," Kailani said, "because you would totally rock a tuxedo, sitting at the tables in Monte Carlo with some buxom blonde with a horrible name like Anita Longdick hanging on your arm, while you're sipping a martini..."

"Shaken not stirred," Benjamin finished for her.

"You definitely missed your calling, John," Kailani continued.

John shook his head. "Not sure about that. My British accent sucks." Which he then proved to them when he said, "I'm too knackered to watch the footie match today," in what was hands-down the worst impression of a Brit Benjamin had ever heard.

They all cracked up.

And suddenly, Benjamin was overwhelmed by the desire to get John to Monte Carlo. And fuck it, he'd take him to Italy and Switzerland too. He'd been to all three places, but something told him he'd enjoy those trips even more if he was with John.

"How about you?" John asked Benjamin. "Any dream vacations still on your list, or have you been everywhere and seen everything?"

"Not quite. Personally, number one on my list is the moon." He was teasing, enjoying the way John and Kailani both rolled their eyes at the same time.

"Lucky for you, billionaires building rockets are all the rage these days," John said.

Benjamin shook his head. "Yeah, you're right. Too gauche. That's for the *nouveau riche*."

The silence that fell was companionable rather than tense. Until John asked, "So what happened between the two of you?"

"Paris happened," Kailani replied. "Benjamin surprised me with the trip. We boarded this jet, but he didn't tell me where we were going."

John's eyes widened. "That's a hell of a surprise."

"It was," she said, the smile on her face so reminiscent of

the one from all those years ago. "It was an incredible trip. We saw it all—the Louvre, the Musée d'Orsay, Sacré Coeur, Notre Dame. We cruised along the Seine, drinking champagne and gorging ourselves on chocolate croissants and macarons."

Kailani darted a glance at him, then forged on. "It's where I...naively...decided that I was in love. That Benjamin and I were soul mates and would be together forever."

John raised a brow. "But you had already joined the Trinity Masters, right?"

"Yes, I knew that any relationships I had should be casual. I knew not to fall in love. But I thought we were Romeo and Juliet. And it wasn't just me. Do you remember what you said?" she asked.

It had been their first night in Paris, Benjamin recalled, the memory seared on his brain. And his heart. "I remember," he said softly, instantly regretting the moment he spoke. Because her expression hardened and her eyes flashed with anger. "I said being with you was the first time I'd ever really been happy."

It had been more than that, more than "happy," but as a stupid twenty-one-year-old, that was what he'd said.

She scoffed. "You got over that quick enough." She looked back at John. "A week later, we headed back to school. Different universities, different states. I thought Paris had changed things. That it was the start of a committed long-distance relationship, but before I could say anything, Benjamin broke things off, gave me a goodbye kiss, and never looked back. I found out from one of my best friends, Theia, who went to the same college as Benjamin, that he had a new girlfriend one week into the fall semester."

"She wasn't a girlfriend," Benjamin said between his teeth.

"So you weren't dating her? Just sleeping with her?"

"I..." Benjamin's teeth ground together as he held back

words that would explain but also make everything so much worse.

"I was heartbroken," she said softly. "Absolutely emotionally devastated, and you can say it was stupid of me. I'll even admit it was. You made it clear exactly how little that summer meant to you."

"It meant something to me. But I didn't know how emotionally involved you were."

"You would have, if you hadn't also decided that the end of our summer fling meant the end of our friendship. You stopped talking to me."

"You stopped talking to *me*," he shot back. "I asked if you wanted to go skiing that winter, and you told me to fuck off."

"Because by that point I'd realized exactly how much of an asshole you were. You used information I accidentally let slip to hurt my family."

"What?" Benjamin sat back, shocked.

"Remember when we went to Costa Rica for the weekend? And we were talking about ecotourism. I told you details about a piece of legislation my uncle was writing."

Benjamin's heart froze in his chest as he realized where this was going, what she must have thought.

"Your family's pet lobbyists made sure the bill never even made it to committee. They knew details about what my uncle was proposing and the preemptive smear campaign they launched meant that multiple groups were already opposed before my uncle even finished the first draft. I told you those things in confidence. I never dreamed you'd turn around and use them to benefit yourself, to hurt my family."

"I didn't..." Had he? Had he mentioned something? He didn't even remember if he had, which made it worse.

"I had to go to my family and tell them it was my fault. That I'd started a relationship with the Dara family heir. That

I'd told him about what my uncle was trying to do, given him details."

Kailani swallowed hard, and the pain he saw in her face made Benjamin want to kill the person who hurt her. But *he* was the one who'd hurt her.

"They reminded me I shouldn't have relationships. I was going to have an arranged marriage. They reminded me I needed to be loyal to my family. They told me they weren't upset, just disappointed."

Benjamin winced. Sometimes there was no greater punishment than to be told your family was disappointed in you.

Kailani turned to John. "So there you have it. That's why I can't stand Benjamin Dara."

John sighed, and Benjamin wondered how a single long breath could make him feel like a total shithead. The thing was...he hadn't grasped how deeply he'd hurt her. Back then, he'd been too caught up in his own horrible realization when it came to feelings.

"Kailani," Benjamin said, hoping there was some way he could find the words to make this right. "I'm sorry. I'm sorry if I said something that fucked up your uncle's bill. I...honestly don't remember if I did. I didn't do it deliberately."

"I figured that, though I did spend a few weeks convinced the only reason you dated me was to get information."

"You thought that?"

"I did."

Benjamin leaned back against the seat, staring up at the ceiling of the plane. "I walked away at the end of that summer because I had to."

Kailani made a dismissive noise, but John said, "What do you mean you had to? Your family didn't like you dating her?"

"No." Benjamin shook his head, still not looking at them. "When we started, after that first kiss, I thought it would be a fun, easy relationship that we could keep going until we were called to the altar." He smiled, but it was grim. "I was twenty-one and I wanted a girlfriend. I knew other legacies who'd managed these no-strings, no-emotions relationships."

"So what happened?" John asked.

"After Paris, I realized I couldn't do it. I couldn't be in a casual relationship with Kailani." Benjamin lifted his head, looking at John, not Kailani. "I realized that I never should have even kissed her, let alone dated her, because she mattered. She was my friend." That wasn't enough, the words too small and simple to express what he felt. "If we'd spent any more time together. If we'd dated any longer—"

The intercom system dinged, the pilot's voice coming through the speakers.

"Mr. Dara, we're not going to make it to upstate New York."

Benjamin blinked, his brain taking a moment to shift gears.

"We're going to die. I knew it." John reached across and tightened Kailani's seat belt. "These little planes are death traps!"

"A weather system on the East Coast has made it inadvisable for lighter-weight aircraft to continue," the pilot continued calmly. "We'll be setting down in Denver and waiting out the storm there."

"No, we have to get to New York. I have to get the other keyholder." Kailani looked panicked as she loosened the seat belt John had tightened.

"Wait, so we're not crashing?" John was staring out the window, hands plastered to the wall of the plane.

"We'll have to rent a car and drive," Kailani declared.

"If we crash here, we're going to crash in the Rocky Mountains." John stabbed his finger at the window, at the view of endless mountains. "We're so dead."

"Or fly commercial," Kailani demanded. "A bigger plane will make it. Can we fly commercial?"

Benjamin looked at them, both panicking for different reasons. This he could handle. He knew how to take control in a crisis.

He'd much rather do that than confess the truth about what he'd realized all those years ago.

CHAPTER TWELVE

The penthouse suite was well appointed, but Benjamin had to admit he wouldn't have thought much of it if not for John standing beside him.

"Holy shit," John breathed.

Benjamin put his arm around the other man's shoulders. He'd meant it to be a friendly, companionable touch, but the moment they connected, Benjamin was aware of John in an entirely different way.

He hadn't let himself think about John like that. He'd found him attractive when he dropped his robe during the binding ceremony, but once Kailani's name was called, Benjamin hadn't allowed himself to fantasize about a relationship with the man.

He cleared his throat. "Yes, well, it will give us some space to spread out until we're able to fly to New York."

"When?" Kailani demanded. "When will that be?" She was calmer than she had been but still focused on getting to New York.

Benjamin dropped his arm from John's shoulders. "As we

both know, everything, including bad weather, is the Dara family's fault. I'll make some calls and see if I can redirect the massive storm hammering the East Coast."

Kailani's skin pulled tight over her cheekbones. "You're such an ass."

She turned and stalked away, heading for the stairs to the upper floor of the two-story suite, where the primary bedroom was.

"Why do you do that?" John asked.

"Do what?"

"Don't play dumb."

"I assure you, when it comes to Kailani, I'm not playing dumb." He just always managed to say and do the wrong things when it came to her.

"Your sense of humor is maybe a little too dry," John replied gently. "It doesn't sound like a joke."

Benjamin shook his head, turning away.

"We should eat something," John said.

"I'm a member," Benjamin said.

"Member?"

"Of the hotel."

"You have to be a member to stay here?"

"No, you can get a room if you're not. There are just certain amenities that are only open to members, including a private restaurant where we could have lunch."

"As interested as I am in seeing what a private restaurant at a hotel is like," John pointed at the dining area with seating for eight, "I think we should eat in, and then maybe get some sleep?"

John turned at the same time Benjamin stepped forward, and they bumped into one another. He grabbed John to steady him. John was shorter than he was but bulkier. Benjamin had always wanted a heavily muscled physique, but unless he sacrificed all cardio in favor of weights, the best he could do were the lean muscles a previous romantic partner had referred to as a swimmer's build.

John felt like he had muscle, the kind of heavy muscle that would make him powerful. Would allow him to manhandle his partners.

John's gaze met his, and Benjamin felt the impact of that connection low in his gut.

They stared at one another, and Benjamin couldn't stop himself from feeling possessive of this man. This man who, by rights, was his. His fiancé. His future husband.

Unless Kailani was made acting Grand Master and she dissolved their trinity.

Benjamin turned away from John, his stomach tight. If that came to pass, it would be a good thing. He didn't want to spend his life as the third wheel in his own marriage. But if it was dissolved, he'd never see these two people again. And that felt...

"I'll order some food," he said, shutting down that line of thought. "We'll eat, then you two get some rest while I check in with the pilot and my travel coordinator for alternatives." Benjamin picked up the sleek land-line phone and looked back at John. "Perhaps you could let Kailani know food is coming?"

John studied him for a moment, then nodded and headed for the stairs.

Benjamin blew out a breath and dialed the concierge.

LUNCH WAS A HEARTY AFFAIR, given that they hadn't eaten breakfast except for a few bites of cinnamon rolls in L.A., and Kailani hadn't had even that much. The meal was full of locally sourced ingredients, served with suggested beer pairings, and Benjamin enjoyed it more than he'd expected. By the time they'd all filled at least one plate from the family-style dishes in the middle of the table, the tension had also almost dissipated.

"Not as good as Kona Brewing, but good," Kailani said as she raised a brown glass bottle to her mouth.

The beer and the relaxed atmosphere, combined with that early bump into John, had Benjamin's thoughts turning to sex.

He watched Kailani swallow and tried to convince himself that he didn't want to run his tongue down her neck. He turned his attention to John, but that wasn't better. He wanted to grab a handful of John's dark brown hair and use it to hold him still for a kiss.

What the fuck was going on with his libido? Maybe remembering that summer with Kailani—which had been romantic, but during which they'd also fucked like it was their job—had broken the seal on his self-control.

John cleared his throat and said, "I meant it, back on the plane."

"Meant what?" Kailani took another drink.

"I'm going to need more details about the sex clubs and kinky sex you two had."

It was as if John could hear Benjamin's thoughts. He certainly felt better knowing he wasn't the only one who was feeling some kind of way right now.

Kailani slowly lowered the bottle, her dark eyes assessing. "Have a little voyeur in you?" she asked softly.

John shrugged. "Partially. I'm also thinking that two rich, cultured kids probably had a way more...interesting...sexual exploration phase than most of the rest of us." John raised his brows, the corner of his mouth kicked up in a small smile. "For example, I don't think most people are quite so thorough."

"You didn't take your summer love to BDSM clubs in Amsterdam, try out being furries in Berlin, or attend private seminars about breath play on a yacht somewhere off Mallorca?"

"Mykonos," Kailani corrected, her fingertips on her throat.

"Ah, right." Benjamin caught Kailani's eyes, and there was a beat of memory before her expression changed and a moment of silent communication passed between them. Kailani raised a brow and hid her smile with her beer bottle.

He knew that expression, remembered it, and knew exactly what she was proposing.

Benjamin leaned back in his seat. "What did we try in Mallorca? Was that where we had a session with a dominatrix?" Benjamin watched John out of the corner of his eye.

"Hmm, yes, it was." Kailani tapped her nails rhythmically on her beer bottle.

"Where was the swingers party?" Benjamin asked.

"Wasn't it at that same hotel where we had the X-rated bachelor auction? The one where you wore a loincloth?" Kailani's expression was the picture of innocent confusion.

Benjamin rubbed his mouth with two fingers to control the grin before saying, "Then there was that retreat where we did the Tarzan role-play."

"And the primal play." Kailani's touched the tip of her tongue to her upper lip.

Benjamin's cock reacted to the sight. He shifted, tugging on the thigh of his pants. Across the table, John swallowed hard.

Benjamin realized the silence had stretched, and it was his turn. "And then there was the sex in the ice hotel."

Kailani shivered. "Oh, that's right. It was a tad chilly."

John's eyes narrowed. "You two are making this shit up."

Kailani broke first, her grin giving them away. Benjamin couldn't help but chuckle, his eyes meeting Kailani's. Another shared moment of understanding. Of remembering when they were friends and could always play off one another because they had similar senses of humor and their minds worked the same way.

"Assholes," John breathed, collapsing back in his seat. "How much of that was true?"

"The first few," Benjamin said.

At the same time Kailani said, "Everything up through the breath play."

John frowned, looking up as he remembered. "So, a BDSM club, furries, and breath play." John looked at them, brows raised. "Furries?"

"We just watched," Benjamin said. "The Germans really enjoy being furries."

"We were also really high," Kailani explained.

"So high," Benjamin agreed.

John took a fresh beer, then paused, glancing between them. "No orgy, then."

"No."

"Who'd you have a menage with?" John asked.

Kailani and Benjamin looked at one another, then away, tension breaking the connection of a moment ago.

"Because from what I heard, which I admit isn't much, most people practice menages once they're members. Sex prepping."

"We never had a menage," Benjamin said softly.

Because at twenty-one, I was unwilling to share Kailani.

"Remember how I said I thought we were Romeo and Juliet?" Kailani had turned in her chair, her body language tense and defensive. "I also thought that our love would be so great that not only would it fix the relationship between our families, but the Grand Master would declare us the only duo-relationship in the whole society. Because we were so strong, so stable, we didn't need a third."

Benjamin closed his eyes, his grip on the bottle so tight that his fingers ached.

"So the two of you have had sex, including kinky sex, but the one kink you should have tried, a menage, you didn't."

John's comment broke the tension, and Benjamin forced himself to relax, smiling as he said, "Have I mentioned we were young and stupid?"

"You mean me," Kailani countered. "I was young and stupid."

"No, I meant what I said," Benjamin countered. "We were both young and stupid."

Kailani shook her head, as if she didn't believe him. Goddamn it, why wouldn't she ever listen to him?

"I wouldn't have had a menage because back then I was unwilling to share you," Benjamin said, frustration making him speak when he probably should have kept his mouth shut. "I would have killed anyone else, man or woman, who put their hands on you."

His words fell like bombs, the silence after they fell, shocking.

"Back then?" John asked softly.

"What?" Benjamin turned to him.

"You said 'back then' you were unwilling to share her. You would have killed anyone else who touched her." John reached out one of those long, muscled arms, grabbed Kailani's chair, and dragged it next to his own.

Kailani let out a squeak of surprise, then turned to John, her eyes first wide with surprise, then heavy-lidded with...

Fuck, he knew that look.

Kailani was aroused.

John looked at her, his gaze searching her face. "May I?"

"Yes," she breathed.

John looked over at Benjamin. "Are you watching?"

Benjamin grabbed the arms of his chair, unable to look away. John's hand cupped the back of Kailani's head, turning her face to his. Then he leaned in and kissed her.

Benjamin's cock reacted to the sight, going from semi-aroused to rock-hard in a single breath.

Kailani tipped her head back, yielding to John's kiss, one hand gripping the front of his shirt. He broke the kiss, their faces inches apart. They looked good together. Maybe Kailani should dissolve this trinity but keep John, find a different third to replace him.

The thought of that, of these two belonging to someone else, made Benjamin want to break things.

"This is probably a mistake," Kailani said, her gaze flipping from John to Benjamin and then back.

Of course it was. She thought everything involving him or his family was a mistake. Benjamin shoved back from the table. "If you'll excuse me."

He was going to lock himself in the bedroom on this floor. And if they decided to fuck on the table, he'd go take a shower so he didn't have to hear anything because it would kill him to—

John grabbed his shoulder, whirling him around and pushing him up against the closest wall.

Benjamin's back hit, his breath whooshing out. Then he was breathless for a different reason as John leaned in, pinning him in place, before sealing their lips together.

The kiss tasted like hops and desire.

Benjamin let out a low moan of need and wrapped his arms desperately around him. He could feel John's hard cock against his thigh and knew John could feel his in turn.

A hand brushed Benjamin's, tugging it until he released his hold on John.

Benjamin lifted his head, looking to the side, where Kailani stood, her hands around his wrist.

"I was trying to get you to let me in," she said softly.

Benjamin looked between the two of them, silently asking if they were really doing this. Kailani's brow creased, and Benjamin could feel the desire-fueled moment of insanity passing.

John, still with his side pressed against Benjamin's chest, wrapped an arm around her, yanking her forward so she fell against their chests.

John cupped the back of each of their heads. He leaned down and kissed Kailani; this time it was hard and fast, and this close to them, Benjamin could hear the small, quiet, needy sound Kailani made. Then John's lips were on his, and as he'd seen with Kailani, this kiss was quick. A demand.

Benjamin let his eyes close, actively suppressing his urge to take control of the situation. He trusted John. Trusted him enough to lead them through this. God knew he had a bad track record when it came to Kailani...maybe when it came to relationships in general.

Pressure on the back of his head made him lean down, yet it was still a surprise when his lips touched Kailani's. This was both familiar and foreign. Their kiss was tentative at first, a decade of animosity lingering between them. But he wanted this, wanted to taste her.

Benjamin cupped her head, his hand on top of John's, and claimed her mouth.

Kailani nipped his tongue, and he sucked her lower lip into his mouth and bit it.

"Enough." John's quiet command broke them apart.

Benjamin lifted his head, panting. Kailani had a faint frown line between her brows.

John shifted his grip to their shoulders and dragged them

both across the room, through the door to the downstairs bedroom. The bed was wide, the comforter a pristine white. Pillows were piled high and deep against the leather-wrapped headboard.

John put a hand on Benjamin's chest and pushed, shoving him back toward the bed. "Strip."

Benjamin stopped, looking from the bed to John to Kailani. John was whispering something in Kailani's ear. She rose on tiptoe to whisper her own response. Benjamin debated walking out, walking away. It would be the smart move.

But dammit, he wanted this. Wanted *them*. Since their fight after the binding ceremony, he'd been sure he'd never share a bed, let alone a life, with them.

And maybe that was why this was okay, why this would work. Because there was no real future for them. There was a good chance Kailani would be the acting Grand Master, and if so, she would dissolve their trinity.

So this might be it. His one chance to experience something he thought he never would. Something he was afraid to admit he wanted even now, as he began to unbutton his shirt.

John and Kailani finished their whispered conversation, and then John turned her to face the bed. Standing behind her, he pulled her thin jacket off her shoulders, then stripped her of the long tunic top she wore under it.

The key she wore on a chain around her neck glinted, but Benjamin's attention was drawn to her breasts, the black bra a contrast against her pale skin. John yanked down her leggings, revealing skin shades darker than her upper body. That summer they spent together, she'd worn bikinis for the aesthetic only. When swimming, she wore a long-sleeved rash-guard or swim top, and based on her tan, she still did that. Somehow the fact that he knew this about her, that he knew her, even after all this time, made it easier for Benjamin to toe off his shoes, then unfasten and drop his pants.

"Benjamin, get on the bed, in the middle, and lean back against the pillows."

He stripped off his socks but left his boxer briefs on. His cock was tenting the front, perilously close to poking out, but he adjusted the fabric as he got into position, stacking pillows so his back was supported while he sprawled in a semi-reclined position.

"On the bed. I want you to kiss him," John commanded.

Benjamin once more fought the urge to take control, to be the one issuing orders.

Still in her bra and panties, Kailani crawled onto the bed and kept crawling. Benjamin spread his legs, making space for her. Her hair fell over her shoulders, dark curtains that framed her face.

She glanced at his cock, still trapped in his boxers. Benjamin held his breath, but she didn't touch him there. Instead, she braced her hands on his chest and leaned in, her lips meeting his.

Benjamin tangled a hand in her hair and squeezed her hips with his knees.

"Touch her," came John's soft command.

Benjamin raised his free hand, sliding it into the space between their bodies to palm her breasts. He squeezed until she moaned, then yanked the cups of her bra down to play with her nipples.

The mattress tipped as John joined them. Then Kailani's bra loosened, falling to lay against Benjamin's chest, and he had better access to her breasts.

John's hand touched Benjamin's where it was tangled in her hair, and Benjamin yielded the position, letting his arm drop. He continued to kiss her and play with her nipples, pinching and tugging in a way she'd loved when they were young and dumb.

Kailani was pulled away from him, her gasp both shocked and aroused. John held her by the hair, forcing her upright as she knelt between Benjamin's thighs. John grabbed the bra, still hooked on one elbow, and threw it aside. His other hand played down her front, teasing her nipples, stroking her belly, tugging her panties down until they were barely covering her.

Desire riding him hard, Benjamin sat up, gripping her hips and then fastening his lips over her nipple. John played with the other one, twisting and pinching harder than Benjamin had.

"More," Kailani demanded.

Benjamin gently bit her, holding her nipple between his teeth and pulling back, tugging the sensitive tip with the vise of his teeth.

"I need you," Kailani demanded.

Who? Who do you need? Benjamin wasn't a moron, so he didn't ask that aloud. He wouldn't like the answer.

"Both of you," she breathed.

"Damn right, you do," John said, his voice hoarse.

The next thing he knew, Benjamin was being pushed back against the pillows, Kailani's back against his chest. John yanked her panties down and off. Benjamin put a hand on her belly, sliding until his fingertips nudged the top of her curls. He stopped, unsure of his welcome.

Kailani gripped his wrist, guiding him down to touch her sex.

She was hot and wet. He dipped a finger into her entrance, drawing her body's moisture up to her clit, but then stopped touching her there. He toyed with her, stroking and spreading her labia. Kailani's nails dug into his wrist, her body arching up off his chest as the back of her head pressed into his shoulder.

John grabbed her legs, forcing them wide, hooking them over Benjamin's bent knees. John knelt between Benjamin's feet. He was naked, his cock erect, condom already on. Heavy curtains muted the afternoon light and created deep shadows in the room, but there was enough illumination that Benjamin could see the wetness at the tip of John's cock.

"Are you going to fuck her?" Benjamin demanded roughly.

"Yes." John leaned over them. He grabbed Benjamin's free hand, guiding it over Kailani's body.

Benjamin expected him to stop at her breasts, expected he'd finger her and play with her tits while John fucked her, but instead, John guided his hand to Kailani's throat.

"I'm going to fuck her while you choke her."

Kailani sucked in a shocked breath, while Benjamin's mouth went dry. He stopped stroking her clit, but let his fingers rest between her pussy lips. It was his turn to whisper in her ear. "If you don't want—"

"I do." Kailani breathed. "I haven't had it since that summer."

"Why?" John demanded.

"Because I have trust issues," she replied.

"But you trust me?" Benjamin asked, curling his hand around her neck.

"Yes...even though you're the reason I have trust issues. I trust you." She let out a mirthless laugh.

Benjamin didn't like the sound, so he stopped it, cut it off with a slight squeeze to her neck.

John watched them, focused and attentive.

Benjamin released her almost immediately, and Kailani shook her head, her temple hitting his jaw as she did.

"Not enough," she said.

"You can have more when his cock is in you." Benjamin emphasized the comment with a stroke to her clit.

Kailani reached for John. "Fuck me. Now."

John's gaze met Benjamin's. "Is she ready?"

Benjamin stretched down, shoving two fingers into her vagina. She clenched around him. "Oh yeah, she's ready to be fucked."

John lowered himself, and Benjamin shifted, managing to recline a bit more, to give John a better angle. John tried bracing a hand on the bed, but that didn't work well, so he gripped Benjamin's shoulder, his other hand on his cock, guiding it to Kailani's pussy.

Benjamin felt the tip of John's cock brush the backs of his fingers. He lifted his hand, which was wet from her pussy, and grabbed John's dick, stroking. He didn't have the reach to work much more than the tip, but the way John's eyes closed and his breath hitched said it was enough.

Benjamin gave him one more quick tug, then let go, and instead spread Kailani's pussy lips. John's gaze was focused on her sex as he guided himself in. Benjamin couldn't see, but he knew what was happening based on her reactions, on the soft, needy sounds she made.

"John...Ben..."

Benjamin didn't like the nickname Ben. Had never gone by Ben and refused to answer to it. The one exception was sex with Kailani, because as she'd told him, when she was really turned on, "Benjamin" was just too many syllables.

John eased out, then slammed in, hard enough to drive both Kailani and Benjamin into the pillows. As he withdrew, Benjamin repositioned his fingers, stroking her clit in a slow, controlled circle that was in direct opposition to the hard, rough fucking John was giving her.

"Please," Kailani said, and he knew what she wanted.

"Deep breath," he whispered in her ear.

Kailani took a breath, and Benjamin tightened his hold on her neck. His hand applied gentle pressure to the front of her neck, heavier pressure on the sides. This might be called breath play, but Kailani liked being choked more than she liked having a hand over her nose and mouth because she needed that light pressure on the blood vessels too. Benjamin was wholly focused on her in that moment, aware of every small movement. John continued to pound her pussy while he stroked her clit and gently choked her.

Benjamin released her neck. Kailani expelled her breath in a desperate woosh, inhaled once, and then Benjamin tightened his hand again.

Kailani had been rocking slightly, her movements limited due to her position, but she'd been moving her hips, her hands roaming over John's body and Benjamin's arm where it crossed over on her. Now she wasn't moving at all, both her hands locked around Benjamin's wrist.

"She's close," Benjamin said.

"So am I," John growled.

Benjamin released her neck.

Kailani let out a needy sob. "Please, Ben, plea—"

He tightened his hold a third time, controlling her air, controlling the very blood in her veins.

John's gaze met his, then his eyes slid closed, a grimace contorting his face. Benjamin added pressure as he circled her clit.

Kailani's body jerked in his arms, an almost violent tightening of muscles as she came. He waited until her body was bowed and tense and then released her throat, released her so she could scream in pleasure.

John's moan was raw and guttural as he too came.

Benjamin's own cock hurt physically, but he didn't expect he'd get to come, at least not until he jerked off in the shower.

He'd be content holding Kailani as she came down from the orgasm.

He was wrong.

Kailani was still panting, riding the end of her orgasm when John jerked back, sliding off the foot of the bed. He grabbed Kailani's ankles, yanking her down, her hair sliding along Benjamin's chest.

"I left you a condom." John jerked his head to the side. Benjamin, no longer pinned by Kailani, looked over to see the silver packet.

"Fuck me," Kailani demanded, tipping her head back to look at him upside down. "Now."

Benjamin leapt off the bed. His fingers trembled as he rolled on the condom. He circled to the foot of the bed. John had lain down beside Kailani, hooking one of her legs over his hip. Spreading her wide. Her pussy glistened, and the hand not buried in John's hair was pulling on her own nipple, being far rougher with it than Benjamin had been.

Need and desire made his blood thick, his muscles trembling as he knelt between her legs.

Then he was in her, and damn but that felt good. More than good. It almost felt like coming home.

Luckily, he was too aroused to follow that train of thought. Benjamin pounded his cock into her pussy as John kissed her neck and played with her nipples.

When he was ready to come, when he knew from the sounds she made that she was close again, Benjamin sealed his lips on hers, stealing her breath as he pushed them both up, up, up, and then they tipped over that edge, falling down into the dark pleasure.

CHAPTER THIRTEEN

J ohn came awake slowly when he heard voices next to him, the roar of the plane's engine serving as white noise that muted their words to some extent. He blinked a few times, trying to rouse himself.

It was rare that he woke up confused and disoriented, but right now, after the past two days...

He scrubbed his face before pressing the button to bring his seat into an upright position.

They'd boarded Benjamin's plane in the middle of the night, leaving Denver around three a.m. They'd managed a few hours' sleep in the hotel, each of them falling into bed about eleven, after an afternoon of what could best be described as debauchery.

The first time they had sex it had been fast, almost frantic. The second time, they put Kailani on her hands and knees and John fucked her mouth while Benjamin took her from behind— a slow, almost punishingly hard fucking.

Then, almost in apology, John had lain her down on her back and settled between her legs. Benjamin stretched out beside her with his hand alternately around her throat and toying with her nipples.

After that they'd silently showered—not together—and crawled into bed. Benjamin had taken the downstairs room by himself, while Kailani had followed John to the upstairs bedroom. John had thought about telling Benjamin to join them, but he'd been too tired to deal with it, so he let it go, planning to talk about it when they woke up in the morning.

Instead, they'd been woken up only hours later when Benjamin came to tell them that the pilot called. They'd been cleared to fly to New York and the plane was fueled up and ready anytime they wanted to leave. Kailani had been unwilling to wait until morning, insisting that they leave the moment the airport cleared them for takeoff.

John didn't blame her for her impatience. She'd been given an important role within the society, and watching the seriousness with which she took it told him the Trinity Masters had selected the right family...the right person for the job.

They hadn't spoken since leaving Denver, exhaustion catching up with them. He'd fallen asleep a few minutes after the flight attendant told them it was safe to take off their seat belts. John had left his on because this fancy-ass plane was still a potential death trap. Benjamin had been snoring softly before they'd even reached cruising altitude.

John still couldn't quite convince himself the events in that hotel suite had truly happened. When he'd initiated that first kiss with Kailani, he'd had reservations, uncertainty. Those doubts vanished the moment his lips touched hers, and they were vanquished forever when he looked over and saw the naked desire, the yearning in Benjamin's gaze.

Benjamin had tried to walk away from him—from them— and that was when the last straw broke.

John wanted this trinity more than he'd ever wanted

anything, and he would fight the two stubborn fools on this plane until the end of time if necessary to achieve his goal.

He'd wasted the past month being too passive, when he should have assumed a strong stance.

Last night, John found his weapon. And he was ready to wield it again.

Glancing across the aisle, he watched as Benjamin sipped coffee, the table before him set with a mouth-watering platter of pastries.

"Thank you," Benjamin said to the flight attendant before spotting he was also awake. Keeping his voice low, he leaned toward him. "Would you like some breakfast, John? I doubt we'll have time to grab something to eat once we land."

John shook his head. Maybe he'd pay for that decision later, but right now, all he wanted was caffeine. "Just coffee, please," he asked the flight attendant. "Black."

"Just bring a pot, Joan," Benjamin said, "and two more cups. I know Kailani will want some when she wakes up too."

Joan excused herself as Benjamin said, "We're about two hours out."

Which meant he'd been dozing for two hours. It hadn't been a restful sleep, so he actually felt as tired now as when he'd boarded the plane.

Kailani stirred, opening her eyes just seconds after the flight attendant delivered the pot and extra cups. "Do I smell coffee?"

Benjamin chuckled, pouring John his requested black coffee. He poured a second cup for Kailani, adding cream and sugar without asking her preference, before handing it across the aisle.

"Thanks," she said, her voice husky from sleep, and so damn sexy, John felt his dick stir as he recalled Benjamin's hand around her throat. He'd never indulged in breath play, but now all he could think about was how much he wanted Benjamin to teach him. Fuck, he wanted to try everything they'd rattled off on that fake list of theirs. Well, maybe not the furries thing.

Benjamin offered Kailani one of his pastries, but like John, she declined.

John breathed in the dark, rich scent of his coffee, taking a sip. "Beats the hell out of the swill they serve at the precinct."

"It's *Finca El Injerto*. I have it imported from Guatemala."

Kailani rolled her eyes. "Pretentious much, Mr. Dara?"

Benjamin chuckled. "Don't complain, tree hugger. It's certified carbon neutral."

Kailani's eyes widened. "Wow. I'm surprised you even know what that means."

John shook his head at the way the two of them continued to pick at each other, though he noticed their comments felt more teasing today, less contentious. Or maybe that was just wishful thinking.

What they needed was time. Time to just sit down and talk. He couldn't help but feel like they were one good conversation away from resolving so many of the issues between them.

And while he was tempted to get the ball rolling now, one glance at Kailani's face told him it wasn't a good time. She kept sneaking peeks out the window and at her watch, her knee bouncing nervously. Her anxiety was almost tangible and it wasn't fair to launch into life-altering topics while her thoughts were consumed by her responsibility as keyholder.

He thought he and Benjamin had done a pretty good job distracting her yesterday afternoon, and while the three separate bouts of sex between the three of them was off-the-charts, he was smart enough to know it was basically the equivalent of putting a Band-Aid on a gunshot wound.

Once this was all over, John was going to do what he should

have done back in Boston. Demand that the three of them hole themselves up somewhere, shut out the world, and just talk. And maybe fuck. He wouldn't mind an encore of last night... every night for the rest of his life.

Kailani looked at Benjamin. "How long until we land?"

"Two hours. Maybe a little bit more," he replied.

She sighed, tapping her toe impatiently.

Benjamin lifted his hand, calling out the flight attendant's name. "Joan?"

She came back to clear his plate, tucking the table away. "We won't need you again," he said. "We'd like some privacy."

"Of course, sir." Joan returned to the front of the plane, pulling a retractable door closed across the bulkhead.

Benjamin rose from his seat. "Why don't we move to the back? We'll be more comfortable there."

The rear of the plane not only boasted a bar, but there was a long leather couch along one wall that was roomy enough for the three of them to sit comfortably if they desired. The chairs across from it swiveled toward the aisle so that the entire back of the plane resembled a cozy sitting area, perfect for conversation and relaxing.

John and Kailani followed Benjamin, who claimed one half of the couch. Kailani sat next to him—progress, John thought— while he took a chair across from them, twisting it until he faced them.

Kailani flipped her hair over her shoulder, her knee resuming its anxious bouncing. "This is taking too long," she said quietly.

"Kailani," Benjamin said. "It hasn't even been forty-eight hours yet. We'll land in two hours, go find the last keyholder, then hop right back on this jet and return to Hawaii. I told the pilot to refuel immediately. We can't go direct; we'll have to stop for a quick refueling on the West Coast. Barring any more weather delays, we should be back on the island by six p.m. island time tonight. It's going to be okay."

She blew out a long breath, her shoulders still too stiff for John's liking.

"I think Kailani needs a distraction," he suggested. He was using sex as his weapon, but he felt no remorse in doing so. Last night had felt like a minor breakthrough, and he was ready to see if he could knock down a few more bricks in the wall between them.

John was aware the society was in peril, and while he was concerned about that, all he'd been able to think of when Benjamin put an actual timeline on today's itinerary was that maybe tomorrow, after they'd gotten back to Hawaii and Kailani did her keyholder thing, they could have an actual conversation, without a crisis or problem distracting them.

Speaking of distracting...

"Distraction?" Kailani asked softly, just breathlessly enough that he could tell she knew what he was suggesting.

Benjamin rested his arm along the back of the couch, just shy of touching Kailani, and John closed his eyes wearily.

One step forward, three steps back. Benjamin was holding back again, unwilling to take the first step for fear of rejection.

Kailani cast Benjamin a sideways glance, then looked back down the aisle toward the cockpit.

"Joan won't come back unless I call for her," Benjamin said, answering Kailani's unspoken concern. Then he looked at John. "What kind of distraction did you have in mind?"

John had taken the lead last night in bed because he sensed that was what they'd needed. Hell, it still felt that way.

Which wasn't a problem. John didn't mind calling the shots. At all.

John grinned. "Given the time and space constraints, I think we're going to have to be a little creative."

Kailani's knee stopped bouncing. "I'm a very creative person."

He chuckled, even as he shook his head. "I'm sure you are, and I can't wait for you to prove it, but...this is my show."

"Thought last night was your show," Benjamin said, revealing what John had suspected. Benjamin wasn't the type of man to typically hold back, to let go of the reins in the bedroom. This time with Kailani was the exception because he still didn't feel wanted.

Baby steps, he decided.

"Are you complaining?" John put some force behind his words, making it clear it wasn't up for debate.

His lovers responded exactly as he expected. Kailani's face flushed with instant arousal, while Benjamin's eyes narrowed— a blink and you missed it reaction—before he schooled his features.

"No. I'm not complaining," Benjamin replied brusquely. In Denver, John had the element of surprise on his side, Benjamin so shocked by Kailani's willingness to include him that he'd followed John's lead without comment, probably afraid of saying the wrong thing and pushing Kailani away.

While the hesitance was still there, Benjamin's true nature was chafing at the bit.

John leaned back in his seat, stretching his legs out and assuming a lord of the manor attitude. He captured Benjamin's gaze, then tilted his head toward Kailani. "Take off her blouse," he demanded. "I want to see her tits."

Benjamin's brows furrowed, and John waited, expecting him to refuse while praying he didn't.

If—when—this trinity was solidified, there would most likely be a day of reckoning for him and Benjamin as far as sex was concerned. For one thing, they both had alpha tendencies. For another, the sexual tension between them was almost suffocating. It would be interesting—and fun—to see how things shook out for them physically. John had never had a dick in his ass, always envisioning himself as the giver, not the receiver, but Benjamin had him reconsidering that stance.

Yet another item for the conversation the three of them needed to have. John wondered if he should start a damn list.

John raised one eyebrow imperiously, shooting Benjamin an, "I'm waiting" look.

Then he released the breath he didn't realize he was holding when Benjamin twisted to face Kailani, unbuttoning her blouse.

"Looks like we're giving the demanding bastard a show," Benjamin murmured to Kailani, though there was no heat to his words. Kailani giggled, and John felt once again that everything about this was right.

Benjamin removed it and her bra, drawing the backs of his hands over Kailani's breasts, her nipples budding. When it became apparent he intended to extend the play, reaching out to cup them, John stopped him.

"I didn't give you permission to touch her. Put your hands down."

Kailani took a shaky breath, whispering, "This is so hot."

John lifted his hand to his mouth, pretending to stroke his jaw so that he might appear stoic, serious. In truth, he was trying to hide his smile.

"Kailani," John said. "Face me, beauty. Let me see you."

Kailani had been sitting in profile, Benjamin getting the full view, but at his command, she turned to look at him.

"Stand up and take off your jeans and panties," he said. "Look me in the eye as you do it, let me see those pretty dark eyes."

Benjamin started to rise, intent on claiming the seat next to John to grab a better view.

John shook his head. "Stay right where you are."

Kailani wasted no time shedding the rest of her clothing. Standing before him nude, she kept her hands by her sides. Unlike Benjamin, she had no problem waiting for orders.

John shifted forward in his seat. The aisle between them was narrow, less than three feet, so it was a simple thing for him to reach up to draw a single fingertip down the center of Kailani's body. He started at the base of her throat, traveling through the valley of her breasts, over her flat stomach until he reached her pussy.

Pushing that one finger through the well-trimmed hair, he found her clit, drawing a circle around it as Kailani's breathing became shallow.

"Please," she whispered.

"Spread your legs apart," he said, nudging at the inside of her ankles to move her along.

As he continued to play with her clit, keeping his touch purposely too light, he glanced behind her. Benjamin was leaning forward on the couch, peering around her waist to watch him.

"Move behind her," John directed, barely sparing Benjamin a glance as he left her clit, pushing his finger between her legs, stroking between her pussy lips. God, she was soaking wet and so fucking hot.

Once Benjamin was in place, John continued drawing a straight line along her slit, from her ass to her pussy to her clit, back and forth. It was just enough to keep her on edge without giving her what she really wanted. He'd watched her last night, seen how she liked a rough touch, pleasure blended with pain.

With his free hand, he crooked a finger at her. "Bend forward."

So far, she'd responded without hesitation, but this time...

she paused. Because following his instructions meant her ass would basically be right in Benjamin's face.

"Kailani," he said sternly.

The threat lacing the tone worked. She bent at the waist, her hands resting on the arms of his chair, her face now level with his.

Benjamin hummed in appreciation.

"Last night I got to eat your pussy, but he didn't. We're going to continue to expand on the threesome experience since the two of you failed to practice back when you had a chance," John said, his lips brushing Kailani's in a soft kiss. "Reach back and grasp your ass cheeks, pull them apart for Benjamin."

He gripped her waist with his free hand, steadying her as Kailani's hands moved, stopped, then moved again, as she struggled to obey.

"Do it, Kailani," Benjamin demanded, the dominant slipping out. "Let me see you. All of you."

"Be quiet," John said to Benjamin, when he saw her stiffen ever so slightly. "Do only as I say." He was speaking to Benjamin, though his gaze was locked on Kailani's face.

She grinned when he winked at her, something that Benjamin couldn't see, trying to set her at ease.

Reaching behind her, she gripped her ass cheeks and parted them.

Benjamin muttered a soft curse. It was pure appreciation. And hunger.

John pulled his finger away from Kailani's clit, and she moaned, annoyed by the loss. He half expected her to complain, to demand he touch her again. John harbored no illusions that if this trinity remained, there would be nights when Kailani would demand to be the one calling the shots.

"Run your tongue along her slit, Benjamin. Taste our woman."

Kailani's stuttered breathing and the way her eyes drifted closed let John know Benjamin had followed his orders without delay.

"Open your eyes. Watch me," John said, pleased when she obeyed. Their faces were so close, he could feel the heat of her breath on his face, smell the sweet coffee.

Leaning back, John unfastened his jeans, lifting his hips so that he could push them down to his ankles.

"Commando," Kailani murmured.

Benjamin's head appeared around her ass, his gaze drifting down to steal a peek of John's hard cock.

John narrowed his eyes at Benjamin, who gave him a shameless grin before disappearing behind Kailani again.

"Jesus," she breathed. Benjamin was clearly enjoying his assigned task.

John gripped his dick firmly, running his hand up and down the thick shaft as Kailani watched. "You're going to suck it for me."

Kailani's head lowered and it was obvious she was ready to do just that, but he stopped her, his hand gripping her shoulder.

"Not yet," he said. "First, you're going to come for me and Benjamin."

Pushing her upward, just enough to serve his purpose, he gripped one of her breasts, drawing it to his mouth.

"Use your fingers with your mouth," he said to Benjamin. "Play with her. Her clit, her pussy, her ass. All of it. Do whatever it takes to make her come...but make her beg first."

"I don't beg," she taunted, her words a lie. But more importantly, a dare.

Benjamin chuckled. "This is going to be fun."

John wasn't sure what Benjamin did, but within seconds, Kailani shuddered, her eyes drifting closed.

"Open your eyes," he said harshly, reminding her of his

earlier command. "If I have to remind you again, Benjamin's going to stop making it feel good and instead, he's going to toss you over his lap and spank that cute little ass of yours."

For a moment, he thought he caught the slightest lowering of her eyelids as if she was tempted to make that threat a reality. Unfortunately, she appeared to change her mind, her gaze finding his once more.

Oh yeah, they were definitely going to spank her.

She moaned, thanks to something Benjamin did. Then the sound grew louder. Especially when John took her tight nipple into his mouth and sucked on it. Roughly.

Her hands flew to his head, her fists closing around his hair. She was tugging it hard enough that it stung, but he didn't call her to task. He wanted her pain, and he was willing to give her his own.

He played with her breasts for several minutes, alternating between hard sucks, sharp bites, and soothing strokes of his tongue, gentle kisses.

It occurred to him—belatedly—that putting her in this position between them meant he was blind to what Benjamin was doing. So he had to call on his other senses, listening to the wet sound of Benjamin's fingers slipping in and out of her pussy, the sweet scent of her arousal.

She began shifting her hips, pushing backward, seeking out whatever Benjamin was doing to her, trying to assume some level of control. John refused to relinquish it.

"Hold still," John said darkly. "Take only what we give you."

Kailani pushed back one last time, a tiny rebellion, before she managed to hold steady.

"God," she groaned.

"What's he doing to you, Kailani?" John asked, pinching

her nipples as he kissed and licked his way along the side of her neck.

"Fingers," she hissed. "Inside of me."

"How many?" John asked.

She started to close her eyes, then remembered his threat, and they flew open once more. "Two," she said. Then added, "Now three. Shit." She went up on her tiptoes. "So deep."

"Harder," John said to Benjamin. "Fuck her harder."

He felt, rather than saw, Benjamin obey as Kailani's body shifted into overdrive.

"Thumb," she said. "God. His thumb. My ass. Fuck."

Pinching one of her nipples, he cupped the back of her neck, pulling her down to kiss her, stealing her cries, her curses.

Releasing her lips, he looked at her and said, "Come for us."

Kailani shattered between them, her body shaking, her grip on the arms of his chair the only thing holding her steady.

They remained there for several minutes, giving her time to land, Benjamin's hands on her hips, his on her shoulders, supporting her.

When Kailani's eyes landed on his cock, and she licked her lips, he grinned.

"You're so fucking sexy," John said, cupping her cheek affectionately. "I'm never going to get enough of you." It was a strong proclamation. Maybe too strong, given the tenuous bond between them, but his concern melted away when she gave him a sultry smile.

"You said something about sucking your cock," she murmured.

John swallowed deeply, his dick doing the impossible and getting even harder.

"Benjamin," he said, the gruffness of his voice betraying his need. "Fuck her."

Neither he nor Kailani looked back when they heard the rasp of a zipper, the crinkle of a foil wrapper. Instead, they merely looked deep into each other's eyes, waiting for their lover...

Kailani groaned as Benjamin stood up and slid inside, then she lowered her head, taking his cock into her hand and her mouth.

For three new lovers in a fairly tight space, he might have expected the choreography to be awkward, but this felt as natural as breathing.

Kailani took him deeper with each pass, moving in time with Benjamin.

On each forward thrust, he felt the back of her throat.

Then the retreat.

The pace started slow, steady, but it built with each return until the three of them were gasping for air, no sounds except the gentle hum of the plane's engines, skin slapping skin, and labored breathing.

John tried to hold off as long as he could, but her mouth was too fucking good. When she reached lower to grip his balls, he was a goner.

"Jesus, Kailani," he said, his fists closed tightly in her soft hair. "Swallow it, take it all."

He came hard, Kailani, the sexy minx, giving him no quarter, no reprieve, sucking and sucking until she'd drawn every single drop.

John finally pushed her away, taking her cheeks in his hands, kissing her, pushing her mouth open, tasting himself on her lips.

Then it was her turn to fall apart. She cried out, her back arching.

"God, Ben. I'm—" It was all she managed to say before she splintered, shattered. John had never seen anything more beautiful than his wife—by God, she *would* be his—in the midst of an orgasm.

As the last tremors faded, he looked over her shoulder and watched as Benjamin's face contorted with the pleasure-pain of his own climax, his fingers holding tight to Kailani's hips as he rode out the storm.

Benjamin was the first to break away, dropping heavily onto the couch behind him, gasping for air. "Jesus Christ," he said.

John zipped up his jeans, then helped Kailani stand upright, kneeling in front of her to help her put her panties and jeans back on. Then he pushed her back to the couch next to Benjamin, who slipped her bra over her shoulders, reaching around behind her to fasten the hooks, stealing his own kiss, though it was too short, too...fuck...

The hesitance was back.

Next time, John was going to make the two of them kiss for hours until this goddamn reticence was a thing of the past.

Next time.

God, please let there be a next time.

CHAPTER FOURTEEN

The stately Georgian Colonial house looked clean and crisp, thanks to the rain, the trim bright white, the brick warm browns and reds. The storm that had grounded them in Denver had battered the Eastern Seaboard, but they were upstate and inland enough that there hadn't been much more than heavy rain.

Kailani felt like she was vibrating, she was so anxious. On the plane, they'd taken away every worry, every thought but them, when they fucked her. John was easygoing outside of the bedroom, demanding and dominant inside of it. And Benjamin...Benjamin who was dominant through and through, who'd excelled and reveled in their exploration of kink and power exchange, had been willing to listen to and obey John. What would happen if the two of them just went at it, fought for control...?

She'd been able to stay relaxed for the rest of the flight, blissed out and still aroused until the intercom dinged, announcing their descent.

Then reality came crashing down.

She'd been jiggling her foot most of the way from the airport and hadn't stopped even when John put a hand on her knee. It was ten a.m. in New York, four a.m. in Hawaii, and it had been over thirty-six hours since she'd gotten the call, assuming she'd done that math right.

Was that too slow? Was she right on schedule?

Kailani had no idea. Frankly, the keyholder protocols were stupid. They needed to be updated, damn it. Encrypted emails would have been instantaneous, just as secure, and all three keyholders could have been in Hawaii within twelve hours of the call.

Now, best-case scenario, they were at the *waihona* this evening Hawaii time.

The chauffeured black SUV pulled into the long, curving drive, stopping at the front door.

Kailani was sliding across John's lap to get out even as the driver asked Benjamin if he should wait.

John exhaled heavily—she might have accidentally elbowed him—as she all but fell out of the car. He followed her. Kailani shivered despite the sweater. She'd packed for Boston, but no matter how many layers she wore, she always felt cold when visiting this part of the world.

Her boots splashed through a small puddle at the foot of the white steps as she raced for the door. It had been a gamble coming here at this hour. The keyholder might be at work. Finding them at their job could prove time-consuming, given what they did for a living, so she'd pinned her hopes on this person being at home.

Kailani dug one hand under the high cowl neck of her sweater and pulled out the key, while the other raised the brass knocker set in the center of the black door.

John stepped up beside her, one hand going to her back in a

faint touch before dropping away. A reassuring "I'm here if you need me" touch.

Footsteps thudded on the other side of the door, and then it swung open.

The man who opened it looked pissed.

He was black, tall and broad, appearing broader when he crossed his arms. The tight Henley he wore clung to the muscles of his arms. His gaze bounced from her, to John, to a spot just over her other shoulder, where Kailani guessed Benjamin was standing.

The man groaned in disgust. "There's three of you. That means this is some cult shit." He turned away from the door, stalking back into the house. "Other cult members are here, and I'm not in the mood for this!" he yelled out as he walked away.

Kailani blinked, glanced at John, then looked the other way, at Benjamin, who'd stepped up beside her.

"Lovely manners," Benjamin said mildly.

There was the clatter of feet on the stairs, at the same time they heard a door open and close somewhere in the house.

A white man wearing thick black-framed glasses approached the open door, his frown of confusion more curious than pissed. A slender woman with Asian features and long dark hair came down the steps, ducking as she did in order to see the door.

"Hello," she said, voice formal and a bit cool as she cleared the bottom step.

"Tell them I still have 'Baby Shark' queued up and I'm not afraid to use it!" The first man's voice echoed from somewhere in the house.

Okay, so these three were...odd. Kailani ignored that, focusing on the woman. "Dr. Tanaka?"

Doctor Selene Tanaka, professor of theoretical nuclear physics at Cornell, smiled as she approached. "I'm Professor

Tanaka." She frowned, glancing between Kailani and Benjamin, then shook her head. "And you are?"

"Members of your same organization," Benjamin said in a cool, collected tone that matched hers.

"So you say," she agreed. She was calm, waiting, but gave off the impression that she was so intelligent most conversations were beneath her.

"Dr. Tanaka—" Kailani started.

She raised one brow. "I prefer Professor Tanaka. Technically professor is a higher title than doctor."

Kailani cleared her throat, refusing to let the fact that she was intimidated by this woman derail her. "I believe you have another title…" Kailani touched the chain, drawing attention to what she wore around her neck. "Keyholder."

Selene's eyes widened, her mouth falling open. She morphed from intimidatingly intelligent and poised to wildly excited. Her expression was now oddly familiar.

"Oh my God, it's HAPPENING. It's happening!" Selene grabbed Kailani's shoulders. "Keyholders. How cool are we?" Selene yanked Kailani into the house.

"Um, Dr. Tanaka…Professor Tanaka. We need to go. There's a private plane set to take us to the—"

"The backup Batcave? Excellent. Where are we going?"

"Oahu, Hawaii."

"Makes perfect sense for a backup Batcave," Selene declared. Then her face went slack. "Oh dammit…where is my key?"

Kailani's heart stopped beating. "You…you don't have it?"

"I have it. I do."

That was not reassuring.

"Can I ask what's going on?" The man in glasses was standing right beside them, but somehow Kailani hadn't really noticed him. He had a lovely accent, and when she looked at him, he was objectively good-looking, which made it all that much odder that she hadn't noticed him.

"I'll explain." John stepped forward.

"John..." Kailani looked at him, a lifetime of keeping this secret, of protecting the very existence of the keyholders and their existence, never mind the location of the *waihona*, balking at the idea of sharing those secrets.

"I'm going to find the key." Selene raced for the stairs.

"You're her husband?" John asked the man in glasses.

"Luca," he said, holding out his hand.

"And the big grumpy dude?"

"Our husband Oscar," Luca confirmed.

"You're both going to want to hear this, and then one of you will need to go pack for all three of you."

"John..." Kailani said again.

"They're her trinity," John replied. "Besides, this is now essentially a joint task force operation, and the only way to run an effective task force is to have all members working with the same information."

Luca's brows rose, but he turned away, returning a moment later with Oscar.

"What fresh hell is this?" Oscar demanded.

"The Trinity Masters is under attack," John said succinctly. "The Grand Master is MIA, which triggered a designated survivor fail-safe."

Both Oscar and Luca stiffened, but neither interrupted as John continued.

"The Trinity Masters set up a secret treasury, or vault, or whatever you want to call it. Whatever's inside is supposed to be enough to ensure the survival of the society, in case the current leadership and/or the headquarters in Boston are destroyed."

"What does this have to do with Selene?" Oscar demanded.

"If you think she had something to do with the attack—"

Kailani frowned. "No, no, of course not. Why would we think she was part of the attack?"

"Er...no reason. Go on."

Kailani eyed the two men suspiciously.

"Why are you here?" Luca asked, his tone making it mere inquiry rather than accusation.

Kailani realized it was too late to turn back now, and even if this trinity was a bit shady, Selene was the keyholder, so there was nothing to do but follow through with her duty.

"It takes three keys to open the *waihona*," Kailani explained, accepting that this wasn't a secret she could keep from these two men. "Three keys that have been passed down through the generations, within legacy families."

Oscar looked to the stairs. "Selene has one of them?"

"Yes. She needs...actually, probably all three of you need to come with us, right now. The sooner we get there, the sooner we know who the acting Grand Master is."

"Wait, what?" Oscar demanded. "Acting...?"

"Each key has its own specific lock in the inner *waihona* door. Whoever's key opens the top lock becomes the acting Grand Master."

"Selene might become the temporary Grand Master?" Luca asked faintly.

"Yes."

"Jesus take the fucking wheel." Oscar staggered back and sat on the steps.

Luca rubbed his hands over his face.

"What?" Benjamin demanded.

"It's...fine," Luca said faintly.

"We're all going to die," Oscar said. "This is it. We thought it was back in that warehouse, but this is it, the moment she flips all the way into being a supervillain."

Kailani relaxed when she realized they were joking. Their words had the rhythm and cadence of an in-joke, though their delivery made it seriously convincing. Selene was a professor; she wasn't actually dangerous...

"I'm not going to become a supervillain." Selene came down the stairs, a duffel bag in one hand. "You two can stop having a fit of the vapors any time now."

Oscar grabbed her around the waist, tumbling her onto his lap as she passed.

"Do you have the key?" Kailani demanded.

"Yes, and I grabbed clothes."

"You have five minutes to pack for yourselves," Benjamin said, his gaze focusing first on Luca, then Oscar.

"They can come too?" Selene asked.

"You need a fucking keeper," Oscar declared.

She patted his cheek. "Awww, you're cute when you're grumpy. Which is always."

"I'll pack," Luca said.

"I didn't think I was even allowed to tell them about it," Selene said. "Just whichever of our kids would have to take over."

"I thought the same," Kailani said. "I think that's probably how it was meant to be...but someone told me that your trinity comes first. You don't, shouldn't, keep secrets from them."

"Damn right," Oscar said.

"And," Kailani continued, "it's possible that whoever attacked the Grand Master knows about us."

Selene slid off Oscar's lap, her expression focused and serious. Oscar stood, resting a hand on her shoulder. Luca headed for the stairs, his hand brushing against his spouses' arms, as he took them two at a time.

"We might all be in danger," Kailani said. "Right after I got the call there was a fire at my hotel...arson."

"Which still feels like a distraction more than an attack," John said softly, so only she heard it.

Talking about this, explaining it, had only increased Kailani's anxiety, her need to go. To get back on the plane and get home as fast as possible.

"You said the Grand Master is MIA..." Oscar was frowning. "What happened to her?"

"We don't know, but whatever it was, the Grand Master and the Boston headquarters are out of commission."

Selene glanced at the stairs just as Luca raced down, a carry-on suitcase in his hand.

Benjamin touched Kailani's shoulder. "The plane is ready. We'll have to stop and refuel or change planes on the West Coast, but I'll get you back to Hawaii as fast as humanly possible."

Kailani nodded her thanks, looked at Selene, Oscar, and Luca, and said, "Let's go."

"Fuck me. That's good bourbon," Oscar said, taking a sip from the crystal glass.

"Better than Crown and Coke?" Luca asked with a quiet smile.

Benjamin smiled too. He wouldn't tell Oscar how much the thirty-year-old bottle of Glenfiddich cost, even if he asked, in case that stopped the other man from enjoying it.

Oscar and Luca had spent a good forty-five minutes exploring the entire jet. Benjamin had worried for a little while that he wasn't going to be able to get Oscar out of the cockpit as he peppered the pilot with questions about the avionics, the dual flight management system, the synthetic vision system, and the weather radar.

Benjamin hadn't asked that many questions when he'd bought the damn jet. Probably because everything the pilot and Oscar had talked about had flown right over his head.

While Benjamin knew that Selene Tanaka had probably come from money if she was a legacy, none of the other men currently on the plane were accustomed to such wealth, and it occurred to Benjamin that he'd become somewhat jaded about his lifestyle, rarely noticing or even truly appreciating everything that he had.

Seeing things from John's perspective the past two days had opened his eyes to just how many things he took for granted.

Benjamin was standing at the rear of the plane, playing bartender, handing John a second beer. He'd already delivered Selene and Kailani mimosas—this was after Oscar and Selene had a mock fight about gin and tonics and an acceptable time to drink them—and the two women settled into the front half of the plane, facing each other over the table between them, eating finger sandwiches, and chatting. He couldn't hear what they were saying, but given their carefree smiles and occasional laughter, it didn't sound like anything too serious. It was almost as if everyone had silently agreed not to talk about the very volatile and dangerous situation they were in...and what would happen when they got to Oahu.

It was probably too early to drink, but after the past thirty-six hours, it was clear he, John, and Kailani had hit a wall. No one could run on adrenaline and stress and sex for hours on end without crashing.

Benjamin harbored no delusions that as they got closer to the islands, Kailani's stress would return. Better for her to unwind now and relax with a few drinks, while she had the time.

"Luca?" Benjamin asked. "You sure you don't want something a little stronger?"

"Vodka," Oscar said. "He loves his vodka."

Oscar and Selene's third was a soft-spoken man with a pleasant, easygoing disposition. Given Oscar and Selene's larger-than-life personalities, Benjamin couldn't help but recall that old *Sesame Street* song, "One of These Things." Because Luca was definitely "not like the others," and he'd wondered if Luca's quiet nature was truly who he was or born of the inability to get a word in edgewise with his spouses.

Luca stared down his husband, shaking his head before looking at Benjamin. "Water is fine. I don't drink much."

Oscar threw his arm around Luca's shoulders affectionately, pulling the man closer to him. "One beer and Luca's out like a light, snoring like a chain saw."

Luca narrowed his eyes, though he was grinning. "I don't snore. Now, you, on the other hand..."

Oscar snorted, and it was clear this argument wasn't a new one. "I don't snore either."

Luca reached for his phone. "Shall I play the proof for our new friends?"

Selene twisted in her seat. "Luca, push play on that damn recording and I'm tossing your phone out of the plane. Isn't it enough that I have to listen to that god-awful sound all night?"

"Told you so." Luca put the phone away and they all laughed.

Benjamin topped up his and Oscar's drinks, then claimed the chair next to John.

Luca and Oscar were sharing the couch, John sitting in the same seat he'd been in earlier when he'd officially earned his mile-high card. Benjamin and Kailani had claimed theirs on the way to Amsterdam, all those years ago.

Benjamin's seat put him essentially in the middle of the

plane, and the two groups, allowing him to listen to both conversations.

Oscar and John launched into a debate about using predictive artificial intelligence to track and anticipate crimes and criminal activity. Luca occasionally interjected a comment here or there.

Meanwhile, Benjamin listened with half an ear, too distracted by his own thoughts to try to follow along intently.

He'd spent the past month anxiously waiting for the phone call that would determine his future...one way or the other. He'd tried to convince himself that dissolving the trinity would be the best thing for all of them.

Now...now there was nothing he wanted less.

He'd hurt her all those years ago, his ignorance of just how deep her feelings ran, no excuse. So did he have the right to ask her to reconsider? To give him a second chance?

He was pulled from his musings when he heard Selene snap her fingers. "I've got it. It's been driving me nuts."

"Excuse me?" Kailani asked.

"How I knew you and Benjamin. You both looked familiar to me, but I couldn't make the connection. You were friends with my younger sister, Theia, when you were all in college. She used to tell me stories about the parties at the legacy house, and who was there."

"Ahhh, okay, I thought something about you was familiar when you were excited. I knew Theia had an older sister, but I didn't realize it was you. Forgive me for saying it, but you don't look a thing alike," Kailani said.

"We have different mothers, and while I took after Dad, Theia got her mother's blonde hair and blue eyes. Just one reason why I'm a theoretical physicist and not a geneticist. The loose mathematical predictability in genetics is brain-breaking."

"You have different last names as well."

Selene smiled. "Theia took her mother's name, while I have our father's. Theia said fuck the patriarchy and all that jazz."

Kailani laughed, but Benjamin's stomach clenched. He and Theia had gone to the same university, and it was Selene's younger sister who'd told Kailani that Benjamin had moved on too quickly after they broke things off.

He hated that Kailani had interpreted that as him not caring. The truth was, he'd cared too fucking much, and leaving her had hurt like a bitch. He wasn't proud of it, but his twenty-one-year-old self had determined the best way to get over her was to fuck her out of his system.

Shockingly...it hadn't worked.

"How is Theia?" Kailani asked. "I'm ashamed to say she and I lost touch over the last few years. I've been busy with my family's hotels, so I don't get back to Boston as often as I should for galas and meetings."

"She's doing well. Anxiously waiting to be called to the altar. To say she's impatient to meet her trinity would be an understatement."

Kailani laughed. "As I recall, she's been ready for her binding ceremony since the first day she officially joined the Trinity Masters."

"It's not her being romantic. It's her being type A," Selene joked. "Patience is not one of her virtues."

"I will make a point to call her soon. I'm so sorry I let so much time go by," Kailani promised.

Selene lowered her voice, leaning forward, and Benjamin tried to subtly shift closer, anxious to hear their conversation.

"Correct me if I'm wrong, but didn't you and Benjamin date once upon a time?" Selene asked.

The seats in the plane had high, wide backs, so he couldn't see Kailani at all. Of course, that also meant she couldn't see more than the side, top part of his head. From her vantage point, he probably looked like he was engrossed in Oscar and John's conversation.

"We did," Kailani answered softly.

Selene was quiet for just a moment, and he realized when she spoke, she'd obviously been trying to recall bits and pieces of stories her sister had told her nearly a decade earlier. "Wasn't it a bad breakup?"

Kailani sighed. "It was."

"And now you're in a trinity?"

"Not exactly," Kailani said.

"Wait, you're not married? When you showed up together, I thought—"

"We're...sort of...maybe engaged."

Benjamin's heart began to race, and while he knew he should feel guilty for eavesdropping, there was no way he was going to stop now. He never went into a business deal without knowing all the facts. Surprises were a surefire way to lose the upper hand.

He was tired of flying blind in regards to how Kailani felt.

While she'd promised to go through with the marriage if the trinity wasn't dissolved, she'd also vowed that she wouldn't share a home, a bed, or a life with him.

After last night and this morning, he couldn't help but wonder if her feelings were still the same.

"What does that mean?" Selene asked.

"We had a binding ceremony, but when we realized who was in our trinity, Benjamin asked the Grand Master to dissolve it."

He hated that he was being credited with that request. What the hell had she expected him to do when she'd essentially vowed to shut him out of their marriage and their bedroom?

"Is that even possible?"

"One of the Grand Master's counselors promised to ask. We've spent the last month apart, awaiting the call saying we didn't have to come back to Boston to get married."

"Oh, Kailani. I'm so sorry. To have so much up in the air. The stress of a new, unwanted trinity would be enough without this whole collapsing society nightmare on top of it."

Unwanted trinity.

Benjamin wished he could see Kailani's face. He couldn't read a damn thing from her tone or responses, and he wondered if her expressions would tell him more.

Either Kailani didn't reply, or it was so soft that Benjamin couldn't hear it because Selene spoke again, and this time, her voice wasn't quiet at all. It was as if she wanted him to hear. "You know," she said, "if either of us become acting Grand Master, we would have the power to dissolve your trinity."

Benjamin grimaced and darted a quick glance in John's direction, and could tell from the dark scowl on his face that he'd overheard Selene as well.

Oscar and Luca were oblivious to the sudden tension, the two men bantering back and forth about what defines a supervillain.

After what felt like three lifetimes, Kailani finally responded.

"I've thought of that, and—"

The plane hit turbulence, and the pilot came over the PA system, asking them to return to their seats and buckle up.

Benjamin and John exchanged a brief glance, but Benjamin didn't know how to interpret John's expression.

He took the last open seat, nodding to the attendant who came by to check that everyone was strapped in before going to secure the bottles in the galley. So much had changed for him in the past two days. He thought he'd understood what happened between him and Kailani. To find out that instead of her feeling battered and bruised, the way he had, she'd been cut deep, dealing not only with the end of the relationship but fallout from it that included her family...

He hadn't had all the pieces of the puzzle. Hadn't even known to look for them. And after touching her, tasting her again...

Lifetimes had passed, but now time was running out. Benjamin knew that despite the way they'd come together in Denver, nothing between the three of them had truly been resolved.

For a man who was used to being in control of every aspect of his life, right now he felt wildly out of control.

And he hated it.

CHAPTER FIFTEEN

Rose waited beside Lachlan, resisting the urge to start snapping at people to hurry up. Yelling would probably scare the tourists.

The sunset behind them was brilliant with shades of the expected yellow and orange, but there were hints of purple and lavender too, as the sun dropped down into the ocean. Tourists had gathered atop the seawall to watch, some simply enjoying, while others posed for pictures.

Lachlan touched his ear. "Preston is on his way down."

Rose nodded as she resisted the urge to relax, to maybe wander over and lose herself in the sunset.

She and Lachlan had arrived on Oahu several hours ago, after a truly grueling twelve-hour direct flight. She'd had a rather spectacular fight with Sebastian, which involved her calling him a useless dipshit, to which he retaliated she was a violent psychopath. Mild-mannered Franco had been the one to step between them, his normally smiling, handsome face set in a snarl. Seeing that, seeing the grief that he wore like a heavy cloak, had nearly broken Rose. She could handle her own pain, but seeing the people she cared about hurt and suffering...that, she didn't handle well.

Sebastian had insisted she go to Hawaii while he stayed in Boston to do "damage control" with the Europeans. Seeing as no one had even listened to her suggestion that they find a dungeon to lock Colum in, she'd agreed to fly out with Lachlan, who was still coordinating the search and rescue efforts, but whose expertise they needed in case there was a second attack. Rose was here to act as both a communications link between Boston and Honolulu, and a counselor to the acting Grand Master, whoever that might be.

They were about to find out.

A Dara family private jet had landed about forty minutes ago, and Lachlan was tracking the two chauffeured cars that had picked up the six passengers. Preston Kim was already here, and as she watched, he walked out the doors of the modern hotel tower. He looked around, then spotted her and Lachlan where they waited in a shadowy corner of the grassy lawn. He started for them, only to stop when a group emerged from the lobby.

Preston looked at Kailani, then at Selene, who walked beside her. Kailani nodded, turned, and said something to the four men behind her. Preston—whom Rose had spoken with when she got here—gestured toward her and Lachlan.

So these were the keyholders. Kailani Iona, Preston Kim, and Selene Tanaka.

The three keyholders fell in step together and walked toward her.

Lachlan raised a hand to his ear, murmuring something to Levi and Tate, the other Warrior Scholars who were here to provide added security.

There was movement above and to the right, and Rose looked up in time to see Tate appear on a balcony high above them. He looked casual in his aloha shirt, but he wasn't gazing in awe at the sunset. He was watching the grounds. Rose wondered if he had a gun.

Lachlan must have had Makani Iona on the comm channel too because he appeared near the entrance to the hotel's famous outdoor bar. He was smiling politely and had a hotel name tag pinned to his mandarin-collar shirt.

Kailani eyed her suspiciously when she got close. Good.

"You don't know me," Rose said in place of a greeting. "But we don't have time to play secret handshake and obscure questions."

Kailani's mouth tightened. "No, we don't."

"I'm one of the Grand Master's counselors. I'm here to help and advise whichever one of you is about to become ringmaster of this nightmare circus."

Selene Tanaka snickered, but Preston nodded solemnly while Kailani just looked grim and anxious.

"I'm Lachlan Howard. A few friends and I, who are here, serve as the Grand Master's on-call bodyguards, security force—"

"And fixers," Rose cut in.

Lachlan raised one big shoulder. "We're here to provide security."

"My brother Makani is in charge of security," Kailani said.

"We've spoken with him, but he has to look out for the hotel and your guests too." Lachlan nodded, and Kailani looked over to where her brother stood.

"Okay." Kailani looked at Rose, then Lachlan. "Thank you for being here...but you can't be a part of what comes next. That's only for the keyholders."

Rose nodded. "Of course."

Kailani glanced at Selene and Preston. Then Rose

watched, an odd but familiar combination of dread and calm filling her, as the keyholders walked away.

PRESTON GINGERLY LEANED back to give Kailani room to work. He'd helped her roll a heavy metal shelving unit away from the wall in the small office. He was conscious of not wanting to knock the shelves and send plates and pitchers and other restaurant necessities tumbling.

Kailani finished opening the door to the large wall safe that had been half blocked when they first walked in.

He hadn't expected that the wall safe was the *waihona*. That was far too simple and straightforward for the Trinity Masters.

The door swung open and he wasn't disappointed.

The safe was actually a doorway, and when Kailani stepped through into the small space on the other side, lights clicked on, illuminating a spiral staircase.

"Okay, that's cool." Selene peered through the door, craning her neck to look up.

"Follow me up," Kailani said.

Preston eyed the wall-safe door. "What if this door closes behind us?"

"Don't worry, there's a handle on the inside."

Preston was cautious enough that he checked, grabbing the lever mounted to the inner surface of the door and turning it, watching the bolts retract. By that point, Selene was halfway up the stairs, only her legs visible, so Preston followed her.

The spiral staircase ended in a small landing. Not enough room for the three of them so he stayed several steps down. The door was dark wood, like the walls, and though there was some light in the stairwell, their bodies blocked most of it, making the door a shadowy, dark thing.

Kailani paused, looked back at him, then at Selene. "All three of our keys should open this door."

Selene nodded and took a key from her pocket. "Let's see if that's true." She fitted her key in the lock and, after a little bit of wiggling, the key turned. Sound echoed down the small stairwell, heavy clicks and thumps coming from within the door.

"Whoa," Selene breathed.

"The interior of the door is a large lock mechanism," Kailani explained. "Part of my duties is to oil it every few months."

Selene grabbed the handle and opened the door.

Preston held his breath, the drama of the moment making his heart pound. It was the same way he felt every time he took the elevator down into their headquarters under the Boston Public Library—somber but nervous, aware that he was one of a select few who got to see, to know, an important and valuable secret.

This moment felt even more momentous. Because even among the Trinity Masters, this was a secret. His family had made a promise generations ago, a promise that had almost been forgotten, but now it was his turn, his duty, to see it fulfilled.

Stale air wafted out of the small room, which was made of the same dark wood. A few dim lights mounted along the ceiling had clicked on when the door opened, barely illuminating the space. Directly across from the first door was a second, larger, and far more ornate one. The center of the door was an etched metal panel with three keyholes, spaced in a triangle.

Preston leaned to the side, craning to see the rest of the room around Kailani and Selene's legs. Gold bars were stacked along the walls. A thrill ran through him when he saw them. Preston's grandfather had told him stories about the vault—his grandfather either hadn't known or hadn't used the term *waihona*. One element that was in every story was the gold.

Where the vault was, how to get into it, that had varied widely, and had always been based on speculation, but the gold, that was a fact. There were ninety-nine gold bars in the vault. Not a hundred, not ninety-eight, but ninety-nine. Preston's great-grandfather had been one of the original three keyholders, and according to Preston's grandfather, their family had been the ones tasked with obtaining the gold bars and placing them in the vault.

Preston's great-grandfather had kept the location of the *waihona* a secret, but he'd passed on the knowledge of the gold. Seeing the gold there, seeing the proof of the family legend, made it all—

Preston narrowed his eyes, scanning the room again.

Kailani was halfway through the door, Selene right behind her.

"Stop!" Preston lunged up the steps, grabbing their arms.

Both women turned to him, their expressions unreadable due to the dim lighting.

"Preston?" Kailani's voice was tight.

"How many gold bars do you see?"

"Why?" Selene demanded.

"How many?" he insisted.

Kailani was already scanning the walls. She sucked in a breath but didn't say anything.

Selene traced a finger in the air as she counted, then turned back to them. "About thirty, why?"

"There should be ninety-nine gold bars." Preston's back and shoulder muscles were tense as the implications continued to fall like dominos. "Kailani, did you or your family remove any of them?"

"No, I—"

"I'm not accusing you of theft," Preston said quickly. "Maybe at some point in the past, the Trinity Masters needed a cash infusion?"

Kailani shook her head.

"How do you know how many there should be?" Selene demanded.

"When the keyholders were created, that's what my family was responsible for—getting ninety-nine gold bars. That information was passed down with my key."

Selene looked from him to the room to Kailani.

Kailani took a deep breath, then her shoulders dropped. "My family didn't steal the gold."

"Okay, maybe they borrowed it," Preston said cautiously.

"Wait, what if the rest of it is inside the inner room?" Selene asked.

According to what Preston had been told, it should all be together in the first room, but he stayed silent, waiting to see what Kailani said.

"I think...I think the vault was robbed." Kailani looked at them. "Recently."

"Shit," Preston breathed.

"The day I got the call, I ran up here to grab the letter with your names. There's a hidden compartment. I didn't really look around. But these stacks... You're right. There should be way more gold. The day I came for the letter, I must not have noticed that these stacks aren't as tall as they should be."

Selene crouched and ran her fingertips along the floor just inside the door. She held up her hand, rubbing her thumb along her fingers. "Gritty dust."

"These rooms aren't totally airtight," Kailani said slowly. "I sweep, when I oil the locks, but..."

Selene reached out with her other hand, touching the top of the nearest brick. "No dust."

"The vault has been robbed." Kailani's tone was somewhere between horrified and disbelieving.

"Out," Selene said. "We need to get out of here."

Preston agreed. He'd had a chance to talk at length with Makani about the arson, about the timing of that event. He looked at the wooden walls of the stairwell and had a vivid mental image of being trapped here as they burned around him.

Less than a minute later, he, Kailani, and Selene dashed out into the hallway; the normal lighting and sign for the restrooms feeling both incongruously normal and safe.

Rose and Lachlan waited there. "Well?" Rose asked with a raised brow. "Which of you is it?"

Preston looked at the others, then to Rose, and said, "We have a problem."

FIFTEEN PEOPLE CROWDED into the meeting room. For a while, the hotel had tried to draw in business clients and had converted some oddly sized and unused space on the first floor of the old hotel into a small meeting room. With the door facing the new hotel, rather than either the picturesque grounds or the ocean, the space had originally been storage, then a conference room, and was now storage again. One of the interior walls was shared with the large kitchen for the two restaurants in the building. The room had its own bathroom, and if she'd been able to walk through walls, she could have gone from this bathroom, through to the elegant main bathrooms, and into the hall where she'd been moments ago.

One wall was lined with stacks of chairs just waiting to be set up on the grass for a wedding ceremony, but the large conference table and plush office chairs were still here.

Kailani felt slightly numb with shock as she dropped down

into a chair. She wanted to sit somewhere by herself and just process everything that had happened, but she didn't have time for that. She looked at John and Benjamin, who sat down as well, flanking her. Protectively? Possessively? Or maybe that was wishful thinking on her part and they—like her—were just too tired to stand for long.

John reached over and took her hand, giving it a squeeze of encouragement.

Benjamin's knee kept brushing against hers every now and then, though she couldn't tell if it was accidental or intentional. They were in the middle of a dumpster fire, their society under attack, and everything—everything except the physical attraction she, John, and Benjamin shared—was a complete unknown, up in the air.

The worst part was, she didn't have time to even think about them, or her feelings, because all fifteen people filing into this room were looking at *her*.

"Please take a seat," Kailani said, her manners and a lifetime of being in hospitality taking over.

Everyone sat, except Lachlan and the man he'd called to join them, Tate. A second man, Levi, was standing guard outside the door.

Preston sat between his wife and husband, as did Selene. Selene had reacted with surprise when she saw Tate, asking about her cousin. Tate, who was apparently married to Selene's cousin, had seemed cold toward Selene and her trinity, but that was probably because he was working as their security. Rose took the seat at the far end of the table, exactly opposite Kailani. Makani sat near her, his brow furrowed with worry.

Kailani took a breath, braced herself, and spoke. "The *waihona* has been robbed."

There were murmurings around the room, and Makani

shoved to his feet, his arms tense as he braced himself on the table.

John muttered, "I knew this felt like a robbery."

"There should be ninety-nine bars of gold. I'd never counted them, but they line the wall, stacked higher than my knees." Kailani had to swallow hard before she could go on. "Two days ago, when I went to retrieve the identities of the other keyholders, I didn't really pay attention to anything other than getting the names. Looking back...looking back, I think maybe some of the gold was missing then. I don't know exactly how much. Today... Today," she was repeating herself, her brain sluggishly trying to work, "as soon as Preston pointed it out, I realized how wrong it looked."

"How and why do you know how much gold there should be?" Rose asked Preston.

Preston and Selene took over, explaining first Preston's family knowledge about the gold, then Selene explained her finding about the lack of dust.

"You're claiming this theft is recent," Rose said in a dangerously pleasant tone.

Makani transferred his hard stare to her. "If you're implying my family—"

"Oh, I am," Rose assured.

"No," Kailani said. "We didn't take the gold. And I'm not going to waste time justifying and defending. Like I said, I think that when I was in there two days ago, some of the gold was missing." She closed her eyes, desperately calling up the memory of that moment. "Yes, some gold was missing." She opened her eyes. "But not as much as today."

"You're saying that over the past two days, someone has been robbing the *waihona* and no one noticed?" Rose's brow went up but she didn't look at Makani.

"The fire," Makani said. "Maybe the fire was a distraction."

"Yes," John said, nodding.

"How did the fire start?" The question came, unexpectedly, from Selene's quiet husband, Luca.

"A remote detonation system," Makani said. "It wasn't homemade. The fire investigator said it looks like the kind used by fireworks companies."

"You can buy those on Amazon," Oscar said.

Why did he know that?

"Why do you know that?" Makani demanded.

Oscar smirked.

"Why isn't *all* the gold gone?" Carly asked. "If they robbed it, why not take it all? Too heavy?"

"Robbing," John spoke with quiet authority. "Not robbed, not past tense. This is a crime in progress, and we need to react accordingly."

"But that..." Makani looked ill, and Kailani wanted to hug her brother.

"However they're accessing the *waihona*," John went on, his gaze focused on the middle distance as he thought it through, "they must be limited in how much they can take out at one time. Clearly they haven't been able to clear everything out at once. They must be sneaking in and out."

"We don't know if anything else is missing, if they made it to the inner part of the vault," Selene added. "We backed out when we realized."

Kailani's stomach went tight with anxiety. She wanted to rush back to the *waihona*, check what was missing. Not that she had any idea what was in the inner vault. If someone had breached the inner room, there might not be any way to know.

"From what you've said, last time Kailani went into the *waihona*, someone, let's now assume the robbers, started a fire," Preston said. "It might be dangerous to be in there."

"I agree," John said.

"But we have to go back," Kailani added.

"If they start a fire with the three of us in there, I doubt we'd all make it out alive. I can only assume losing the keyholders would be—"

"Catastrophic," Rose said.

"Problematic," Preston finished.

"I don't know most of you, and you don't know me," John said. "Hi, I'm John, and I'm a major crimes detective. Robbery, homicide." John pushed to his feet. "I'm going to investigate the crime scene."

"Take Luca," Selene said. "If the place is rigged to catch fire, he can deal with the detonator."

Luca cleared his throat. "Hi, I'm Luca, and I—"

"Blow things up," Selene said with a serene expression.

Lachlan rubbed his forehead.

"Have some experience with munitions," Luca finished.

"I'll go with you." Kailani moved beside John.

"You're one of the keyholders," Preston protested. "If something happens to you—"

"If something happens to me, Makani takes my key. You'll still have three keyholders." She headed for the door, John at her heels, Luca rising to follow. "And besides, without me, you can't get in."

CHAPTER SIXTEEN

L ight. The first thing they needed was light.
      There was a reason all crime scene units carried
      enough lighting to turn a nighttime street bright as day
—illuminating a crime scene wasn't just metaphorical; it was a
practical necessity. John appreciated the drama of the low
lighting in the stairwell, and then in the *waihona* itself, but that
wasn't going to work for them.

As soon as he saw what he was dealing with, he backed out,
taking Luca and Kailani with him. He asked Tate, who'd
accompanied them, to get them some light. Ten minutes later,
they had a heavy work light wedged in the corner at the foot of
the stairs, and several more in hand, the extensions cords
trailing out the open safe door into the office.

Luca quietly asked to go first, and John let him. Luca examined each step as they went up, then spent a long time studying
the door itself. Kailani passed him the key to let him open the
door. He studied the edge of the door, and the frame, before
entering the small room.

John glanced at the inner door, at the three keyholes. Now

wasn't the time to think about what would happen after they were, finally, able to open that door.

Luca examined the room inch by inch, working his way to the other door. Once he'd reached the other side, John slid in. He set his own light on the floor, angled up, and looked around.

He found it right as Luca said, "There's C4 on the door."

The presence of an explosive took precedence, so John turned to Luca, ignoring Kailani's horrified gasp.

Luca pointed out the small lumps along the edges of the door, the wire that had been taped down leading away from it. The brown electrician's tape blended with the dark wood of the door, and the C4 had been shaped into small bricks about the size of a deck of cards. Those too had been covered in tape, hiding the pale gray color of the explosive. Given how ornate the door was, they blended right in.

"Oh my God," Kailani breathed when Luca showed her. "Do we need to run? Evacuate the hotel?"

"I already disabled it," Luca said calmly. He held up the end of a wire. "We're safe. C4 is very stable."

"The detonation wire goes up into the ceiling?" John asked, raising the light to trace the wire. "That makes sense, given..."

John backed up to the center of the room and angled the light. As he did, the ceiling, which had appeared smooth, now had four faint lines. The outline of a hatch.

"Ah," Luca said.

"That's...that wasn't there." Kailani sounded ready to cry.

John took out the heavy flashlight he'd stuck in his waistband and raised it, using the tip to push up on the ceiling. The concealed panel moved, giving just a bit.

"This is how they're getting in," John said. "An easy access point, where they can drop in, grab a few bars, pull themselves back through, and then just walk out of the hotel with them.

All the gold at once would be heavy and bulky. Hard to move. Take two or three at a time, and you don't have to worry about that."

"And they tried to open this door." Luca pointed to a few marks on the keyholes on the inner door.

"I'm a thief," John said, putting himself in the culprit's shoes. "I find a room full of gold, and I start stealing it, little by little. But there's also a locked room that I can't get into from above." John looked over at Kailani, hoping she'd have more information about the inner room.

"The heart of the *waihona* is surrounded by steel," she said softly. "It's a self-contained fireproof box. Built by someone who repaired ships down at the harbor."

"That explains why they couldn't come in from above. So I'm a thief, I'm thinking if there's gold in this room, just imagine what's in that room." John pointed to the door. "I'm planning to take my time. After all, I don't want anyone to know that I robbed the place. But one day I hear, or see, the owner of the hotel coming to look at the gold. I realize I'm probably about to be found out, so I quickly set a fire somewhere else so she'll leave. I plan to just grab all the rest of the gold while she's distracted..." John paused, thinking it through, the pieces clicking into place. "But she doesn't call the cops and report a robbery. Instead, she leaves, and I think maybe she didn't notice, maybe I have a bit more time. Not a lot. I have to get through that door soon, but first, I'll finish stealing the gold."

"The placement of the explosives...it's how I'd do it if I were trying to open a bank vault," Luca said.

John pointed at him. "Exactly. The robber knows what they're doing. They've done this before."

"Why haven't they already blown it up?" Kailani demanded.

"My guess? They're waiting for something loud."

"Ahh," Luca said. "They're hoping to cover the sound."

"Wouldn't the building shake?" Kailani asked.

"Not if they are very good. This is a small, controlled explosion," Luca said. "It would sound like pops rather than a boom."

"How often do you get thunderstorms?" John asked.

"All the time. It rains most days, and it's the wet season, so...so it would make sense that they were waiting for a big storm."

"It's a gamble." John looked from the door to the hatch. "They were gambling on you not coming back before they could get all the gold and blow that door. They knew if they did it at a time when everyone heard, that they'd attract attention, and there'd be no chance of cleaning out whatever's inside. Especially if it's something heavy like more gold. That takes time to move." John looked at Luca. "There's no chance of this exploding?"

Luca started peeling C4 off the door. "No."

"Wait, if that's the case, if this is a robbery...it's possible this had nothing to do with Trinity Masters." Kailani sounded hopeful.

"I'd bet my badge this is a good old-fashioned heist." John looked up. "I'm going to see if I can get to that hatch from above, check for any evidence." He glanced at Kailani. "Tell your brother to round up the construction crew. I have some questions."

KAILANI LED the way up the spiral staircase once more. She wanted to be with John while he questioned people and searched for their robber, but this was more important. She was a keyholder, and this robbery was just one more delay. Watching, listening, to John solve the crime had been a vivid illustration of what an amazing detective he was.

She nearly tripped when she failed to lift her foot enough and it caught on the lip of a step.

"Careful," Preston said behind her.

She nodded, grasping the railing to steady herself before she continued on. She wasn't sure she'd ever been this tired in her entire life. She'd done a cross-country jaunt—twice—in the past forty-eight hours, only managing a few hours of sleep in the Denver hotel and a few odd restless naps on Benjamin's private jet. Her eyes were dry, her body weary, her brain sluggish at best.

She wanted to blame her exhaustion on just the lack of sleep, but she knew it was more than that. Kailani feared a twelve-hour nap wouldn't even cure what ailed her.

Whenever she was overstressed at work, her brain shut down. It had always been that way, and she'd had to figure out ways to overcome it, or else she'd watch hour after hour of true crime documentaries instead. In order to compensate, she'd learned to break her tasks down into manageable chunks rather than looking at the whole picture.

There'd been no breaking the past two days down into anything resembling manageable. It had been barely controlled chaos. An insane sprint peppered with forced downtime.

If she'd only had to retrieve Preston and Selene, things most likely would have been fine. The weather delay would have upset her, but she could have dealt with it.

Instead, Benjamin and John had been with her, adding a completely different set of emotions to the mix, both of them looking to her for...God, she wasn't sure what? Answers? A change of heart?

Two days ago, she was certain nothing on earth would change her mind about her feelings toward Benjamin, toward their trinity.

Now?

Now...

Now...

Fuck. Her brain was done. Cooked.

Kailani entered the first room, waiting as Selene and Preston stepped in behind her. They'd left the work lights, and the room seemed oddly smaller now that she could see everything more clearly than when it had been illuminated only by the battery-operated motion lights.

Preston's expression was somber and serious, while Selene was back to the coldly intelligent woman who'd first come down the stairs of her home in New York.

Kailani rubbed her eyes wearily, trying to stifle a yawn. She'd prepared for this moment her whole life, and now that it was here, all she wanted to do was crawl beneath the cool duvet on her bed and sleep for a week.

Unfortunately, she was still hours away from that even being a possibility. Once they knew who the acting Grand Master was, there was work to be done, plus dealing with the outcome of John's investigation...

Kailani's heart began to pound, so hard it almost hurt. Because she was here now, moments away from discovering if she would be the acting Grand Master. Her chest tightened and she closed her eyes, fighting like the devil to find the courage to do what came next.

"Do we take turns trying our keys in the top spot?" Selene asked, clearly ready to begin.

"No. Well, yes, but all three keys have to be in." Kailani tried to draw from the other woman's energy, her confidence. "Even the right key won't turn in the top lock unless the other keys are also in place."

"We'll try your key in the top spot first," Preston said.

"It would make the most sense for it to be you," Selene agreed.

Kailani stepped forward, placing her own key in the top lock. She wanted this over with. One way or the other.

She waited as Preston and Selene put their keys in the bottom two locks, and then she held her breath. The three of them turned the keys and...

Nothing.

Her key didn't move.

It wasn't her.

She blew out a long, slow sigh, hoping the other two didn't notice, then she turned her head, blinking rapidly several times to bat away tears. She wasn't a crier. Not by any stretch of the imagination, but it felt as if every emotion—the confusion, anger, fear, anxiety, sadness—that had been battering her over the past two days was suddenly demanding to be released.

She swallowed hard, refusing to let the tears fall. She wasn't sure how Selene and Preston felt about stepping up as acting Grand Master, but if they were as stressed out about it as she had been, it wouldn't be fair to act relieved.

Which she was.

The brief moment of weakness passed quickly, mercifully, so that when she faced them again, she was able to give them some semblance of calm.

"Not it," she said, briefly touching the tip of her nose, trying to bring some levity to the situation.

"And then there were two," Selene murmured.

LACHLAN SET DOWN THE TOOLBOX. It thunked, the table groaning. John looked up from the list of construction workers that Makani had provided. The crew that had been on-site working today—unlike normal construction crews that stopped at a normal quitting time—was still there. The Hale'ekolu construction had been going nearly around the clock in order to complete renovations as fast as possible, so it had been a relatively simple task to sequester the crew in a staff area of the hotel. The company owner, as well as anyone else who'd worked at the Hale'ekolu, had been called and were on their way in.

While Makani rounded people up, and John planned who to question first, Lachlan had decided to do a little recon, including breaking into the construction vehicles parked in a designated section of the hotel's underground garage. And he'd found what he was looking for...or at least some of it.

"What's that?" John asked him.

"Found it in one of the cars. A gray truck." Lachlan rattled off the plate number. Makani wrote it down and then went to a computer he'd balanced on top of a rolling catering cart in the hallway they were using as a makeshift command post.

John walked over, and Lachlan undid the latches on the box, opening it. He lifted out the upper tray, which held a messy assortment of vises, colored tape, and pliers.

John stared down at the gold bars hidden in the bottom of the toolbox.

"Four," John counted. "Any more in the truck?"

"Not that I could find, but I didn't take the panels off or rip up the seats."

John's brows rose. "Where was this?"

"In the cab."

"And the cab was unlocked?"

"No."

"You broke in?" John winced. "We won't be able to use this evidence, it's fruit of the..." John trailed off.

Fruit of the poisoned tree was a legal term. The man was thinking like a cop. It made sense, since he *was* a cop, but they wouldn't be worrying about evidence and making a case.

Lachlan would serve as ultimate judge, jury, and, if needed, executioner.

"Yeah, I wasn't planning on turning this guy over to the police," Lachlan told the other man.

John looked pained. "Right. We'll have to handle this ourselves."

Lachlan nodded. "Quietly." He was prepared to add another black mark to his soul if necessary. He'd hoped to be done with that when he left the service and moved to Boston to study, but right now the Trinity Masters needed him.

"That truck is registered to one of the electricians," Makani said. "But he hasn't been on-site in weeks. The wiring is mostly done, and they won't come back until after the walls are up to do some finishing work."

"Meaning, he shouldn't be here," John said. "I'm guessing he's in that room." He pointed to where they'd rounded up everyone.

"No," Makani said. "I just talked to him. He's one of the people we called in, along with the rest of the electrical crew."

"So why is his truck here, and who's driving it?" John posed the question before he stuck the crew list to the wall, studying it.

This was like watching a detective show. Lachlan leaned back against the table and grinned.

"Who do we question first?" Makani answered.

John looked over at Lachlan. "I realize this is more your operation, so if you want to take the lead..."

Lachlan repressed a soul-weary sigh. "I can handle the questioning, just tell me what answers you want, and I'll get them. I mean, they're not always reliable, but—"

John held up a hand, cutting him off. "If I say 'interrogation', what are you picturing?"

"We don't have time for sleep deprivation, so waterboarding." Lachlan knew his words would probably shock most people, but he didn't have time to be anything but truthful and direct.

"*Kahaha*," Makani said in a tone of surprise and possibly disgust.

That was fine, Lachlan knew what he was.

"No," John said slowly, drawing out the vowel. "We don't torture people."

"Maybe *you* don't."

John put his hands on Lachlan's shoulders. "Torture bad. No torture."

Lachlan let out a surprised bark of laughter. "If you say so."

"I do...also pretty sure torture by definition is bad. We're going to use our words to ask questions."

Lachlan was smiling for the first time since Franco called him. "If I handle the questioning, it's going to be straight out of the CIA's playbook."

"Okay, then you... Just...stay here," John said with a sigh.

Lachlan watched the detective walk away, and he called out, "I can stand in the corner and look threatening."

John just shook his head, and Lachlan allowed himself a moment to enjoy the smile. If John didn't get the information they needed, well...Lachlan's soul was already forfeit. He'd do whatever it took to protect the Trinity Masters.

CHAPTER SEVENTEEN

W hen in doubt, food and wine.
Benjamin felt helpless, and he hated that feeling. Hated that he could do nothing but wait. Wait for Kailani and the keyholders to finish opening the *waihona*. Wait for John to find the thief.

He wasn't the only one waiting, and after looking around at the odd collection of people who, like him, had no specific role to play at this moment, he'd taken charge.

Luckily, it was the same hostess from two days ago, and he'd been able to arrange for them to have a large table in the back corner of the downstairs restaurant, Hibiscus. It was late, so not all the tables were occupied, and those that did have diners were the ones on the lanai with views of the ocean or Diamond Head. Their large table was in the back corner, near the door that led out to the bathroom hallway—and the entrance to the *waihona*. An interior wall and the bar area blocked any views, both their views of Oahu's coastline and any other diners' views of them. Benjamin and the server designed a quick family-style meal based on the menu, and he selected several good wines. After that, the restaurant staff left them alone.

Benjamin plucked the bottle of California white out of the bucket and circled the table, checking to see if anyone needed a refill. They'd only been here for a few minutes, but Rose's glass was already empty.

It was an odd collection of people—Carly and Lance, Preston's spouses, were seated together, her shoulder against his chest while his arm rested on the back of her chair. Oscar, Selene's husband, had angled his chair so he could see out the restaurant doors to the hallway. He was watching for Kailani, Preston, and Selene to appear.

His husband, Luca, was next to Rose, and as Benjamin finished filling her glass, he heard the tail end of their conversation about the best and most exciting ways to blow things up. Well, that was...alarming.

Benjamin returned the wine bottle to the bucket and braced his hands on the back of his chair. His arms and shoulders were tight with the need to do something. Anything. He wanted to help Kailani and John, but they didn't need him.

They didn't need him.

Now feeling sick, Benjamin dropped into his seat. Like Oscar, he'd selected a chair that allowed him to see the hallway.

"Hey, man," Oscar said. "I hope you know how difficult you made my life."

Benjamin turned to him, brow raised. "Excuse me?"

"My wife is absolutely going to want to buy a private jet now."

Benjamin relaxed. "I wouldn't actually recommend buying. If it has wheels or wings, I'd suggest leasing."

"You lease?"

"No, but I own a whole airline, so maintenance of the jet is easy for me to arrange."

"Wait, so what I'm hearing," Oscar sat forward, his mouth unsmiling, but the corners of his eyes crinkled, "is that you can get me a sweet discount on booking a private jet."

Benjamin snorted, mouth opened to reply, when the sound of a raised voice had him turning.

"Sir, sir! Please let me—" The hostess was almost yelling.

Most likely at the man who came barreling around the corner into the restaurant at a sprint.

The man's eyes were wide as he stared at them. "Bomb!"

Benjamin's whole body went cold with fear—but then he narrowed his eyes, examining the man. He was slender, with dark hair and a thin face. He wore long shorts and a short-sleeve button-down. He was nondescript, the kind of man Benjamin wouldn't look at twice in normal circumstances.

"There's a bomb in the building! Get out!" the man repeated.

Benjamin looked at his companions, none of whom were jumping to their feet and running.

The man was poised to run deeper into the restaurant, to scare all the nice tourists enjoying the nighttime ocean views, but their lack of response apparently stymied him.

"D-didn't you hear me?"

"Another one?" Oscar said with a snort, echoing Benjamin's feelings. "Not fucking likely."

"We know there was a bomb," Benjamin said to the man as he pushed to his feet. "Why...how do *you* know?"

The wide-eyed panic left the man's face, replaced by a wary expression. "You need to get out," he stammered. "There's a—"

"Was," Benjamin interrupted. "There *was* a bomb."

Luca cleared his throat, drawing everyone's attention as he reached into his pocket and pulled out chucks of gray material. The guy was keeping C4 in his pockets?

Okay, then...

"What the fuck?" the man demanded, falling back a step.

"Take him," Rose commanded.

Benjamin grabbed the man by the shoulder. He saw the punch coming, and twisted, taking a fist to his shoulder rather than face.

Then Lance was there, coming up behind the man and hooking an arm around his neck.

Benjamin saw the wide-eyed hostess standing in the restaurant doorway, a phone to her ear.

Lance, who'd either killed the man or rendered him unconscious with the chokehold, was already lowering the man's body to the floor.

"Everything is under control," Benjamin told the hostess. "No need to involve the authorities, but if you could let Mr. Iona know we'd appreciate him stopping by, that would be helpful."

The woman swallowed, nodding jerkily, responding to the calm command in his voice.

"Nice," Oscar said. He hadn't even gotten up from the table.

Rose walked over, standing over the unconscious man. "Is he dead?"

"No." Lance crouched, touching the man's neck. "Er, let me check. It's been a minute since I tried that. Yep, alive."

"That's some Seal Team Six shit," Oscar declared, but he was looking at his husband. "Luca, do *not* put that explosive back in your pocket."

"It's stable."

"I don't care, you shouldn't keep shit that can go boom that close to your dick."

Benjamin suppressed the urge to start laughing. It was probably exhaustion that had him on the verge of cracking up.

Rose nudged the man with the toe of her high heel. "Who thinks this is our robber and he was going to use a bomb scare to evacuate this building and then finish clearing out the gold and blow the inner door?"

Everyone raised their hands.

"I lide him..." Rose looked around. "Under the table?"

Everyone scooted out their chairs.

"Wait, let me check his pockets." Luca frisked the man, pulling out several things, including a small bright-yellow box with a big black button. "Detonator."

Benjamin was crouched, and when Luca said that, Benjamin was as close to murder as he'd ever come in his life. This man could have killed Kailani. He curled his hands into fists to stop himself from choking the man or banging his head against the floor.

Benjamin helped Lance shove the unconscious man under their table as Rose put her phone to her ear. "Lachlan? I think we caught the bad guy. Come get him."

SELENE REMOVED her key from the bottom right lock. There was a moment of hesitation, as if none of the three of them were sure what to do next, so Selene decided for them. She slid into the middle, nudging Kailani to the side.

Preston, cool and calm, didn't seem bothered by the fact that she was trying the top position next. Selene gave him a quick wink anyway, and his lips quirked, amused.

"Keys in," Selene declared.

She waited for the other two to fit their keys into the bottom locks, then slid hers into the top one.

They turned the keys.

The locks gave way, the sound of cascading tumblers and

clicking metal loud in the quiet room. There was a final *thunk* and then quiet.

The door was unlocked.

Holy fuck.

Selene stared at her hand, still on the key, and then at the others.

It was her.

She was the acting Grand Master of the Trinity Masters.

OSCAR STARED AT THE HALLWAY. The queasiness he'd experienced from all that fucking turbulence on the plane had finally lessened...after two sleeves of saltines and three glasses of ginger ale...but it wasn't completely gone. It was why he hadn't gotten up to help with the bad guy, whom Lachlan had just finished pulling out from under the table. Lachlan stuffed him into a large laundry cart and rolled him away. Bad guy disposal service. Nice.

He should get up and get another ginger ale from the bar. He should get up and confiscate that fucking C4 that Luca had absolutely put back into his pocket.

Movement caught his eye. The door to the staff office opened, Kailani and Preston emerging, Selene right behind them.

"They're back," Oscar said.

Everyone else turned to look, waiting attentively in tense silence as the keyholders walked into the restaurant. Oscar refused to take his eyes off Selene, searching for some hint, some sign of what the fuck had happened in that vault.

"Well?" Rose asked with an arched brow. "Who is it?"

Kailani and Preston stepped aside, and from that point, everything switched into slow motion as Selene stepped forward.

No. Sweet baby Jesus, *no.*

"Selene is now the acting Grand Master," Kailani announced.

Oscar's residual sickness was abruptly cured by a mix of pride and horror. Motherfucking son of a bitch. The cult was out of their fucking minds. What stupid fucker thought this was a good idea? Selene's ancestor who'd originally been given the key was...probably...normal. But Selene as Grand Master... Jesus fucking Christ.

He loved his wife. He would kill for her.

And he knew to the marrow of his bones that they were now royally fucked because as much as he loved Selene, she could be chaos in human form. Give her power and she went full supervillain. It had happened before, the last time they'd gotten sucked into solving some Trinity Masters mystery.

And now she was the Grand Master.

Oscar turned his head, staring at Luca.

Luca's eyes were wide as their gazes met.

"Grand Master." Rose inclined her head. "I think you'll want details about exactly what's happened. And then there are decisions we need to make."

Selene was smiling. "I'm great with decisions."

Luca made a choking sound. Oscar covered his face with his hands and groaned.

Someone poked him in the arm. He spread his fingers, staring up at Selene with one eye.

"Don't be such a drama king," she said.

"Baby, you are brilliant and amazing and you know I love you, but..."

Selene narrowed her eyes. "But what?"

"But your risk tolerance is insanely high," Luca said. "Your willingness to create, and run headlong into danger is terrifying for the rest of us."

Selene stared into the middle distance, probably remembering the last time they'd been on an adventure. She smiled.

"That smile isn't reassuring," Oscar growled, only half teasing. Selene really wasn't someone who should have their hand on the proverbial button. And now...

Selene rolled her eyes. "But did you die?"

Oscar crossed his arms on the table and laid his head on them.

Selene...no, the Grand Master...turned and walked away, still smiling.

THEY WERE BACK in the little conference room, everyone except John, Makani, Tate, and Levi, who were dealing with the robbery. Lachlan had deposited the presumed bad guy somewhere and was back, standing beside Selene at the head of the table.

Kailani and Preston were seated together on Selene's left, while Rose sat on her right.

"My first decree—" Selene started.

"Decree?" Oscar interrupted.

"Interruptions will earn you twenty lashings," she said.

"Baby, they think you're joking," Oscar said slowly.

"I am, about the lashings. Not about my decrees. I think that sounds better than orders. Proclamations?" Selene seemed to relish the word, but then her expression turned serious, her gaze, sharp and intelligent, sweeping the room.

"First, Lachlan, you are now my warlord."

Lachlan blinked. "Warlord?"

"We're under attack. You're the warlord."

"General," Oscar said under his breath. "Could have said general."

"Your first priority is to find and rescue the Grand Master."

Lachlan nodded.

"Next, I want a private meeting with all the counselors."
Selene looked to Rose, who was holding out a phone.

A voice came from the phone, but Benjamin couldn't hear
exactly what was said. Selene's response made him raise his
eyebrows though. "If you want, we can meet in person. Bring
the hostage if he's cooperative, otherwise put him in...Guan-
tanamo Bay or something like that until you get back to
Boston."

Rose smiled.

What hostage? Had they caught whoever took the Grand
Master? Benjamin hated not knowing what was going on.
Information was, after all, a form of control. He shifted rest-
lessly, checking the urge to demand answers.

"Third," Selene went on, "from here on out, my warlord
has the right to draft any member of the society into his strike
team." Selene looked at Lachlan. "If you need anyone in this
room, take them with you when you go back to Boston."

"Yes, Grand Master." Lachlan's expression was calm,
almost blank as he accepted his orders.

"Sebastian, you're now in charge of an all-society roll call."
Selene was speaking to the phone in Rose's hand.

Sebastian? Hmm, probably Sebastian Stewart. It felt odd
and a little unsettling to know the names of all the counselors. As a legacy, Benjamin was used to feeling like he
knew more than most members, but this...this was next-level
shit.

"I want to know who else is missing," Selene was saying.

Had other people been taken? Benjamin reached for his
phone, needing to text his family, to make sure they were all
right.

"Your priority is to find the Grand Master, but we need to
find our other people too," she said to Lachlan.

"With your permission, Grand Master, I'll continue to expand on our current search and investigation efforts."

"Absolutely, Warlord."

This time Lachlan didn't blink at the title.

Selene turned to her right. "Preston, Kailani, catalog the interior of the *waihona*. It's supposed to have what we need to protect the society, so I need to know what's in it."

"Yes, Grand Master," Kailani murmured.

Benjamin looked at her. Kailani. His Kailani. They must have opened the door, that's how they knew which key worked, but maybe they hadn't wasted time looking around inside, or maybe everything was boxed or sealed up. Benjamin wanted to ask Kailani. Wanted her to look at him.

"What weapons I have at my disposal," Selene said with a relish that was alarming.

There was a low groan from Oscar that might have been amusing under other circumstances.

"While I remember...Benjamin."

Benjamin jerked when she said his name, his attention snapping to the Grand Master.

Selene looked directly at him. "I understand you made a formal request after your binding ceremony. Request granted. Your trinity is dissolved."

CHAPTER EIGHTEEN

Benjamin froze. With four fucking words, Selene had thrown his entire future out the window. He glanced across the table and found Kailani's gaze.

She'd done it. Asked Selene to dissolve the trinity.

He wasn't sure when, but she'd had plenty of moments alone with Selene, during the long flight back to Hawaii and even here, though they'd certainly hit the ground running since returning to the hotel.

They stared at each other for several long moments, as Benjamin waited.

For her to say something. Anything.

Maybe "thank you" to Selene?

Or "fuck you" to him?

Damn it, she owed him *something*.

Instead, she simply sat there, looking at him, giving him nothing.

So what the hell did he do now?

Reject Selene's goddamn decree? How could he do that?

He'd been the one to request the trinity to be dissolved, even though that wasn't really what he wanted. Not at all.

When the Grand Master had called out Kailani's name at the binding ceremony, Benjamin's immediate, split-second, unguarded response had been joy.

Unmitigated joy.

Because the thing he hadn't said, the thing he hadn't finished confessing on their flight from L.A., was that he'd never stopped loving her.

Then he'd seen her face, read the anger in her eyes, and that happiness had died.

When Kailani told him their marriage would be in name only, he'd gone with the knee-jerk reaction, asking Devon for a way out, because fuck if he was going to be shut out of his own marriage.

He'd done everything wrong that day, and he knew it. He'd done everything wrong a decade ago, more wrong than he'd known until a few days ago.

Kailani continued to hold his gaze, but he didn't have a clue what she was thinking or how she was feeling.

He wished John was here.

John understood Kailani better. Understood him better.

No, it wasn't understanding as much as a willingness to put in the hard work. John hadn't shied away from their anger, but had faced it head-on. More than that, John had put his own pride on the line by offering them all of himself, sharing his painful past as well as his hopes for the future. He'd led them to bed, bridging what had seemed like an endless chasm between Benjamin and Kailani, and given Benjamin something he hadn't expected.

Hope.

Hope that they could overcome their problems and become a true trinity.

Because he'd been in love with Kailani Iona since she was nineteen years old, and while it seemed insane, he was already halfway in love with John.

John. Jesus.

What would he say if he was here?

Benjamin didn't have to search for that answer for long. He knew exactly what the sexy detective would do. He'd stop this fucking meeting and set Selene straight.

God knew that was what Benjamin wanted to do, but he was leaving it to Kailani. He'd made so many mistakes before, that this time he was going to be smart and shut up. If things had changed for her over the past few days, she'd say something. Right now.

He wouldn't stop this, save their trinity if that wasn't what Kailani wanted. He didn't want to give her yet another reason to hate him.

Her silence was all the answer he needed.

She'd clearly gotten what she wanted. What more was there to say?

Benjamin had walked away from her all those years ago because he'd fallen so deeply in love that he knew if he didn't, his heart would be broken when the two of them were assigned to their trinities. He'd thought he'd been so smart, avoiding the pain, minimizing the hurt.

Now, there was no reprieve, and his heart didn't just break, it shattered.

She really didn't want this. Didn't want *him*.

He swallowed heavily. He couldn't stay on this island, couldn't stand the thought of John's response when he found out...

Would he be as devastated as Benjamin?

Or would he be as relieved as—apparently—Kailani was?

"Kailani?" Selene said, her voice cutting through the fog. "Did you hear me?"

Kailani's attention jerked to Selene. "I'm sorry. No," Kailani said softly.

"I need you and Preston to inventory the *waihona* now. It can't wait until morning."

Kailani nodded. "Of course, Grand Master."

Preston had already risen, and Kailani followed suit. Benjamin watched her progress, all the way to the door, feeling like a fool because he was still waiting. Still hoping.

Kailani never looked back.

And though the meeting wasn't finished, he was. With all of it.

Benjamin rose, and without a word, he walked out.

No one here needed him. For anything.

He was going home.

"LISTEN, man, I get it. We all have that one family member." John actually didn't have that one family member, since he was family-less, but it was a line he knew most people could relate to.

He rested his hand on Liam Lee's shoulder. Poor guy had a name with an unfortunate amount of alliteration, and also a shitty cousin. Turns out, the man Lachlan had tied to a chair in their makeshift holding cell—which was undoubtedly an improvement over being hogtied and stuffed in a laundry cart—was Liam's cousin.

"Take me through it again," John said.

"Please, I know I made a mistake, but I don't... Can I talk to Ms. Iona? Apologize?"

John shook his head, frowning as if he were sad that he

couldn't do that for his new friend, Liam. "Just take me through it again, and I'll see what I can do."

"My cousin, Mark, he's the oldest, but he's kind of a fuck-up, you know what I mean?" Liam said.

"Absolutely," John agreed.

"My uncle insists he has potential, and he does. He's smart. Dropped out of MIT, but my uncle acts like he graduated."

"What was he studying at MIT?"

"Electrical engineering. I'm a licensed electrician. I make good money. But I just went to a trade school so it's like it doesn't count." Liam was getting worked up, which was great.

"Wait, wait, so your uncle thinks his dropout son is better than you, when you're the one with the skilled profession?" John said, much of his outrage on Liam's behalf genuine. The thing that made his job so hard was that he could usually see where people were coming from, could empathize with the reasons behind the bad decisions. That ability was also part of what made him good at his job.

"Right?" Liam leaned forward, elbows on the small table John had found for use in his mock interrogation room. "And so my uncle pressures my dad, who pressures me, that I should let Mark tag along on some of my jobs. Because maybe Mark will think it's interesting enough that he'll want to do it too."

John shook his head as if he couldn't believe the audacity. Honestly, he sort of couldn't.

"And if he did decide it was interesting enough for him," Liam went on, "I would have had to vouch for him to my boss."

"So you bring him with you to work. Here, at Hale'ekolu." They'd already been over this once, and John needed to redirect if he didn't want this to devolve into cousin-bashing.

"Yeah. I brought him for a few days, including the day I was redoing some of the wiring in the old hotel. They're upgrading to energy-efficient fixtures and adding more lighting, and that wiring was too old, with way too many junctions for that."

"Where do you have to go to do that? Were you on the roof?"

"In the ceiling, actually. There's not much space. You can't even really sit up, but if you lay flat you can get it done."

John knew that from experience, since he and Makani had investigated the other side of the hatch.

"You and Mark were up in the ceiling?"

"Yeah, and then Mark isn't paying attention to what he's doing, and he puts a knee through the drywall. I'm thinking *shit*, because the restaurant is still open, and I just messed up their ceiling, which means they'll have to close while we fix it. But Mark checks and he says he's not over the restaurant. That he's over a storage room."

"And did you go over and look in, see what was in the room?"

"No." Liam shook his head. "I didn't."

Liar. He absolutely looked. But John nodded.

"I told Mark to leave it, that I'd ask the drywall guys to fix it, but he says he'll fix it. I just...I just needed to finish my stuff, so I left Mark to it."

"And this was all in one day?"

Liam looked down at his hands. "No. Mark came back with me a couple days in a row. He went down into the storage room. Said he couldn't fix it all from above. But I never went in. Never."

That, John believed. He was pretty sure Liam saw the gold, knew what his cousin was going to do, and turned a blind eye.

"Mark fixed it. He even painted the drywall patch he made. He did a good job."

John leaned in. "But it's not a patch, right? It's actually more of an access hatch."

Liam blanched. "It was just so he could get in because he said the door into that storage room was locked from the outside, so he had to go in and out through the ceiling."

"Or you could have told your boss, told the hotel, what happened. They would have opened the door for you to fix it."

Liam looked down at his hands. His fingers were shaking.

"Mark fixes the hole," John said, pulling back from the accusations. "You finish the rewiring in the ceiling. Then what?"

"Then...nothing. I was done at that point. I got assigned to a different project with the understanding I'd come back, toward the end of the renovation, to help with some of the installs, but the electrical prep work was done."

"I get it." John stood, hands in his pockets. Casual, nonthreatening. He frowned, as if he'd just thought of something. "But didn't we find your truck in the parking lot today?"

"I loaned my cousin my truck," Liam said, dejected. "I've been driving my wife's car."

"When did he borrow it?"

"A week, week and a half ago."

"And he's had it all this time?"

Liam nodded, looking miserable.

"But your truck, it's the one with a sticker pass on the window. A pass that gives the vehicle access to this hotel's parking lot."

"I...I kept the sticker on that truck because I was coming back," Liam stammered. "I was coming back to do the finishing work—"

"That makes sense, but, Liam, you have to realize that if Mark was driving your truck, he could just drive it right into the hotel because security would see the sticker and let him through."

"I...I didn't think that he'd..."

"And it's your truck we searched. Your toolbox where we found some of the contents of that storage room." John dropped into his chair, elbows on the table. "Because it's a storage room, but not for mops and toilet paper. The Iona family stored valuables there. And you knew that because you saw what was in there, didn't you?"

"No. No!"

"You saw, but you weren't going to take anything."

"Yes! I didn't take anything."

"You're not a thief."

"No, no, I'm not."

"And you didn't actually *see* your cousin steal the gold bars."

"I didn't see him take anything," Liam said vehemently, not reacting to the mention of gold bars. Yep, he'd seen what was in there.

"But you suspected what he'd do, didn't you, Liam? You know your cousin is an asshole. Know he'd rather steal than work."

Liam opened his mouth, but no words came out. He closed his eyes, braced his hands on the table.

"When he asked to borrow your truck, you knew what he'd do. Knew he was stealing all that gold you'd both seen."

Liam didn't look up.

"What I want to know is, did you know about the bomb?"

At that, Liam's head jerked up. "The *what?*"

John put the detonator Luca had taken from Mark's pocket on the table. "The room you saw...that's just storage. But there's a vault. I'm betting you could tell, from what you saw in the ceiling."

"No." Liam's voice was firm, if shocked. "I mean it. I don't know about any vault. Or a bomb."

John believed him but pointed at the detonator. "Do you know what this is?"

Liam nodded. "Only because we did a couple days on demolition during training. I've never seen one in real life. You have to believe me." Liam swallowed. "Did…did Mark hurt anyone?"

"No, but it was close." John sat back in his chair. "Let's go over it again."

John was fairly certain he had the whole picture. Mark, who'd been a suspect in several robberies on the East Coast after dropping out of college, had seen his cousin Liam's job at one of Waikiki's oldest and most expensive hotels as an opportunity. He'd bullied his cousin into bringing him to work, hoping to find something to steal, either from the hotel itself or one of the wealthy guests.

Instead, he'd crawled around in the ceiling and found the *waihona*. John would put money on it not being wholly an accident. He'd gone up into the ceiling space. And while the top of the steel container that was the inner part of the *waihona* wasn't immediately visible, if you poked around, you'd notice it. Mark may have seen that and wondered what it was. When he couldn't get in through the steel plate, he probably hunted around until he found a bit of ceiling he could punch through.

He made a hole, saw the gold, and when he actually dropped down into the room, he saw the inner vault door, and started picturing dollar signs. Mark started smuggling out the gold bars one or two at a time, but then Liam finished his work. Mark wanted the rest of the gold, but more than that, he wanted to get into the main vault. So he borrowed his cousin's truck and showed up every day like he's one of the crew, smuggling out gold in between attempts to break into the vault.

What John didn't know was how Mark had known that Kailani had entered the *waihona*. His best guess was that Mark may have actually heard or seen her and closed the trap door. The idea of someone in the ceiling looking down on Kailani, possibly wondering if he should grab her, hurt her, silence her, made John's blood run cold.

"Let me go talk to...some people." He'd almost said "the D.A.," which was what he would have said if this were a normal interrogation and he could list possible charges as a pressure point.

John walked out into the hall where Makani was waiting, standing guard in front of the large cage where they'd stuck Mark, who was trussed to a chair. The cage was actually a secure storage area for the construction crew, meant for tools and materials. It was a great makeshift cell.

John studied the man, who Lachlan had gagged with a few pieces of tape over his mouth.

"Was he in on it?" Makani asked, with a nod to the door John had just come in through.

"Willfully ignorant. He knew, but desperately pretended it wasn't happening."

Makani nodded and lowered his voice. "You think there's any connection to our society?"

"No, I think this is a weird, dangerous coincidence." John looked toward the plastic-sheeting doorway, as if he could see through it to the old hotel, to the meeting room where Lachlan said everyone was gathering. John wanted to be there, to know what was going on. It was odd for him to want to walk away in the middle of a case like this, especially when he'd reached his favorite part—fitting the final pieces of the puzzle into place.

But he wanted to be with them, to stand with Kailani and Benjamin as they dealt with whatever came next.

John shook his head, trying to dismiss the need to go find them, and went to question Mark.

CHAPTER NINETEEN

Kailani held a notebook, jotting down everything Preston said as they explored the inner room of the *waihona*, grateful her task was simple.

Preston had taken charge of the inventory, cataloging and counting what was there, then dictating it for her to write down. They had some of the big work lights from earlier, but even with those, the room was full of long shadows, thanks to the contents. Roughly six by six, the steel box that was the heart of the *waihona* was hot, the air so stale that they hadn't been able to enter when they first opened it. They'd propped the door open while they had that meeting, which had improved the air quality somewhat, but the air in the outer room and stairwell wasn't exactly fresh. Used to a constant gentle ocean breeze, the stale stillness was making Kailani feel ill.

Or maybe that feeling had nothing to do with the air.

The largest thing in the vault was a vintage paper storage cabinet. Preston said it was called a cabinet letter file. Apparently someone in his family had one of these, and it was now a valuable antique. Rather than large drawers where papers were inserted vertically, like a modern filing cabinet, this one had shallow, horizontal drawers, each slightly wider than a piece of paper. Pages were placed flat in the drawers.

This cabinet was massive—nearly as tall as the doorway, with three columns, each with seventeen drawers. There were library card-catalog-style brass label holders and pulls on each drawer. If they'd ever had labels, the ink had faded, the paper brittle and yellow.

Besides that, the vault contained a few heavy chests that absolutely looked like they held pirate treasure, several modern hard-sided silver briefcases, one large cardboard moving box that was completely out of place and, weirdly, three chairs. The chairs were ladder-backed, simple things. The fabric and thread on the upholstered seats had been mostly leeched of color, but the embroidered pattern was visible—a hand-stitched triquetra.

Given the air quality, and the space issues—there wasn't much room to move—they'd decided one person would investigate while the other took notes. Kailani hadn't protested when Preston stepped into the vault. Normally, her curiosity would be driving her crazy, but right now...

Simply recording what he said was the limit of her abilities at the moment.

Because she was numb.

Completely numb.

Selene had dissolved the trinity, announcing it in the middle of what was essentially a war council, as if it was just one more item ticked off her new to-do list as Grand Master.

The moment Selene had made the pronouncement, Kailani had looked across the table at Benjamin, expecting—hoping?—that he would speak up.

But he didn't.

He didn't say a word, which...confused her. But more than that, she'd been surprised by how much it hurt.

She hadn't been certain that he still wanted the trinity dissolved. Though perhaps that was just wishful thinking on her part.

After all, he'd been the one to ask for it.

God. She couldn't put the blame for that on him. It had been her behavior, her insistence that the marriage would be in name only that had prompted his request, which was why she'd really expected him to speak out against Selene's proclamation.

So now what?

Kailani rubbed her temples, the beginning of a headache forming, fueled no doubt by the lack of sleep and fresh air, paired with an abundance of stress and regret.

This was her fault. All of it. She'd made a terrible mistake, and she knew it, just as she knew she needed to fix it. But she wasn't sure how.

Probably because she was drifting on fumes.

Kailani blinked a few times, her eyes scratchy and dry from exhaustion. Once again, she was fighting not to cry, and she hated it. Hated feeling so tired, so weak, so confused.

She swayed slightly where she stood. Part of her wondered if she closed her eyes, if she could actually sleep right here, just like this, standing up.

She was that fucking tired.

No. She shook her head, wishing she'd thought to grab a cup of coffee from the restaurant before the meeting...or even before coming back here, though given Preston's delicate handling of everything he touched, she doubted he would have let her walk in here with a to-go cup of coffee.

"This is incredible," Preston said, not for the first time. He had one of the drawers in the cabinet file pulled out and was leafing through the papers inside.

While she was distracted and stressed out, he resembled a kid in a candy store as he uncovered more and more of the secret society's "hidden treasure."

She hadn't even been able to muster up excitement when he opened one of the silver briefcases and revealed that it was stuffed with cash. Not just cash but Hawaiian overprint notes from WWII, which were worth considerably more than their face value.

Kailani simply wrote down everything he said.

"Damn." Preston's tone turned sober, almost grim, with the next item.

"What?" she asked, his tone waking her up enough that some of the exhaustion fog lifted.

"Do you know what the term 'broken arrow' means?" He tilted the page he held so she could see it. It looked to have been written on a typewriter, the letters a little uneven. The heading was "Broken Arrow."

"No, what is it?"

"Broken Arrow is the military's term for things like missing nuclear bombs."

"Missing?" Kailani looked at him, hoping he was joking.

"Yes, I think there's something like six, or maybe eight acknowledged missing warheads."

"What the fuck?" Kailani breathed, horror acting like a shot of espresso.

"Except according to this...three of them aren't actually missing. Saying they're missing was actually the cover-up because the Trinity Masters put them in storage."

"We have nuclear bombs? Please tell me they're not on any of my islands."

"Nope." He pointed to an address on the paper.

"Wow," Kailani breathed.

Shoulder to shoulder, they looked at the cabinet file.

"How many drawers have you gone through?" Kailani asked.

"Three."

"Three drawers. Out of...fifty-one. Plus, everything else in here." Kailani looked over her shoulder, then back at the cabinet file. "They'll probably all contain something horrible," she said.

"No, not horrible. Secrets, yes, but not all horrible. Not exactly." He closed the current box, then pulled out the one above it. "Let me get your opinion on this." He handed her an old paper photo envelope, the kind where the developed pictures went in the back, while there was a small place in the front for the negatives.

He'd mentioned this already. Kailani had put "picture negatives" on her list and was too tired to ask for more specifics. Though now that she thought about it, it was odd that he just said there were negatives, without any hint about the subject of the photos.

Carefully, she took one strip of negatives out, holding it so the light shone through. The first picture showed a wide street with a park on the far side and a scattering of pedestrians on the sidewalk. To the left were brick buildings, with arches above the top-floor windows. The photographer was slightly above street level, looking down on the road and the sidewalk.

The second shot was the same scene but a slightly different angle, more of the brick buildings and street visible. The left side of the photo was black, as if something in the foreground, close to the photographer, had blocked the camera.

The third photo was from the same spot, but now there were a few vintage-looking cars and a couple motorcycles on the street. Oddly, the cars were driving down the middle of the street rather than in a lane. The black on the left side of the photo was now gray and had a curve at the top. She studied it for a moment, deciding it looked like someone's shoulder, that person standing in front of the photographer.

The fourth and final photo on the strip was clearly a minute later, chronologically. The person was farther away, their silhouette clearly visible but dark, as if they stood in shadow, while the rest of the picture was bright with sunlight. The cars were closer in this shot. Definitely vintage, and one of the cars, the convertible, was long, with what looked like three rows of seats. She could just make out four heads, the people in the back rows. One of the heads was oddly square on top. She peered closer. It was a hat. One of those pillbox hats—

"Holy shit!" Kailani jerked up. "Is this..."

"Someone taking pictures from the grassy knoll?" Preston grinned. "I think so."

Kailani carefully put the negative back into the folder, resisting the urge to check the other strips and find out if there really had been another shooter. She put the photo envelope into the drawer and looked at Preston.

"I'll get my pen and paper." Kailani added "JFK" to the "photo negatives" listing. For a few minutes, the horror from the Broken Arrow list, and excitement of the photo discovery, bolstered her energy, but as they slogged through things like old war bonds, articles of incorporation, and the deed to some massive piece of land, exhaustion and the stifling heat of the vault covered her like a wool blanket, making her too drowsy to concentrate.

She'd had to scribble out countless things because her sluggish brain couldn't spell.

After the third time she asked Preston to repeat something he'd said, he stopped and looked at her. He frowned. "When was the last time you slept, Kailani?"

"Um...when did I get the keyholder call?"

Preston's eyes widened. "You mean to tell me you've been

awake since you got the call to institute the keyholder protocol?"

She gave him a tired grin. "No, I've slept, but not well or a lot. It's not like you and Selene were just down the road waiting for me to fetch you. You couldn't even make it easy by living on the same coast."

Preston chuckled. "I guess we didn't."

"We had a layover in Denver because of bad weather, and I managed to grab a few hours' sleep there." After some marathon sex she couldn't bear to think about. "Other than that, I dozed on the jet a few times, but...you know how it is sleeping on a plane. It's never a very sound sleep, is it?"

"No, it's not. I can finish this on my own, Kailani. Why don't you head into the hotel? I bet the owner would give you a room to sleep in," he joked.

Kailani shook her head. Even if they were finished with their task, she wouldn't be able to go to sleep. The minute she put her head down, she knew all she'd be able to do was think about Benjamin and John.

"I...I can't... I need to find...I have to..."

Preston reached out and took her arm, drawing her into the *waihona*. He pushed on the seat of one of the chairs, then said, "Seems sturdy enough. Sit down for a minute."

She started to refuse because even as uncomfortable as the chair looked, standing up was the only thing keeping her awake at the moment.

That and the stress.

And the painful tightness in her chest.

Unfortunately, her body took the decision away from her, dropping down heavily on the uncomfortable chair.

Taking stock of what was in the *waihona* had been keeping the panic at bay, but now...as she looked at this seemingly endless task, she wanted out of here. Suddenly overcome with the desire to see Benjamin and John, to talk to them.

"Can I ask you something, Kailani? And if it's too personal, you can tell me to go take a flying leap," Preston said, smiling.

"What is it?"

"Carly and Lance mentioned that your trinity was still in the binding month, and things weren't going well."

Kailani's shoulders sagged. "That's an understatement."

"But now it's dissolved..."

Kailani swallowed hard to dislodge the lump in her throat. "Yeah."

"You don't seem happy about that."

She looked up at him. He had been a complete stranger a couple of days ago, yet she felt a bond with him, forged by their shared heritage and their role within the society.

"I'm not."

Preston nodded slowly. "I didn't think you were. And it was clear Benjamin wasn't either."

His comment sliced through her exhaustion. "What?"

"I was looking right at him when Selene told him she'd granted his request. He looked miserable."

He did?

Kailani had been looking at him too, but she hadn't seen that. Why hadn't she?

"Are you sure?"

Preston gave a slight shrug. "I realize I don't know Benjamin as well as you do, but I can recognize a man in pain."

Pain.

Oh God.

"I need to talk to him," she said, standing, resisting the urge to run from the room in search of Benjamin, hating the thought that he was hurting, alone, without her and John.

She didn't move, though, because the Grand Master had given her a direct order.

Preston seemed to understand her reticence. He looked around the *waihona*. "This is going to take days to go through, not a single night. Why don't you take the list of what we've found so far to Selene, give her a progress report?"

"Progress report?"

He was giving her a way out.

"Yeah. I'm tired too," Preston lied. He looked well-rested and too intrigued by everything they'd uncovered so far to quit now. "We can start back again in the morning."

"Okay," she said, tearing the top few pages from her notebook so that she could leave it and the pen behind for him. "I think that's a good idea."

He took the notebook from her, giving her a gentle smile. "Can I tell you a secret?"

She nodded. She genuinely liked this man.

"I was glad it wasn't me."

Kailani grinned. "I was too."

"I know you want to talk to Benjamin, but can I give you some advice?"

She nodded.

"Get some sleep, Kailani. I have a feeling after you've gotten some rest, things will look clearer to you, and you'll be better able to figure out where to go from here. You're in love with Benjamin?"

She nodded, unable to deny that truth any longer. "And John, our third," she added, acknowledging that the sexy detective had stolen her heart within mere days.

"Then you'll definitely need to sleep. Because it sounds to me like you have a trinity to fight for."

CHAPTER TWENTY

J ohn walked into the little conference room, aware that he'd missed the meeting Selene had called earlier. He'd finally wrapped up the investigation of the theft, getting the answers he wanted from Mark, who'd at first smugly asked for a lawyer and threatened to sue all of them.

When John calmly explained that he wasn't a Honolulu police officer, and that he therefore had no legal obligation to let Mark call a lawyer, the man's tune had changed rather quickly. Having Makani standing there, periodically making vaguely threatening statements like "my family will take care of this, we don't need to involve anyone else" had helped. It hadn't taken long to get Mark talking.

Tate, one of the Warrior Scholars, had taken Mark's keys and gone to retrieve the gold bars that Mark had stashed in his father's garage.

The question of exactly what would happen to Mark and Liam was one John was leaving to Tate, Levi, and Makani, though he'd threatened to arrest them for murder if they went so far as to kill the men. John knew the Trinity Masters hadn't kept their secrets and maintained their power by being all sweetness and light, but there was a point of no return, and for John, murder was it.

Levi had cheerfully informed John that there were plenty of ways to deal with someone without killing them, but that hadn't actually made John feel better.

What had made him feel marginally better was when Tate said it would be some variation of blackmail for Liam, and Mark would end up in prison for something else—probably drugs. John might have stayed to get details, but the need to see Kailani and Benjamin was biting at him, so he abandoned Mark and Liam to their fates.

He'd expected to find Kailani and Benjamin waiting for him, but instead, the only people still present in the meeting room were Selene, Rose, and Lachlan, who were all sitting grouped together at one end of the long table looking at something in a notebook, speaking in hushed tones, while Luca and Oscar remained at the other end. Neither man was talking; rather, they were looking down the table at Selene.

Luca gave John a pleasant smile as he passed by them, but Oscar merely grunted.

Selene glanced up as he approached. "You've questioned the thief."

"I did. Got a confession." John gave a report as if Selene were his captain or an ADA, walking her through the timeline of the crime, along with their evidence.

"So it was just a robbery," she mused, her words not necessarily a question, but he answered as if they were.

"Yeah. An old-fashioned heist that came at the worst possible time as far as the Trinity Masters is concerned."

"It certainly did." Selene looked over at Lachlan. "My warlord tells me someone has gone to recover the gold bars, so it seems that's one problem solved."

Warlord?

John exchanged a glance with Lachlan, but either the man was cool with the nickname or had a rock-solid poker face.

"Levi and Tate will take care of the punishment part of crime and punishment," Lachlan told her.

"If you think about it, there are so many good options for body disposal here. What about sharks?"

"Selene, baby, this is when you start to sound like a supervillain," Oscar said slowly.

"Oh, like I'm the only one who was thinking we could dump the bodies into an active volcano."

"You were, Grand Master." Lachlan's face showed not a hint of emotion.

Selene pointed her finger at him. "I expect more creativity from my warlord." She turned back to the table. "It's a missed opportunity, and I'm disappointed in all of you."

Oscar scrubbed his hands over his face while Luca patted his back.

"Quick question," John said, ready to get out of there and see Kailani and Benjamin. "Where's my trinity?"

Selene frowned momentarily then raised a brow. "You don't have a trinity."

John's heart stopped. "What?"

Selene tapped her finger on the table. "Your binding, your trinity, has been dissolved."

John scowled, his temper flaring. "What the fuck did you do?"

Lachlan's attention shifted to John, and it felt like he'd just been sighted down the barrel of a rifle.

A chair slid across the floor behind him, loudly.

"Watch your fucking mouth when you talk to her," Oscar snapped.

"Why would you do that?" John asked, struggling to sound

calm. His tone was still rough enough that Oscar growled in warning.

John was typically better at keeping his emotions under control. In his line of work, it was necessary, but he was completely incapable of doing so now.

"Wait. Do you even know them? I thought you were all avoiding each other."

"Where are Benjamin and Kailani?" he asked through gritted teeth.

Selene stared him down, not angrily but curiously. "Kailani was cataloging treasure and weapons, but just left to get some sleep after delivering a partial list of what's in the *waihona*. I have no idea where Benjamin is. He walked out a few minutes after I dissolved the trinity."

John held her gaze, fighting to temper his tone when he said, "Un-dissolve it. *Now*."

Oscar had been hostile, protective of his wife up until that point, but John heard the man's heavy groan. "Fuck. You're in love with them."

"Shit," Selene muttered. "When did that happen?"

John glanced over at Oscar and recognized...a kindred spirit? "They're mine."

Oscar turned to Selene and it appeared as if he might intervene on John's behalf, but she shook her head, the same pity he'd seen too much of in his life reflected in her eyes. "I'm sorry, John, truly I am, but neither Benjamin nor Kailani protested. They didn't speak up after I dissolved it. They didn't say a word."

John paused, raking his hand through his hair as he let the implications of that soak in. "Neither one of them said anything?"

Oscar placed a comforting hand on his shoulder. "I'm sorry you fell in love with dumb assholes."

John turned and walked out of the conference room.

The stars sparkled above him, beautiful and mocking as he crossed from the old hotel to the new building, walked across the lush grass, between giant elephant ear leaves and under gently swaying palms. He stepped through an arch, into the open-air first-floor hallway, and was overwhelmed by a fury and a bone-deep hurt that told him something he hadn't had time to truly consider.

John *had* fallen in love with them. He'd opened himself up to Benjamin and Kailani, given them pieces of himself he'd never offered another living soul because he'd thought... hoped...*believed* they would be a family.

The request to end the trinity had been made during that nasty fight after the binding ceremony a month ago. After the past few days, he'd genuinely thought Benjamin and Kailani would be able to overcome their issues and move toward building an amazing life together.

He swallowed heavily.

"Goddammit," he muttered to himself as too many truths rained down on his head. It wasn't supposed to be like this. He'd joined the Trinity Masters because he wanted a chance to be a part of something real, something lasting.

A family.

And he wanted it to include Benjamin and Kailani.

But they hadn't spoken up, hadn't fought for it.

For *him*.

That was the part that cut deep, bringing back old feelings he thought he'd overcome. Now he stood there, feeling like that same little boy, carrying his meager bag of clothes to the social worker's car as yet another home, another family, turned him away.

That was when it struck him that he'd been the only one fighting for this all along.

So what did he do now?

He had no idea where Benjamin and Kailani were, which suited him just fine. Until he got his emotions under control, talking to either of them would be a bad idea.

John stood in the hallway, the ocean at his back, staring at the doorway into the lobby, which in turn led out onto the street, trying to figure out his next move.

He needed to...fuck...what?

He wished he wasn't so goddamn tired. He hadn't slept much in the past few days. A breeze ruffled his hair and shirt, and it was cool and smelled of sea and night. It was too late to head to the airport. Even if it wasn't, the idea of hopping back on a plane wasn't one he wanted to entertain at the moment.

He was beyond exhausted, so his best bet was probably to just head to bed. He'd sleep and sort out his next move in the morning.

Heading toward the lobby, he planned to book a room for the night.

"John!" The sound of Kailani calling his name froze him in place. She looked frantic, and her panic muted his own feelings of hurt as he turned, ready to help her, protect her, whatever she needed.

"What is it?" he asked as Kailani rushed up to him. "What's happened?"

"It's Benjamin," she said almost hysterically. "He's gone!"

John frowned. Selene told him Benjamin had walked out of the meeting. An asshole move, but not surprising, not really.

"And?" he asked, his voice wooden even to his own ears.

He noticed the dark circles under her eyes, the panic laced with weariness when she said, "He left the island. I went to find him, to talk to him about..." She paused, not meeting John's gaze.

So Benjamin hadn't just excused himself from the room. He'd really left.

No, not left, run away. With the trinity dissolved, Benjamin had decided to move on with his life. Yet another arrow to the heart. He hadn't even bothered to say goodbye.

"Selene told me she dissolved the trinity." John fought to keep the fury he felt from slipping out.

"She did," was all Kailani offered in return.

"And you both just sat there and said nothing."

The fact he knew clearly took her aback. But not for long. She pushed her hair behind her ear. "I should have said something, should have spoken up. I wanted to. So badly. I just..."

"You just what?" This time, the words came out too sharp. Too loud.

John couldn't go easy on her. Discovering they'd remained silent rather than speaking up for their trinity cut deep. Too deep. There was a gaping hole in his chest left behind from where she and Benjamin had ripped his heart out.

When Kailani spoke, her words were soft. "I should have stopped her. Should have asked her not to do it."

"Why didn't you?"

"Because Benjamin—"

John exploded. "Goddammit! Don't fucking tell me it was because of your past relationship with Benjamin! That's ancient history, Kailani, and it's time to move on. I thought you had, thought the two of you were making strides toward working things out."

"We were," Kailani said. "Or at least, I thought we might be able to. If I'd been Grand Master, I wouldn't have dissolved our trinity. Maybe...we could have talked and—"

"How the hell were we going to talk if the two of you weren't even capable of opening your mouths to ask Selene to stop?"

John never spoke with this kind of malice, this kind of anger. Shit. He wasn't sure he'd ever been this angry.

A childhood filled with disappointment had taught him not to set his hopes too high because the second he started to care about something, life had a way of pulling the rug out.

This time...with them...he'd dropped his guard, lowered the walls he'd built to protect himself because of false security.

The Trinity Masters had promised to give him a family.

"I made a mistake, John. Today. And after our binding ceremony. I'm sorrier than I—"

"Why didn't you speak up?" he asked again, aware he'd cut her off, afraid she would tell him that her feelings hadn't changed, that she still didn't want a true marriage with Benjamin.

"I was waiting for Benjamin to say something. Selene was addressing him. Dissolving the trinity was his request."

On the surface, her response made sense. But it was still a lame excuse.

"You didn't give him much choice, vowing to cut him out of the marriage," he said, though he was starting to feel like he was kicking a dog that was down. Especially when she wiped away a tear. Now was not the time for this conversation. His temper was only rising.

"I know. John," she said. "I'm so sorry. For everything. I hope that you can find it in your heart to—"

"And Benjamin may have been the one to talk to Devon, but *you're* the one who told Selene about it."

"I know, I know. I'm sorry—"

"It's late," he interjected, uninterested in her apology. It was just words. And he'd learned a long time ago, those were worthless. It was actions that mattered, and all hers and Benjamin's actions had shown him was that they weren't as invested in making this work as he was. They didn't care enough to say one word.

No. That was all they'd had to say, and John was certain Selene would have changed her mind. From Selene's point of view, she was probably protecting Kailani. If Kailani had said something, anything...

So it was time for him to figure out how to do the same. Time to harden his heart. To cut his losses. After all, he'd had a lifetime of practice.

"What do we do?" she asked, looking to him for answers he didn't have.

"Right now? We go to sleep. We've been up for forty-eight-plus hours with just a few cat naps scattered here and there. Neither one of us is in the right state of mind for this conversation. Nothing is going to get resolved tonight."

Actually, fuck that.

There was nothing *to* resolve. Their trinity was no more. Though he didn't say that aloud.

For a moment, he thought she might disagree with that decision, insist they board yet another plane in search of the man who was so anxious to get away from them, he hopped on his jet and escaped without a word.

"You're right. We need to sleep. I'll get us a room." She paused as she looked at him. "Two beds. I know you're angry, and you have every right to be—"

"No. I can't...I can't be here." He started walking through the lobby, headed for the grand front doors.

"John, where are you going?"

"I'm going to go get a room in another hotel. There's a million right here, aren't there?"

"Okay, I'll call and—"

"No. I'll handle it myself."

His luggage was in storage somewhere in the Hale'ekolu, but fuck it. He didn't need luggage.

"John, please stay."

At that, he stopped, looked at her. Exhaustion was etched on every inch of her face.

"We can talk in the morning. Over breakfast...or maybe even brunch," she said, as if realizing how late it was and how badly they both needed sleep.

He nodded, though not necessarily in agreement. He wasn't sure what else there was to say.

Kailani looked at him, and though he knew it was wrong, he couldn't stop himself from wanting to bend his head and place his lips against hers.

He could imagine it. A soft, short kiss. If he kissed her now...it would be their last one.

So if he did kiss her, he'd make it hard and hot, his tongue brushing hers, her hands fisting his shirt.

But he didn't kiss her. They stayed that way, looking at one another, and he wished he knew what she was thinking.

"Let me know if you don't find a place with vacancies...are you sure you won't let me arrange your room?"

"No, Kalani."

She nodded once, her expression tight. "Good night, John."

"Good night," he said aloud.

Goodbye, he said in his head.

The trinity was broken, Benjamin was gone, and as far as John was concerned, his current duty to the society was done. He'd helped Kailani find the keyholders, he'd gotten a confession from a thief, and he'd helped them recover their stolen gold.

Game over.

Time to return to L.A. Home. Alone.

The more things change, the more they stay the same.

CHAPTER TWENTY-ONE

Kailani rolled over, finally feeling semi-human...and discovered she'd slept until nearly noon. Crap. She checked her phone, no message from John. He was probably still asleep too. She sent him a good morning text and suggested a restaurant. Given that he hadn't wanted to stay here last night, she suggested the name of a restaurant not in the Hale'ekolu.

After a super-quick shower, she braided her hair and rummaged through her suitcase for her least dirty outfit to wear. She really needed to return to her house at some point today, just to grab clean clothes.

When she'd originally packed her bag, she'd thought she was heading to Boston for her wedding, which meant she'd included way too many overly dressy and cold-weather outfits. Not enough tropical island day-wear. And even though she'd been back in Hawaii since yesterday evening, there'd been zero time for her to head home to change clothes.

She checked her phone. No message. She considered calling, anxious to continue the conversation she and John had started last night, especially now that she'd had some sleep and felt like herself again, but decided not to. If he was still asleep, clearly he needed the rest.

For the past few days, she'd been more zombie than Kailani, and she was looking forward to proving to John she could be a reasonable, pleasant person versus the stressed-out lunatic he'd been exposed to since meeting her.

Taking the elevator to the first floor, she'd just stepped off the elevator when she heard her name.

"Kailani." Oscar walked over to her. "I was looking for you."

She was surprised by that, simply because she couldn't imagine what the two of them had to talk about.

"You look like you got some sleep," he said, in what she was learning was his usual gruff tone.

"I did. I'm happy to say I actually feel human again. Slept ten hours and I'm pretty sure I never rolled over once."

He grunted in response.

"Did you have a restful night?" Despite her urge to find John, her "be polite to a guest" training kicked in.

With one eyebrow raised, Oscar pierced her with a sardonic stare, speaking in a hushed tone when he said, "My wife is the fucking Grand Master. I think it's safe to say sleep isn't going to be a thing for me anymore."

Kailani laughed, though she wasn't entirely sure he was joking. "Hopefully, it will only be for a short while," she said, watching her words, given the fact they were in the middle of the hotel lobby.

"I hope so. Listen, I've got a message for you."

"From Selene?"

Oscar shook his head. "John."

"Oh," she said. "When did you see him?"

Oscar scowled, though she didn't get the sense he was angry, just...uncomfortable? "Listen. Don't shoot the messenger, but he left for the airport a couple hours ago. He came by to pick up his suitcase, and I just happened to be in the lobby. I'm pretty sure he's in the air, on his way back to California by now."

He'd left her too.

Just like Benjamin.

"Did he...say anything else?" she asked, a little more hostile than she'd intended.

Oscar nodded. "He wanted me to say he was sorry things ended the way they did, and that he hopes you have a good life."

Kailani narrowed her eyes. "Have a good life?"

Oscar stiffened at the obvious anger in her voice. "Yeah, but, um..." He pointed at himself. "I'm just the fucking messenger, remember?" he said as he took one step back.

She might have laughed at the absurdity of a big guy like Oscar being intimidated by her, but she was too...fuck...hurt and pissed off.

Kailani spun away from Oscar without another word, storming toward the back door of the main hotel, the one that led to the courtyard gardens.

She hit the bar to open the door too hard, the loud banging noise echoing through the wide foyer. Kailani kept going, storming across the grass until she reached the seawall. There was a bench there that faced southeast, with a perfect view of Diamond Head and well-shaded by the loulu palms that also formed a curving privacy wall.

Whenever she was stressed out or upset, she came here, to her special spot. Dropping heavily on the bench, she bent forward, her elbows resting on her knees, her eyes cast downward at the stone walkway.

Last night, when she'd discovered Benjamin gone, she'd been too tired to think straight, too upset over the fact that he'd left without a word.

Now she'd had some sleep. She could see his departure for what it was.

Cowardice.

It was an easy thing to recognize because she'd been a coward too.

Selene had dissolved their trinity and she'd said nothing. And rather than stay to face her and John, Benjamin had left without a backward glance. He'd done the same damn thing to her a decade earlier. Back then, she'd cried about it, but this time...

She sat up, staring at the bright blue sky.

Not this time.

Benjamin's departure she could deal with. She *would* deal with it, and him.

But she never—not in a million years—would have expected John to do the same. He'd been angry last night, and rightfully so. Because she and Benjamin had been wrong not to speak up in that meeting.

Kailani had no problem owning up to that. It had been a mistake, one that she regretted. One that she'd intended to apologize for again this morning.

She drew in a long, deep breath, the floral scent of pikake and gardenia tickling her nose and calming her. She took another breath. Then another.

It had been thirty-two days since her trip to Boston, since she'd led with her emotions rather than her head and sent her trinity into a downward spiral.

For four weeks, she'd stuck her head in the sand, praying the Grand Master would dissolve the union.

She hadn't given them a chance, hadn't spent time with them. Then this crisis forced them together and...and they became a trinity. Somewhere over the past few days, her feelings had changed. She'd realized it last night when talking to Preston. Might have recognized and acknowledged that sooner, if she hadn't been stressed as fuck about getting the other keyholders and existing on next to no sleep.

God, she had a hard time believing the three of them had only been together for four days.

Just four.

It felt as if a lifetime had passed. They'd embarked on a crazy, insane, stressful, whirlwind of an adventure, and all she could think was she'd do it all again, every sleepless second of it, if it meant she could be with them.

Yes. She'd fucked up. A lot.

But now, her head was as clear as the gorgeous, cloudless sky above her, and she knew exactly what she wanted.

She was going to go get it.

Go get *them*.

"Selene." Kailani burst into the little conference room in the old hotel. Bringing everyone here yesterday had been a matter of availability and proximity. Today, the chairs that had been stored here had been cleared out, and there was now an elegant desk set at an angle in the corner.

Selene sat behind the desk, the handset of a landline phone sandwiched between her ear and shoulder.

Kailani pulled up short when she saw that, switching to look at the people gathered around the conference table—Rose, Lachlan, and Preston.

Rose and Lachlan were both on their computers, while Preston was having a cup of coffee.

"Did you get some sleep?" Preston asked.

Kailani nodded but focused on Selene, whose serious expression made Kailani's stomach muscles tight with worry.

"I did."

"If you're ready, I am. We can start." Preston raised his cup, taking a long final sip.

The inventory. Shit.

"Preston...I can't."

That got Lachlan's attention. "Is there a problem?"

"Benjamin and John...they're both gone."

"Gone as in missing?" Rose asked.

"No. No, they... They left."

"Ah, I'm sorry," Preston said softly.

Kailani looked down at her hands. Her fingers clenched tightly in a fist, as if she was bracing for a physical fight. "They're my trinity and—"

"No, they're not." Selene, phone call apparently over, joined them at the conference table.

"You shouldn't have dissolved it," Kailani told her.

"Why not? Benjamin asked for it. I thought you wanted it gone. It was a crazy match anyway. You and Benjamin have way too much history."

"We do... No, we did. Past tense. We were working through it. John...John made us work."

"Your trinity is dissolved." Selene raised a brow. "I did it as a favor to you since you're a keyholder and you would have done it yourself if you'd become Grand Master."

Rose snorted as if that was amusing, though Kailani didn't know why.

"I wouldn't have," Kailani said.

"Then why didn't you say something when I made the proclamation?" Selene spread her hands in the air.

Lachlan mouthed "proclamation," the corner of his mouth ticked up in a grin.

"I was waiting for Benjamin to say something because I didn't want to force him into—" Kailani cut herself off, shaking her head. "Selene, Grand Master, I just came to let you know I'm leaving for a few days."

"No, you're not." Selene smiled slightly, but it wasn't a joke.

"I have to go after—"

"You have to finish the inventory," the Grand Master said.

Kailani shook her head. "Please, they're my trinity—"

"They're not." Selene was merciless.

"Dammit, *please*. I love them!" Kailani snapped. "I love them, and I'm going no matter what you say!"

Lachlan pushed back from the table. A silent threat. Kailani felt like the walls were closing in.

"Grand Master, I can handle the inventory alone." Preston waved his fingers above his head, vaguely gesturing to where the *waihona* was.

Selene shook her head. "I saw the picture you took, that's at least a two-person job. And besides, it takes all three of us, and all three keys, to open it."

Kailani nodded, leaning in. "I know, I know, and I've thought of that. I'll give my key to Makani. If I were hit by a bus, he'd probably be the person who'd get it anyway."

"And Makani is going to take over your job helping with inventory?"

"Sure," Kailani said. She'd lie if that was what it took to get out of here.

Lachlan shook his head. "He's busy for the next few days reporting the crimes we 'discovered' Mark committing."

It took Kailani a minute to remember who Mark was—the cousin of one of the construction crew, the man who'd stolen the gold and tried to break in. They must be planning to frame him for an equivalent crime since they couldn't tell Honolulu PD the truth. Between dealing with that, and keeping an eye on the hotel in general, Makani was already stretched thin.

"He can do it," Kailani insisted, promising she'd make it up to him somehow.

Lachlan shook his head, Preston looked pained, and Rose had one brow raised.

Kailani fought the urge to just run—run out of this room and straight to the airport and damn the consequences. "Please," she said instead. "Please, they're my trinity."

Selene started to speak, but Kailani cut her off. "I know technically they're not. I know I screwed up when I didn't say something last night. But they're *mine*, and if I don't go find them, don't fix this, now, I'll lose them forever."

"I was going to say," Selene said slowly, "that I sympathize. I know what it's like to find your trinity. To love them, even if you don't have any of the formal society approvals."

Kailani's heart jumped. "Will you call us to the altar? Put us back in a formal trinity?"

Selene leaned back. "Oh, no way."

Damn it. "Selene, please."

"We are at war." She gestured to Lachlan. "I dissolved it as a favor to you. To be honest, I don't even know what goes into calling a trinity to the altar. And, frankly, it's not a priority right now."

"Then you have to let me go to them. I can't—" Kailani bowed her head, panic and rage churning through her. Plus fear. Fear that it was too late, that she'd lost them forever.

"Isn't your cousin here?" Preston asked.

Kailani looked up to find that he was staring at Selene.

"Yes, Roman's here, but he just came because he's married to Tate."

"Is he related to you on the keyholder side?"

"Yes, why?"

"The actual keyholders have to be one person from each of our families, right?" Preston pulled his key from his pocket.

"I'm with you so far," Selene said.

"But as far as access to the *waihona*, from what I understand, it's members of keyholder families." Preston looked at Kailani. "I'm assuming you were in there, at least the outer room, with the previous keyholder."

"Yes, to learn the maintenance things and where the letters went."

"So anyone from a keyholder family is allowed inside the *waihona*." Preston smiled. "If Kailani gives her key to Makani, he can come with us to unlock the door." Preston gestured from himself to Selene. "But for the inventory, Selene's cousin Roman, who is here and not currently busy, could join me."

"That's splitting hairs," Rose said. "I like it."

Kailani checked the urge to throw her arms around Preston in a desperate hug.

"And everyone keeps insisting *I'm* a scary Grand Master. With that kind of thinking, you'd be great." Selene shook her head, but she was smiling, looking almost relieved.

"I'm just good at putting elements together to get the outcome I want," Preston said.

Selene looked at Kailani. "The *waihona* inventory comes before dramatic romantic gestures, but if you can get your brother, and my cousin, to agree, then you can go. But, Kailani... this is temporary." Selene outlined the restrictions, and Kailani nodded, knowing better than to argue.

"Thank you, Grand Master." Kailani leaned over to hug Preston, then raced out the door.

. . .

It took longer than she'd wanted not just getting Makani and Roman on board with the plan but figuring out exactly where she was going. She'd called in a lot of favors with friends who worked at the airport in order to learn where John and Benjamin had gone.

John, not surprisingly, had flown back to L.A.

However, Benjamin's private plane had filed flight plans to Seattle.

The problem was, she had no idea where in Seattle he'd be. As far as she knew, the Daras didn't have a family home there, so he was probably at a hotel, which meant she'd either have to call him and ask where he was, and risk him hanging up on her, or hire a PI to figure out where he was while she was in the air.

That was what she'd planned to do...until she realized she'd missed the last direct flight to Seattle.

Kailani had been near panic as she looked at alternate itineraries. For the most part, taking any non-direct flight basically got her there at the same time tomorrow that she'd arrive if she just waited for the first direct flight out tomorrow morning. Resigned to the wait, she went home to pack and plan.

First, she had to figure out where Benjamin was. Now that she had more time, she scrapped the idea of a PI in favor of working the legacy members' gossip chain.

A call to another friend and she had an address. Not of a hotel but of an apartment owned by one of Benjamin's many companies. The mutual friend had crashed there several times and even attended a large party Benjamin threw there not long after that summer in Paris.

Thinking of that summer had given her several ideas, and in the end, Kailani was glad for the evening in her own home to not only rest and figure out what she wanted to say but to pack everything she'd need.

And at six a.m. the next morning, she boarded a plane for Seattle. Once more, she was on her way to find people, but this time something far more important than the fate of the Trinity Masters hung in the balance. Because if she screwed this up, she'd lose her trinity. Forever.

CHAPTER TWENTY-TWO

K ailani stepped out of the taxi, thanking the driver as he pulled her suitcase from the trunk and placed it on the curb for her. She'd packed based on a best-case scenario. Her goal was to fix things with Benjamin, and then, the two of them could travel together to win back John.

Previously, she might have flipped the order, going to John first and leaning on him to help her deal with Benjamin, but John... He had been so angry with them, and rightfully so. It would mean so much more to John if she and Benjamin showed up together.

But first, she had to make things right with Benjamin.

It was probably the most complicated two-part plan in history, but as she crept closer and closer to Seattle, her determination to succeed continued to grow.

Glancing up—and up and up—at the high-rise apartment building, she tried to imagine the view from the top floor, which was apparently where Benjamin resided while in the city. From that incredible height, he no doubt had an amazing view of the Space Needle and Elliott Bay.

A Starbucks across the street caught her eye. If he wasn't home, she'd kill some time there, waiting for him.

With that contingency plan in mind, she walked to the entrance of the building, smiling at the doorman who opened the door for her.

She headed toward the elevator, crossing the large foyer, complete with a front desk and perky clerk who gave her a sunny smile and hello. She was briefly worried she might be stopped by the clerk, but the first eleven floors of the building were actually a boutique hotel, the condos occupying the thirty floors above that.

She'd done a bit of research about the building on the flight from Hawaii, needing the distraction more than the information. It was an impressive—expensive—place, and she couldn't help but wonder what John would say about it if he were here.

Thinking of John produced the same reaction she'd had since waking up yesterday to find him gone. Her heart began to race, her chest grew tight, and she felt the uncharacteristic desire to cry.

Entering the elevator, she pressed the button to the forty-first floor. The button didn't light up—the residential floors required a security code to access. Kailani had half expected this and pulled a thick card out of her purse. It was a well-kept secret in the hotel industry that keycards weren't actually all that secure. After all, the keys need to be quickly and easily replaced since guests tended to lose them. She had a master key that worked in most hotels—and hotel elevators. The other part of the hotel security secret was that one company made ninety percent of the card-reader-style locks, so it was possible to get a master card that worked on multiple properties.

She popped the master keycard into the slot on the elevator, pressed the button again, and the number forty-one lit up. She took a calming breath as the doors slid closed. She had no idea what sort of welcome to expect from Benjamin, but given the way he'd left Hawaii without a word, she was certain he wasn't going to be happy to see her.

Once she reached the top, she stepped off and looked around. There were five penthouses on this floor. Of course, one of the Dara family companies owned the largest, most expensive one.

Bracing herself, she walked to his door and prayed he was home. She'd been psyching herself up for hours, and she wasn't sure she could maintain this level of confidence if she had to wait any longer.

Lifting her hand, she knocked on the door. She thought she heard movement inside the apartment, her gaze flicking between the small security camera on the doorframe and the peephole in the door. Was he in there, looking out at her?

She'd had hours to gird her loins for this confrontation, so she couldn't blame him if he needed to take a moment before facing her.

After about thirty seconds—that felt more like an hour—the door swung open, and there he stood.

Benjamin.

Her Benjamin.

She drew in a breath as she looked at his beloved face, and all the words she'd practiced on the flight vanished.

She'd intended to start with an apology, but instead, when she opened her mouth, what fell out was, "We have a problem."

And because he was Benjamin—her Benjamin—he snorted sarcastically and said, "No shit."

Before she could reply to that, a door opened across the hall. She looked over as an older woman with one of those frou-frou purse dogs stepped out of her apartment.

She turned back to Benjamin, who stepped aside to let her in, his attitude about doing so begrudging at best.

Kailani stepped into the condo but didn't travel more than a few steps inside when he shut the door behind them.

"Hate to break it to you, but you didn't need to travel all this way to state the obvious," Benjamin said, his arms crossed.

Kailani started to retort but decided the best way to make her point was to prove it, not state it. So she reached out, gripped his muscular forearms, and used them to help propel her up on tiptoe.

She caught only a glimpse of Benjamin's startled expression before she pressed her lips against his and kissed him. He didn't return it immediately, but she didn't give a shit. She wasn't stopping until he gave her the response she wanted. The fact he didn't immediately shove her away told her he wasn't as averse to this as he might want to seem.

Kailani didn't have to wait long. Benjamin uncrossed his arms, shaking off her grip so he could wrap his arms around her. His tongue pressed through the seam of her lips, demanding entrance to her mouth as he spun her, pushing her backward, until her back was pressed against the door.

She slipped her arms around his neck, holding him tightly, refusing to let him go. She twisted her head as Benjamin did the same, both of them seeking to deepen the kiss, to devour each other.

This kiss was hard enough to leave bruises, but she didn't care. She needed more. She nipped his lower lip, felt him jolt in pain or shock or both, tasted the metallic tang of blood.

Benjamin didn't call her to task. At least not with words. His hands found their way to her hair. She'd pulled it back into a low ponytail before leaving Hawaii. Benjamin ripped the band out, then took her hair in his hand, twisting it around his fist, tightly, pulling it to tilt her head farther back in yet another attempt to deepen the kiss.

Her scalp stung, but the pain traveled down her body

making its way to her pussy, which was throbbing, pulsating. She whimpered, and Benjamin, the clever, wicked man, knew exactly what was wrong.

He kicked at the inside of her ankles, forcing her legs apart before bending his knee and driving it between. Her hips began to move of their own accord, humping him in an attempt to find some level of relief.

Benjamin had always held the keys to her arousal. One twist in the ignition and within seconds, he had her flying a million miles an hour, out of control.

Maintaining his grip on her hair with one hand, his other traveled down her side until he reached her ass. Adding his strength to her motion, he pressed her pussy tighter against his thigh, which was now moving in tandem with her thrusts.

Through it all, they kissed, their tongues fighting for dominance, their teeth tugging as they swallowed each other's groans and sucked in each other's labored breaths.

She gasped as the angle shifted just enough that her panties were rubbing against her clit, and she gave herself up to the madness. Thrusting harder against him, desperate to reach that—

"Fuck!" Benjamin shoved away from her so quickly, she almost fell. He caught her immediately, his hand on her elbow, steadying her, even as he shook his head.

"Fuck, Kailani," he said again, his voice softer this time, less angry. "What the fuck was that?"

Jesus. She'd meant to prove a point, but that had escalated quickly. So quickly, it was taking her a second to remember why in the hell she'd started that and to figure out why in the hell they couldn't finish.

She took a couple deep breaths, leaning heavily on the door, though Benjamin still held her arm. Even furious, he took care of her.

And she recalled all the things he'd done for her the past few days. Supplying the plane, preparing her coffee just the way she liked it, making sure she had everything she needed to retrieve the keyholders and bring them back to Hawaii. She considered how stressed out she'd been, then realized that anxiety would have been next level without Benjamin—and John—sharing the load. She could have done it all on her own, but it would have been a hell of a lot harder.

"That," she said, once she had her breathing back under control, "is our problem."

He frowned, confused, so she explained.

"We've always been good at the physical aspects of our relationship."

Benjamin might be pissed, but that emotion faded in comparison when stacked next to his arrogance. "Better than good," he corrected.

She resisted the familiar urge to put him in his place because his cocky comment was only helping to prove her point.

"We are amazing together in bed, and until John, I was pretty sure there was nothing we could have done to improve on it."

"God. You're not kidding. The three of us..." Benjamin said.

"Fireworks," she finished. "But this's what I'm saying, Benjamin. We come together and everything else in the world vanishes."

She waited, giving him a chance to shoot yet another smart-ass line back at her, so she was surprised when he nodded. "It does."

"We've always been so good in bed that we let it carry the relationship. It's the other places where we fall apart."

"Other places?" he asked.

"Our communication sucks."

He snorted, and this time, it was driven by amusement rather than anger. "You can say that again."

"There are times when you talk," she said, "that it takes all I have not to rip your throat out."

Benjamin laughed loudly. "Jesus. That's beautiful," he teased. "You should write greeting cards."

"The problem," she said, stressing the words, "is I've been letting my feelings overwhelm me and rather than talk about them, I keep shutting down and walking away."

Benjamin nodded slowly.

She raised one eyebrow at him when he didn't say anything. "And you," she said, pointing her finger at him, driving it into his chest as she spoke each word, "do the same. Damn. Thing."

He gave her a rueful grin. "You're right. I do."

"I was devastated when you broke up with me after Paris, but I didn't tell you that, didn't let you know how much it hurt me. Didn't confront you about the confidential information I thought you shared. Not once in ten long years."

"I wish I'd known. I don't know how I could have fixed things, but I would have tried. I swear to you."

She had trust issues when it came to Benjamin, but right now, she believed every word he said because she knew he was telling her the truth.

"You left Hawaii without saying goodbye." Old Kailani might have tempered those words, spoken them in a "couldn't care less" tone. Or she might not have said them at all.

This Kailani let him see how much his departure hurt.

And for the first time, he cracked open the door to his emotions as well, though she was slightly surprised by what she saw. "You asked Selene to dissolve our trinity, Kailani. What did you expect me to do? Stick around so you could kick me some more?"

"I—" she started, but Benjamin cut her off.

"How else would Selene have known about my request? Are you telling me the counselors briefed her on our fucked-up binding ceremony? That our shit was a priority during a crisis?"

"I told her about your request. On the plane. But, Benjamin, I didn't ask her to dissolve it." She paused, recalling the conversation she and Selene had had on the jet. Selene had pointed out that if one of them became Grand Master, they would have the power to set Kailani's trinity aside. Kailani had actually had that same thought herself, but she'd dismissed it after the night they'd all spent together in Denver.

"I didn't think Selene would dissolve the trinity after becoming the acting Grand Master for the very reasons you just said. The society is at war. I thought she would be too overwhelmed by the fact our leaders and members are going missing and our headquarters is compromised, to give a shit about one unhappy trinity."

"Then why didn't you speak up?" he asked.

"I...should have, but when you didn't say anything, I thought..." She paused. "I didn't realize you thought I'd asked Selene to do that."

No wonder he left.

No wonder he'd looked so...devastated.

Kailani had thought her heart had already broken yesterday, when she woke up and realized both Benjamin and John were gone.

Now...

"God, Benjamin," she said, stepping toward him, placing her hands on his waist, desperate to keep him from walking away again. "I'm so sorry. I didn't ask Selene to dissolve the trinity because that isn't what I want."

He stared at her for just a moment, and she could practically see the wheels spinning in his brain as he tried to decide whether or not to believe her. "You don't want the trinity broken?"

She shook her head. "No. That's why I'm here. I want this, want you and John, but I'm so afraid..." Kailani blinked rapidly, hating the tears suddenly blurring her vision. She wasn't going to cry, wasn't going to use tears, when she asked for his forgiveness.

She took a steadying breath, then forged on. "This is what I mean. We're both too hot-headed, too impatient. We shut down at the first sign of adversity. I let you leave after Paris without telling you how I felt. I lost my shit in Boston, reacting rather than thinking, and then...I left. Without talking to you. When Selene dissolved the trinity, I didn't speak up because I was afraid you didn't want me."

"And instead of sticking around, telling you what I thought, I left. Fuck, Kailani. I'm sorry I didn't stay."

"I don't want to do this anymore. Don't want to keep hurting you."

Benjamin cupped her cheek with one hand, tilting her face up, his thumb stroking away the one traitorous tear that escaped. "I don't want to hurt you anymore either."

"Can you forgive me for the things I said after the binding ceremony? For threatening you and walking away in Boston without giving us a chance?" she asked.

He placed a soft kiss on her forehead. "I can forgive you for that if you can forgive me for the way I ended things after Paris."

"I still don't understand why—" she started.

Benjamin cut her off. "I was in love with you, Kailani."

She frowned. "I...I know. I mean, I loved you too, and at the time, I was sure you loved me." She eyed him. "But when you broke up with me, I questioned it."

"When I say I was in love, I don't just mean sort of in love. Or young love. I knew...I knew when I was twenty-one that what I felt for you was the kind of thing that would never fade."

Kailani's heart clenched.

"I meant what I said on the plane. You were my first love... and I thought that if I didn't break up with you, walk away from you, you'd be my only love."

"What?"

"Kailani, I fell in love with you then, and I'm still in love with you now."

Kailani gasped, her world tilting on its axis.

"If we'd stayed together the way I'd planned—a casual but hot relationship that lasted years—I would have been so irrevocably in love with you, I wouldn't have been able to let you go. I was already thinking about what we'd do. Where we could go, where we could disappear to that the Trinity Masters would never find us."

His words shocked her, but she understood. Remembered feeling the same, remembered her fantasies about them being married, but in her fantasies, it was only ever just the two of them.

"I was so in love with you," she confessed. "It killed me when Theia called and told me you were dating someone just a couple weeks after we split up. It made me think what we'd shared hadn't meant anything to you."

"It meant everything to me. I was desperate to *not* love you, so I did what any twenty-one-year-old guy would do. I tried to fuck you out of my system."

Kailani rolled her eyes. "That's not how you nurse a broken heart."

"Of course it is," he said with the kind of complete authority only Benjamin could manage.

She shook her head, but she was smiling.

His expression softened. "I kept trying to find ways to forget you, but instead, all I found were women who couldn't hold a candle to you."

"That's ridiculous." There was no heat behind her words, just faint shades of the way they used to be, back when they were friends and playfully gave each other shit.

"No, it's not. What did you do?"

"What everyone does," she said. "I ate gallons of ice cream and cried myself to sleep for months."

"That's what everyone does? Did I miss a how-to manual or something?" The joke was so Benjamin, she couldn't help but laugh.

"Why are you such an ass?" she teased.

He gave her a one-shoulder, good-natured shrug. "That's just my personality shining through."

"You really loved me?" she asked again, uncertain why it was so hard to accept those words. Benjamin had certainly proven that fact to her, both now and a decade ago. It was just hard to overcome ten years of feeling...rejected.

"I've never stopped loving you," Benjamin said, opening his arms. She stepped into his embrace, soaking up his warm hug. "That was why I had to walk away."

She sighed, her brain telling her the things her heart had refused to accept all those years ago, too hurt by his desertion and then his betrayal. Now she could see he'd been right to leave. "I know that. I just..."

He released her, placing a soft kiss on her forehead. "Neither of us was free to choose. We're members of the Trinity Masters, legacies with way more than a working knowledge of how the society functions. We both knew back then that we were going to be called to the altar someday and that we would live the rest of our lives with whoever was beneath the robes. I never expected, never even let myself hope, that the Grand Master would place me in a trinity with you."

"You left because you knew the longer we were together, the more it would hurt." Kailani wished her younger self had been that smart, that strong.

"That's what I thought at the time, though I'm not sure walking away helped. It still hurt like fuck. And every time I thought of you, bound to two other people, shit..." He raked his hand over his head. "I was so blinded by jealousy I couldn't see straight."

She shook her head sadly. "All these years...I harbored the hurt instead of thinking it through rationally, like you had."

"I thought you understood why I'd broken things off. Thought you'd see things the way I had, that you would have known our relationship could never be more than a summer fling."

Kailani gave him a crooked grin. "I *should* have known that," she admitted. "But a nineteen-year-old in the throes of first love isn't exactly a logical creature. I led with my heart, and I guess my brain never caught up."

"And afterward, I was desperate to have you back in my life. I wanted my friend back. And when you said no to that..."

"To me, that made it seem like Paris hadn't meant the same thing to you as it had to me. Because I was still heartbroken."

"So was I. But I missed you."

Kailani swallowed against the tears. "I missed you too."

"I'm also sorry about betraying your trust, about my carelessness hurting your family. My actions weren't intentional. Just stupid."

She gave him a kiss on the cheek. "Forgiven," she whispered.

He cupped her face in his large palms, and she saw him— the Benjamin she'd fallen in love with all those years ago. "If I'd been free to choose anyone in the entire world, I would have picked you, Kailani, and..." He paused. "And John."

Kailani was so relieved to hear Benjamin admit not only his feelings for her but for John as well. "I always believed we were enough on our own, but with him, we're so much better."

"So much more," Benjamin added.

This time, she gave up the fight, tears—happy ones— streaming down her cheeks. "Given the choice, I would have chosen you and John too."

Benjamin bent his head, this kiss the polar opposite of their previous one. It was soft, an apology and a promise. One she would never forget.

Kailani wrapped her arms around his waist and felt his erection brush her stomach. She tilted her head back, narrowing her eyes at him.

"It's not my fault. He's missed you," Benjamin joked, adjusting his dick in his pants.

Kailani laughed. "I've missed him too." A few minutes ago, Benjamin had her pushed up against the door, her arousal raging out of control, yet even then she'd known...she wouldn't have let it go all the way. She couldn't. "But—"

"But this isn't just about us anymore," Benjamin interjected, reading her mind.

"It's not."

"We're not a couple. We're a trio."

She smiled sadly, wishing that was true. She didn't tell him about Selene's refusal to reinstate their trinity because it would be a moot point if they couldn't convince John to forgive them, to take them back.

"Where is John?" Benjamin asked.

Just like that, the tears that had been joyful changed to

sorrow and her throat clogged, so that when she answered him, her words sounded thick and rough.

"He was angry when he found out the trinity had been dissolved."

"At Selene?" Benjamin asked, though Kailani could tell he already knew where John's anger lay.

She shook her head. "At us. For not speaking up, for not fighting for our trinity."

Benjamin swallowed heavily, taking the words hard. "I wanted to. I swear to God, I wanted to."

Kailani gripped his hand, squeezing it tightly. "I wanted to say something too. I keep trying to tell myself if I hadn't been so damn tired, maybe...I'd like to hope..."

"We were all exhausted, which I'm sure didn't work in our favor. None of us was operating at one hundred percent. I flew directly here from Hawaii and slept the sleep of the dead for close to ten hours."

"I did the same, but I'm not sure that's a good enough excuse. Not where John is concerned. He was just as tired, yet he knew...he would have done the right thing. Would have swallowed his pride and fought for us."

"He would have. We need John, Kailani," Benjamin said sadly. "I know it's only been a few days, but he's..."

"The part of us that we were missing," she replied. "Do you think he'll forgive us? Throughout all of this, he's been the one always working toward creating something lasting. He never gave up when I'm sure anyone else would have been running—not walking—to the nearest exit to get away from us. We didn't make any of this easy for him. He deserved so much better."

"He did." Benjamin crossed his arms, his gaze focused in the middle distance before it sharpened as he focused on her. "So we're going to make it up to him. Going to find a way to fix all the things we screwed up."

"That's what I was hoping you'd say." Kailani smiled, but doubt crept in. "You really think we can?"

"There's no other choice. We have to get him back, Kailani. There's no us without him."

She smiled, relieved Benjamin felt the same way she did. "I agree."

Benjamin took her hand and led her into his apartment. She was amused when she realized they'd worked out ten years of misery and anger while standing in the foyer by the front door.

She gasped when she looked out the floor-to-ceiling windows of the living room. She'd been right. His view was breathtaking as she looked out across the bright sunshine gleaming off the bay.

He gestured to the couch. She sat down and he joined her, their sides pressed tight. Apparently, she wasn't the only one who felt the need to keep touching him, afraid of him disappearing if she didn't keep him close.

"Despite our behavior the past few days, I think we're both intelligent and creative," Benjamin said, and Kailani caught a gleam in his eye. "Not to mention, we're both filthy rich with unlimited resources."

"You already have a plan," she said. "I have one, or at least the start of one too, but I want to hear your ideas."

He nodded and smiled, rubbing his hands together like some villain out of an old Bond movie. "I have the perfect plan. You and I are going to get our husband back."

CHAPTER TWENTY-THREE

"Wilson."

John looked up at the sound of his name, spotting his captain standing in the open doorway of his office. "Yes, sir?"

"My office. Now." The chief beckoned him with a quick flick of his hand before reentering his office.

John glanced at his computer, sighing heavily at the report he'd started working on an hour earlier. He'd made zero progress on it, the form still empty, except for the case number and date. It wasn't even really his case, which was part of the problem. He was assisting a detective over in automotive, which meant no one was relying solely on him to find justice, so if his attention wandered and his heart wasn't in it...

It was his first day back to work since returning from Hawaii the day before yesterday. As such, he was in work limbo, wrapping up the loose ends he never seemed to find time for when in the thick of a homicide investigation.

All that meant was, he was left with too little to occupy his mind.

Though he couldn't decide if that was a good thing or a bad thing because he was too distracted by...

God.

By them.

He'd never come so close to true happiness, so the fact that it had slipped through his fingers was killing him.

John tried to shut down that line of thinking as he rose and walked to the captain's office.

"Come in and shut the door," Captain Danielson said, in his typically gruff manner, from where he sat behind his desk. If the chief had an organizational scheme for his shit, John couldn't understand it. As it was, the captain's desk was covered with countless untidy piles of paper and books, stacked so high they seemed to defy gravity by not toppling over. There were three dirty coffee mugs, the ceramic stained so dark inside, he wondered if they'd ever been washed properly—with soap— or if the chief just swilled them out with water before refilling them each day.

John closed the door, then dropped down in the chair across from his boss. "Is everything okay?"

"Yeah. It's fine. Listen, I know you just got back from vacation, so I hate to do this to you," Captain Danielson said, "but I just got off the phone with 100 West."

John raised his brows, but inside he was cursing—100 West was the address of LAPD Headquarters, meaning, his captain had just gotten a call from someone higher up the chain of command.

Did this have something to do with the Trinity Masters? Had Selene used her new pull to make something happen? Maybe they were pissed he left, but technically he wasn't even supposed to be there. And the task he'd taken on, handling the robbery, was done. He sure as shit had no personal reason to stay.

"And *they* just got off the phone with Interpol."

"Interpol?" That...wasn't what he'd expected the captain to say.

Captain Danielson pointed at him with a dirty coffee mug. "Exactly."

"Are we getting visitors?" John asked, wondering if Interpol was chasing down someone in L.A. and needed some local help.

"Actually, they are. You're joining a task force."

John blinked. "Interpol is in Europe."

"Technically the U.S. is a member of Interpol."

"Huh. Didn't know that."

"But this *is* about Europe," his captain confirmed.

John shook his head. "I've never even been to Europe."

"You have a passport?"

"Yes."

"Good, because you're going to..." Captain Danielson picked up and then discarded several pieces of paper before finding the one he wanted. "Monaco."

"Monaco?" John usually wasn't the guy who just repeated what he'd been told, but this was seriously unexpected. At least now he knew it had nothing to do with Trinity Masters, since it was in Europe.

"Interpol's NCB in Monaco is coordinating the ask on behalf of the Criminal Investigations Department of Public Security."

"Monaco is requesting something from us?" John asked, wondering what the hell the LAPD could offer that would require him, apparently, playing errand boy.

"Not something. Someone. You."

"Me? Why?"

The chief picked up a retractable pen, clicking it open and closed, open and closed. John had worked for Chief Danielson for six years, so he was accustomed to his boss' annoying habit. It had driven him crazy the first year or so he was here, but now he'd learned to ignore it—mostly.

"Apparently, you closed a case last year, and they think someone in that case is involved in one of their cases, and they want you, in person, to weigh in."

"What case?"

"They won't tell me. As your captain, I demanded to know and was told that the LAPD is happy to do this favor for our friends at Interpol." Captain Danielson grunted. "Meaning, my bosses told me to shut up and not ask questions because they're happy to stick your ass on a plane if it means they can ask Interpol for a favor in the future."

"I'm guessing that means they also aren't willing to email the case files to me so I can look at them from the comfort of my slightly broken chair."

"Damn it, I told you I'll put in a requisition for a new chair."

John grinned. The issue of his chair was, at this point, a comforting routine. As was the way the right arm periodically fell off.

Captain Danielson shook his head. "Whatever this case is, details are sensitive or need to know, but they think you can help."

John leaned back, thinking. As a major crimes detective, he worked both robbery and homicide cases. He doubted this had anything to do with a homicide, but there had been a few robbery cases where he hadn't been satisfied at the time that all players were accounted for. It had to be one of those.

"And I have to go in person." John was seriously sick of planes.

"I tried to get you out of it, but like I said, the LAPD is happy to stick you on a plane in exchange for some goodwill from Interpol. They gave me this number." Again, papers fluttered in a haphazard way that made John's eye twitch. "They want you on a flight today, and this is the travel coordinator's number. Said there's a red-eye tonight that will get you to Monaco the fastest."

"Tonight?" John asked, wondering what the hell the rush was. He hadn't even unpacked his bag from the trip to Hawaii, although that had less to do with a lack of time and more to do with a lack of energy, fueled by depression.

He'd dropped the suitcase onto one of his brand-new, gorgeous armchairs. Looking at the furniture hurt.

"Yeah. I told them that was a quick turnaround, but they insisted. Flight leaves in," the captain looked at his watch, "six hours, so I'm giving you the rest of the day off. Go home and pack and get your ass to the airport. Rush hour will be a bitch, so give yourself plenty of time to get there."

John rose, forcing a grin because his boss would be suspicious as hell if he didn't feign enthusiasm. This was a sweet opportunity for a simple LAPD detective. His captain had no idea just how many damn planes he'd been on in the past four days. "Monaco...maybe I'll go to Monte Carlo, huh? Beats the hell out of working that shooting out of South," he said.

The more he thought about it, this trip felt like it could be the answer to a prayer. Perhaps a change of scenery and a juicy case would keep him distracted enough that he wouldn't spend every single minute of the day and night thinking about Benjamin and Kailani, wondering where they were, what they were doing.

The captain rolled his eyes. "Yeah, yeah. Do me a favor and keep this trip to yourself. If the rest of the guys find out you're flying to Monte Carlo, I'll have a mutiny on my hands, everyone pissed off that you're going instead of them."

"I won't say a word." John was absolutely going to tell

everyone else about it and gloat when he got back. Maybe he'd bring the rest of the squad keychains.

Monaco. Home of Monte Carlo. He was about to travel to his dream location, so he was shocked he wasn't more excited. However, thoughts of Monte Carlo no longer replayed in his mind as a Bond movie. Instead, all he could see were Kailani and Benjamin's amused faces on the jet when he told them about his love of *GoldenEye* and all things James Bond.

"Pack enough for at least a week or two. Interpol said you could be there for a while."

"Okay," he replied with a bit too much of a heavy sigh.

The captain studied his face closely, and John realized he'd let his mask slip, the misery he felt coming out in his tone. As far as his captain knew, he just got back from vacation and should be relaxed and happy.

"Think I'll need a tuxedo? Just in case I need to play super-spy?" John joked, trying to recover.

"I think you can leave the tuxedo at home, Double-O-Seven." His captain was well aware of John's love for the spy. Every time one of the new Bond movies came out, John dragged a bunch of people from the precinct—the captain included—to go see it.

Because he'd reached the ripe old age of thirty-five as a bachelor, he looked forward to the times when he didn't have to do shit alone. As such, he had a weekly Thursday happy hour with a couple other detectives and a standing Monday night dinner date with his next-door neighbors, an older retired couple, whose adult kids all lived in other states.

"Try not to lose a bundle at the craps tables," his captain warned as John headed for the door.

"I'll do my best." John returned to his desk, shutting down his computer and grabbing his stuff, considering it a win that he wasn't dreading the idea of spending another night alone.

He'd never cared much about his house, never thought of it as a home as much as just a place to lay his head at night. But now, thanks to the furniture Benjamin had bought, the place felt almost cozy. And while Kailani and Benjamin spent barely a full hour there, he still felt their presence.

John had always been a loner, which wasn't surprising considering his upbringing, but he'd never really considered himself lonely. Since returning from Hawaii, he realized just how empty his life was.

Benjamin and Kailani had shown him how amazing it was to be with someone. Those hours on Benjamin's private jet, just talking and getting to know each other, had been some of the best moments of his life.

Which was sad as fuck now that he considered it.

He walked to the parking lot, recalling how Kailani had mentioned once that she had trust issues, something he certainly understood.

Compared to Kailani and Benjamin, he was a latecomer to the Trinity Masters, not joining the society until he was twenty-six years old. Up until then, he'd done a fair amount of dating, but he'd never managed to move from casual hookups to committed relationships because he'd never opened himself up, never let himself be vulnerable.

Then the Trinity Masters had recruited him, and he'd felt relieved.

That was the predominant emotion.

Relief.

It felt as if the society had just made things easy for him. They would give him spouses and he could have the family he wanted—one that would always stay—and he didn't have to invest or try or leave himself open for the inevitable pain associated with being rejected...left behind.

For a few weeks after joining, he'd been flying high. Then

he caught sight of an ex—a lovely, sweet woman he'd dated for several months in his early twenties—in the grocery store. She was with her husband and pushing twin toddler boys around in one of those carts that resembled a car, complete with a steering wheel. The couple was laughing at something one of the boys said. She looked so happy, so in love, and he'd thought...*that could have been me.*

He'd gone home and spent hours reevaluating their relationship, recalling all the ways she'd tried to get closer, only to have him push her away time after time.

Then he recalled that relief he'd felt after joining the Trinity Masters, and he had realized he'd never have the family he wanted unless he made some changes. So he'd done the hard thing and made an appointment with a therapist, who'd helped him work through his issues with trust. He had been seeing her for years, proud of the strides he'd made, so when the call to the altar came, he'd felt ready...ready to meet his spouses, to share parts of himself he'd never shown anyone else, to be the type of husband they could rely on and trust.

He'd given them all of that...and it still hadn't been enough.

John reached his car, climbing behind the steering wheel.

Regardless of how it all ended, he missed them.

He missed the hell out of them.

Loneliness had settled over him, enveloped him like a mummy, the feeling suffocating, irritating, miserable.

What made it all worse was neither Benjamin nor Kailani had reached out to him. Part of him had expected—maybe hoped was the better word—that they'd try to contact him, even if it was just to say goodbye.

When they didn't, he'd gotten pissed off all over again.

His initial anger toward them had lasted until he'd boarded the plane in Hawaii. Taking his seat, crammed in the too-tight economy section, the rage faded, morphing to sadness, as he realized he would never see them again.

Not unless he started attending Trinity Masters events, which he knew he wouldn't. The idea of running into them at some gala or meeting, the chance that they might be there with their new trinities, was something he simply couldn't face.

Now, his feelings fluctuated between misery and fury, and he hated it.

Fucking therapy. Figured he'd manage to fix his emotional issues just in time for life to take another goddamn swing at him.

John closed his eyes and strengthened his resolve. He'd go to Monte Carlo and focus all his energy on the case. When he came back to L.A., it would be with a clean slate as he put the past month behind him and moved on.

JOHN STEPPED OFF THE PLANE, following signs to the baggage claim area. He'd been shocked when, after calling the number to book his ticket, the email confirmation showed that Interpol had sprung for a first-class seat. He hadn't been looking forward to the fifteen hours of travel crammed into an economy seat, but he'd been sure there was a mistake. He tried to call back the number, but this time instead of answering on the first ring, he'd gotten voice mail.

When he boarded, he'd been pleasantly surprised to discover no mistake had been made. He'd been set up in one of those comfy pod things, where he'd watched a couple movies, then slept a full eight hours, after which he enjoyed breakfast before landing. Instead of being tired and sore, he was well rested and refreshed when he reached his destination.

It had been bliss, yet he still hadn't managed to stop

comparing the commercial flight to the unsurpassed comfort of Benjamin's private jet.

Jesus. Benjamin had ruined him in just one week, and John felt fairly disgusted with himself for finding first class lacking. It was time to return to real life, one where he was grateful for shit like first class.

He sighed as he glanced outside at the darkening sky. It was going to take him a couple of days to adjust to the time difference because while it was ten a.m. in his head, it was actually seven p.m. here in Nice, France.

Mentally, he made a plan for next steps. He was a little nervous too. The signs in the airport were all in about four different languages, but based on his googling on the plane—first class had Wi-Fi—once he actually got to Monaco, signs would be in French and Monégasque, and while a lot of people spoke English, there were no guarantees.

He'd downloaded a couple translation apps, just in case.

The plan was to grab his suitcase from baggage claim, go through immigration, and then, according to the itinerary he'd been emailed along with the plane ticket, someone would meet him here at the airport to help him get the thirty kilometers from Nice to Monte Carlo. There were taxis and a train, but John was glad someone was going to meet him and point him in the right direction, especially since it was evening here.

Once he got to his hotel, he'd have some free time. The next thing on the itinerary was for him to meet someone in his hotel lobby tomorrow morning, which meant he was on his own tonight, so once he was checked in, he'd head out for a late dinner.

He also hoped to go to Monte Carlo Casino tonight, since he wasn't sure how much time he'd have once he started working the case tomorrow.

He was ridiculously excited to see the actual casino where

GoldenEye was filmed. And while he hadn't packed a tux—mainly because he didn't own one—he had brought a suit and tie, since he assumed Interpol agents were like feds and a suit was part of the uniform. The casino had a dress code, so even if he hadn't wanted the suit to look presentable and professional for work, he would have brought it so he could visit the casino.

He'd spent half an hour on his phone learning how to play baccarat so he could give it a try. He was determined to go all-in on this James Bond adventure, and while the idea of doing it alone rather than sharing it with Kailani and Benjamin, bothered him, he was trying to ignore that emotion.

As he cleared the last doorway in customs, emerging into the bustling airport, he was surprised to see his name on a card held by an honest-to-God chauffeur. The guy was even wearing a hat. John had expected his contact to be someone from the cab company, or maybe an airline employee who would just point him in the right direction.

This looked...fancy.

He approached the driver. "Um, *bonjour.*" Okay, that was all the French he was comfortable with. "I'm John Wilson," he said hesitantly, introducing himself. "But I'm not sure you're here for—"

"Mr. Wilson, yes. I'm here for you. Please, allow me." The chauffeur spoke in elegantly accented English and took his bags before John could protest. "If you'll please follow me?"

"Oh. Okay, great." John didn't even bother to hide his surprise, and he was suddenly thinking perhaps he should consider a career change. Because the LAPD certainly didn't fly cops first class or send fancy drivers to pick them up at the airport.

In fact...it didn't feel like the kind of thing Interpol would do either.

No publicly funded law enforcement agency threw around money like this.

As John fell into step behind the man, his Spidey senses were tingling.

Shit. He'd hopped on that damn plane last night without asking enough, or asking the right questions. Initially, he hadn't been excited about the trip, but then the opportunity to get away had been so appealing, he let himself just follow orders.

His brain hadn't engaged enough to tell him...that this was wrong.

Interpol might be fancier than the police, but he'd worked with feds before, the closest equivalent, and they didn't travel like this.

He should have questioned a bunch of shit before now, but he'd been too grateful for the opportunity to escape his lonely, furniture-filled house. It wasn't out of the realm of possibility that Interpol would request his help, but that they'd fly him first class to his bucket list/dream city...

John was already slowing, eyeing the driver's back, and he pulled up short when the man walked over to a limousine— fuck him, a goddamn limousine—and popped the trunk to put his suitcase inside.

"Hey," John said, trying to stop the man. "Who hired you?"

The driver paused, clearly confused.

"Who hired you?" he asked again.

He had a damn good idea who was behind this, and that suspicion was confirmed when the back door of the limo opened...and Benjamin emerged.

CHAPTER TWENTY-FOUR

"John, welcome to France." Benjamin could almost see John trying to decide if he should grab his bag and the first flight back to the States, so he prayed John's desire to see Monte Carlo would win out. That and the fact it would suck to hop back on another thirteen-hour flight after just getting off one, which he was ready to point out if needed.

"Benjamin..." John looked around the busy airport.

The sounds and smells were just as disgusting as Benjamin remembered from commercial air travel.

"Get in the car, John," he said, stepping toward John on the curb, ready to chase him down if he needed to. John was clearly a flight risk at the moment, evidenced by the way he looked over his shoulder at the airport, then back at his suitcase in the trunk.

"Please," Benjamin said softly.

John shook his head, the reaction less *no*, more *disbelief*. "Fell for it all, didn't I?" he said, more to himself than to Benjamin.

Benjamin grinned. "I was hoping you wouldn't put two and

two together until you were on the plane. There were a lot of points during the plan where I was worried your detective brain would kick in. That's the main reason I made sure there was a sense of urgency. Less time for you to think."

"Who did I talk to on the phone?"

"Someone at one of my travel agencies."

"The first-class ticket should have been a giveaway," John muttered.

"When did you figure it out?"

John clearly didn't want to respond, then he huffed. "When I saw him," he said, pointing at the driver.

Benjamin didn't bother to mask his smile. "Damn, man. That's not good," he joked.

He'd expected anger from John, so he was relieved when the easygoing cop chuckled. "It's fucking terrible. Might need to turn in my badge. How the hell did you convince the LAPD you were Interpol?" John frowned. "Impersonating a law enforcement official. That's...a fairly serious crime."

"Oh, it was Interpol who called the LAPD. I just bribed an official in Monaco to make it happen."

"And that's an even more serious crime." John pressed his hands over his eyes. "Benjamin..."

"Don't worry, I won't get caught, and if I do, I'm rich. I won't go to jail."

"That doesn't make me feel better," John declared in exasperation. Then his expression hardened. "I'm leaving."

"No. You're not," Benjamin said, willing to do whatever it took to get John where they wanted him, needed him, to be.

"Holding my suitcase hostage? Weak play." John turned, starting to stalk back into the terminal.

"If you leave, Interpol will report to LAPD that you refused to assist in their investigation."

"That's blackmail," John snarled, turning back.

Benjamin raised a brow. "Yes. It is."

John's jaw clenched but then he hung his head. "I can't believe I didn't figure this out. My only excuse is...I've been distracted."

Benjamin put a hand on his back, but John twisted away from his touch, stalking to the car angrily.

"You're here so we can talk," Benjamin said. "I don't want to force you to stay, but I will, if that's what it takes."

"You have my phone number," John spat. Benjamin didn't expect this conversation to be easy, but he was determined to see it through. "And you know where I live."

"Yeah," he said shamelessly, "But I thought you might be more inclined to listen in Monte Carlo."

John shook his head, clearly annoyed. "Is this how rich people buy their way out of their fuckups? Instead of flowers or candy, you fly someone first class to some swanky city?"

"Something like that."

"You seriously think that's going to work with me?"

"Not really," but this time when Benjamin put his hand on his back, John let himself be led to the car. Benjamin gestured toward the open door.

"Where are we going?" he asked.

Benjamin winked, hoping to take this from angry blackmail to teasing. "Where do you think, Double-O-Seven?"

John glanced at Benjamin, who was dressed to the nines in a tuxedo, then down at himself. Benjamin had to admit the sexy cop looked damn fine in faded blue jeans and a dark green button-down.

"Even if I did want to play along with whatever this is, I'm not exactly dressed for the spy gig...or the casino," John said.

Benjamin waved him off. "Don't worry about what to wear. It's all been taken care of."

"Of course, it has," John muttered disgustedly, though he

was no longer trying to leave, which Benjamin was calling a win.

Unfortunately, there were still a shit-ton of battles left to wage before he could claim victory in this war.

John stepped off the curb and climbed into the back of the limo.

Benjamin followed him in. The driver slid into his seat and then they pulled away from the curb. John stared out the window, his profile silhouetted by the lights as they left Nice.

Benjamin pointed to the bottle of champagne on ice. "If you're interested in a drink, we can pop the cork on that. Then when we get to the casino, we can order those shaken-not-stirred martinis."

John turned down the offer of champagne. "I know it's evening here, but I've only been awake a few hours. I don't know about martinis for breakfast."

They were getting somewhere. At least John was talking.

"Sleep okay on the flight?" Benjamin asked, feeling slightly stupid for the inane question.

"Like a baby. Not sure if it was because that pod thing was so comfortable or if it was the past few days catching up with me."

"Probably both," he suggested. "I made sure you were on one of our newer planes."

"For fuck's sake, I forgot you own that airline." John shook his head.

"Er...sorry?" Benjamin did his best not to smile. "But I'm glad you slept. I feel like I'm still playing catch-up too. Two whirlwind cross-country trips in as many days with practically no sleep was probably the most insane thing I've ever done."

"Same." John fell silent, though Benjamin knew his thoughts weren't quiet. He kept waiting for John to ask him the hard questions. Like why he was here. Where Kailani was. Why he didn't speak up when Selene dissolved the trinity.

John asked none of them. Which relieved Benjamin, because he didn't want to have those conversations without Kailani present.

But it also bothered him.

John wasn't passive by any means, so the fact he wasn't calling Benjamin out told him just how angry he was.

John gazed out the window. "I've never been to Europe," he confessed.

"During the day, this is a scenic drive."

"I didn't realize you couldn't even fly directly to Monaco."

"As an American, I can assure you, you'll find it shockingly small."

Benjamin waited for the next question. Waited for him to ask about Hawaii, about Kailani. Instead, they spent the thirty-minute drive in awkward silence.

The silence changed from awkward to awed, at least on John's part, when the driver dropped them at the Hotel de Paris.

"Jesus," John murmured in appreciation.

While it was nighttime, the square was overflowing with well-dressed people and the mouthwatering smells from the Michelin-star restaurant Louis XV-Alain Ducasse. It was also humming with the engine sounds of Ferraris, Lamborghinis, Bentleys, and Rolls-Royces.

John was in danger of getting whiplash as his head jerked from side to side, his eyes unable to take it all in fast enough.

The hotel, which was right next to the casino, was illuminated, and even though Benjamin had seen it before, this time he was seeing it through John's eyes and he had to admit...it was truly beautiful.

Benjamin escorted John through the wide lobby, with its

ornate marble floor, stained glass skylight, and sculpted arched ceiling, to their suite. The journey was slow as John's gaze took in everything, remarking more than a few times that he'd never seen anything like it.

The Diamond Princess Grace suite he'd reserved was beyond exceptional, but Benjamin didn't give John time to admire it, instead gently pushing him into one of the bedrooms, where a freshly pressed tuxedo was waiting for him.

John studied the garment, and for a tense moment, Benjamin thought he would refuse. He could blackmail John to stay in Monaco, but he couldn't force him to change into that tux...or force him to listen.

When John slipped into the bathroom, Benjamin heard the shower turn on, so he stepped out onto the balcony, took his phone from his pocket, and sent a quick message. He took a few minutes to enjoy the view of the French Riviera, then he gave into his own desire and slipped back into the bedroom. John emerged from the bathroom with a towel around his waist, and one draped over his head as he scrubbed his hair.

Benjamin leaned against the open doorway, watching.

John hesitated when he pulled the towel off his head and saw him. Benjamin waited, willing to retreat at the first sign John didn't want him there.

Instead, John dropped both towels.

Benjamin's stomach muscles tightened at the sight of all that pretty flesh.

John's face was unreadable as he picked up the pair of black socks and black silk briefs, sliding the latter on.

Benjamin said nothing, watching the way the silky fabric hugged the curves of John's ass.

He'd been right about the suit and shoe size, and while the break of the pants wasn't perfect, John looked delicious in his simple tux. Benjamin finally pushed away from the doorway when it was time for the bow tie.

He took it from John's hand. "May I?"

John hesitated, then nodded.

Benjamin slid it under John's collar, brushing the corner of his jaw and neck as he did. "I would offer to teach you to tie a bow tie," Benjamin said softly.

"Except...you know I don't need to know? Since I'm not exactly a tuxedo person."

"Except, if you knew how to do it, you wouldn't need me to do it for you."

John closed his eyes, his jaw muscle working. "Benjamin," he warned.

The fact that John seemed affected by his presence, his touch, was hopefully a good sign.

"Come on." They were in dangerous territory and the faster they got out of this hotel room, the better.

In a matter of minutes, they were downstairs, and as Benjamin walked out the front doors, the valet hopped out of the silver Aston Martin, passing Benjamin the fob.

John's expression made it all worth it as he slid into the passenger seat.

"Want to drive around the block first?" Benjamin asked.

"How far are we going?"

Benjamin pointed across the square. "There."

"First, is that a castle? And second, it's literally next door. Why are we driving?"

"That's the Monte Carlo Casino. And we're driving because the car makes this fun noise." Benjamin revved the engine.

"Around the block," John breathed, the stiffness in his shoulders relaxing. Benjamin hoped that was an indication that his anger was fading.

Traffic prevented them from doing anything to really appreciate the speed the car was capable of, and after ten minutes, they pulled up in front of the casino, joining the line of high-performance luxury vehicles waiting for the casino valet.

"Did you rent an Aston Martin just so we could drive it for ten minutes?" John asked as they pulled up to the doors.

"Of course not." Benjamin put the car in park. "I bought it."

"You mean you already owned it."

"Nope." They climbed out of the car, Benjamin tipping the valet quietly and handsomely. "I bought it." Benjamin didn't think right now was a good time to say that he'd bought the car for John.

"When?"

"This morning."

They mounted the steps into the casino, passing through the atrium, which was filled with elegant and rich people, though often they were one or the other, not both. At the doorway of the Salle Europe room, a porter approached Benjamin.

"Monsieur Dara, your plaques."

Benjamin accepted the handful of credit-card-sized markers the casino used for higher denominations. "*Merci.*"

With a hand on John's back, they stepped into the most famous of the casino's various rooms. A handful of card tables, as well as a single craps table and a French roulette wheel, were elegantly arranged under the massive chandeliers. The walls and high, curved ceiling were art in and of themselves, with their plasterwork and frescos. A bar on one side of the room had a handful of people perched and leaning. Most of the seating areas, elegant armchairs and couches, were empty. It was early still.

They got drinks—John ordered a Vesper martini—and then Benjamin guided him over to the roulette table. He passed the table manager one plaque from his pocket, accepting a small dish of twenty roulette chips.

They found an open space, near one of the table's croupiers, and Benjamin set down his container of chips.

"What do you think of the casino?" he asked as he plucked up two chips, placing an outside bet on red with a nod to the croupier.

"This is amazing." John was watching the wheel, the people. A French roulette table was like a dance.

The ball dropped, and it bounced along the wheel before landing on black. There was a flurry of activity, and a croupier collected Benjamin's chips. For the next round, Benjamin put another couple down on red, then added two more chips to "*impair*."

"You're betting on odd?" John asked, reading the English word for "odd" printed in small type below *impair*.

"Three is an odd number." Benjamin looked at him. "And it's my lucky number." He gestured to the table, to the red square with the number three in it.

"And on a roulette board, it's red, which is why you're betting on red." John took a sip of his martini.

He looked good doing it.

Unable to resist, Benjamin grabbed John's hip, tugging him close. John's eyes narrowed briefly, but he didn't pull away. Then he looked around. "Are we okay..."

"It's safe to be openly bisexual or gay in Monaco," Benjamin assured him.

"Black twenty-four," one croupier said, repeating it in both French and English, before announcing the winners of the various other bets. Someone had placed a column bet and was paid out with much cheering from the players. Benjamin took

John's glass so he could clap, as the croupiers used their rakes to collect the rest of the chips.

"Maybe...maybe three isn't a good bet. At least not this three." John's gaze was on the glass he'd taken back, his refusal to look at Benjamin almost painful.

Benjamin took a stack of five chips and looked at the croupier. "Straight up on three," he said in French, before reaching over and placing the chips on the number. "I'm willing to gamble." He slid his hand up John's back under the tux jacket.

"Really? Because historically, it's not going to be a winner."

A few new people had joined the table, and the ball hadn't dropped, so Benjamin plucked more chips off the stack, then held his hand up to John's mouth. "Blow."

John's lips quirked, but he blew on the chips. Benjamin reached over, adding them to the stack on three. As he straightened, John caught his arm.

"Benjamin, how much are those chips worth?"

Benjamin watched, waited for the ball to drop, meaning it was too late to get the chips back, before saying, "Five hundred euro."

"Each?!"

He took a plaque from his pocket, holding it up for John to see. The elegant marker said *Societe Des Bains De Mer* across the top—the company that owned Monte Carlo Casino as well as several others—and €10,000 embossed across the middle.

"I traded this in for twenty roulette chips," he said.

"You have ten chips on red three." John was tucked up against him, gripping his shoulder so hard Benjamin had to force himself not to wince. "You bet five thousand dollars—"

"Euro."

"Euro, on three."

"And I'll do it again."

The ball bounced to a stop. Black six.

"You just lost all that money," John breathed.

"Three black in a row. I should have been betting on black," Benjamin mused.

He only had four chips left, but when he reached for them, John stopped him.

"Benjamin, don't waste your money."

Benjamin met his gaze. "This bet isn't a waste."

John's gaze softened, but there was a sadness to the set of his mouth that said he wasn't there yet. That was fine. This was just the prelude. Benjamin's phone buzzed in his pocket.

"I can't believe you have enough money to just throw it away."

"We," Benjamin corrected.

"What?"

"*We* have enough money." He picked up the remaining chips and put them in John's hand. "Here."

"I am not betting your money."

"Our money." Benjamin shifted, so he was slightly behind John. "Come on, you know you want to."

"This is two thousand euro."

Benjamin gripped his hips. "Sure you don't want to play?"

John pressed back against him, just a little, nothing raunchy. "Not this game."

"Okay, then come on." Benjamin led him to the table manager, where they traded in the remaining roulette chips for a two thousand euro plaque. Benjamin slid it, plus one of the ten thousand denomination ones, into John's pocket.

"Penny slots," John said, somewhat desperately. "I'll play those."

"Absolutely not." Benjamin guided John back through the series of salons to the atrium. "Besides, there's someone I want you to meet."

Benjamin guided him nearly to the front doors, before grabbing his shoulder and forcing him to turn. The atrium entrance was a study in hand-carved warm wood columns with ornate designs. The center was two stories tall, with second-floor balconies that looked down onto the marble floor.

"What are we..." John's words trailed off as he took in a sharp breath. It was appropriate. She was breathtaking.

Kailani wore an azure-blue dress. The shimmery material flowed down from one shoulder, hugging her breasts, waist, and hips before flaring at the bottom in soft layers that seemed to float around her even when she stopped walking, one hand on the railing as she looked down at them. Her hair was pulled back on the left with a sapphire and diamond clip in the shape of a flower, and a heavy sapphire bracelet hung on one wrist.

"I was afraid she wasn't here," John murmured.

Benjamin once more put his hand on John's back. "That's the woman I want you to meet."

John looked over, one brow raised.

"Come on," Benjamin said, ignoring the questioning look. "I'll introduce you."

CHAPTER TWENTY-FIVE

She beat them to the Salle Blanche, which was on the first floor at the opposite end of the building. The plan was for her to meet them at the bar inside. The bar itself was beautiful—curved and tiled in turquoise, blue, and gold, with a glass top—but her face felt hot from nerves, so she slipped out onto the Salle Blanche Terrace. A few French roulette tables had a scattering of patrons, but a glass half wall divided the gambling space from a narrow strip of the terrace meant for nothing but enjoying the view.

The water was black, except for the lights reflected off the shorelines. Against that blackness, the glittering city of Monte Carlo hugged the shore, bright and golden.

She felt them coming, knew they were there with some sixth sense. The clack of roulette balls and murmur of conversation covered the sound of their steps until they were right behind her, but Kailani didn't jump, wasn't surprised when Benjamin's hand landed on her shoulder.

"Kailani."

She turned, stupidly nervous. "Benjamin." For a second,

she couldn't look at either of them, so she studied the casino tables, the chandeliers that hung over each of them, despite the outdoor setting.

"There's someone I'd like you to meet."

She met Benjamin's gaze, and it grounded her. He was there, solid and capable. Yes, high-handed and controlling, but he was there, and with him at her side, she could do this. They would do this. They would seduce their third and fix this trinity, and...

And damn, John looked good in the tux. The slightly wary expression on his face was also attractive, the suspicion in the way he looked at her unexpectedly arousing.

This was supposed to be a restart that would lead to an honest, unhurried conversation. But as Kailani stood there, her blood heated with a visceral desire. No, not desire...need.

"This is John Wilson," Benjamin said.

"John." Kailani held out her hand. "It's nice to meet you."

"Kailani Iona," Benjamin said as John took her hand. "Her family and mine have some...history."

"It's nice to meet you." John took her hand in a fast, brief shake.

Shit.

Kailani looked at Benjamin. The last text she'd gotten said John was pissed, but she'd hoped he'd have softened up by this point.

"What do you mean history?" John said, the question almost accusatory.

"You need another drink," Benjamin declared.

Kailani looked at Benjamin, who tipped his head, eyeing her meaningfully. It appeared that things weren't going well so they were going to fall back on one of their many backup plans, the first of which was to ply John with expensive booze.

John turned away from them to look out at the sea.

Benjamin shot Kailani another telling look, then flagged down a porter. Kailani turned so she too was looking at the ocean.

"It's a beautiful view," she said softly.

"It is."

Conversation moved on to mundane things as Kailani asked John about his flight.

Benjamin passed her two glasses, and Kailani handed John the martini. She took a small sip of her own beverage.

The three of them literally discussed the damn weather as John finished his martini, and Benjamin ordered him another.

The conversation faded, but the silence was more comfortable than it had been.

"Would you like to play?" Benjamin asked, gesturing to the roulette table at the far end of the terrace, which was empty, a velvet rope sectioning it off.

"With pennies, sure," John said with a slight smile.

Kailani moved down the terrace, and to her relief, John followed, Benjamin bringing up the rear. "Pennies?"

"Earlier, your...friend...Benjamin lost five thousand euro on red three."

"A straight-up bet is no way to play roulette," she said, stepping through one of the openings in the glass wall. The croupier spotted Benjamin and opened the velvet rope for them to pass through. This French roulette table was smaller than the ones inside, and lower, so players didn't have to stand. Kailani sat as Benjamin held her chair. Since he was bent over her, and John was occupied ordering another drink from the server who'd appeared at their table, she twisted to look at him.

"I don't think our plan is going to work," she breathed.

"No," he agreed. "He's about to be too drunk to have a serious conversation about our relationship."

"Sex?" she asked quietly.

"If we cut him off when necessary. Don't want to take advantage of him."

"I was thinking the same thing."

Benjamin slid his hand under the back of her hair, caressing the nape of her neck. Kailani shivered.

Then Benjamin went to talk to the croupier.

"So, Kailani," John said, the martinis relaxing him enough that he was still willing to play along. "Where are you from?"

"Oahu, Hawaii. My family has a hotel there that we've run for generations."

"Do you work for the hotel?"

"I do." Kailani took a few minutes to talk about herself, before asking John about himself. A smile flirted with the corners of his mouth as they chatted. She asked what he'd studied in school and told him about her advocacy work that she did in addition to running the hotel.

Benjamin dropped into his seat, and it took a few moments for them to get organized—each of them trading in their plaques for roulette chips, each of which was a different color to make it easy to distinguish different players' tokens.

They chose one-euro denomination for the chips, at John's insistence, so it took a minute for the croupier to make the necessary change from the ten thousand plaques Kailani and Benjamin handed in. John exchanged a two-thousand-euro card.

After that, they ordered drinks—Benjamin ordering each of them a mixed drink—before finally placing their first chips.

"Not a fan of gambling?" Kailani asked John after watching him hesitantly place one chip.

"I've never had enough money to gamble with." John studied the stacks of chips in front of him. "Having me here is probably ruining your fun. I can't exactly play in your leagues." He held up the one-euro token, then pointed at the stack of plaques Kailani had left on the table. Thirty thousand euro sitting casually at her elbow. She was well off, but this was mostly Benjamin's money because hotels didn't generate cash the way some of the Dara family businesses did.

"The amount of money you risk is just a way of making the outcome matter. Raising the stakes. But there are other ways to do that." Benjamin looked like an ad for some expensive perfume, lounging at the table, one hand flipping a chip between his fingers.

"You mean other things to gamble with," John said.

"Exactly."

"Like?" John looked at them suspiciously, and it was clear he was asking what the rules of this game were.

"Information is a good one," Benjamin said quietly as the croupier's rake picked up their chips. "Whoever wins the most, or loses the least, on this next roll gets to ask for a piece of information. Five-euro bet."

"How about one euro?" John grumbled, but counted out five chips.

"*Orphelins*," Kailani said, setting down five chips. The croupier caught them with the rake, then placed them on the appropriate spaces and borders for the "orphan" numbers.

"Hold on." John scooted his chair closer to her, studying the board. "What did you just do?"

Kailani was far from an expert, but she did her best to explain call bets in French roulette. She liked this, sitting next to him, playing a game. John nodded, but ended up hesitantly placing three chips on black, and two on *pair*—even.

"That's simply rude," Benjamin said.

"Ha," John replied.

"He's betting the opposite of what I did downstairs with my outside bets," Benjamin explained.

John's simple strategy won when the ball landed on ten black.

"You win," Benjamin said. "What do you want to know?"

John took a sip of his drink, considering. "You said your families are adversaries...so why are you two here together?"

Kailani took a long swallow of her pleasantly icy champagne before answering. "Benjamin and I had a relationship when we were young."

"And you're trying to get back together?"

"No. We realize the two of us...don't work."

John's mouth tightened. "You want a therapist. A mediator. Someone to be a bridge."

Kailani shared a look with Benjamin, who shook his head before addressing John. "No. I want, *we* want, the same thing anyone else wants."

"And what's that?"

Benjamin sat back. "We should place our next bets."

John's jaw muscle flexed. "Fine."

She won that time, the *orphelins* bet that she'd made again paying off, thanks to seventeen black. It was her turn to collect her "winnings," but she turned back to Benjamin. "You didn't finish paying your debt. Finish answering."

"What I want?" Benjamin let out a little huff of air. He sat forward. "To be loved."

Kailani's breath caught, the simple statement heavy and honest.

"And have someone to give love to in return. Us." He gestured between himself and Kailani. "We were close to having that. Maybe as close as most people get, but it wasn't close enough." Benjamin's eyes met hers, but he spoke to John. "I will always love her. I fell for her when I was twenty-one, and despite trying to fuck her out of my system, I'll love Kailani until the day I die."

She rolled her eyes. "Yes, breaking up with someone then fucking other people is exactly how you show love."

"It is when you know that love is a really bad idea."

"No, it's not." Kailani took a breath, reminding herself they'd already had this conversation/fight; they didn't need to have it again.

"Sounds like you just need some counseling, and then you'll be perfect for each other," John said, voice hard.

Crap, this wasn't going the way she wanted.

"I know we've just met," Kailani said. "But I'm not normally so...defensive."

"How are you, normally?" John asked.

"I like to think I'm smart. Kind. Maybe a little ruthless when it comes to protecting my family."

"A little," Benjamin snorted.

"Loyal," she said with a bite, eyeing Benjamin.

"You are all those things," John said softly.

They played again, then once more, in silence. Kailani won again once, and then Benjamin won big the last time.

John shook his head, looking at the wheel. "It landed on red three."

"Told you it was a good bet."

"I think Kailani still has some winnings to collect, before you get yours."

"Okay, you go, Kailani," Benjamin said. "What do you want to know?"

She licked her lips, looking from John to Benjamin. "I want to know about you two."

"Us?" John blinked. "What about us?"

"I wanted to fuck him back at the hotel when he was changing," Benjamin said softly. "But we would have been late."

"You're dating?" Kailani asked.

"I did just buy him a car," Benjamin said.

"What?!" John's eyes were round. "That's not my car."

"It is," Benjamin assured him.

"You can't buy people... I don't even know why I'm bothering to say this."

"Are you seriously bribing him to love you?" Kailani meant it to be teasing, but it came out too serious.

"If that's what it takes."

"That's not how love works," John said.

"Fine. Maybe not." Benjamin grinned, and damn he had a sexy, good smile. "But you like the car."

John pointed at him with a chip. "I'll fuck you for the car. Fuck you, not love you. Gotta have a line."

"Hmm, sex for a car, that's a fun game. Can I watch?" Again, she tried for teasing, but it came out serious.

"You want to watch Benjamin and me together?" John asked. He was close enough that, below the table, his knee brushed hers.

"Yes. I want to see who'd be on top." Kailani's libido was screaming at her to drag these two into a closet.

"I don't think you're in a position to demand anything, since you're out of money," Benjamin said.

"What?" Kailani looked down to see the table in front of her empty. She'd had plenty of chips...

"You stole my chips," she said softly, not wanting to accidentally cause an incident in the casino. They wouldn't like her explanation that Benjamin was just playing around. She smiled at their croupier, to whom Benjamin must have paid a fortune for him to both ignore what they were saying and to allow them to pause this much. He had a bland "I'm not even here, I certainly can't hear you" expression on his face.

Benjamin looked down at the stacks of two clearly different-colored chips in front of him. "Hmm, nope, both mine. But I'll loan you money."

"Oh?"

"Not a loan," John said. "How about you just pay her for services rendered...or to be rendered."

They both looked over at John, who was clearly feeling the drinks.

"You two started it," he muttered.

Benjamin selected five of her chips, holding them out to her. "Want these?"

"Depends. What do I have to do to get them?"

"You're going to let my boyfriend put a plug in your ass."

Kailani choked on air.

"Subtle," John told Benjamin. "You're just so subtle."

"Do you want subtle?" Benjamin leaned forward. "Or, do you want to take her to a private room, bend her over a craps table, pull up that sexy dress of hers, and fuck her pretty ass with a plug?"

Kailani had her legs crossed at the ankle, but now she went to cross them at the knee, wanting to squeeze her thighs together. Benjamin grabbed her knee, stopping her.

"Then," he murmured to John, "push her dress back down and take her around the casino, making her walk, knowing with every step she's got that plug in her ass."

"Benjamin," she breathed in warning. "Tonight isn't about me."

"What is it about?" John asked, his hand on her chin forcing her to face him. With Benjamin's hand still on her knee under the table, she was pulled between them.

"You," she said. It was time to stop pretending that they didn't know one another. "It's about trying to win you back, starting with a redo of our first-time meeting. The woman I've been when I'm around you...it's not who I am. Not who I can be."

"I don't know about all that," John said after a moment, studying her face.

Kailani's stomach fell. It was too late. They'd fucked up too badly, and John wouldn't come back. Beside her, Benjamin stiffened.

"But maybe," John said, "that's because all I can think about is getting my hands on the two of you."

Kailani exhaled. They needed to talk, but maybe they needed to touch one another, reconnect, more.

John leaned in, brushing his lips against the corner of her mouth. It was fleeting, not enough, and then he sat back.

"Do you want these chips?" Benjamin jiggled them in his cupped fingers, mocking her.

Kailani raised her chin. "Yes."

"You remember the price?"

"I do." She took the chips. "Safe bet, since I doubt you have a plug and lube in your tux pocket."

"I don't," he conceded. "The toys are in a briefcase in the car."

She and John both stared at Benjamin.

"Is he joking?" John asked.

"I can't tell."

"You should be able to tell. He's your ex."

"Well, he's your boyfriend," she shot back, with the same teasing tone.

"Place your bets," Benjamin said.

Kailani lost all five chips with one drop of the roulette ball.

"Want more?" Benjamin asked, holding up her chips.

"Yes."

Benjamin passed the stack to John. "You'll have to ask him what you can do to earn them."

John looked down at the chips in his hand. "Normally, I'd say I'm a good person."

"Fuck being a good person," Benjamin said.

"A shocking opinion from you, really." Kailani just barely stopped herself from rolling her eyes.

"I don't care if other people think I'm a good person. What matters is protecting and providing for the people you love."

"Providing for someone doesn't have to mean this..." John gestured at their night-dark view of the Mediterranean.

"True, but if you can, why not?"

Kailani put a hand on John's arm. "Why are you doubting you're a good person?"

"Because of the things I want to make you do, in order to earn these."

Kailani's body throbbed with arousal. "I'll say no, if I don't want to do them. You're not forcing me."

John looked pointedly at the croupier. Benjamin asked in French for him to get them some water. The man didn't leave the table, he couldn't, but he shifted as far away as possible, leaning back against the glass wall and waving to a server.

John set down a stack of chips. "For these, you have to fuck Benjamin. I want to see what happens. If you two are as... aggressive...with one another *in* bed as you can be out of bed."

He wanted to watch them hate fuck. Okay, then.

John carefully selected and stacked up a second set of chips. "These? I want you on your knees. Naked. Maybe plugged. Maybe hands tied behind your back. While Benjamin and I take turns fucking your mouth." He added one more chip to the stack. "And you have to swallow."

Kailani's gaze met John's, her breathing shallow, her hard nipples rubbing against the fabric lining of the dress with each inhale.

"Damn, man..." Benjamin was eyeing John. "Where were you hiding this?"

"Should I stop?" John asked softly.

"No," Kailani and Benjamin said at the same time.

"These?" John put a final stack of chips on the table. "You accept your punishment."

Kailani swallowed hard.

"Punishment for being so damned stubborn...and for not fighting for us."

Kailani looked down at her hands, shame mixing with arousal. But she cleared her throat. "I wasn't the only one who stayed silent."

John half rose, then grabbed a stack of Benjamin's chips. Benjamin grabbed his arm, and for a moment they stayed that way, both tense, gazes locked. Then Benjamin slowly let go. John set Benjamin's chips down in the middle of the table.

"Want these back?" John tapped the top of the stack.

"Yes," Benjamin growled.

"Same deal as her. You accept your punishment."

Kailani looked at Benjamin. She knew he was wondering the same thing she was—how would John punish them?

Benjamin cleared his throat and sat forward. "I think it's time to cash in our chips."

CHAPTER TWENTY-SIX

"Your car, sir."

"I won't be staying. Leave her here." The tuxedo-clad detective/secret agent opened the trunk of the sleek silver sports car. A quick check to make sure no one was watching, and then he reached into the trunk. The item he needed was still in its case, but he slipped it out of the package and into his pocket, along with a small liquid-filled packet.

Tense music kept time with his footsteps as he returned to the casino. A guard at the door eyed him, but the detective/secret agent walked in like he had every right to be there. Walked like he had a license to kill.

The second floor was quieter, the sounds of the casino floating up, but muted the deeper he went into the sprawling building. He knew a private spot, where no one would hear them. As long as his associate had managed to get their target into place.

A dark-haired Asian woman stood in a dim side hall, a glass of champagne in her hand. Across from her, leaning casually against the wall, was a tall black man in an immaculate tuxedo.

He looked up, and the detective/secret agent patted his pocket. That was their signal. Without moving, the man reached to the side, turning a doorknob and thrusting the door open. The woman turned, peering into the open door.

That was all the detective/secret agent needed. He didn't stop, didn't pause. His hand slipped around her waist and he whirled her into the room. Behind them, the other man slid into the room, carefully, quietly, closing the door.

"What do you want?" she demanded.

The detective/secret agent took the glass from her hand, passing it back to the other man. "The same thing you do." He grabbed her hip and jerked her forward. Their lips met in a brutal, heated kiss.

The kiss ended, and the woman breathed a name. "John."

A SECOND TOO LATE, Kailani realized she'd broken the game by using his name. The spy-movie-esque setup had been Benjamin's idea. John's delighted smile had made her all too willing to play along. Tonight was all about being a different, maybe better, version of themselves.

John's hands slid down her hips to her thighs. He curled his fingers, bunching up her skirt.

"Do you actually have..." she asked.

"Why don't you check?" John said.

Kailani put her palms on his chest, felt the lump under one hand. John grabbed another handful of skirt.

Another hand brushed over her bare shoulder, and Kailani turned her head to look at Benjamin. He half sat on the game table in the center of the room. It was long enough to serve as either a craps or French Roulette table, but right now the top was unmarked tan felt.

John made an impatient sound as he released the handfuls

of fabric, only to stoop and catch the hem of her dress. He yanked it up around her hips. Kailani gasped as cool air touched her thighs. She was wearing a black lace thong, which instantly chilled, thanks to the fact that their conversation at the roulette table had made her wet enough to soak the fabric.

John's hands went to her legs, skin on skin, her skirts pooled on his forearms.

"I'm going to bend you over that table. Benjamin is going to hold you down and then I'm going to play with you before sliding a plug into your ass."

The words weren't quite a question, but she moaned a quiet, "Yes, please."

John's hands slid to her ass. She knew what he wanted, and Kailani hopped as he lifted her. Her legs went around his hips, his hands under her bare ass cheeks, and he carried her over to the game table.

Just before he set her down, Kailani gasped, "The table."

Benjamin seemed to know what she meant because he slid off his jacket, laying it down lining-side up on the edge of the table.

John set her down, her body sliding against his chest. She kept her arms around his neck until Benjamin took her wrists, tugging them away from John. She wasn't sure what he was doing as he reached into John's jacket. She had a momentary flash of a clear glass toy, before Benjamin, now in his shirt sleeves, headed for the small wet bar in the corner.

John's thumbs stroked the inside of her knees as he spread her thighs apart. Then his fingers were at her core, pressing the damp fabric of her thong between her pussy lips as he explored her sex. She arched her back, throat working, as his fingers grazed her clit. Even with the sensation-dampening barrier of fabric, the touch was electric. Their words, hell, their very presence had her desperate and needy.

Behind her, there were the sounds of Benjamin washing the toy. How very Benjamin-like to always be thinking of the details, to take care of them.

John's lips brushed her cheek, her ear. "Do you think I should let you come now?"

"Let me?" Kailani tried to make it a challenge, but it sounded more like a plea.

"Let you," he confirmed. "You don't get to come unless I say so. And if you're thinking of playing with yourself, just remember..." He straightened, adjusting her skirts to make sure her pussy was visible to Benjamin, who walked up beside them. "There's two of us, and one of you."

Benjamin was watching him with a hungry expression. He handed the now-washed plug back to John, who accepted it, examined it.

"Flip her over," he ordered.

Benjamin didn't hesitate. He yanked Kailani off the table and spun her around. Kailani's skirt fell to cover her legs as she reached out, ready to brace herself. Benjamin's hand between her shoulder blades forced her to bend over the table. She shivered in arousal and just a hint of, if not exactly fear, nervousness. She trusted these men, both together and separately, but that didn't change the fact that some deep survival instinct was desperately pointing out that they could, and would, easily control her body.

She reminded that instinct that they would both stop the instant she said anything, and that this pseudo helplessness was hot as fuck.

Kailani braced her hands on Benjamin's jacket, the satin smooth and slick under her palms.

But that wasn't enough. He kept up the pressure between her shoulders until she dropped onto her elbows.

"All the way," Benjamin commanded, voice dark and rough.

Kailani shifted her weight from foot to foot, thighs rubbing against one another, as she lowered her upper body. Her cheek lay against fabric that smelled like Benjamin, her arms tucked in against her sides, palms under her shoulders. Her ass was in the air, the heels she wore adding height so she was bent at an acute angle.

John's palms skimmed up the backs of her legs, taking her skirt with it, until once more, she felt cold against her thighs and arousal-dampened panties.

"Look at her." John's voice was low and husky.

"Oh I am." Benjamin perched a hip on the table beside her and leaned over to look. Kailani could see him examining her out of the corner of her eye.

"Is she wet?" Benjamin asked.

"Very." John's fingers skittered over her wet thong. He paused, and then he made another pass, and this time it felt like he deliberately forced the fabric between her labia, molding it over her clit.

"Very pretty," Benjamin murmured.

Kailani wasn't sure whose hands were whose. Maybe if she hadn't been panting with arousal, she would have been able to tell, but as it was, she was nearly overwhelmed with sensation as fingers played with her pussy lips—now splayed on either side of the thong—and stroked her ass.

"But not what we're here for. Hold her thong out of the way."

Fingers hooked the back of her underwear, pulling it to the side where it made a tight line across one butt cheek. The tension pulled the fabric harder against her clit and she rocked forward.

"Spread her ass for me."

Benjamin leaned over her, his side braced against her waist as he palmed her butt cheeks and spread them. Cool air kissed her anus, and twin threads of embarrassment and need slithered through her.

"Fuck, that's hot." John's words dissipated her embarrassment.

Kailani tried to look back over her shoulder, but the bulk of Benjamin's body blocked her view. Instead, she heard a small ripping sound.

"I grabbed one of the sample lubes," John said, probably for her benefit. "But don't worry, Benjamin got a big bottle. For later."

Thick gel dropped into the crack of her ass. It was warm, probably from being in John's pocket, and it felt good as it slid down her rear entrance.

Kailani wasn't sure what she expected next. More playing maybe, his fingers to tease her.

Instead, the cool tip of the glass plug rubbed through the lube, spreading it. John centered the toy on her puckered anus, and Kailani instinctively clenched.

"No," Benjamin scolded. "You know better than that. Relax your ass."

Kailani did, and then the plug breached, opening her. She gasped as John applied pressure. She leaned forward, legs tense as she stood on her toes.

"You can take it," John soothed.

At the same time, Benjamin pinched her ass, his voice sharp. "No. Don't fight it."

Her two men, so very different from one another, but together? Perfect.

She was stretched to the point it started to hurt, to burn in that sweet, dark way, and then it was in. Kailani's muscles spasmed as they tightened down around the neck of the plug.

"It's thick," she whispered.

"This isn't a long-wear style," Benjamin said. "It's for anal training, to make anal sex easier."

"How does it feel?" John was stroking her ass and thighs.

"Big. Full."

"Good." His fingers pressed down on her clit for a moment, grinding it against her pubic bone. Unexpected bolts of sensation shot through her, and she hissed out a breath.

Benjamin released her ass cheeks, letting them close on the plug. One of them—she thought it was John—moved her thong back into place. Her dress was smoothed down her legs, and then strong arms helped her up. Kailani wobbled for a second on her heels before finding her balance. Benjamin slipped his jacket on, while John kept his arm around her waist, steadying her.

"You know," John said. "We could walk over to the hotel."

Kailani turned wide eyes on him. "I'm going to have a hard enough time walking to the car."

"Who said we're going to the car?" Benjamin took a few plaques from his pocket. "I still have money to spend."

"You cannot be serious," she hissed.

"Why wouldn't I be?" Benjamin's hand slid down her ass, and he gently pushed against the base of the plug.

Kailani moaned in need, aware that now not only were her panties soaked, her thighs were slick. "I need you, both of you, inside me."

"If I remember correctly, John's first...service...was you on your knees." Benjamin tucked his hands into his pockets, casual and elegant. "We could take care of that here." He gestured to the empty room.

"No," John said. "I want us near a bed."

Benjamin inclined his head.

John released her waist, offering his arm. "May I escort you?"

Benjamin passed back her forgotten glass of champagne. Kailani finished it in one long swallow then nodded, and, arm-in-arm with John, walked out into the casino, the plug shifting with each step.

BY THE TIME they'd walked back to the hotel and reached the suite, Kailani was frantic with need. The well-lubed plug had come perilously close to slipping out several times. At her frantic whispers, Benjamin had tucked in close behind her, pressing the base of the plug to shove it back into place as his and John's bodies hid what was happening.

Worry about the damn toy in her ass had muted some of her arousal, but when Benjamin opened the suite door, gesturing for them to precede him, desire roared back full force.

Before the door had fully closed, Kailani pressed John against the closest wall and kissed him. She felt him smile against her lips, and she wanted to growl at him. But then his lips parted, his tongue touched hers, and all she could think about was what would come next. Him naked. Her naked. Benjamin naked.

It was Benjamin who pulled her away from John. His arms banded across her middle, imprisoning her.

"Our wife is feeling needy," Benjamin said.

The word *wife* made her heart leap even as her pussy pulsed, even as Kailani tensed, worried how John would react to the word.

"Shall we give her what she needs?" Benjamin grabbed Kailani's hair, forcing her to arch back, as if he were offering her to John.

Please, please, Kailani thought. *Please, John.*

John had a strange expression on his face. Then he shook his head. "No. I want what those chips earned me."

"You want to watch me fuck Benjamin." Kailani would have preferred both of them.

The "wife" comment had been too much. He still wasn't there yet. Hopefully they hadn't ruined the momentum. She was worried about fucking Benjamin, about it being just the two of them after John's comments about how all they needed was a therapist.

Maybe she could convince John to join in once they were naked.

"Yes," John said. "But I don't just want you two to fuck. I want to see what it's like, when it's just the two of you."

Benjamin's arms dropped from around her waist, releasing her own arms.

Kailani wanted to ask John why. Wanted to beg him to come to bed with them. This situation felt so dangerous.

"Plug in or plug out?" Benjamin asked.

John pursed his lips but walked away. They followed him through the suite into a large bedroom, the bed massive and inviting. John turned. "Let's say the two of you met up here, in Monte Carlo, and decided to sleep together. How would that have gone down?"

"It wouldn't," Benjamin said simply. "Kailani would have thrown a fit—"

"Fuck you," she yelped, stung by Benjamin's words.

Benjamin grimaced. "I didn't mean it like that. You wouldn't have stayed in a room with me long enough for us to get to the point of a possible hate fuck."

"Is that what it would be?" John asked. "A hate fuck?"

Benjamin's gaze slid down Kailani. She wanted to kiss him and slap him and kiss him again. John was wrong. Because she and Benjamin, as a duo, were no good. Not just because of their past but because of who they were now.

Kailani turned and stalked into the bathroom. To her surprise, John followed her in.

"He can be an ass," he said.

Kailani eyed him, wondering why John was apologizing for Benjamin. "I want you to know that there's no way in hell I'd have been willing to...play...with him. I wouldn't have agreed to being plugged in a public place for him."

"He's the one who suggested it," John said mildly.

"But you were there. You...you're why I agreed to it."

John inclined his head as he walked up behind her, their gazes connected in the mirror. "Then how about I take the plug out?"

Kailani nodded, her body once more, heavy with need.

John kissed her bare shoulder, a tender touch, but then his words were a hard command. "Bend over the sink."

Kailani bent, sighing in pleasure as he raised her skirt. She kept her head up, watching him in the mirror as John examined her exposed ass before gripping the base of the plug. She moaned as he tugged, the feel of it sliding out a sweet, dark pleasure. The smooth glass rubbed the sensitive nerve endings in her anus as he removed it, before placing it in the sink.

"I think you're done with this, don't you?" John slid the thong down and off.

Kailani stepped out of it and started to straighten, but John put a gentle hand on her shoulder.

"You're wet. I'm guessing close to coming."

"Yes."

"Is that making it too easy on him?" A small smile played over John's mouth.

"If I say yes, will you...help me?"

"Definitely." Rather than bend her over the bathroom vanity again, John helped her straighten, and then pulled her back against his chest. Together they watched in the mirror as John pulled up her long skirt, his hand disappearing under the fabric.

"Spread your legs," John whispered in her ear, and Kailani obeyed, stepping wide to give him space to work.

Then his fingers were on, in, her pussy. One thrusting up into her, the heel of his hand tight against her clit. He fucked her with his finger, a small movement using only that finger while his palm worked in small circles against her clit.

It wasn't enough. She wanted more. She wanted to be filled with not just his cock but Benjamin's too. Yet she was so on edge, so needy, that in less than two minutes he had her coming, one of her hands fastened around his wrist, the other reaching up and back, tangled in John's hair.

She panted through the pleasure, but when it was done, instead of release and relief, she just wanted more.

John kissed her shoulder, dropping her skirts. He studied her face in the mirror, then looked at the jeweled hair clip that was holding back her hair.

"Flower behind the left ear?" he asked.

"Means taken."

John frowned, then nodded once and released her. When they opened the bathroom door, Benjamin was there. He'd stripped down to his pants and shirt, the jacket, bow tie, shoes, and socks already gone.

He raised a brow. "Did you enjoy yourself?"

Kailani should have been mellow from pleasure, but his tone—smugly amused—made her stiffen.

"Listening in? Pervert."

Benjamin's gaze raked her up and down. "Say you don't want me to fuck you. Say it, and mean it, and I'll walk away."

"I don't want you to fuck me," she purred.

Benjamin's brow rose. "Say you don't want me to fuck you...in front of John."

Kailani's throat worked. Damn him.

"Come on," Benjamin taunted. "Say it and mean it."

Kailani stalked forward and grabbed him. One hand on the back of his head, forcing his face down to hers so she could kiss him. He nipped her lip; she bit him in return. It was a repeat of when she'd gone to see him in Seattle, but this time they wouldn't stop...because John was here. He'd positioned an armchair so he had a perfect view of the bed. He was lounging in it, his legs stretched out, but his gaze sharp and watchful.

Benjamin pulled her hair so she'd stop biting his lip. Her neck arched, and he took advantage, nipping the sensitive skin below her ear. She yelped and scrambled with the fabric of his shirt, finding the center. She yanked, heard fabric tear.

"I'm wearing shirt studs," he said, his tone slightly irritated as he released her hair.

"Pretentious ass." She examined the shirt. Rather than the buttons popping off, since he had shirt studs in place of buttons, the fabric had torn on one side.

Benjamin's big hands gripped the back of her dress. Kailani reached back to grab his forearms. "Don't you—"

Benjamin yanked, his big arm muscles flexing, and her dress tore.

"Asshole," she hissed.

"You started it."

"I liked this dress."

"I'll buy you another."

"Fuck you and your money."

"Oh, I plan to fuck you." Benjamin flicked the strap off her shoulder, and the ruined dress slithered to the floor, the broken zipper glinting in the dramatic lighting of the elegant bedroom.

Kailani now stood before Benjamin, naked, except for her

strappy stiletto heels. If he sneered at her, or made a rude comment...

"She's breathtaking," Benjamin said simply, but he wasn't talking to her. He was talking to John.

In response, Kailani reached for his shirt studs, carefully undoing them one at a time, sliding them into the pocket of Benjamin's pants. A truce. As she did that, his hands traced her sides from hips to breasts and back down. His thumbs traced against her breasts, never quite touching her nipples.

She pushed his torn shirt off his shoulders, and then Benjamin stepped out of his pants. His cock was hard, jutting up. Both naked, they looked at one another. This naked felt soul-deep, their baggage weighing them down. Instinctively, Kailani started to turn to John, but Benjamin's fingers closing on her nipple stopped her. She moaned as he pinched, first gently, then harder. The quiet, soft intimacy of a moment ago was burned away in the fire of desire that slapped her.

Kailani grabbed Benjamin's dick, curling her fingers around the base and pumping. He grunted, eyes half-lidded, and twisted her nipple. Sweet pain made her cry out. Then Benjamin was sweeping her into his arms. He didn't lay her on the bed, he tossed her, and she bounced, barely settling before he came down on top of her.

Kailani rolled, trying to get on top, but Benjamin pinned one arm to the bed, then bent his head, taking her nipple between his teeth. He pulled, her nipple pinched and extended. She raked her free hand over his shoulder in response. He let her nipple slip from between his teeth and it was a sweet pleasure-pain.

"Again," she demanded.

"So demanding." Benjamin flicked her nipple with his tongue and she arched into his mouth.

Kailani wiggled her free hand between them, finding his cock where it was pressed to her hip. She gripped it, her thumb rubbing the slit. Benjamin froze, a groan of need rumbling up through him.

"So demanding," she mocked him, rubbing the pre-come that leaked out over the soft head of his cock.

Benjamin surged up. Kneeling above her, he looked huge and dangerous. When he grabbed her hips, flipping her onto her stomach, Kailani struggled to turn back, but he held her down. She started to crawl away, so he grabbed her hips, yanking her ass up so she was on her knees, shoulders and head on the pristine white duvet.

His thumb rubbed through her folds, toying with her clit. Kailani pushed back against his hand as she got her elbows under her, preparing to push up on her hands and knees.

Benjamin's thumb moved off her clit. "You want me to touch you there? You'll keep your head down, ass up."

Outrage and fierce desire ripped through her. "Asshole," she breathed, "I don't need you. I can get myself off."

She reached down between her own legs, but Benjamin grabbed her arms. He forced her wrists to the small of her back. Now she had no way to hold herself up, and her head and shoulders hit the bed. She yanked against his hold.

Her reward for that was a spank. A hard swat to one ass cheek that made her yelp. Then Benjamin was circling and stroking her clit, bringing her to the edge. She ground back against his hand, but it wasn't enough. He must have felt the same because behind her, his cock bumped against her thigh, butt, and then finally her pussy. She angled her hips, and he slid into place, his cock notched against her entrance.

Big, warm hands closed over her hips. He squeezed once, and she nodded, cheek against the bed.

Then he surged into her, filling her with one toe-curling thrust.

Kailani shrieked, Benjamin moaned. He fucked her. Fast and hard, keeping her pinned and helpless under him, her pants and moans muffled against the bed. She knew he was about to come when he bent over her, his heavy body pressing down on her while he reached between her legs to circle her clit. It was against Benjamin's personal code to come before his partners, and this time was no different. The orgasm ripped through her, hard and hot and fast, and he followed a moment later, his guttural cries raw and rough.

Kailani's knees couldn't support their combined weight, so she straightened her legs, falling flat on the bed, Benjamin on top of her, the tip of his cock still in her pussy.

They lay like that, panting, for only a moment. Then Benjamin rolled off onto his back, and Kailani pushed up on her elbows. She glanced at Benjamin, then at John, where he sat watching them. The black tux pants made it hard for her to see if he was hard, but when he shifted, tugging the fabric on his thigh, she knew he had to be.

Kailani sat up, one nipple aching, her pussy still throbbing in the aftermath of the orgasm. She looked at John, who spread his legs and pointed to the floor between his feet.

"On your knees."

CHAPTER TWENTY-SEVEN

J ohn rose from the bed, walking over to the window to gaze out at the sun rising over the French Riviera. His internal clock was completely out of whack, and despite the fact they'd stayed up quite late, he'd struggled to sleep, tossing and turning enough that he had decided to get out of the bed lest he wake Benjamin and Kailani.

He would probably pay for that decision later, but he was too wired, too keyed up to continue making the attempt.

Benjamin and Kailani were still asleep, naked, wrapped up in each other's arms, Kailani on her side, her long black hair fanned out on the pillow as Benjamin spooned her from behind, his arm snaked around her waist, his hand hanging just beneath her bare breasts. The sheets only covered them from below the waist, leaving him plenty of skin to enjoy. John studied them, admiring how beautiful they both were, perfect specimens of male and female.

As amazing as yesterday was—the super-spy games, the casino foreplay, even the high-stakes gambling—John couldn't shake the fact they'd still been playing roles. Kailani and

Benjamin had asked for a do-over, and while they'd given him bits and pieces of who they were and what they wanted, they'd still avoided any meaningful talk.

The only glimpse of real, unguarded truth he'd seen was when they'd returned to the room and he'd watched Benjamin and Kailani fuck.

And while it had been hot as hell, it hadn't exactly set John's mind at ease. Because their hot-blooded, fiery, aggressive natures had been just as prevalent in the bedroom as they were any other time Benjamin and Kailani were together. That had been a battle as much as it had been sex.

John was annoyed with himself because he'd gone along with everything that happened yesterday too easily, and that was what had caused his restlessness all night.

He was still pissed off at them.

It was as simple and as complicated as that. He didn't know how to overcome the hurt they'd caused because it had been a damn long time since he'd let anyone get close enough to do that to him.

Of course, he wasn't sure that last "close" relationship could be used in comparison. It certainly hadn't been a romantic one. That hurt had come from a foster family, one he'd truly believed had cared about him, when he was eleven. He'd let himself believe—hope—that he'd finally found his forever home. Then they'd gotten divorced and decided they wanted a clean slate all the way around...which meant he got shoved back into the system.

Kailani and Benjamin were leaps and bounds ahead of him when it came to relationships and love as well. His dating record was a long string of casual hookups and failed attempts at romance. He'd never said the words "I love you" to anyone.

Ever.

But there had been several times when he'd looked at

Benjamin and Kailani last night and felt...well, if it wasn't love yet, it was the closest he'd ever experienced.

There wasn't a doubt in his mind that if things had gone down differently in Boston, if Kailani and Benjamin hadn't been at odds, hadn't walked away, he'd already be halfway in love with them right now.

He'd let things go too far last night, leading with his dick—and too many martinis—instead of his brain. Even now, the fucking thing was making demands, growing hard as he looked at his lovers, recalling how, after she and Benjamin fucked, John had demanded that she get on her knees. Her blowjob had been hot, sensual, sexy as fuck, but it wasn't what he'd demanded in the casino, wasn't what he wanted.

She played with him for several minutes, the tenor not changing until Benjamin stepped next to him, his dick growing thicker, harder, despite coming just a few minutes before. That was when shit got real, he and Benjamin taking turns fucking her mouth, using her roughly, neither stopping until they'd come down her throat.

They'd fallen asleep after that.

He hadn't fucked them, not truly, not the way he'd wanted to, buried deep inside Kailani—or Benjamin—and he knew neither of them would refuse if he woke them up and rang the bell on round two.

No. He wasn't crawling back into that bed. Wasn't expanding on his mistake.

Willing his hard-on to go away, John tiptoed across the room, rummaging through his bag for a pair of boxers. Pulling them on, he padded to the French doors that led to the suite's private terrace.

Despite the very early hour, the weather was quite balmy, a warm breeze blowing in from the water, and he drew in a deep breath of the salty sea air. The suite boasted its own infinity pool, the clear water so inviting, he was tempted to simply dive in.

Instead, he dropped down at the edge, dipping his feet in. The water was bath-like, warm, soothing. He let his legs hang over the edge, the water reaching him mid-calf.

John looked out over the breathtaking skyline, the cityscape lined with castle-like spires and turrets, the gorgeous panorama encompassing not only Monaco but France as well.

He sighed heavily, so many regrets crashing down around him. He'd gone along with Kailani and Benjamin, swept away by the romance, the magic of this place, even though he knew it was wrong.

And while they'd played and fucked, the one thing they hadn't done was talk.

He leaned forward, resting his elbows on his knees, looking down at the shiny surface of the water, his feet beneath.

Where the hell was he supposed to go from here? The trinity was broken, dissolved, so why was he staying? He should walk away from them, should get on a plane and return to his normal life.

That was what a smart man would do.

But he couldn't make himself take the first step.

Because his normal life sucked, and even as fucked up and crazy as things were between them, the time he'd spent with them had been, God, amazing.

"John?"

He lifted his head, looking over his shoulder as Kailani emerged from the bedroom. She'd thrown on a T-shirt and panties, but nothing else. Benjamin was behind her, and like John, he was still shirtless, wearing a pair of lounge pants slung low on his waist.

"What are you doing out here?" Benjamin asked.

John lifted one shoulder. "I couldn't sleep."

Kailani lowered herself to sit next to him. "Mmm," she hummed as she dipped her feet into the warm pool water. "That feels good."

Benjamin pulled a lounger closer, placing it just behind and between them before perching on the end of it.

There was an case between them. He was comfortable around them in ways he'd never experienced before. He kept everyone else in his life at a distance, always able to make a quick escape. The space between the three of them was almost nonexistent, and yet he kept finding himself seeking to close it even more.

John leaned back just slightly, letting his shoulder bump into Benjamin's knee. He tried to pretend it was an accident as he shifted forward once more, but Benjamin reached out and gripped the back of John's neck, pulling him toward him, encouraging him to lean against him. Then Benjamin kept his hand on his neck, his thumb drawing circles in a touch that was familiar yet far from friendly. The stroking was fucking hot, distracting, making it difficult to keep his dick in the down-boy position.

"I left today's itinerary wide open—either for sightseeing, more gambling, sunbathing on the beach, or just hanging out here—so we can schedule a nap later. I think we'll all need one." Benjamin leaned forward, kissing the side of John's head. "You have a preference, Double-O-Seven?"

Before he could reply, Kailani spoke. "Maybe before we make plans for the day, we should tie up loose ends from last night. There's still one thing left on our list. One last debt to pay."

Punishment.

In the heat of the moment, when they were playing with those markers, John had demanded Kailani and Benjamin accept their punishment.

For walking away from this...

From him.

When John added it to his list of demands last night, he'd intended to follow through, countless forms of erotic punishment flashing in his mind.

Now...

Now he couldn't go through with it. Because the punishment—like everything they'd done last night—wouldn't fix a goddamn thing.

John drew one leg out of the water, twisting until it was bent beneath him, so that he was facing both of them. "I think this is a good place for us to cut our losses. I'm heading back to L.A. today."

Benjamin and Kailani both froze, exchanging a look before focusing on him.

"What are you talking about?" Kailani asked. At the same time Benjamin shook his head, simply saying, "No."

"Last night was a mistake."

Kailani's face fell. "No," she whispered. "It wasn't."

"I shouldn't have let things go so far. Nothing's changed between us."

"Bullshit," Benjamin said.

"A vacation and some sex doesn't fix the problems."

Benjamin sighed, exchanging a glance with Kailani. "We know that. To be perfectly honest, we hadn't intended to lead with sex," he insisted.

"We wanted to talk things out," Kailani added. "To try to fix things between us."

"So why didn't we have that conversation?" John asked.

"The plan was to talk first, but you didn't seem ready." Kailani glanced at Benjamin.

"You were pissed," Benjamin confirmed.

"Plus..." Kailani grinned. "How shallow does it make me

sound if I admit it was because you both looked hot as shit in those tuxedos?"

John rolled his eyes, though he was amused. "I can't call you shallow for that because I felt the same way. That dress, Kailani...you took my breath away."

"Don't leave, John," Benjamin said, putting them back on topic. "Let's make a list of the problems, find a way to fix them," Benjamin said.

"I don't know if..." John sighed. "You didn't speak up. Neither of you said a damn word. You didn't fight for us."

"I should have," Kailani admitted.

"I thought Kailani had asked Selene to dissolve the trinity," Benjamin added.

"And rather than stick around and ask, you hopped on your jet and disappeared into the night. This," John said, gesturing between them. "This is the problem. You both act on emotion, jump to conclusions, then cut and run without ever solving a goddamn thing."

"You're right," Kailani agreed. "That's exactly what we do. Benjamin and I are both stubborn, opinionated. We don't work together."

"Kailani," Benjamin said, clearly ready to argue that point.

She lifted her hand. "We don't work without you. John, Benjamin and I have talked more the past week and a half than we have in the decade before. All because you called us on our bullshit. I'm sorry," she said. "So sorry for all of it. How I acted in Boston, then in Hawaii, after Selene dissolved the trinity."

"I'm sorry too," Benjamin added. "Cutting and running in Hawaii was the act of a coward."

John scowled. "It was," he said, aware that it was only Kailani who'd felt the full brunt of his anger in Hawaii.

Kailani reached over and took John's hand. "We were both

scared to say something, so we took the easy way out. And by doing that, we lost something important. *Someone* important."

Benjamin placed his hand on John's shoulder, squeezing it. "I regretted getting on that plane two seconds after it took off. I was wrong not to stay...to try to fix things."

"You didn't even say goodbye," John said. "You just left." That was the part that had truly hurt. That Benjamin didn't even think he was worth the few minutes it would take to say goodbye.

"I know this isn't a good enough excuse, but I was angry at Kailani, hurt that she would ask Selene to break our trinity."

"I hate that you thought that," Kailani whispered.

Benjamin bent forward to give her a kiss on the top of her head. "I dealt with both of those emotions poorly, and you got hurt for it, John. I'll never forgive myself for that. All I can do is promise to do better in the future."

John sighed heavily, refusing to be swayed by words when actions spoke louder.

Then he considered where they were, the great lengths Benjamin had gone to, in order to bring them all together here in Monte Carlo.

"John," Kailani said. "You left too. When I woke up in Hawaii, and Oscar told me you were gone...I was devastated, and, well, pissed off."

He wasn't sure how to respond to that. Mainly because it was the truth. He'd known that night that she regretted not speaking up, that she was upset Benjamin had run away, and that she wanted to talk to him over breakfast the next morning. She'd said all of that, but he'd been so furious, so devastated, that he'd taken a page from their book, acting on emotion and running away instead of returning to face their issues head-on.

He looked at her, then Benjamin, swallowing hard to dislodge the lump forming there. He didn't share his pain, ever, so it didn't come naturally. It was why he'd spent years in therapy. But they were here now, and they were talking, and he... wanted to let them in. "I didn't think you wanted me. You both gave up, and it took me back to a dark place, reminded me of when I was a kid, getting shuffled to the next foster home."

Those were probably some of the hardest words he'd ever had to say.

Kailani pressed her fingers to her lips, her lashes wet with tears. "Oh God."

"No. Please, Kailani. Don't cry," John said. "I'm not saying that to hurt you. Only to explain why I left the way I did."

"Never again," Benjamin said, steel in his voice. "You will *never* feel like that again."

John breathed out a soft laugh, despite the heaviness of the moment, the seriousness of their conversation. Because only Benjamin Dara could make a statement like that and believe it so completely that he almost convinced John.

He shook his head, letting go of his anger. It served no purpose, and besides, they were hard people to stay mad at.

"John." Kailani took his hands. "Please forgive me. Us."

John sighed but didn't say anything. Mainly because he didn't know *what* to say. His past and present were waging a major battle. The scared, abandoned, street-smart kid was telling him to run fast and far, while this man—the one who longed for a family more than anything—desperately wanted to believe in this...in them.

"I need you to tell me what we're doing here," John said. "I need to know exactly what you're hoping to achieve."

Benjamin leaned forward, his elbows on his knees. "Kailani chased me down in Seattle, and you want to know the first thing she said? 'We have a problem'."

"I should have said crisis," Kailani countered. "Because, John, losing you...it's a crisis."

Benjamin smiled. "Want to know something? I'm great in a crisis."

"He really is." Kailani nodded.

John felt a smile twitch his mouth.

"You want to know something else?" Benjamin leaned in, conspiratorially. "I usually get what I want."

"Except for me," Kailani said.

Benjamin raised a brow. "Did I or did I not fuck you last night?"

"Asshole," Kailani breathed, but there was no real heat behind it.

Benjamin's attention shifted to John. "As you know, I'm a betting man. I take big risks, for big rewards, and I go after what I want."

"And what do you want?" John asked, but he knew the answer.

"Us," Benjamin said.

"What we have, it's special," Kailani said. "Like the song says, sometimes you don't know what you've got until it's gone."

"Yeah, well. I may not be a legacy like you two, but I read the fine print when joining the society. Our trinity doesn't exist anymore," John said. "Do you think Selene will change her mind?"

Once again, Benjamin and Kailani spoke over each other. "We'll convince her," Benjamin insisted. While Kailani said, "She won't."

Benjamin scowled as he looked at Kailani. "What do you mean, she won't?"

"I asked her to reinstate our trinity before I left Hawaii. She refused."

"And you don't think that information might have been something you should have shared with me in Seattle?" Benjamin asked hotly.

Kailani's shoulders stiffened, her eyelids narrowed. "Would it have changed anything? Would we still be here?"

Benjamin scowled, and John closed his eyes wearily. "Here we go again."

But then Benjamin switched gears, his voice calmer. "It wouldn't have changed a damn thing. We'd all still be here. Besides, it doesn't matter if Selene changes her mind or not."

Kailani frowned. "It does matter. I want us together. I want us, this, as my trinity. We...I, made so many mistakes, but I'm hoping that together, we can deal with the reinstatement of our trinity."

Benjamin shrugged. "I can fix it."

John rolled his eyes. "You don't seriously think this is another one of those problems you can just throw money at and make it all go away?"

"I absolutely can throw money at it. Because Selene doesn't have any of the official record books, so all she has is a verbal declaration."

John frowned. "She's the Grand Master. That's enough."

"Not if no one heard it."

"What?" John asked.

Kailani blinked, then laughed.

"What?" John demanded again.

"He's going to pay off everyone who was in that room. Pay them to pretend they didn't hear Selene dissolve our trinity."

"That's bribery," John said slowly. "And it's a crime."

Benjamin shrugged. "If that doesn't work, there's always blackmail."

John covered his face with his hands. "I'm pretty sure we've gone over this before, but let me remind you again, also a crime."

"I guess you'll just have to stay with us to turn Benjamin away from his life of crime," Kailani said sweetly.

"You've only seen us at our absolute worst," Benjamin said. "Will you give us a chance to prove to you that we can do better, be better?"

"How? By buying expensive cars? Jetting us off to Italy? Switzerland? Dropping thousands in a casino?" John waved his hand at the view. "None of that is real."

Benjamin shrugged. "Actually, it is real. In my world, it's very real. And I want you and Kailani to be my world."

"One month," Kailani whispered.

"What?" John asked.

"Give us one month. The month we should have had after our binding ceremony before I fucked it all up and walked away. We'll take the time to get to know each other."

Benjamin smiled. "I like that idea." He reached out and gripped John's shoulder. "Don't go home yet. Give us another day."

John knew there was a smart answer to their request. It was the one the old John would have given them. People in his life didn't get two chances to hurt him. One and done. It had been his motto since he was just a kid.

If he walked away now, there'd be another trinity. The Grand Master, when they returned, would assign him to a new trio...and those strangers wouldn't, couldn't, make him feel the way Kailani and Benjamin did.

So he was going to give the un-smart answer, going to open his heart, going to give them his trust. And then he was going to pray that this time...everything would turn out differently.

"We need a do-over," Kailani said, pulling her legs from the water to stand.

Benjamin followed suit, clearly curious about what she had in mind.

"Didn't we try that last night? Pretend we were meeting for the first time?" John asked.

"That was just playing. I mean this, a true second try."

John stood as well, the three of them in a small circle that reminded him of the first time he'd met them at their binding ceremony.

It was apparent that was what Kailani meant by starting over. "I know we're not wearing robes, but we don't need that pomp and circumstance."

"You're right," Benjamin agreed. "We don't. So let's take it from the top. I believe the Grand Master started with you," he said, looking at John.

Kailani said his name, solemnly. "John Wilson."

He'd bared his soul to them once before and it hadn't ended well. But unlike all those other people in his past, the ones who'd rejected him, who'd left him behind, Benjamin and Kailani had done something no one else ever had.

They'd come back.

John reached down, shoving his boxers down, a symbolic gesture meant to mimic the shedding of his robe, and his unspoken vow that he was coming to them freely, without reservations, holding back nothing.

He held his breath as they both looked at him, then Kailani said, "Benjamin Dara."

Benjamin didn't hesitate for a moment, stripping off his lounge pants, and John drew from the man's confidence, from his seemingly unshakable belief that this trinity was his for the taking.

John took a moment to admire Benjamin's body, neither of them winning any battles in self-control, both of them hard, erect.

Benjamin took over the Grand Master's duties, as he said, "Kailani Iona."

Kailani gave both of them a smile that was as sweet as it was sexy. Then she drew her shirt over her head and pushed down her thong.

Kailani reached out, holding her hand palm up as she started to recite the last line of the binding ceremony. "A trinity marriage isn't easy."

"But if we love and trust one another," Benjamin added, placing his hand on top of hers.

"We'll never be alone," John finished, the power of those words shaking him to the depths of his soul. He reached out and took their hands in his.

John wasn't sure who moved first or if they all three shifted forward as a unit. Kailani kissed him, but with their vows taken, all traces of hesitance were gone. He pressed his tongue into her mouth and met hers. He felt Benjamin's breath, hot on his cheek, knew he was waiting his turn, somewhat impatiently.

As his kiss with Kailani ended, Benjamin was there, cupping John's jaw, his lips taking his with a roughness, a hunger that sparked John's.

John broke the union, sucking in much-needed air, as Benjamin turned to Kailani, the two of them sealing their own vows with the same aggression and need he'd witnessed from them last night.

Nothing would ever be simple with these two, and they would definitely keep him on his toes, but for some reason, he was looking forward to it. Imagining a fuck-ton of makeup sex in his future.

When it looked as if Benjamin and Kailani planned to return for seconds on the kisses, John stepped away, shaking his head.

Kailani looked concerned, Benjamin determined, when he broke the close circle completely.

"Last one in goes down on the other two," he said, turning

and jumping into the pool, creating a huge splash that drenched his lovers.

He heard Kailani laugh as they both jumped in as well, at the exact same time.

They surfaced and splashed, teasing and playing, until Kailani popped up to sit on the side of the pool. Her expression was serious, and John swam over, grabbing her ankles as he looked up at her. "What's wrong?"

"I wish...I wish we could stay here for a month. To stay away from everyone and everything and just make sure our trinity is strong."

"But?" John asked as Benjamin swam up beside them.

"But...I have to go back. Selene gave me five days before I have to be back at the *waihona*. My brother and her cousin took on my keyholder duties, but it was a temporary reprieve. Leaving time for travel...my time is almost up." Kailani looked at Benjamin.

"I have a flight arranged for tomorrow," Benjamin said. "I'd like us all to be on that plane together. LAPD thinks you're working for Interpol for a few weeks, so you can come with us."

John looked at Benjamin. "You're going with her?"

"Yes, I can work from anywhere, so I'm staying with Kailani. To help her, support her." Benjamin's hand slid down John's back, under the water. "As her husband."

John looked at them, and he looked at her as another thought occurred to him. "You have to stay in Hawaii, don't you? I mean long-term. Benjamin and I would need to move there."

Kailani's expression was pinched with worry as she nodded once.

"Everything is negotiable," Benjamin said, uncharacteristically playing peacemaker. "We know your career is with the LAPD."

John reached up, grabbed Kailani's waist, and tumbled her into the pool. She yelped, floundering for a moment before pushing up.

John laughed and kissed her. "I'm going with you tomorrow. And I'll move to Hawaii, transfer to Honolulu PD." John grinned. "I'm gonna be a 5-0."

Knowing that their time to play and escape in Monte Carlo was limited made the kiss they shared all that much sweeter.

CHAPTER TWENTY-EIGHT

There were places he'd planned to take his spouses, things they could enjoy doing together. And yet, as they walked inside, still damp from the pool, supposedly to take showers, all Benjamin could think about was getting his hands on them.

He wanted both of them, his husband and wife, and he'd had the opportunity to fuck Kailani last night. He and John, however...

John was walking with his hand casually on Kailani's very nice ass, the two of them in front of Benjamin. He reached forward and wrapped his arm around John's waist, dragging him to a halt.

Kailani turned, brows rising in question. John too tried to turn, but Benjamin yanked him back. John's back hit his chest, and Benjamin braced himself as John's weight pushed against him.

John was shorter than he was but broader, with a football player's build rather than Benjamin's own swimmer's build, and Benjamin liked feeling the weight of the other man's body pressed to his chest.

"Benjamin?" It was Kailani who asked the question.

"I think I've been pretty good up until now," Benjamin said.

Kailani's expression morphed into skepticism. "In what way?"

"I've been very good about not taking control. About repressing every instinct in my body and letting John take the lead."

Kailani's eyes widened, her gaze shifting to John, then back to him. "Ah."

"Letting me?" John tugged at his arm, but Benjamin held fast.

"Letting you," Benjamin confirmed. "Because I knew I'd probably fuck it up, especially with Kailani being—"

"Do not finish that sentence, Benjamin," she snapped.

"Cautious around me." That wasn't what he'd been planning to say, but he could learn. He'd learn, and be better, for them.

"Mmmmhmmm." That from Kailani, while John shifted his weight, his ass rubbing against Benjamin's dick as he asked, "So what are you saying, Benjamin?"

"I'm saying that from now on, I'm in charge."

John snorted. "And you think I'm going to agree to that?"

"Yes."

John gripped his wrist, and though Benjamin braced himself, muscles tensed, John spun out of his hold and, with a quick shove, had Benjamin stumbling back. His back smacked the wall beside the bed, and then John was on him.

Benjamin bared his teeth in a grin as John pinned one wrist beside his shoulder, John's hips grinding into his. Benjamin rotated his hips, and felt the bulge of John's semi-erect cock against his own.

A dragging sound had them both looking over. Kailani was dragging the armchair John had used last night closer to the bed. She stopped when she realized they were watching her.

"Don't mind me, just want a good view for this."

"And what is it you think you're about to see?"

She plopped into the chair. "Your first time together, just the two of you. Because while I'm selfish and love having my needs met, you're not putting me in the middle every time we have sex."

Benjamin met John's eyes. Damn, but the man had gorgeous eyes. For a moment, Benjamin considered something softer, sweeter. He raised his free hand, the one John didn't currently have pinned to the wall, and cupped the back of John's head. John's gaze slid to Benjamin's lips, and Benjamin pulled him in, ducking his own head for the kiss.

It started off slow and sweet, with just a press of lips, chaste and almost reverent.

Benjamin's patience broke first, desire roaring through him. He tightened his fingers in John's hair, forced the other man's head back, and deepened the kiss. John yielded, let him in so their tongues could touch and dance. They broke apart, both panting. At some point, John had released his wrist and now they were holding each other.

John nipped his lower lip, and Benjamin ran his hands down John's bare back to his equally bare ass. Benjamin had pulled his lounge pants back on before they came inside, but John was naked.

Benjamin gripped his ass, felt the muscles tighten.

"It was killing you not to take control, wasn't it?" John's voice was low, intimate.

"I've been dying inside every day for the past five weeks,"

MARI CARR & LILA DUBOIS

Benjamin replied. "But I'd get on my knees and submit every time if that's what it takes to keep you. Both of you."

John opened his mouth, but Benjamin cut him off.

"But since it's not necessary, right now, you're mine. You're going to submit to me. Let me fuck this tight ass." Benjamin dug his fingers into John's buttocks once more.

"Bossy," he said, but his cock was rock hard against Benjamin's thighs.

"Later, I'll let you fuck Kailani while I fuck you."

"Let me?" John's eyes narrowed and he shifted, grabbing Benjamin's hips and shoving him away.

Benjamin allowed it, only to give him space to grab John's arm and spin him toward the bed. He'd intended to shove him face down over the edge of the bed, the perfect position to play with his ass, plug him, in preparation for anal, but John anticipated the move. He turned, landing on his back on the bed and yanking Benjamin down on top of him.

Benjamin landed, hands braced on either side of John's shoulders, arms in a push-up position, their faces inches apart.

John grinned, then raised his head and kissed Benjamin. He lowered himself, and for once, he didn't bother to keep some of his weight on his hands. He lay on John's muscled chest—a move that would have crushed Kailani—and kissed him, long and slow and sweet.

It didn't stay sweet. Soon, they were once again dueling for control of the kiss, their tongues tangled, breath mingled. They battled for dominance, and Benjamin suspected their lives would be one long string of alpha battles in their bedroom. He looked forward to it.

Benjamin pushed up. John had a hand on the back of his head because Benjamin's hair was too short for John to use as a handle.

"I would never do something you don't want," Benjamin

whispered. "And if you don't want me to fuck you right now, that's fine. If you don't want me to ever fuck you, that's fine, but if that's the case, know that I *will* seduce you. And I can be very persuasive."

"You always get what you want," John said, smiling.

"Yes." Benjamin looked over his shoulder at Kailani, at the one person he'd wanted desperately and thought he'd never have. "Yes, I do."

"And right now you want..."

Benjamin looked back at John, saw the uncertainty in his eyes. He raised a brow. "Are you doubting how much I want you?" Benjamin rolled his hips, grinding his dick against John's.

"Well, I kissed you first. I came on to you, back in Denver."

"You think I didn't want to kiss you first? That I wasn't desperate for both of you?" Benjamin shook his head. "I was the asshole no one wanted. I couldn't let myself want you, knowing there was no chance I'd get to be with you."

John's expression softened, and his hand stroked Benjamin's cheek. Benjamin turned into it and kissed his palm. This wild swing from battle to tenderness shouldn't have felt as natural and easy as it did.

"I want," John said, "you to fuck me. Then I want to fuck you. And after that, well... We'll have to battle it out to see who gets to be in control."

Benjamin pushed to his feet, looking down at John, whose erect cock jutted straight up, the curves and hard planes of his muscles on beautiful display.

"Slide up, I want you in the middle of the bed."

John inched back, until his whole body was on the mattress. Benjamin looked back at Kailani, who jumped out of her seat.

Benjamin reached for John's legs, planning to use them as leverage to flip him over, but John braced himself, smirking.

"Roll over and get that ass in the air," Benjamin growled.

"Make me."

Kailani was at Benjamin's shoulder. He looked over to see what she held, and smiled. Then he looked down at John, who was smirking while looking up at him through his lashes. Benjamin shoved John's ankles apart, kneeling between them. When John went to shift away, Benjamin pinned his thighs to the bed. He started to sit up, so Benjamin stretched out on top of him. They both jolted when their cocks brushed against one another. Then Benjamin kissed him, bearing him down into the mattress. John's hand roamed over Benjamin's back and ass, his fingers restless, stroking and kneading.

Benjamin shifted to the side, stretched out next to his lover with one of John's legs trapped between his own. He kept kissing him, but now Benjamin had access to stroke John's naked front. He followed the lines of his pecs, rubbing his thumb across John's nipples, and stroked his belly as his hand worked south.

Benjamin rested his hand on the velvety-soft skin below John's belly button, his fingers splayed.

John made a noise of frustration, his hips arching up.

"You want me to touch your pretty cock?" Benjamin asked.

"Fuck. Yes."

"Then spread your legs. Wider. Good. Bend your knee."

Benjamin kept one of John's legs trapped between his own. Now John's other leg was spread to the side, his foot flat on the bed, knee raised.

In reward, Benjamin gripped the base of John's cock, squeezing. He arched up, air hissing between his teeth. Benjamin worked the shaft, then shifted his grip up. His palm and fingers wrapped around John's dick, his thumb on the head, teasing the slit. Pre-come already wet the tip of his dick, and Benjamin spread it over the head.

"Fuck. Fuck," John panted.

Benjamin looked at Kailani as he released John's cock. She was there, ready to help. Since Benjamin was propped up on one elbow, Kailani helped him put on the black glove, then dribbled lube onto his fingers.

John had his head up, watching what they were doing. His face was tight, his eyes bright with desire.

Benjamin lowered his hand to John's ass. The position wasn't ideal, but it would work, and this way he could watch John's face.

He slid his lubed fingers between John's butt cheeks. John dropped his head to the bed, exhaling heavily.

Benjamin found the tight ring of muscle by feel and started to stroke the rosette with the pad of one finger. John's cock bobbed as his muscles clenched in response to the stimuli.

"Why does that feel so good?" John moaned.

"Lots of nerve endings here." Benjamin kept up the caress, adding a little pressure but still stroking.

Kailani took a seat on the edge of the bed, a towel spread out on the mattress next to her with the other things she'd grabbed. She'd pulled on a robe at some point and her nipples were two hard peaks against the silky fabric.

"Lube," Benjamin said, lifting his hand. Kailani dribbled more of the thick lube on his fingers.

This time, Benjamin didn't stroke. He put the tip of his index finger against John's anus and pushed.

"Fuck." John's hips came up off the bed.

"Relax," Benjamin chided, adding pressure.

"Oh fuck," John breathed as his body yielded.

Benjamin pressed his finger into John's ass up to the first knuckle, watching a fresh bead of pre-come leak from the tip of John's cock.

Benjamin thrust in and out, slow and gentle, almost stroking John's ass. When his hips started thrusting up in sync with the movement of Benjamin's finger, he carefully withdrew. Stacking his middle finger atop his index to form a wedge, he once more invaded John's ass. John sighed with pleasure when the tip of Benjamin's middle finger was in, stiffening as the tip of his index finger joined it.

This time, Benjamin worked in stages, working his fingers in a half inch at a time. When his second knuckles breached the ring of muscle, and John's cock was so erect it was practically lying on his belly, Benjamin looked over to Kailani once more.

Without a word, she passed him the washed and already lubed plug.

Benjamin carefully withdrew his fingers, smiling in satisfaction at John's disappointed moan. Then he wiggled the plug into place.

"Is that the plug?" John had his eyes closed. One of his hands gripped Benjamin's shoulder, the other fisted in the duvet.

"Yes. Relax." He applied gentle pressure, and the tip of the plug slid in. When John moaned in pleasure, Benjamin planted the heel of his hand against the base and pushed the rest of the plug in with one long, firm thrust.

John's hips came up off the bed, his chest heaving as he panted. Benjamin tugged on the base to make sure it was firmly seated, making John swear.

Benjamin's own cock was rock hard, wet, and aching.

The need to fuck John was riding him, making him grit his back teeth to maintain control, but he wanted, needed, John to enjoy this. The need to pleasure his husband was stronger than any selfish desire to come.

Benjamin stripped off the glove, tossing it onto the towel, before once more gripping John's cock. He swiped his thumb across the head, then brought his hand to his mouth, tasting the salty essence of his lover. John was watching him through slitted eyes, a flush riding high on his cheeks and the upper part of his chest.

Benjamin palmed his dick once more.

"I won't last long if you do that," John warned.

"Do what? This?" Benjamin worked the shaft, grazing the head at the top of each stroke.

"Yes, that... Fuck. The plug is..." John's garbled, panted words were sweet music.

"I don't want you to last long. I want to see you come. I want to see you lose control and let go for me."

John's eyes opened, and their gazes met. Benjamin continued to work his cock, felt it jerk in his hand at the same time John's eyes slid closed.

Every muscle in his body went tense as the orgasm gripped him. His fingers were digging into Benjamin's shoulder so hard that he knew he'd have bruises tomorrow. Watching John come undone, watching him be wholly subsumed in pleasure, was one of the most erotic things Benjamin had ever seen.

He angled his dick so John's come splashed across his own chest. And when John was done, when his body went limp, Benjamin gave in to his own burning need.

He pulled the plug out of John's ass, making him arch up. Then Benjamin was between his legs, pushing his thighs wide as John bent both knees.

"I like being your first," Benjamin murmured.

Benjamin rolled on the condom Kailani passed him, with shaking hands. He stretched out over John, bracing himself on his elbows because he wanted to see John's face as he fucked him.

Benjamin shifted his hips, finding the lube-slicked crack of John's ass. He notched his cock against his entrance, but held there. He waited until John's gaze met his, and only then did he thrust in.

They both moaned in pleasure as the head of Benjamin's cock breached John's ass. Sweat dampened Benjamin's back as he slowly worked himself into his body. John's hands roamed his sides and back, gripping his hips to urge him deeper. When he was fully seated, Benjamin dropped his forehead to John's, their breaths mingled.

There were things Benjamin could have said, wanted to say. *I love you. I need you. We need you. Please don't ever leave me. Don't ever leave us.*

But Benjamin was shit with words, so he held still, their breaths damp and hot.

Then he pulled halfway out and thrust in again. It felt so good, so fucking good. And even better when a dip in the mattress had him turning, seeing Kailani beside them, watching them with a hungry gaze.

Benjamin didn't last long, a dozen hard strokes and then he was coming, John's arms wrapped around his body, Kailani's hands stroking both their shoulders.

He'd thought touching Kailani felt like coming home, but he'd been wrong...because this? Wrapped up in their arms?

This was home.

CHAPTER TWENTY-NINE

"What do you think of Monte Carlo, John? Everything you imagined?" Benjamin asked as he refilled all of their wineglasses. After their exciting morning, they'd all gotten dressed, then moved to the spacious living room to enjoy a continental breakfast. It was strange, but after repeating the ceremony, it was as if they could all finally breathe again.

They decided to make the most of their remaining time by going out to put a few miles on Benjamin's—though he kept insisting it was John's—brand-new Aston Martin, Kailani squished into the barely there backseat. After a scenic drive, they came back and had a late lunch al fresco at Le Grill, the Michelin-starred restaurant on the eighth floor of the hotel, then Benjamin had arranged for all of them to have Swedish massages—John's first.

Devoid of stress or uncertainty, all of them had completely relaxed, and John realized Benjamin had been right. He hadn't truly met them.

Kailani was playful and funny, and she had this amazing

smile that achieved something John wouldn't have thought possible. It made her even more beautiful.

Benjamin could be impatient, and he had a sarcastic wit that, though it often came off as him being an asshole, spoke to John's own smart-ass side. The two of them had begun to banter back and forth, good-naturedly ribbing each other.

"Monte Carlo is so much better than I imagined. Though I have to admit, I have precious little to compare it to. The first time I'd ever left California was when I flew to Boston to join the Trinity Masters when I was twenty-six."

"Really?" Kailani asked, though with less surprise than she might have earlier in the day. If there'd been one recurring theme today, it had been his awe and wonder as he'd been exposed to no fewer than a hundred new and unique experiences.

The entire day had passed like a dream, yet underlying it all had been a different sort of tension to the one that had been so pervasive this past month or so.

The sexual tension was almost palpable, as John felt it ebbing and flowing between them throughout the day. They'd stolen countless kisses and glancing touches, and Benjamin, the maniacal man, was a master at sexual innuendos, drawing too many racy images in his mind.

He'd spent a good portion of the day dealing with an erection, trying to keep his arousal banked. It was a fight he'd lost more than he'd won.

Even now, as they dined outside on their private terrace, the incredible nighttime skyline as their backdrop, all John could think about was pushing away from the table, grabbing his lovers and dragging them to bed so that he could have his wicked way with them again.

The only thing holding him back was the fact that Benjamin had gone to a lot of trouble—or perhaps expense was a better word—to arrange for this romantic candlelight dinner.

Benjamin had hired a private chef, who'd prepared a five-course tour of the Mediterranean menu. The sommelier who'd selected and poured their wines had helped serve, but once all the dishes were out, Benjamin asked that they simply leave the dessert and port and dismissed them, so that their trinity could be alone.

"For the first thirty-four years of my life, the sum total of my travels," John said, "included that one trip to Boston. Then, a month ago, I returned to Boston for our binding ceremony."

"That's terrible, John," Benjamin said. "It's a huge world, so many places for you to see and explore."

"Oh, don't worry about it," John said. "Since you two steamrolled into my life, I've made up for all of that. Because in the past nine days, I've been to Hawaii, Colorado, and upstate New York. I've flown cross-country in a private jet...twice. And now I'm sitting in a bougie-ass suite in Monaco. All of that in just *nine* days," he repeated, stressing the number. "Nine. Days."

By the time he'd finished his list, Benjamin and Kailani were cracking up.

"All I'm hearing is we've been a good influence on you. We're broadening your horizons," Benjamin said, grinning as he tapped his wineglass against John's in a toast.

John shook his head. "Maybe so, but we're not all used to the jet-setting life, Mr. Dara. I could stand to take a little bit of a break between those horizons. I've been in so many different time zones, my body is struggling to keep up and my sleep schedule is legit fucked."

"I agree." Kailani took a sip of wine, sighing peacefully. "All this travel has been utter madness. I wish we could stay here forever."

"I love this city," John said.

"Back to Hawaii tomorrow," Benjamin grumbled, clearly unhappy to have their trip cut so short.

Kailani stiffened. "I'm sorry—"

John was prepared to jump in, cut the budding argument off, but he didn't have to.

Benjamin held up his hand. "I'm sorry, I didn't mean to sound like I'm blaming you. I know you have a duty, and I... we...are going to do everything we can to support you."

Kailani relaxed, nodding. They'd been lucky Selene had given them this time at all, and they each knew it.

The question of getting their trinity reinstated was still up in the air, but Benjamin's confidence was infectious. He said he'd make it happen, and John believed him. Maybe he was a deluded fool for doing so, but that was a worry for another day and time.

"It's a shame we have to rush back because Venice is amazing this time of year," Benjamin mused. "And I was hoping to take John to Eilean Donan Castle while we're on this side of the Atlantic."

John leaned forward. "Seriously? In Scotland?"

The World Is Not Enough was one of his favorite Bond movies.

"Of course. I know you're partial to Brosnan's Bond, so I started doing a little research, contacted a few people. We could stay in the castle if you'd like."

John wasn't sure he'd ever get used to Benjamin's ability to snap his fingers and basically have anything and everything in the world rolled out for him.

"Scotland is always cold," Kailani grumbled, clearly not on board when it came to that trip. "Look out there," she said to John, gesturing to the sparkling water, made colorful by reflections of the lights along the shoreline. "Warm is good. Sunshine is good."

John chuckled. "Spoken like a true Hawaiian."

"If we go to Scotland, the two of you will wear too many clothes," she said.

"Speaking of Hawaii." Benjamin pulled up real estate listings on Oahu, and John, who thought he was impossible to shock, thanks to L.A. real estate prices, almost fell out of his chair when Benjamin started discussing the market prices.

Kailani's current house was in the Nu'uanu Valley in the center of the island. Benjamin found a house in Kaneohe—John made a note to start studying how to pronounce Hawaiian words and names—that had views of both Kaneohe Bay on one side, and the vegetation-covered mountains on that other. With eight bedrooms, five bathrooms, and six thousand square feet, it actually looked like a fairly normal house, except for the size, but the price...

John lunged for Benjamin's phone when the man casually said, "Look, there's a buy-now button."

John managed to yank the phone away, thankfully discovering that there wasn't actually a buy-now button for real estate.

"Asshole," John said, stealing Kailani's term of endearment for their husband, while she laughed.

Despite the fancy meal, they were dressed casually, wearing what they'd put on upon their return to the room after massages left them loose and lethargic. For him and Benjamin, that meant loose-fitting shorts...sans shirts. Kailani had slipped on a lightweight sundress...sans bra.

All they had to lose were three pieces of clothing between the three of them and they'd be completely naked.

Rising, Kailani walked over to John, her nails scraping

along his back as she kept moving around the table until she was standing between him and Benjamin.

"Am I to assume dinner is over?" Benjamin asked.

They'd all finished eating, though they hadn't had the dessert course yet.

"Dessert in bed?" Kailani suggested.

That was all John had to hear.

"Later," he said, pushing his chair away from the table but not rising. "First, it's time to tie up loose ends."

Kailani tilted her head, confused.

"There's still the issue of your punishment."

His words hovered in the air for just a split second before he reached up, gripped Kailani's arm, and pulled her onto his lap. She didn't have time to settle there before he flipped her over, face down.

"What the f—" Her words were cut off when he lifted her dress and placed two hard smacks on her bare ass.

Kailani tried to push herself upright, but he didn't relent, holding her down with a firm hand between her shoulder blades.

"You said you would accept your punishment," he reminded her, though he didn't seek to continue the spanking.

Kailani stilled. "I did," she admitted after a moment.

John ran his fingers along her slit, grinning to himself when he discovered how wet she was.

Kailani sighed blissfully, parting her legs to grant him better access. "More," she demanded when he stopped stroking her.

"That's hardly a punishment," John said, looking over at Benjamin, who remained in his seat, watching...waiting.

"I can help," Benjamin offered. "Hold her down for you across the table."

John shook his head. "No. You're being punished too, remember?"

Benjamin scowled. "How?"

"You can look, but you can't touch. Can't join in."

Benjamin was ready to argue that point, but John cut him off.

"You're going to sit there without touching yourself. You're going to watch me spank our naughty wife, going to watch her come apart on my fingers, all without moving. Consider your punishment a time-out."

Kailani giggled, her response tweaking Benjamin, who really wasn't happy about his punishment.

"John," he started.

"You agreed," he reminded him.

"Yes, but I thought..."

"You thought all was forgiven. And it is. Mostly. This is the last step."

Before Benjamin could continue the argument, John raised his hand and brought it back down on Kailani's ass. This time he didn't stop. Instead, he spanked her until her tanned skin was red. Kailani squirmed on his lap, though he'd recognized the moment her struggles became less about escape and more about arousal.

He paused several times between smacks, driving two fingers roughly inside her. He'd thrust until he could tell she was on the brink of coming, then he'd withdraw, beginning the spanking again.

John looked over at Benjamin, could see from the tenting of his shorts how much he was enjoying the show.

He lifted his chin. "That looks painful," he said, in regards to Benjamin's raging hard-on.

Benjamin's jaw clenched. "It is."

"You want to push down your shorts, don't you? Want to grip your cock tight in your fist, stroke it as roughly as I'm finger-fucking our wife."

Benjamin started to unfasten his shorts.

"Put your hands on the arms of your chair. Don't you dare fucking touch yourself or the next person to find themselves bent over will be you. And I won't use my hand, I'll use my belt."

"Fuck," Benjamin breathed, "me."

Kailani twisted, looking over her shoulder and up at John.

"Looks like you uncovered a kink."

John fought the urge to chuckle. "Face down," he said sternly. "We're not finished here."

He backed that up with a few more slaps, but they weren't as hard as the previous ones, used more to heat up the already red flesh rather than increase the stinging.

"Promise me," John said, as he slipped two fingers back inside her, while looking at Benjamin.

"Promise you what?" Benjamin asked, his voice gruff, pained.

"You never walk away again. Either of you. We have a problem, you stick around to talk it out...to work it out."

Kailani groaned when he curved his fingers inside her, finding her G-spot.

"Say it, Kailani. Say you promise and I'll let you come."

"I promise, John! I'll never stop fighting for us. Never."

John added a third finger to the other two and gave her exactly what she needed. She came, loudly, within seconds, her body bending forward over his lap, as her orgasm rocketed through her.

Through it all, Benjamin white-knuckled the arms of the chair, his gaze locked on John's fingers buried deep in Kailani's pussy.

John slowed his strokes until Kailani lay limp, replete. Then he looked at Benjamin. "I'm still waiting."

Benjamin cleared his throat. "I swear to you, John. I'll

never walk away again. You're mine," he said, John amused by the way his husband felt the need to possess everything. Then his heart skipped a beat or three when Benjamin added, "And I'm yours. Always."

Kailani pushed herself up, and John helped her, allowing her to settle on his lap. He grinned when she narrowed her eyes at him, her ass obviously sore.

"I think Benjamin has suffered enough," John whispered in her ear.

Kailani nodded, the two of them on the same page when she shifted off John's lap, crawling over to where their lover sat. Benjamin unfastened his own shorts, in too much of a hurry to wait, seduction out the window.

Shifting to the edge of his seat, Kailani knelt between his outstretched thighs and took him into her mouth.

Now it was John's turn to white-knuckle the chair, the image of Kailani sucking Benjamin deep into her mouth one that John would carry with him for the rest of his life.

They were beautiful.

They were perfect.

They were his.

Benjamin had been pushed too close to the edge, so his climax came quickly.

Kailani held him in her mouth, swallowing every drop, and then she released him with a soft pop.

As one, his lovers turned to look at him.

While they'd both come, John was hard and hurting, and he didn't doubt for a second he'd come just as fast as Benjamin had.

"Forgiven?" Kailani asked softly.

"Forgiven," John said, though, in truth, that forgiveness had already been granted this morning.

"Good. Because I think it's time this relationship was fully consummated," Kailani said, rising from the patio, wobbling slightly.

Benjamin gripped her elbow to steady her. "What did you have in mind?"

Kailani gave them both a wicked grin, her ass swaying as she walked away from them, tugging her sundress over her head. "You're going to fuck my pussy, Benjamin, while John fucks my ass," she called out over her shoulder, just before she stepped inside the bedroom.

John was only half a step behind Benjamin, the two of them following their wife before she'd finished speaking. He paused in the open doorway when he spotted Kailani, crawling naked to the center of the large bed.

Benjamin was across the room, digging through the nightstand drawer. John knew exactly what he was seeking, grinning when Benjamin held up the tube of lubrication, wiggling it before tossing it to the bed, where it landed next to Kailani on the mattress.

Kailani shifted onto her back, crooking her finger at Benjamin.

Benjamin pushed off his shorts, then followed her direction, laying on his back before pulling her over him. "Come lie on top of me, kiss me, while John gets you ready to take that thick cock of his in your ass."

Kailani shivered as Benjamin wrapped his fist in her hair, tugging it in a way they'd both discovered was a hot button for her.

"Kailani," John said, stripping off his own shorts and crawling onto the bed, kneeling next to his lovers. He placed a kiss on her shoulder. "You're so beautiful."

She twisted, lifting her head so that he could kiss her briefly.

Then John shifted, nudging Benjamin's knees apart so that

he could position himself directly behind her. Kailani's legs opened even wider, her thighs outstretched over Benjamin's hips.

John wrapped his arms around her, taking her breasts in his hands, squeezing them, pinching her nipples.

"God," Kailani gasped. "The two of you will..." Her words fell away, devolving into panting moans.

Curious, John glanced down, watched as Benjamin drove two fingers inside her.

"Bend down. Kiss our husband," John demanded. "And put that cute little ass of yours up in the air for me."

Benjamin reached for Kailani, drawing her back down. She lowered her head, her lips finding Benjamin's, his strong, muscular hand gripping the back of her neck, reminding John of their first time together, how they'd indulged in breath play.

His lovers were a portrait in contrasts, Kailani's lightly bronzed skin next to Benjamin's dark brown. Looking at them always made John wish he possessed the ability to paint or draw or even take a decent fucking photograph.

He could watch them all night and never get his fill.

Benjamin broke their kiss and glanced over her shoulder at him. "Anytime you're ready, John. We're not getting any younger here."

John laughed, and then, because he felt the desire to reclaim the upper hand he'd relinquished this morning, he reached between Benjamin's open legs and gripped his balls, squeezing them with just enough force to catch his husband's attention.

Benjamin groaned, a deep, guttural, hungry sound that proved the three of them weren't going to scratch the surface on all their kinks tonight. God willing, they'd convince Selene to change her mind—because John really hated the idea of bribery or blackmail—and they'd have a lifetime to explore all their deep-seated needs, desires, hungers.

Fuck. A lifetime wouldn't be enough.

John reached for the lubrication, ready to move them to the next part. The idea of him and Benjamin taking their wife—claiming her—so arousing, he felt light-headed.

Opening the cap, he put a generous amount of lube on his finger, recalling the care Benjamin had taken with him this morning.

Working it in slowly, he grinned when Kailani groaned, tilting her hips to allow him better access.

John barely restrained his own groan, painfully aware of just how good...how tight this was going to feel. Fuck. It took everything he had to stop himself from shoving in, but he couldn't do that. He knew he needed to make sure Kailani was prepared or this would be painful.

Benjamin's hands stroked up and down Kailani's back as he whispered wicked, descriptive details of how it was going to feel when she was stuffed full of both their cocks.

One finger became two, then he added more lube, as two became three. Kailani grunted, but there was no pain in the sound.

He began to thrust, building force and speed, as Kailani's breathing grew louder, more labored, and soon she was pleading. Just one word. Over and over.

"Please," she whispered. "Please."

Benjamin caught John's gaze. "Our wife is ready for us."

John nodded, withdrawing his fingers, pulling Kailani upright, her back to his chest.

Benjamin's fingers tightened on her hips as he lifted her, and Kailani reached down, guiding Benjamin's cock to her pussy, slowly sliding down to engulf him.

They both froze when he was buried deep, John's arm circled tightly around her waist.

Kailani started to lift back up, but John stopped her.

"No. Wait for me."

She glanced over her shoulder at him and whispered, "Always." Then she lowered her upper body back down, kissing Benjamin briefly.

John looked down at where their two bodies were joined, Kailani's pussy stretched wide over Benjamin's thick cock.

"John," Benjamin said, capturing his attention.

John pulled on his condom, quickly lubed it up, and then...

He pushed the head of his dick inside, Benjamin and Kailani both moaning this time. John's restraint was gone, a thing of the past, as he pressed forward, not stopping until she'd taken every inch of him inside her tight ass.

"Fuck, John," Benjamin breathed. "I can feel you."

Benjamin lost the fight first, but only by seconds, Kailani coming loudly, calling out Benjamin's name—and his.

John wanted to hold on, hated the idea of leaving this paradise he'd only just discovered, but he couldn't do it. His balls tightened and he cursed as his own climax crashed down on top of him. His vision went gray, his muscles tight, as the pleasure felt as if it was being ripped from his very soul.

None of them moved for a few minutes, the three of them breathing heavily, slick with sweat. John finally found the strength to push away, to withdraw. He rose from the bed, then padding to the bathroom to dispose of the condom. He washed his hands and splashed some water on his face before returning to his lovers.

Benjamin was almost down for the count, lying on his side, his arm over Kailani's stomach, his eyelids opening and closing in a way that told John he was about to lose the fight, sleep overtaking him.

She gave John a sweet, tired smile as he climbed into the bed, claiming her other side. She twisted to face him, wrapping her arm around his waist, her head pillowed on his shoulder. Benjamin reached around her, adding to the embrace, his hand resting just over John's heart.

John lay there, feeling lost and found all at the same time.

Lost in them, in their arms, in this trinity.

And that was when he realized he'd done it.

Found his family.

At last.

EPILOGUE

Boston

Twenty-four hours since the kidnapping

FRANCO STARED at the now empty-feeling suite. Rose and Lachlan were in the air, on their way to Honolulu. The acting Grand Master, whichever of the keyholders it was, would need one of the counselors there to help explain what was going on, and what to do.

Sebastian and Rose had a rather spectacular fight before Rose left. If Juliette were here, she wouldn't have allowed it. She would have shut them both down and had them working together. Without her...

Franco rose to pace, unable to sit still.

It had been a full day since they were taken, and as far as Franco could tell, they were no closer to finding Juliette and Devon.

The teams of investigators Lachlan had dispatched had

uncovered lots of information. They now knew exactly how Juliette and Devon had been smuggled out of the library. They'd been loaded into a truck, and someone had tracked the truck through the city, following its trail from camera to camera. But then the trail went cold, the truck disappearing off any security camera Bennett's people were able to get footage from. The truck itself belonged to a moving company and had been reported stolen three days ago.

The investigation into Izabel, Rowan, and Brennon's kidnapping had hit similar dead ends.

Lachlan had, before he left, promised that there were still leads, that the best people the Trinity Masters had were working on this. But the fact remained that Lachlan had made a strategic decision to go to Honolulu. The fact that other members had been kidnapped, plus the arson on Oahu, was an indicator that the keyholders might be in danger, and right now...right now, the society needed a leader.

If Juliette was here, she would have made the same call. Would have sent Lachlan to Hawaii, but Franco wanted to scream at everyone. To demand that no one do anything else, that they all focus only on finding Juliette and Devon.

"Elle says there haven't been any calls to your house." Sebastian came up behind him, placing a hand on Franco's shoulder.

Lachlan had also treated this as a possible kidnapping for ransom. Last night, after they'd initiated the keyholder protocol by calling Kailani Iona, Sebastian had called his husband Grant, and wife Elle, and sent them over to Franco's house. They, along with a K&R tech, were waiting to see if any calls came in. Franco's cell phone was being monitored by Bennett security for the same reason.

Other people with similar experience in K&R had gone to the Serra and Reyes families, as both Izabel and Brennon were legacies. Rowan's family didn't know anything about the Trinity Masters and didn't have any money anyway. Lachlan had tapped their phones in case they did got a call and sent someone to watch and protect them.

So far, there had been no ransom call.

"You sure you don't want to go home?" Sebastian asked.

Franco shook his head. He couldn't be in his house, their house, without Juliette and Devon.

"Okay, then you have to eat something," Sebastian insisted.

Colum walked up on Franco's other side, handing him a cup of milky tea. "I'm a hostage who makes tea."

"You're not our hostage," Sebastian said wearily. "You told the Fleet Admiral that, right?"

"Sure enough. He says it's grand. Drink your tea," Colum said.

Franco took a sip.

"Did you talk about it? What the keyholder covenant says?" Colum asked after a moment.

Franco's stomach sank.

"I'm still pissed off that you had a copy of this keyholder thing when I didn't even know about it," Sebastian said to the Irishman.

Colum shrugged. "Your ignorance is hardly my problem."

Franco turned away from the window, glancing at his wife's best friend, who was glowering at Colum. Something on his face must have given away Franco's worry, because Sebastian looked from Franco to Colum and back.

"What is Colum talking about? What else does the keyholder document say?"

Franco's hands were shaking, and he had to walk over to the table and set the cup down.

"Franco, if there's something else, I need to know about it. Now."

"Two weeks." Franco didn't look up, couldn't bear to look at Sebastian.

"Two weeks of what? Until what?"

Franco braced his hands on the table, letting his head drop between his arms. He hadn't cried, wouldn't let himself. Rage was safer than fear. And if he had to tell Sebastian what was coming, if he had to give voice to the possibility, the fear and the tears would come.

Colum put a hand on Franco's shoulder blade, a silent question. Franco nodded, a tiny movement.

"Your keyholder covenant doesn't just ensure the society will survive by creating a cache of valuables and identifying an acting Grand Master," Colum said.

Sebastian cursed quietly. "Fuck, what else does it say?"

"You have two weeks to find your Grand Master. And if you don't, if she's still missing after fourteen days...then she can no longer *be* Grand Master."

"What the fuck?" Sebastian exploded.

"I suspect it's meant to ensure that the society doesn't exist in limbo for too long. Either way, if you don't find your Juliette in the next two weeks, you'll have to choose a new Grand Master."

Franco straightened and looked at Sebastian. A wealth of understanding passed between them with that look because it wasn't as simple as choosing a new Grand Master. The position was hereditary, passed down from Adams to Adams. There were old rules, protocols, for how to choose a new Grand Master if there was no Adams to take up the mantle, but if they had to do that... Well, there were other problems that would arise. Other secrets that might break the society that right now felt fragile as glass.

"We'll find her," Sebastian said. "We'll find both of them, long before the two-week deadline."

Franco nodded, but some part of him, a cold, analytical part, said that this wasn't going to be fast, that whoever had taken them had done too good a job.

"Thirteen days," Franco said softly. "We have thirteen days left to find them."

READ THE ENTIRE TRINITY MASTERS: **Crossroads**
Contempt
Forgotten Promise
Stolen Faith
Jagged Salvation

AND CHECK out these other series...all part of the Trinity Masters world.

FALL of the **Grand Master**
Elemental Pleasure (Preston, Carly, and Lance's story)
Primal Passion
Scorching Desire
Forbidden Legacy

SECRETS AND SIN
Hidden Devotion
Elegant Seduction
Secret Scandal
Delicate Ties
Beloved Sacrifice
Masterful Truth

. . .

MASTERS ADMIRALTY
Treachery's Devotion
Loyalty's Betrayal
Pleasure's Fury
Honor's Revenge
Bravery's Sin

THE HAYDEN BROTHERS
Fiery Surrender
Necessary Pursuit (Selene, Oscar, and Luca's story)
Joyful Engagement (a novella featuring Warrior Scholar
Tate and Selene's cousin, Roman)
Wrath's Storm

THE MAFIA
Suspicion's Fire
Desire's Addiction
Danger's Heir

WARRIOR SCHOLARS
Hollywood Lies

CALLING ALL FACEBOOK FANS! Did you know there's a group
for fans of the Trinity Masters series? Come join Mari and Lila
for behind-the-scenes stories, contests, exclusive sneak peeks,
and hilarious text threads. Join the society right HERE.

ABOUT THE AUTHORS

Virginia native Mari Carr is a *New York Times* and *USA TODAY* bestseller of contemporary sexy romance novels. With over two million copies of her books sold, Mari was the winner of the Romance Writers of America's Passionate Plume for her novella, *Erotic Research*.

Join her newsletter so you don't miss new releases and for exclusive subscriber-only content. You can visit Mari's website at https://maricarr.com or email her at mari@maricarr.com.

Lila Dubois is an award winning author of erotic, paranormal and fantasy romance. Her book J is for..., the tenth book in the bestselling checklist series, won the 2019 National Readers' Choice Award. Additionally, she's been nominated for the RT Book Reviews Erotic Novella of the Year for Undone Rebel and the Golden Flogger.

Having spent extensive time in France, Egypt, Turkey, Ireland and England Lila speaks five languages, none of them (including English) fluently. Lila lives in California with her own Irish Farm Boy and loves receiving email from readers.

You can visit Lila's website at www.liladubois.net. She loves to hear from fans! Send an email to author@liladubois.net or join her newsletter.

Made in United States
North Haven, CT
06 May 2023

36311478R00225